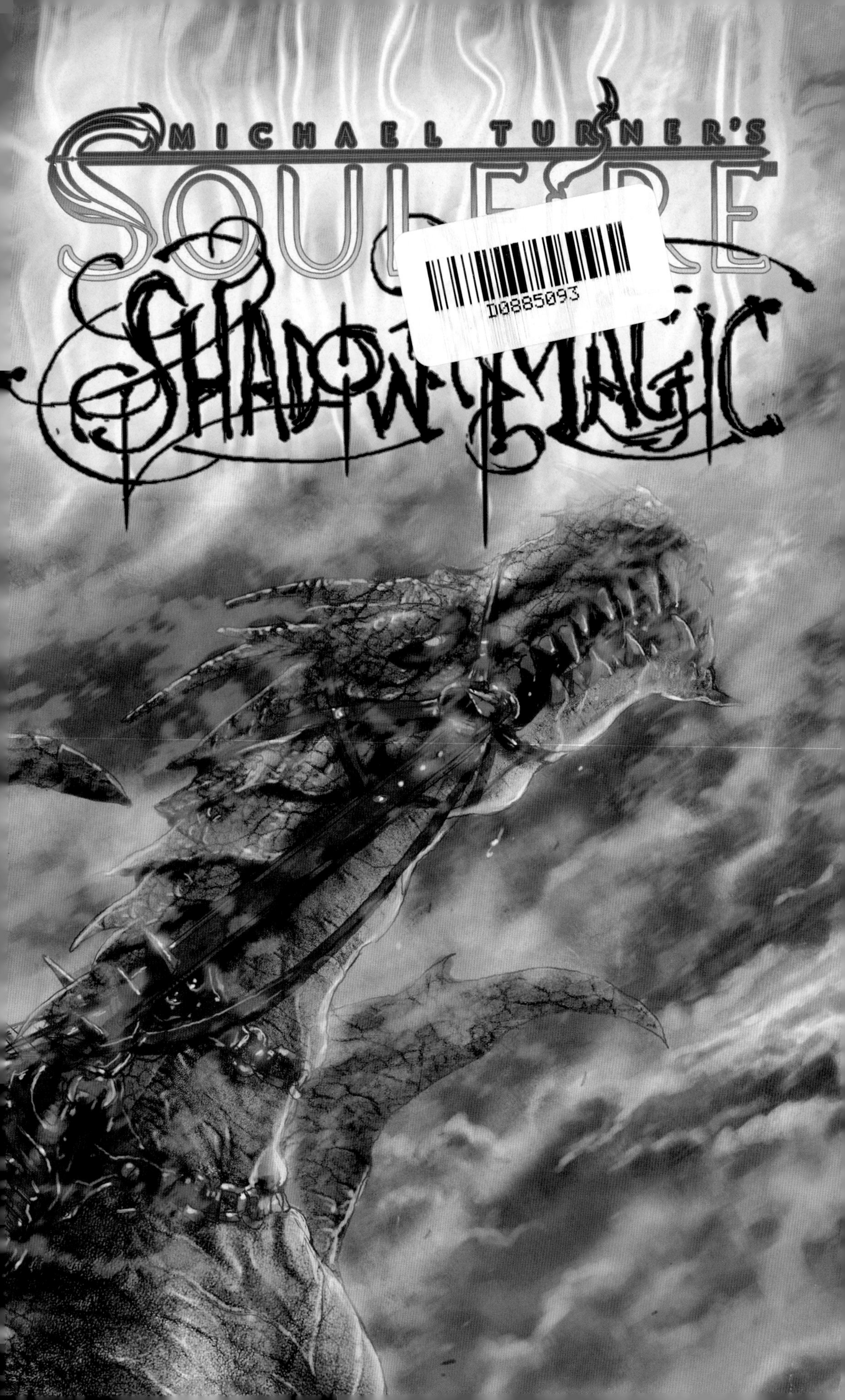
MICHAEL TURNER'S
SOULFIRE
SHADOW MAGIC

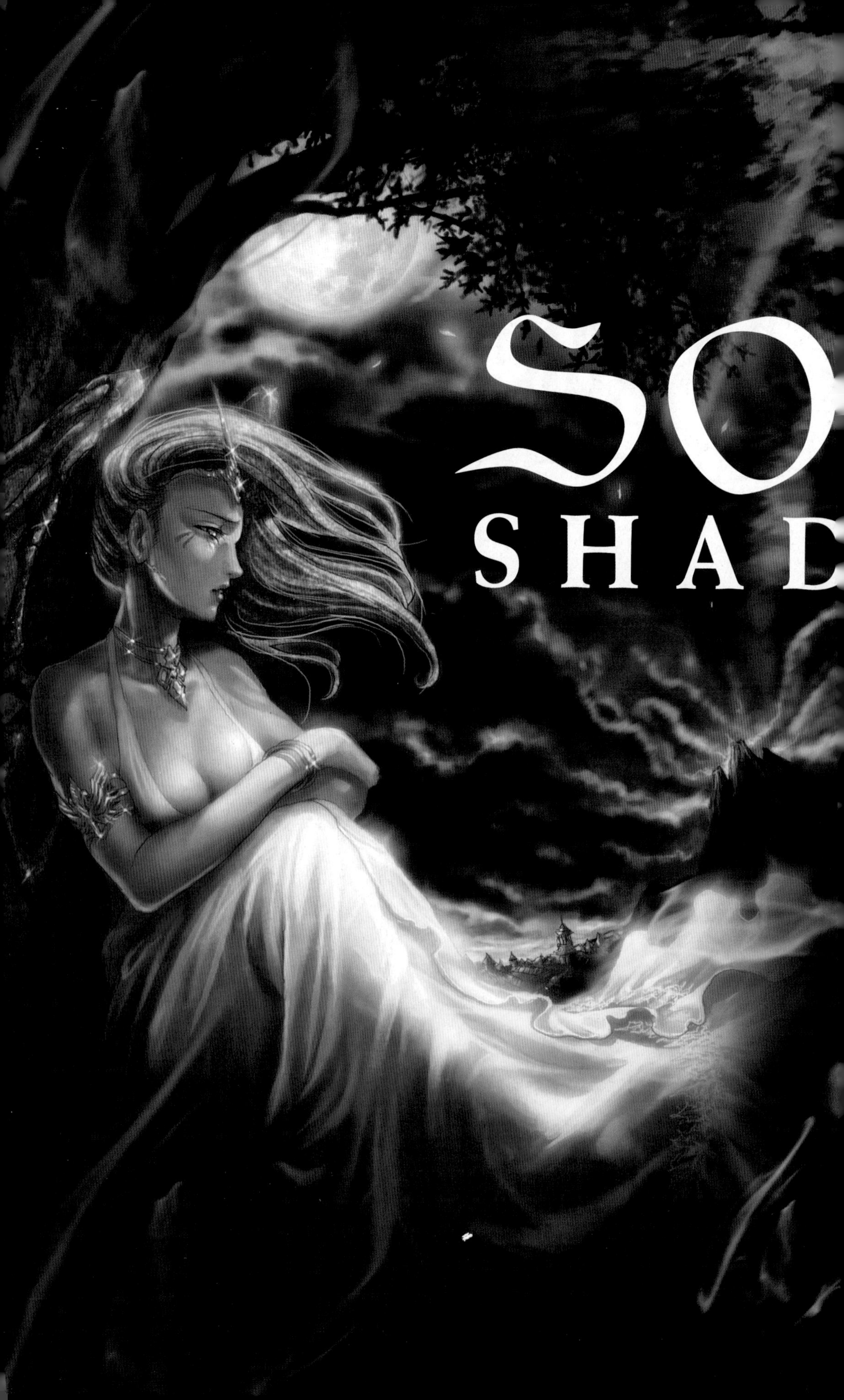
SO
SHAD

ULFIRE:
OW MAGIC

written by
Vince Hernandez

illustrations by
Sana Takeda

lettering by
Josh Reed

MICHAEL TURNER

SOULFIRE: SHADOW MAGIC™ VOLUME 1
ISBN: 978-0-9823628-7-7 FIRST PRINTING, REGULAR EDITION 2018. Collects material originally published as Soulfire: Shadow Magic 0,1-5

Published by Aspen MLT, LLC.
Office of Publication: 5701 W. Slauson Ave. Suite. 120, Culver City, CA 90230.

Address correspondence to:
SOULFIRE *c/o Aspen MLT LLC.*
5701 W. Slauson Ave. Suite. 120
Culver City, CA. 90230-6946
or fanmail@aspencomics.com

Visit us on the web at:
aspencomics.com
aspenstore.com
facebook.com/aspencomics
twitter.com/aspencomics

Original Series:

Editor: **Frank Mastromauro**
Assistant Editor: **Josh Reed**

For this Edition:

Supervising Editor: **Frank Mastromauro**
Editors: **Andrea Shea** and **Mark Roslan**
Cover and Book Design and Production: **Mark Roslan**
Logo Design: **Peter Steigerwald**
Cover Illustration: **Sana Takeda**

For Aspen:

FOUNDER: MICHAEL TURNER
CO-OWNER: PETER STEIGERWALD
CO-OWNER/PRESIDENT: FRANK MASTROMAURO
VICE PRESIDENT/EDITOR IN CHIEF: VINCE HERNANDEZ
VICE PRESIDENT/DESIGN AND PRODUCTION: MARK ROSLAN
EDITOR: GABE CARRASCO
PRODUCTION ASSISTANT: JUSTIN VANCHO
OFFICE COORDINATOR: MEGAN SHIRK
AspenStore.com: CHRIS RUPP

TO FIND THE COMIC SHOP
NEAREST YOU...

comicshoplocator.com
888-COMIC-BOOK
1-888-266-4226

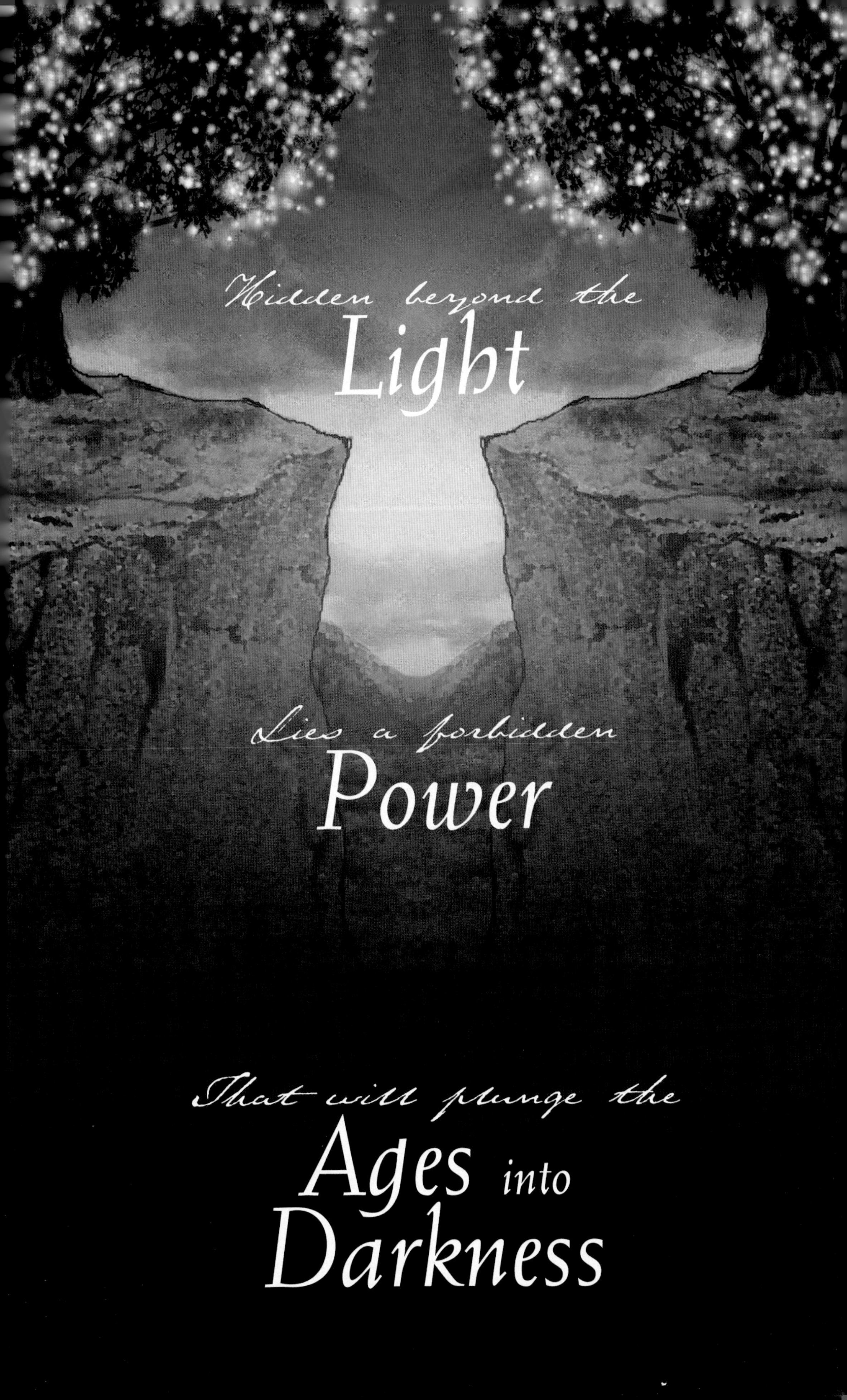
Hidden beyond the
Light
Lies a forbidden
Power
That will plunge the
Ages into
Darkness

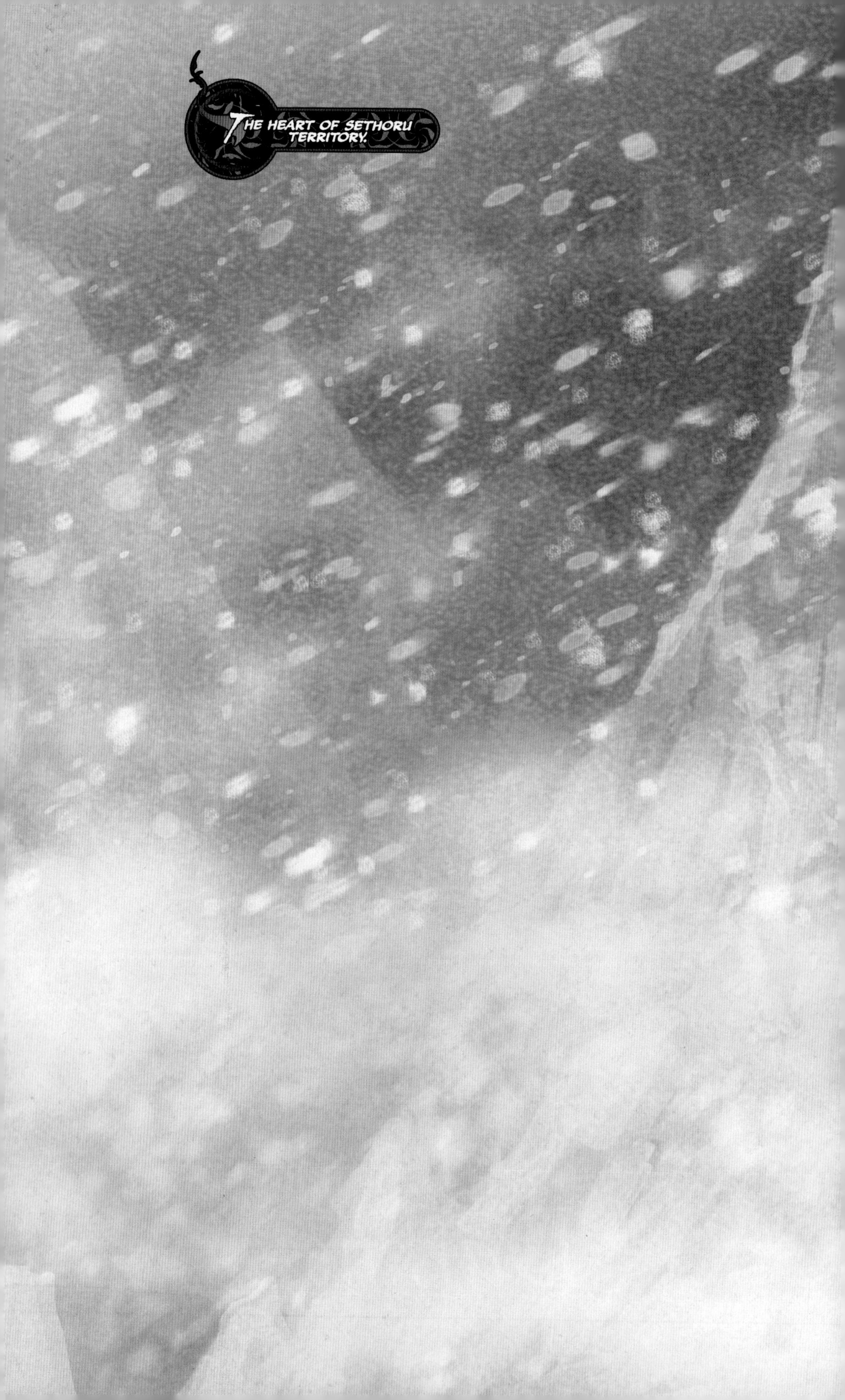
THE HEART OF SETHORU TERRITORY.

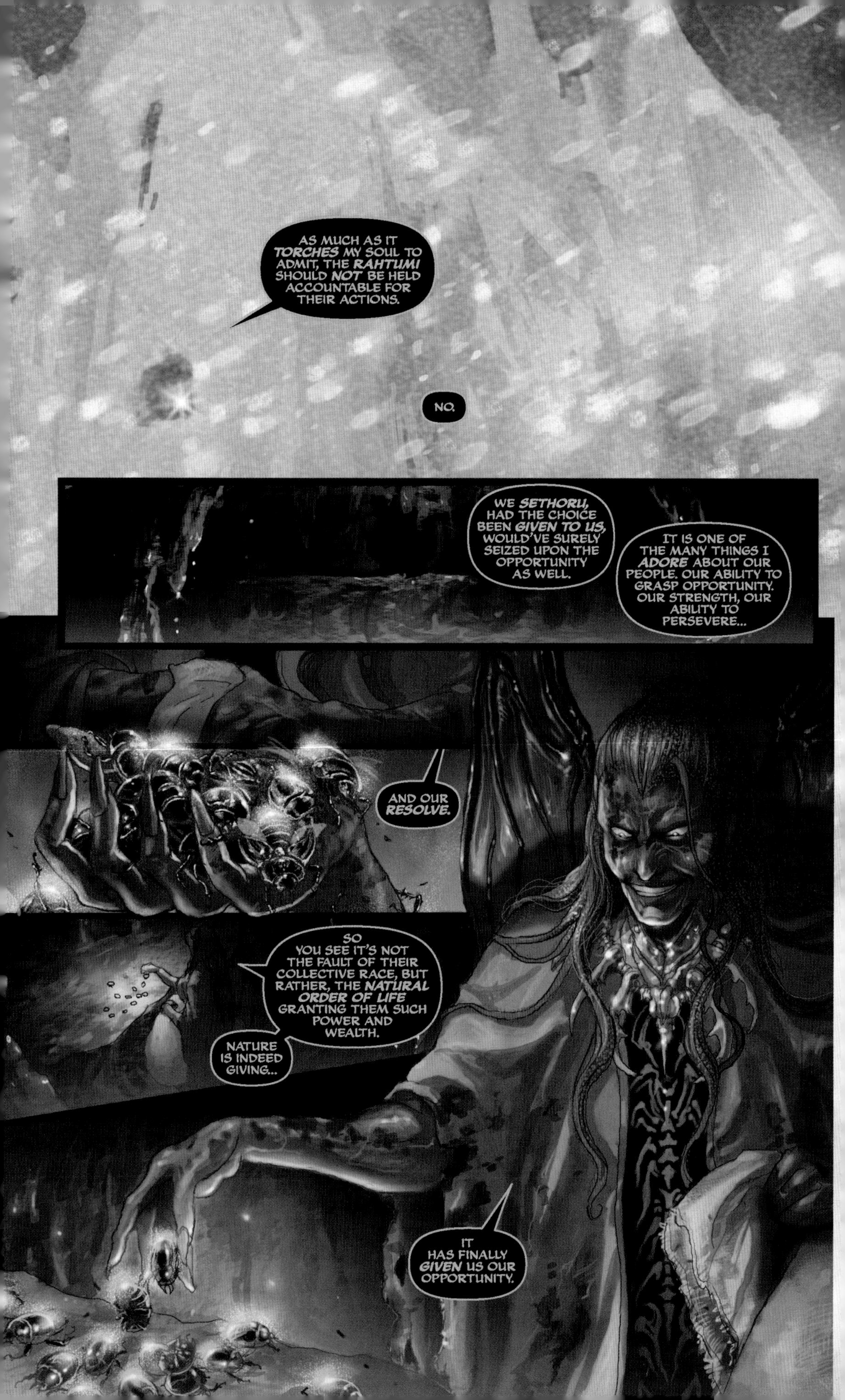
AS MUCH AS IT TORCHES MY SOUL TO ADMIT, THE RAHTUMI SHOULD NOT BE HELD ACCOUNTABLE FOR THEIR ACTIONS.
NO.
WE SETHORU, HAD THE CHOICE BEEN GIVEN TO US, WOULD'VE SURELY SEIZED UPON THE OPPORTUNITY AS WELL.
IT IS ONE OF THE MANY THINGS I ADORE ABOUT OUR PEOPLE. OUR ABILITY TO GRASP OPPORTUNITY. OUR STRENGTH, OUR ABILITY TO PERSEVERE...
AND OUR RESOLVE.
SO YOU SEE IT'S NOT THE FAULT OF THEIR COLLECTIVE RACE, BUT RATHER, THE NATURAL ORDER OF LIFE GRANTING THEM SUCH POWER AND WEALTH.
NATURE IS INDEED GIVING...
IT HAS FINALLY GIVEN US OUR OPPORTUNITY.

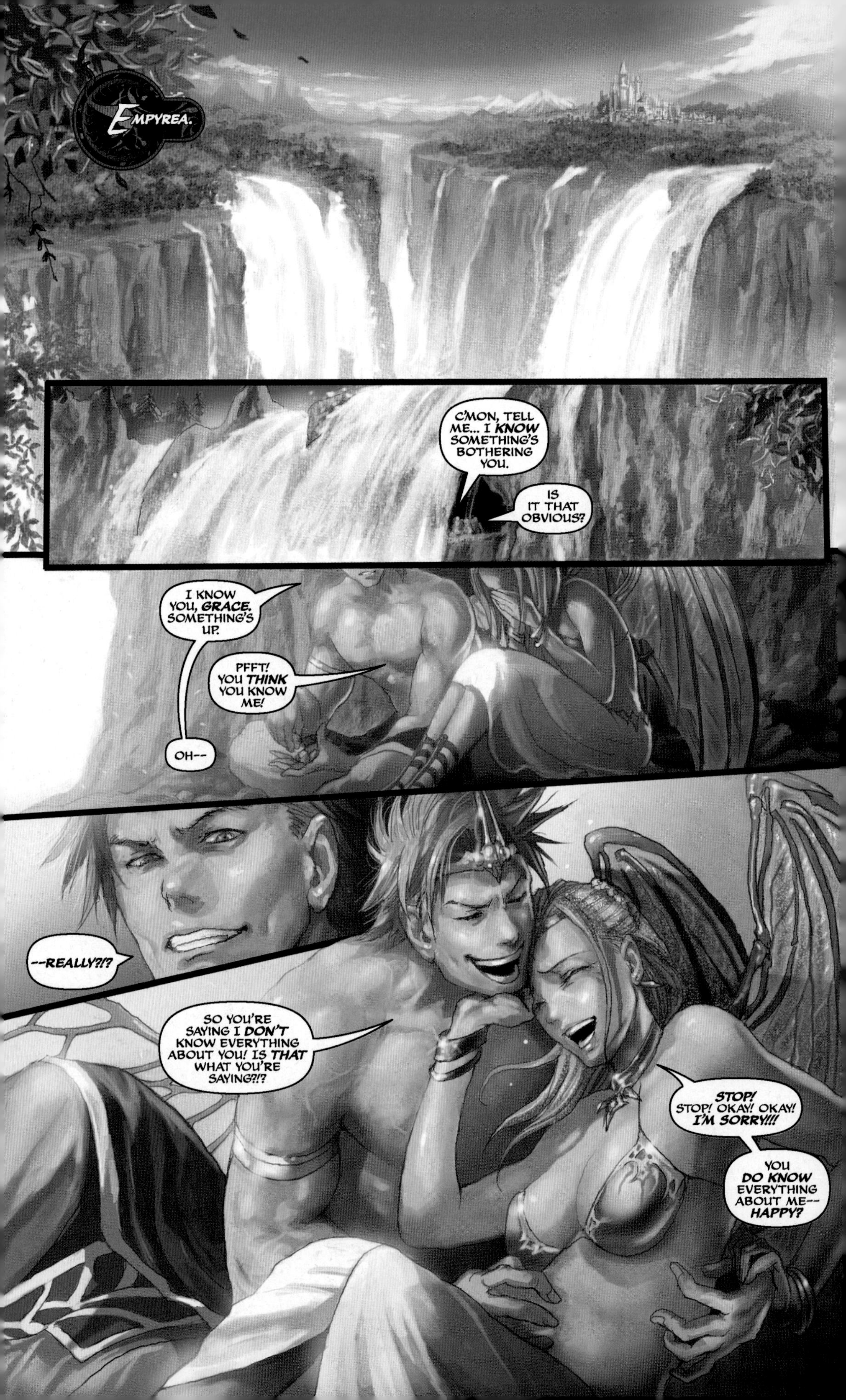
EMPYREA.
C'MON, TELL ME... I KNOW SOMETHING'S BOTHERING YOU.
IS IT THAT OBVIOUS?
I KNOW YOU, GRACE. SOMETHING'S UP.
PFFT! YOU THINK YOU KNOW ME!
OH--
--REALLY?!?
SO YOU'RE SAYING I DON'T KNOW EVERYTHING ABOUT YOU! IS THAT WHAT YOU'RE SAYING?!?
STOP! STOP! OKAY! OKAY! I'M SORRY!!!
YOU DO KNOW EVERYTHING ABOUT ME-- HAPPY?

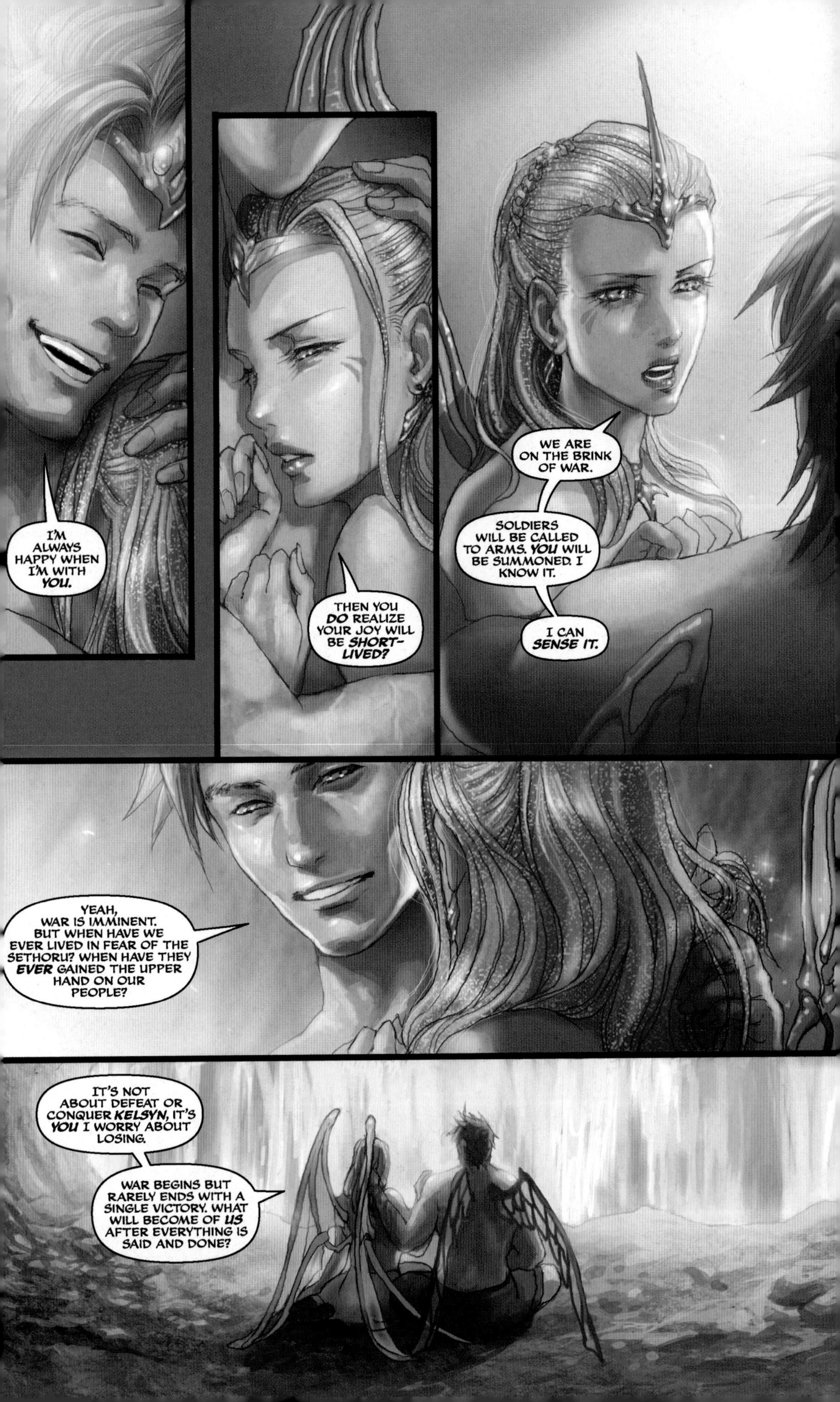
I'M ALWAYS HAPPY WHEN I'M WITH *YOU.*
THEN YOU *DO* REALIZE YOUR JOY WILL BE *SHORT-LIVED?*
WE ARE ON THE BRINK OF WAR.
SOLDIERS WILL BE CALLED TO ARMS. *YOU* WILL BE SUMMONED. I KNOW IT.
I CAN *SENSE IT.*
YEAH, WAR IS IMMINENT. BUT WHEN HAVE WE EVER LIVED IN FEAR OF THE SETHORU? WHEN HAVE THEY *EVER* GAINED THE UPPER HAND ON OUR PEOPLE?
IT'S NOT ABOUT DEFEAT OR CONQUER *KELSYN,* IT'S *YOU* I WORRY ABOUT LOSING.
WAR BEGINS BUT RARELY ENDS WITH A SINGLE VICTORY. WHAT WILL BECOME OF *US* AFTER EVERYTHING IS SAID AND DONE?

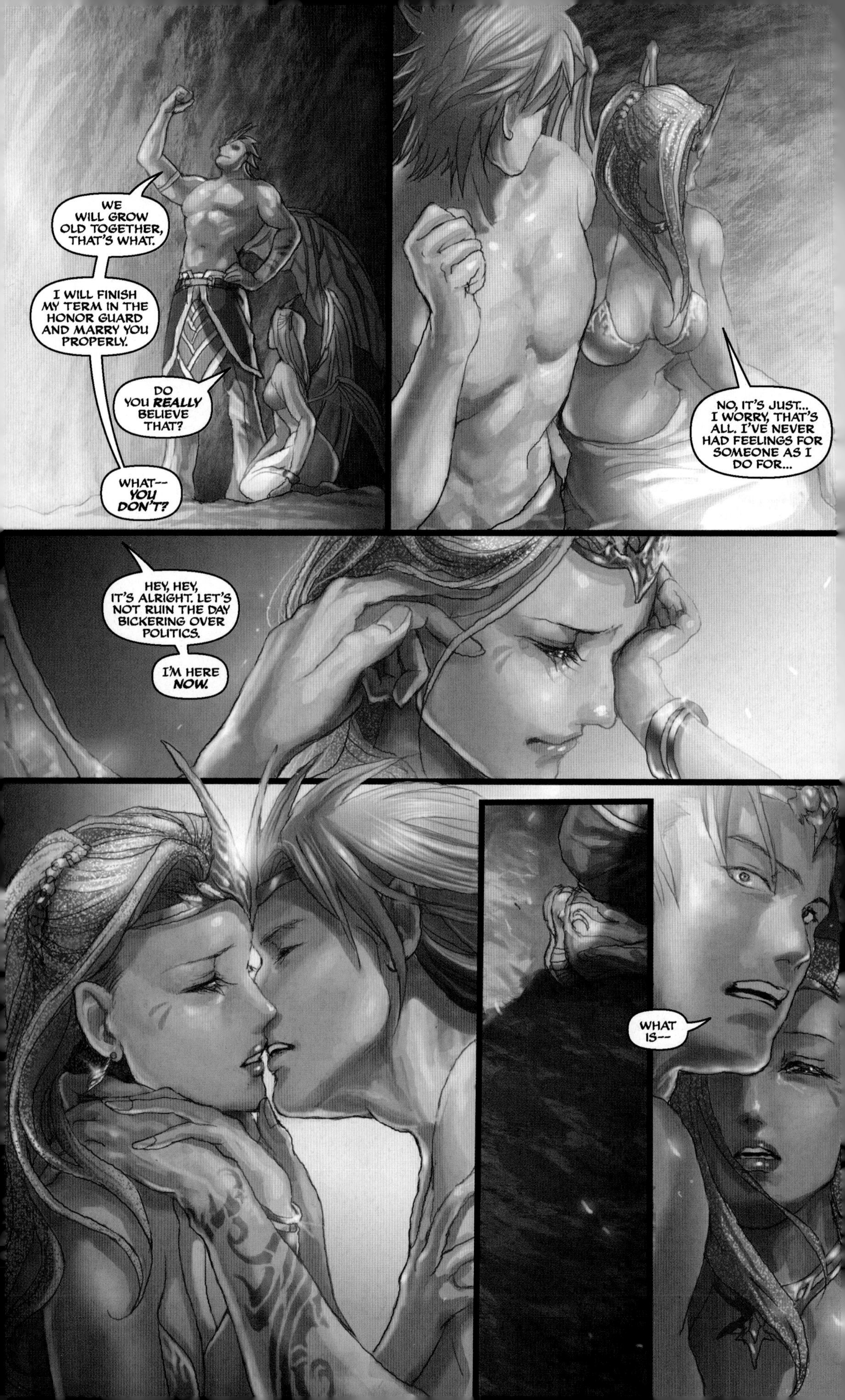

WE WILL GROW OLD TOGETHER, THAT'S WHAT.
I WILL FINISH MY TERM IN THE HONOR GUARD AND MARRY YOU PROPERLY.
DO YOU *REALLY* BELIEVE THAT?
WHAT-- *YOU DON'T?*
NO, IT'S JUST... I WORRY, THAT'S ALL. I'VE NEVER HAD FEELINGS FOR SOMEONE AS I DO FOR...
HEY, HEY, IT'S ALRIGHT. LET'S NOT RUIN THE DAY BICKERING OVER POLITICS.
I'M HERE *NOW.*
WHAT IS--

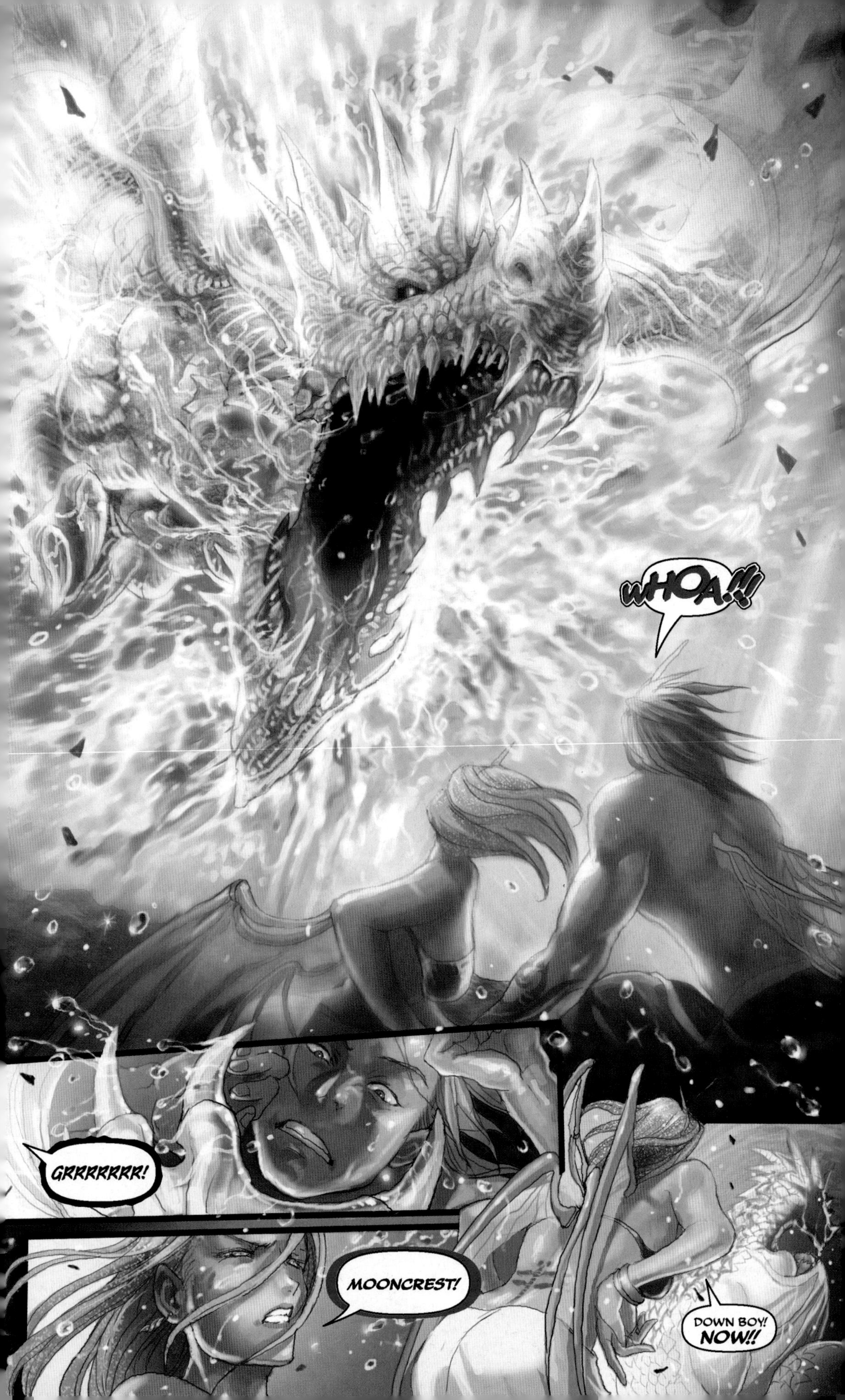
WHOA!!
GRRRRRRR!
MOONCREST!
DOWN BOY! NOW!!

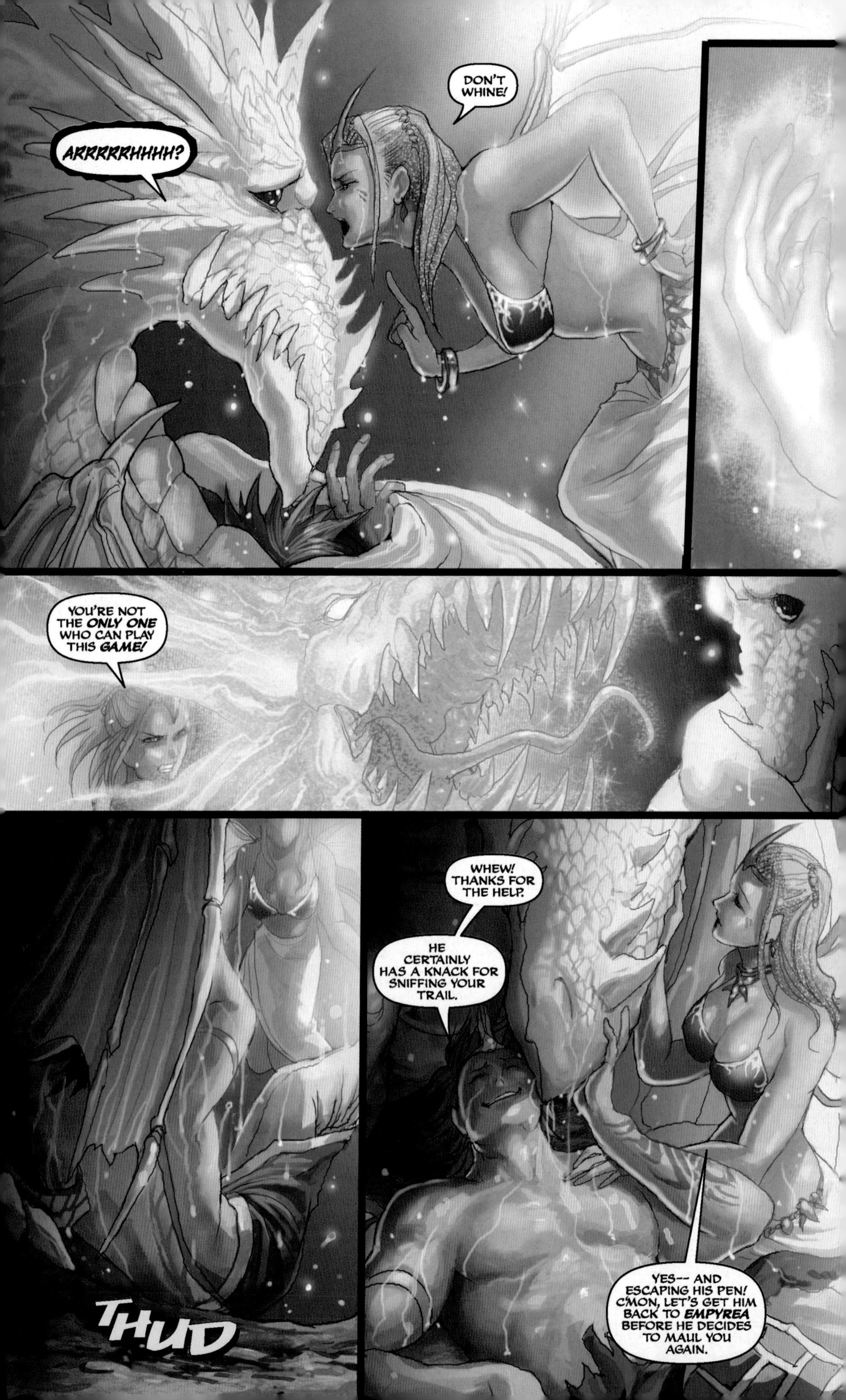
DON'T WHINE!
ARRRRRHHHH?
YOU'RE NOT THE ONLY ONE WHO CAN PLAY THIS GAME!
THUD
WHEW! THANKS FOR THE HELP.
HE CERTAINLY HAS A KNACK FOR SNIFFING YOUR TRAIL.
YES-- AND ESCAPING HIS PEN! C'MON, LET'S GET HIM BACK TO EMPYREA BEFORE HE DECIDES TO MAUL YOU AGAIN.

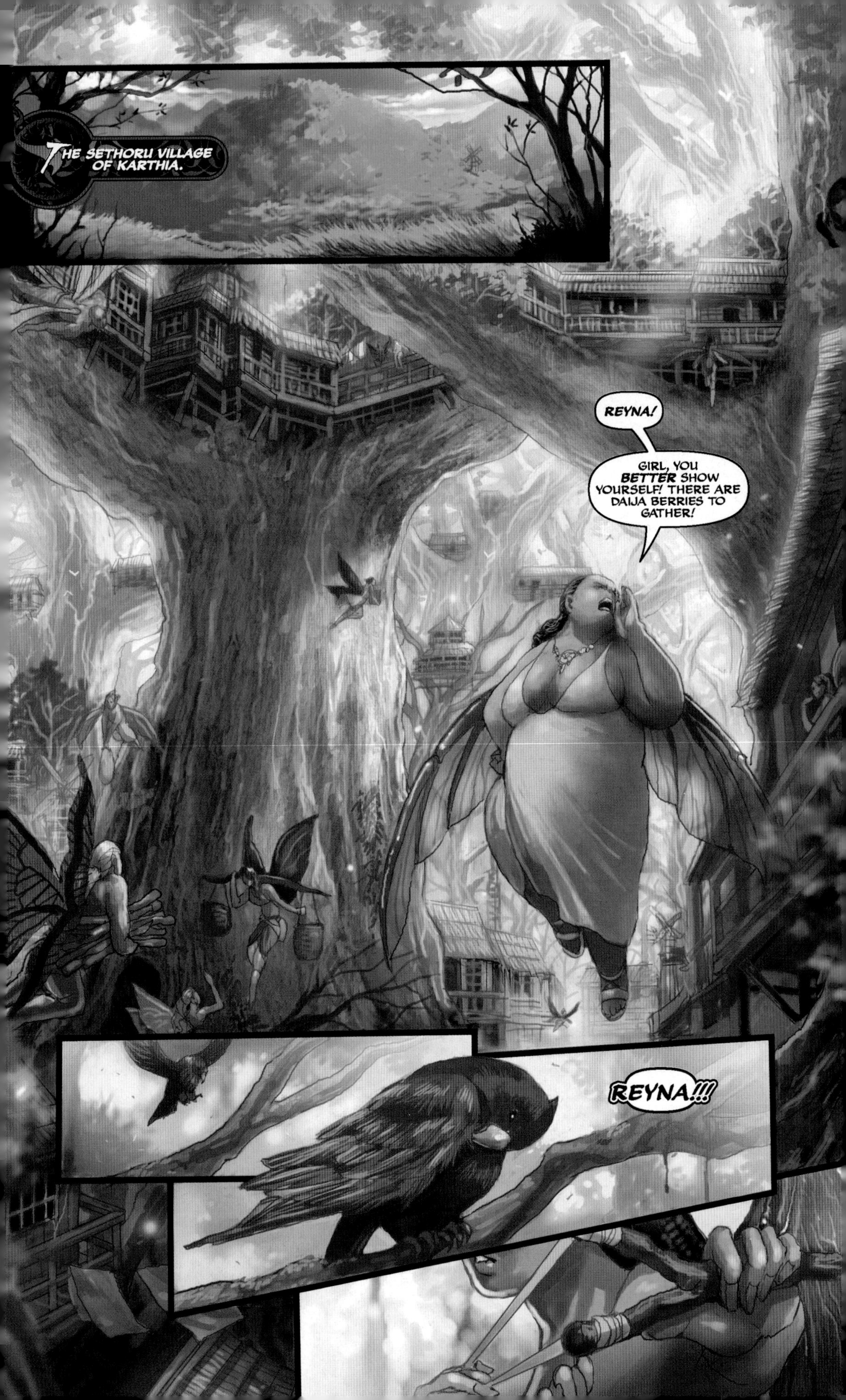
THE SETHORU VILLAGE OF KARTHIA.
REYNA!
GIRL, YOU BETTER SHOW YOURSELF! THERE ARE DAIJA BERRIES TO GATHER!
REYNA!!!

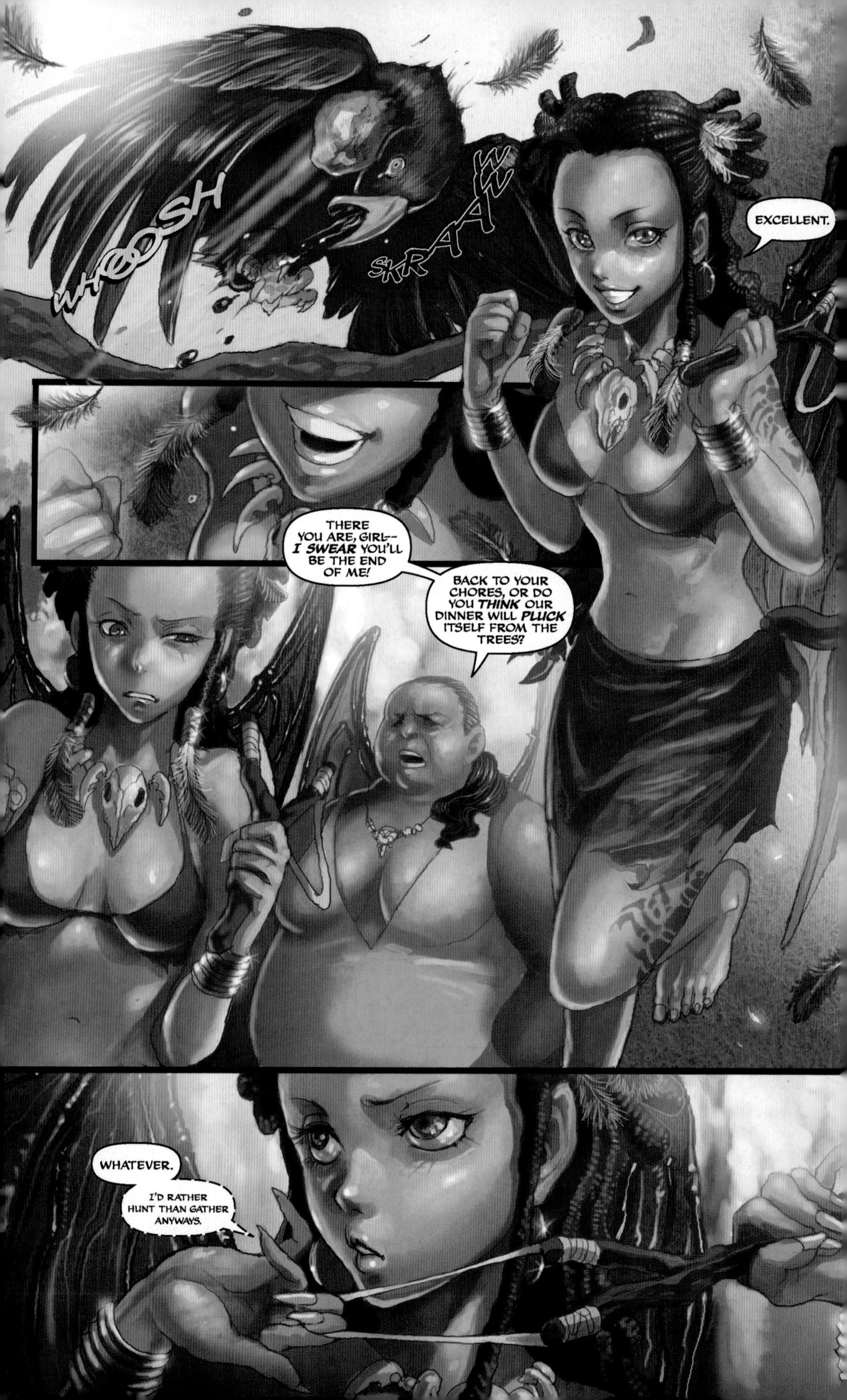
WHOOSH
SKRAAW
EXCELLENT.
THERE YOU ARE, GIRL-- I SWEAR YOU'LL BE THE END OF ME!
BACK TO YOUR CHORES, OR DO YOU THINK OUR DINNER WILL PLUCK ITSELF FROM THE TREES?
WHATEVER.
I'D RATHER HUNT THAN GATHER ANYWAYS.

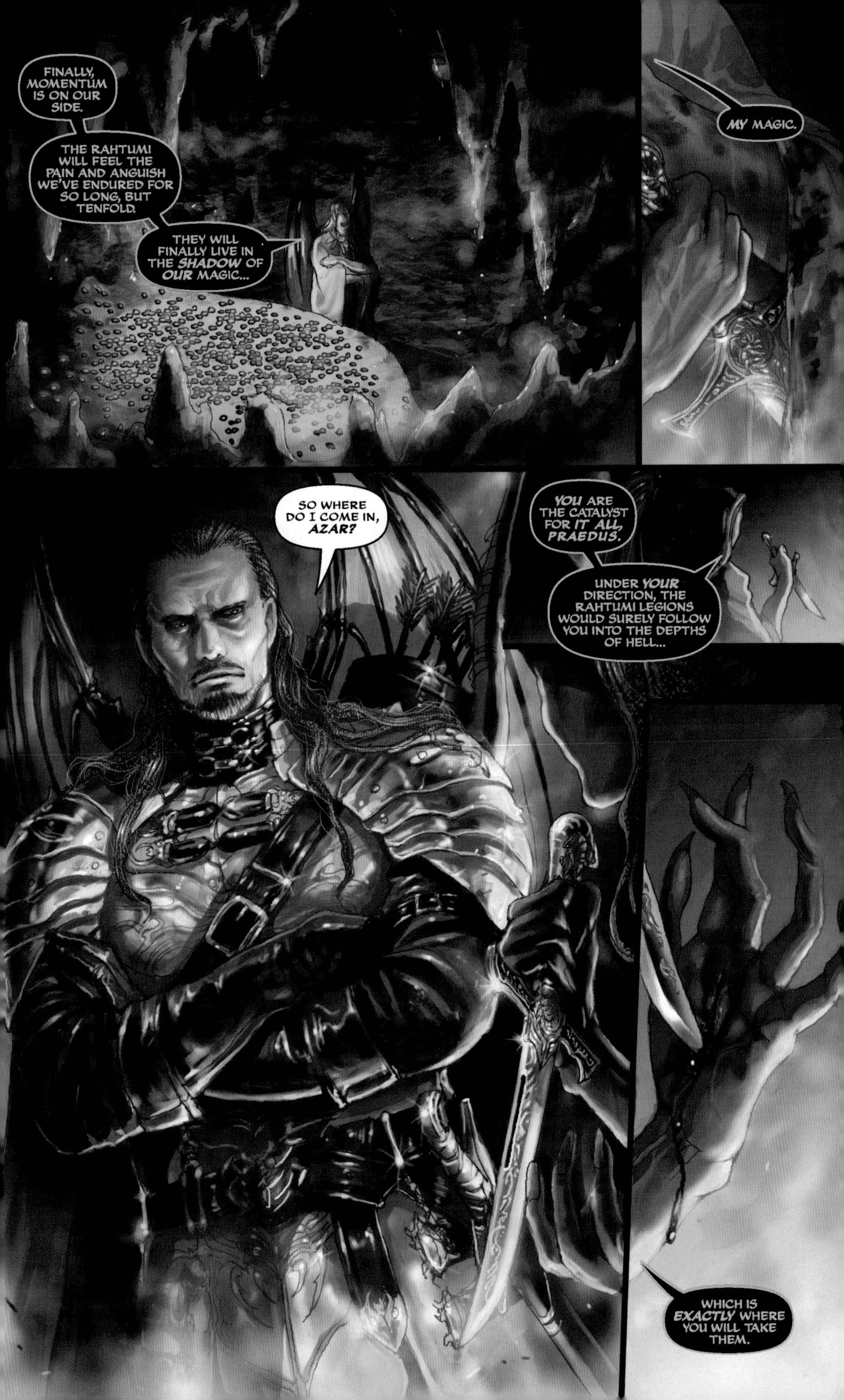
FINALLY, MOMENTUM IS ON OUR SIDE.
THE RAHTUMI WILL FEEL THE PAIN AND ANGUISH WE'VE ENDURED FOR SO LONG, BUT TENFOLD.
THEY WILL FINALLY LIVE IN THE *SHADOW* OF *OUR* MAGIC...
MY MAGIC.
SO WHERE DO I COME IN, *AZAR?*
YOU ARE THE CATALYST FOR *IT ALL, PRAEDUS.*
UNDER *YOUR* DIRECTION, THE RAHTUMI LEGIONS WOULD SURELY FOLLOW YOU INTO THE DEPTHS OF HELL...
WHICH IS *EXACTLY* WHERE YOU WILL TAKE THEM.

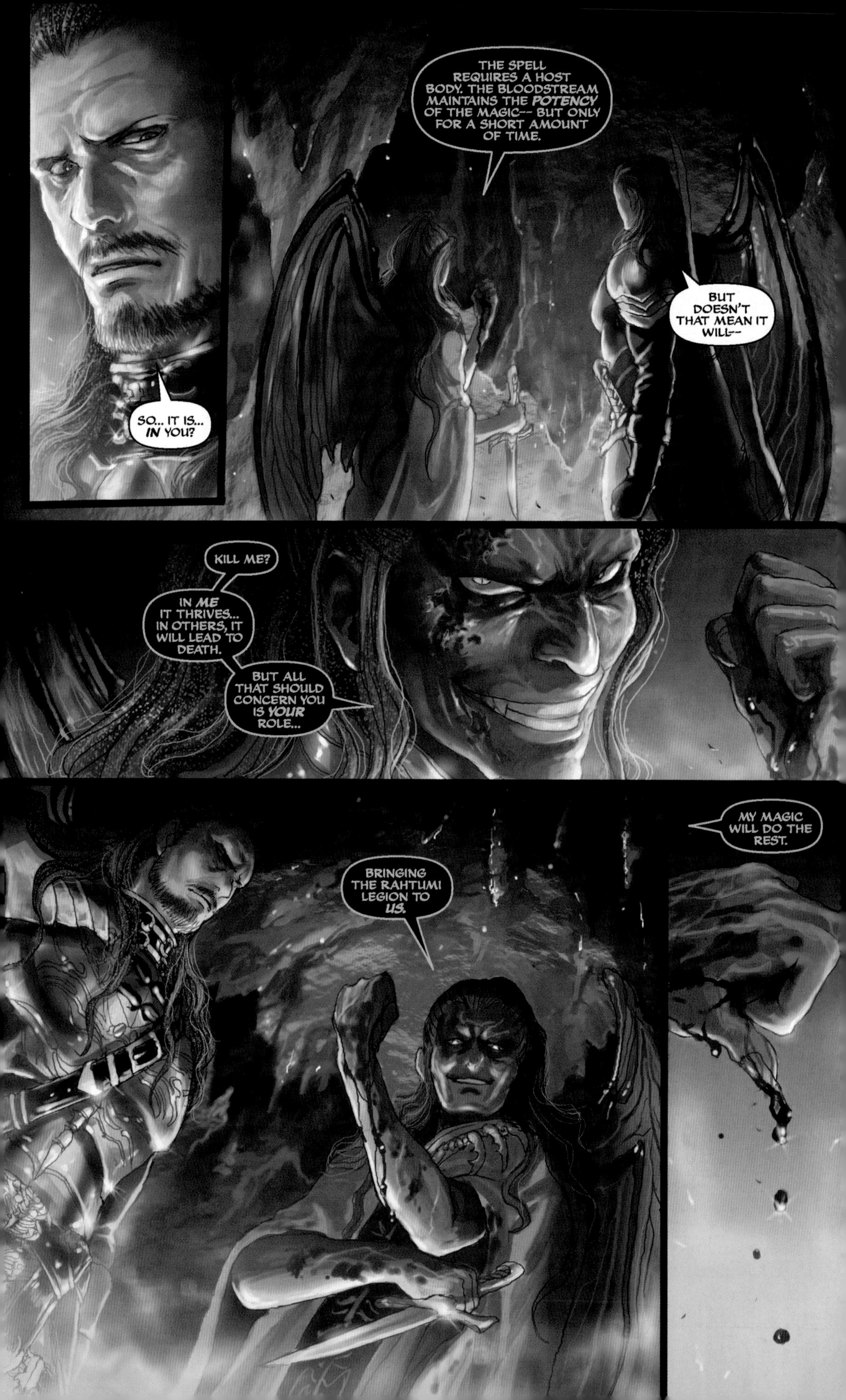
THE SPELL REQUIRES A HOST BODY. THE BLOODSTREAM MAINTAINS THE POTENCY OF THE MAGIC-- BUT ONLY FOR A SHORT AMOUNT OF TIME.
SO... IT IS... IN YOU?
BUT DOESN'T THAT MEAN IT WILL--
KILL ME?
IN ME IT THRIVES... IN OTHERS, IT WILL LEAD TO DEATH.
BUT ALL THAT SHOULD CONCERN YOU IS YOUR ROLE...
BRINGING THE RAHTUMI LEGION TO US.
MY MAGIC WILL DO THE REST.

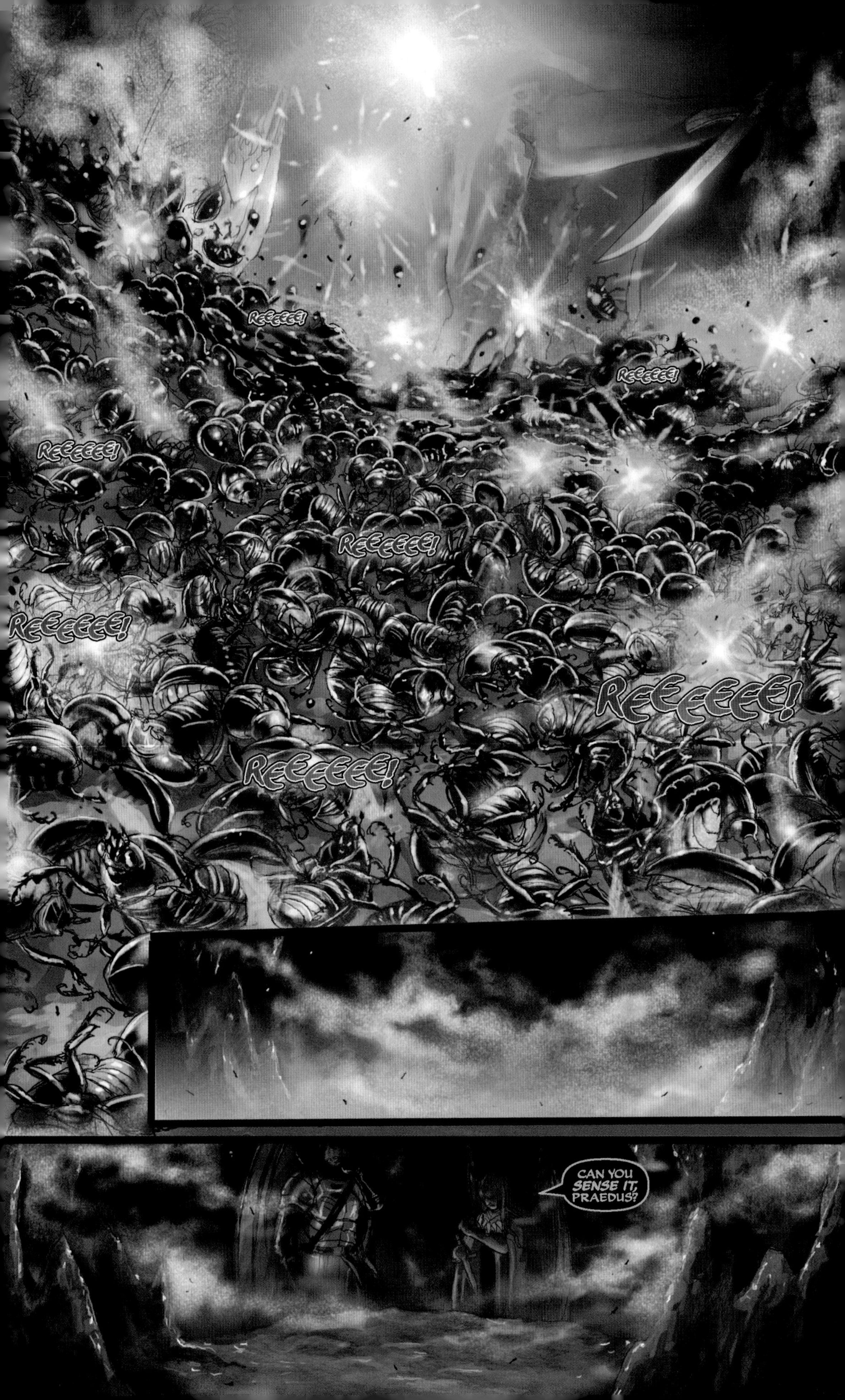
REEEEEE!
REEEEEE!
REEEEEE!
REEEEEEE!
REEEEEEE!
REEEEEEE!
REEEEEEE!
CAN YOU SENSE IT, PRAEDUS?

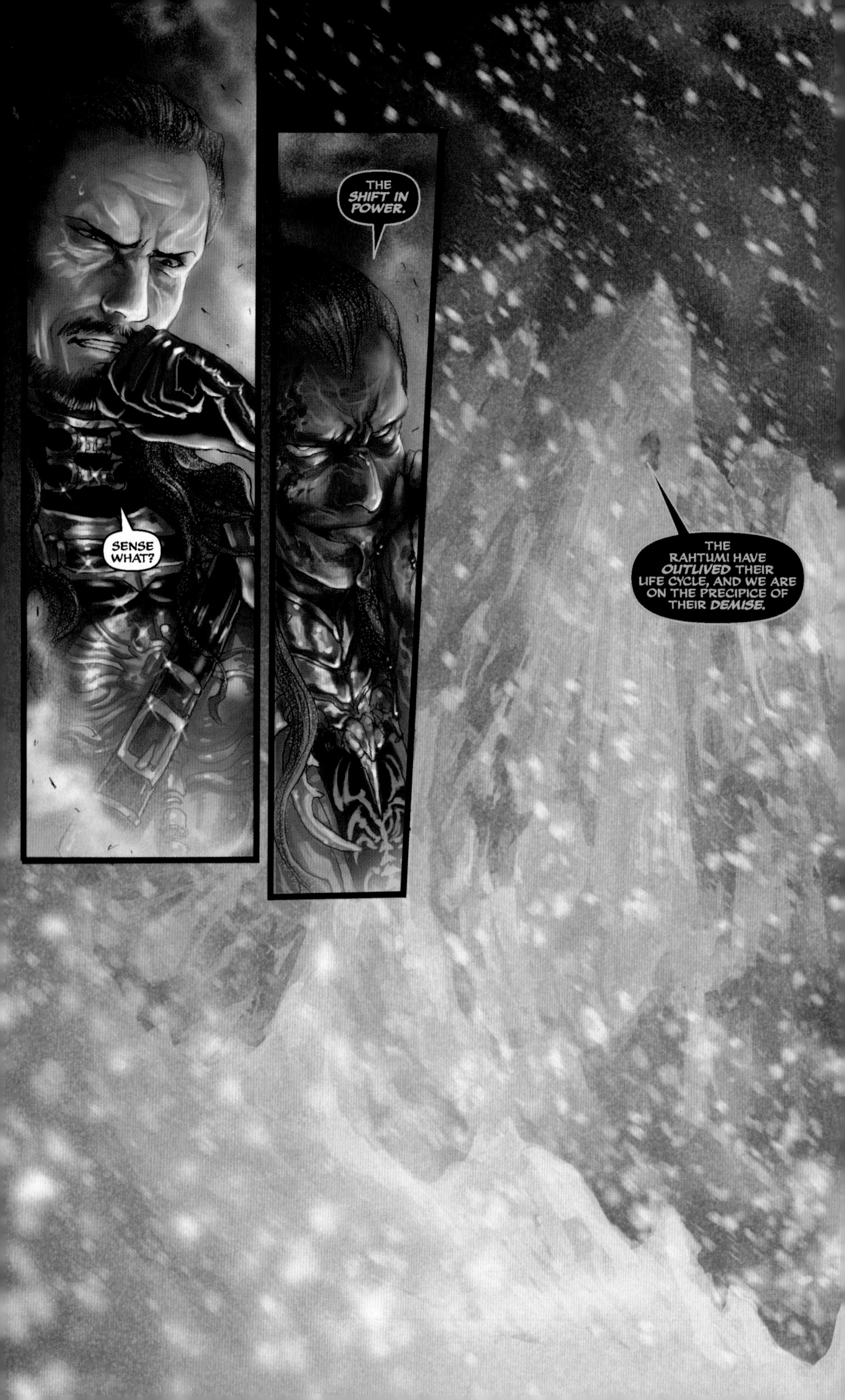
SENSE WHAT?
THE *SHIFT IN POWER.*
THE RAHTUMI HAVE *OUTLIVED* THEIR LIFE CYCLE, AND WE ARE ON THE PRECIPICE OF THEIR *DEMISE.*

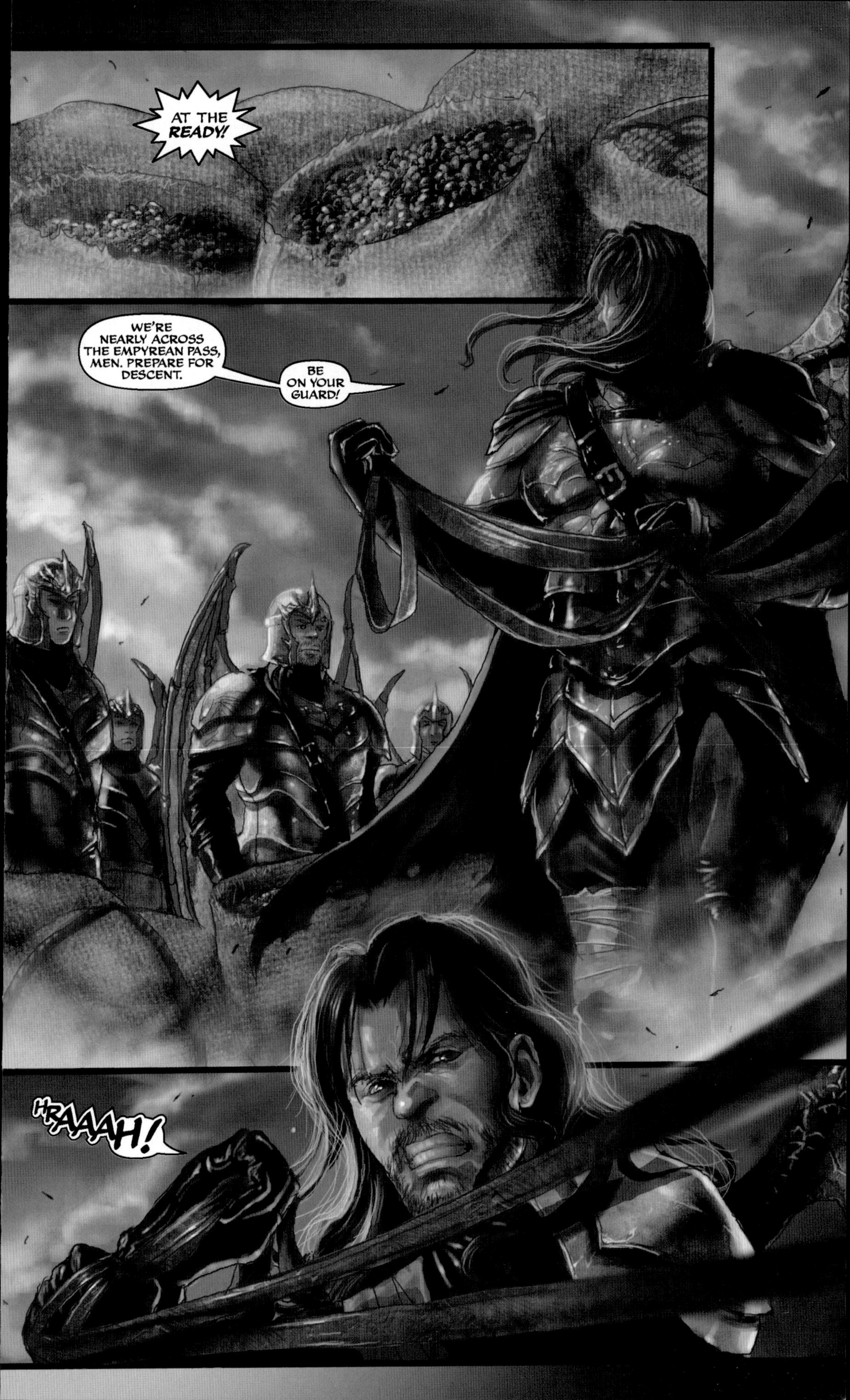
AT THE READY!
WE'RE NEARLY ACROSS THE EMPYREAN PASS, MEN. PREPARE FOR DESCENT.
BE ON YOUR GUARD!
HRAAAH!

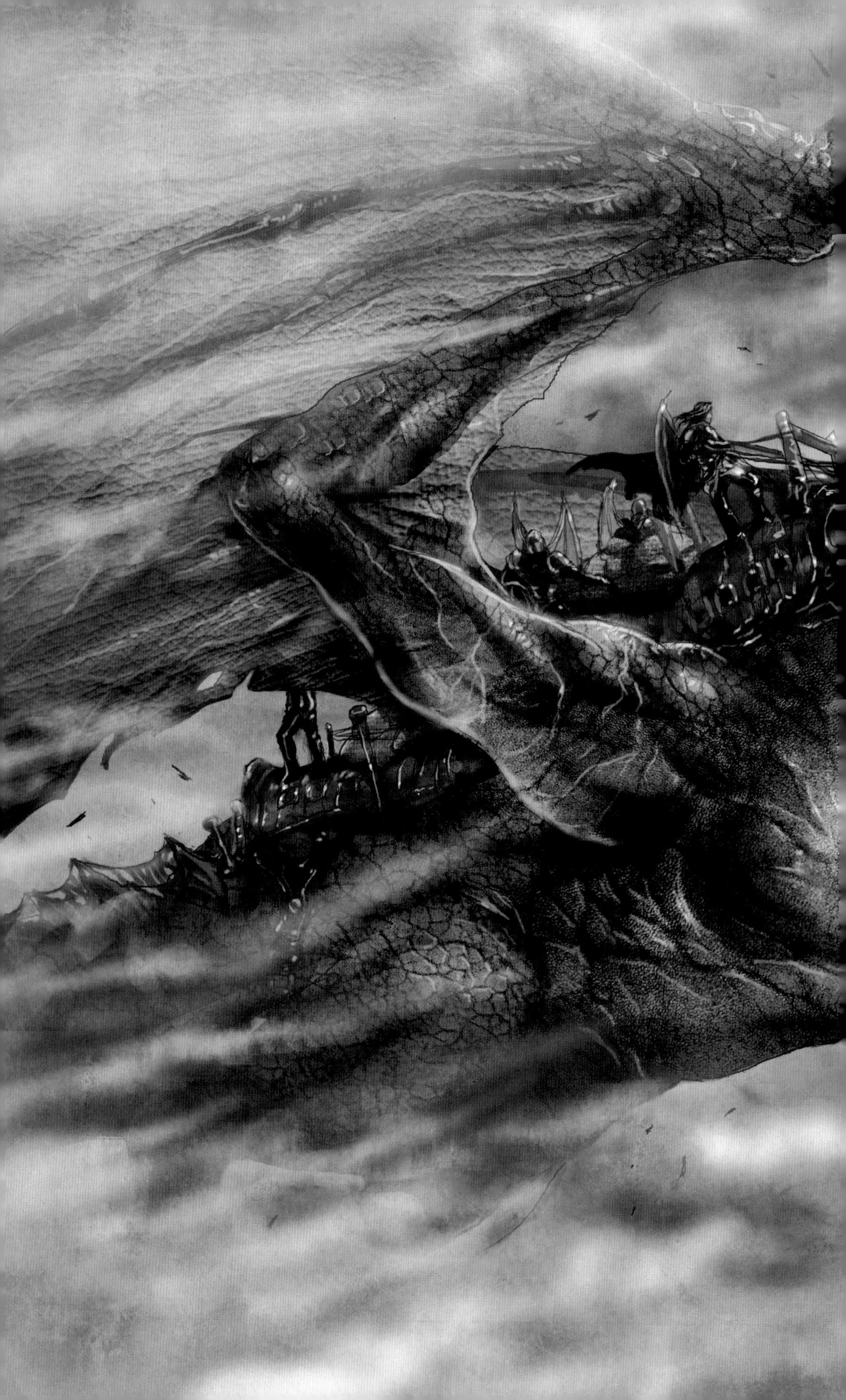

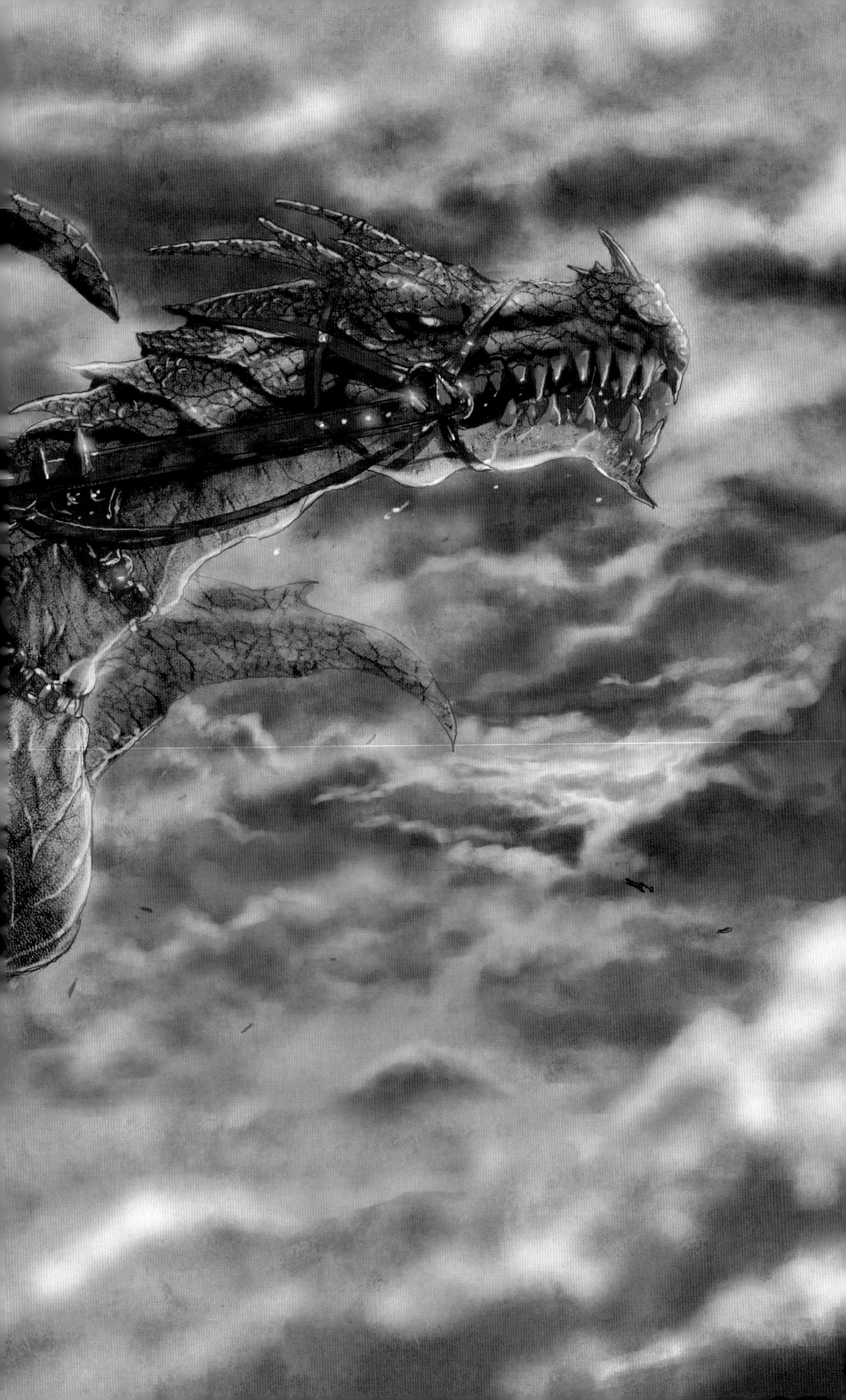

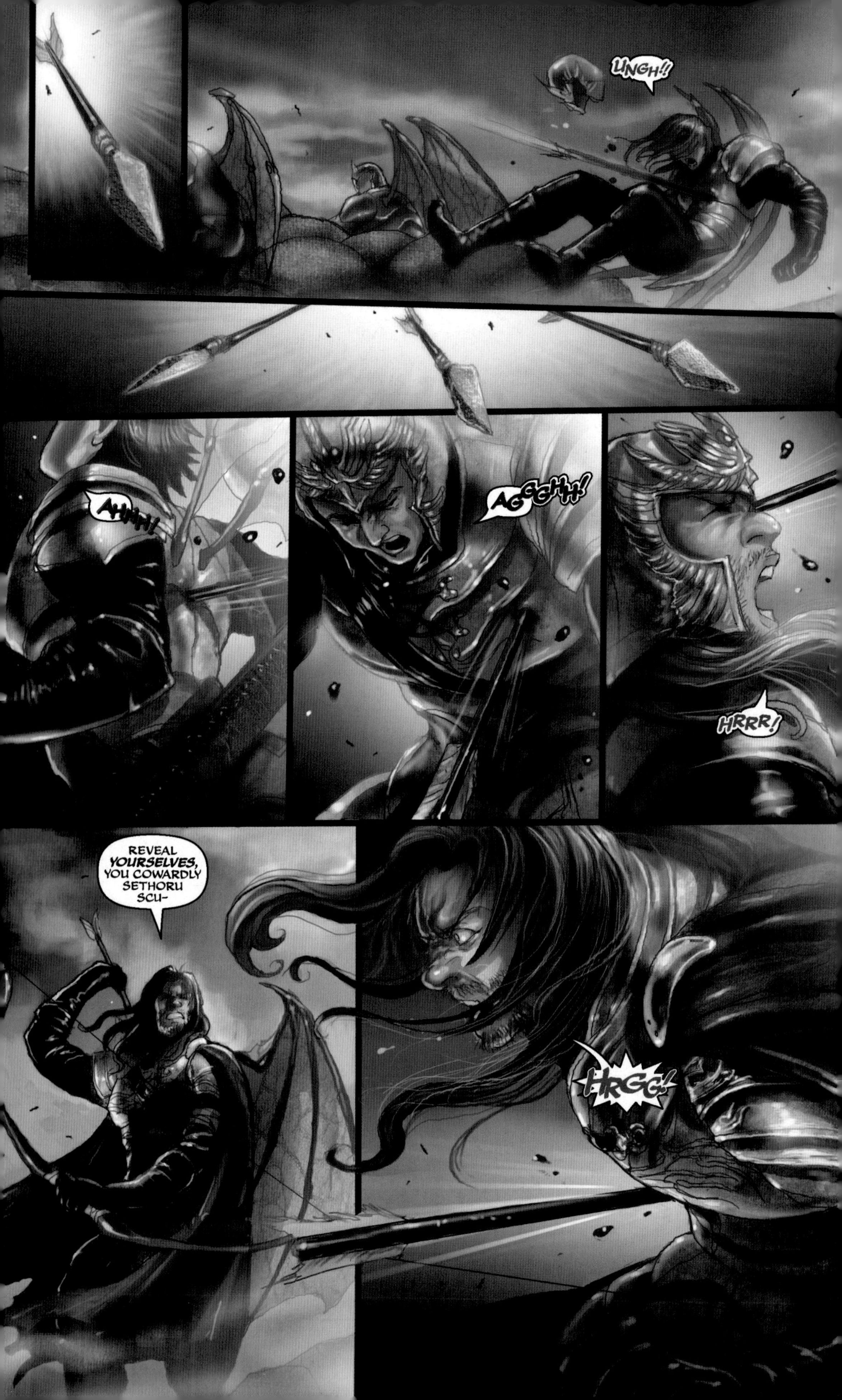
UNGH!!
AHHH!
AGGGHHH!
HRRR!
REVEAL YOURSELVES, YOU COWARDLY SETHORU SCU-
HRGG!

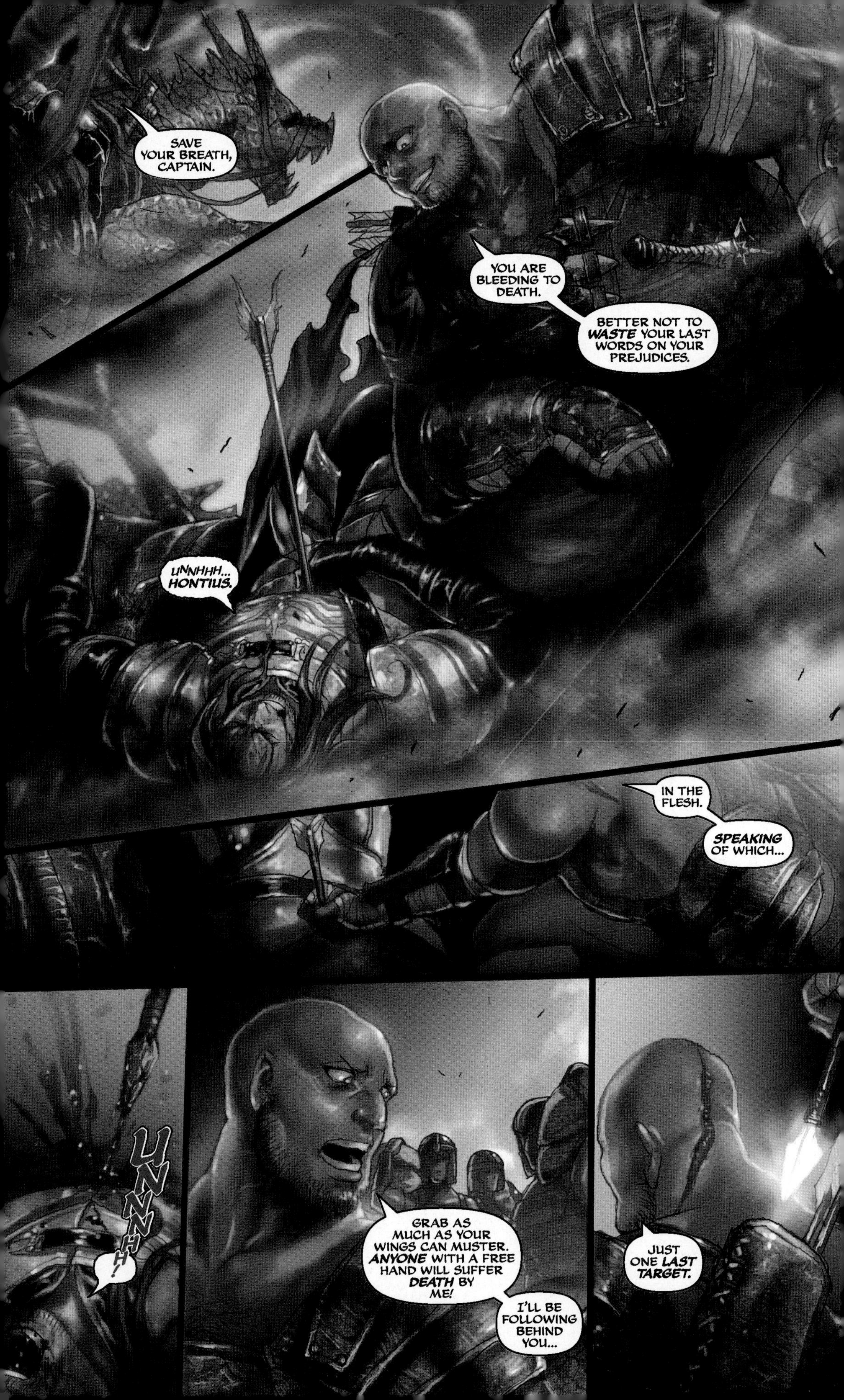
SAVE YOUR BREATH, CAPTAIN.
YOU ARE BLEEDING TO DEATH.
BETTER NOT TO WASTE YOUR LAST WORDS ON YOUR PREJUDICES.
UNNHHH... HONTIUS.
IN THE FLESH.
SPEAKING OF WHICH...
UNNNHH!
GRAB AS MUCH AS YOUR WINGS CAN MUSTER. ANYONE WITH A FREE HAND WILL SUFFER DEATH BY ME!
I'LL BE FOLLOWING BEHIND YOU...
JUST ONE LAST TARGET.

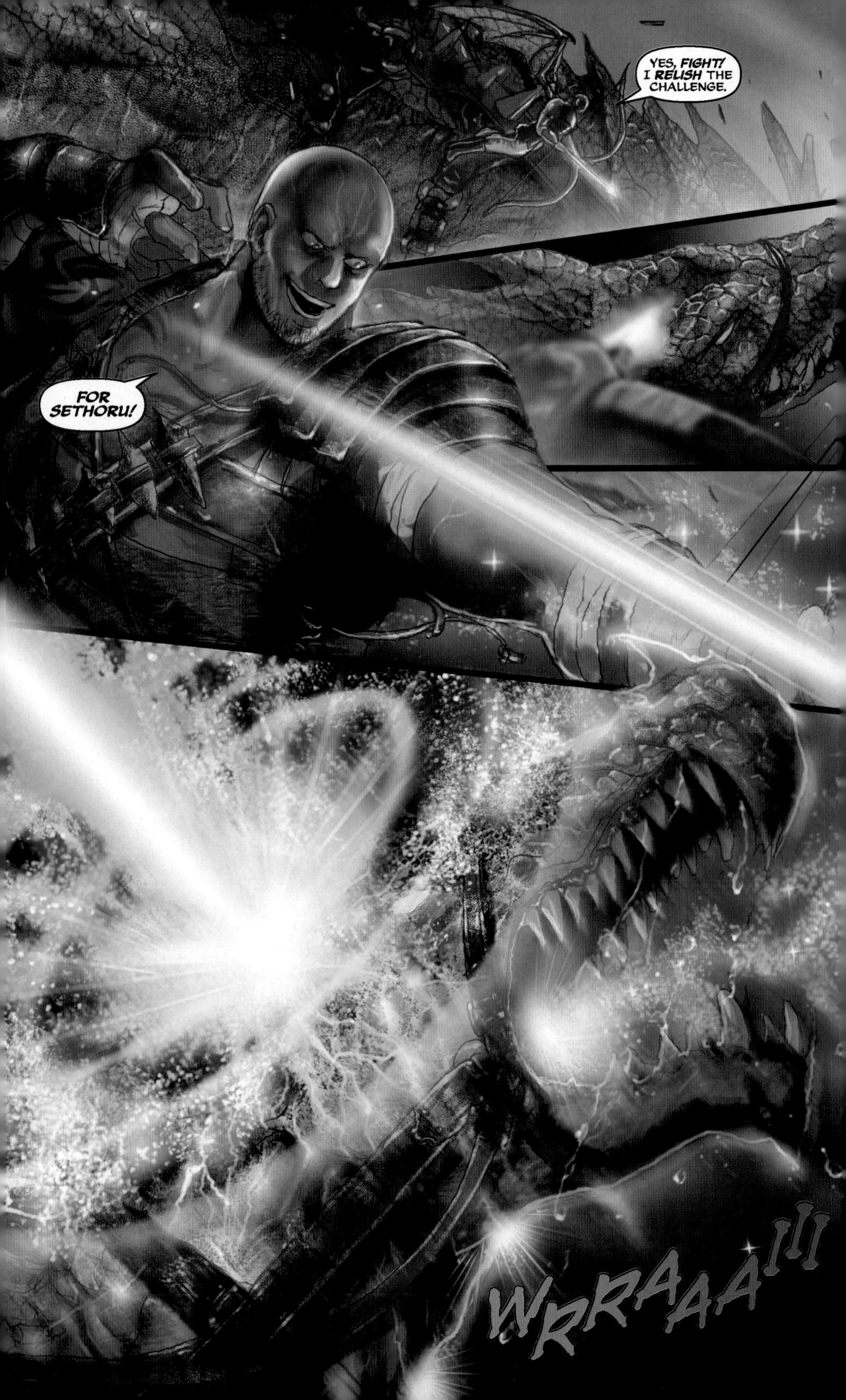
YES, FIGHT! I RELISH THE CHALLENGE.
FOR SETHORU!
WRRAAAIII

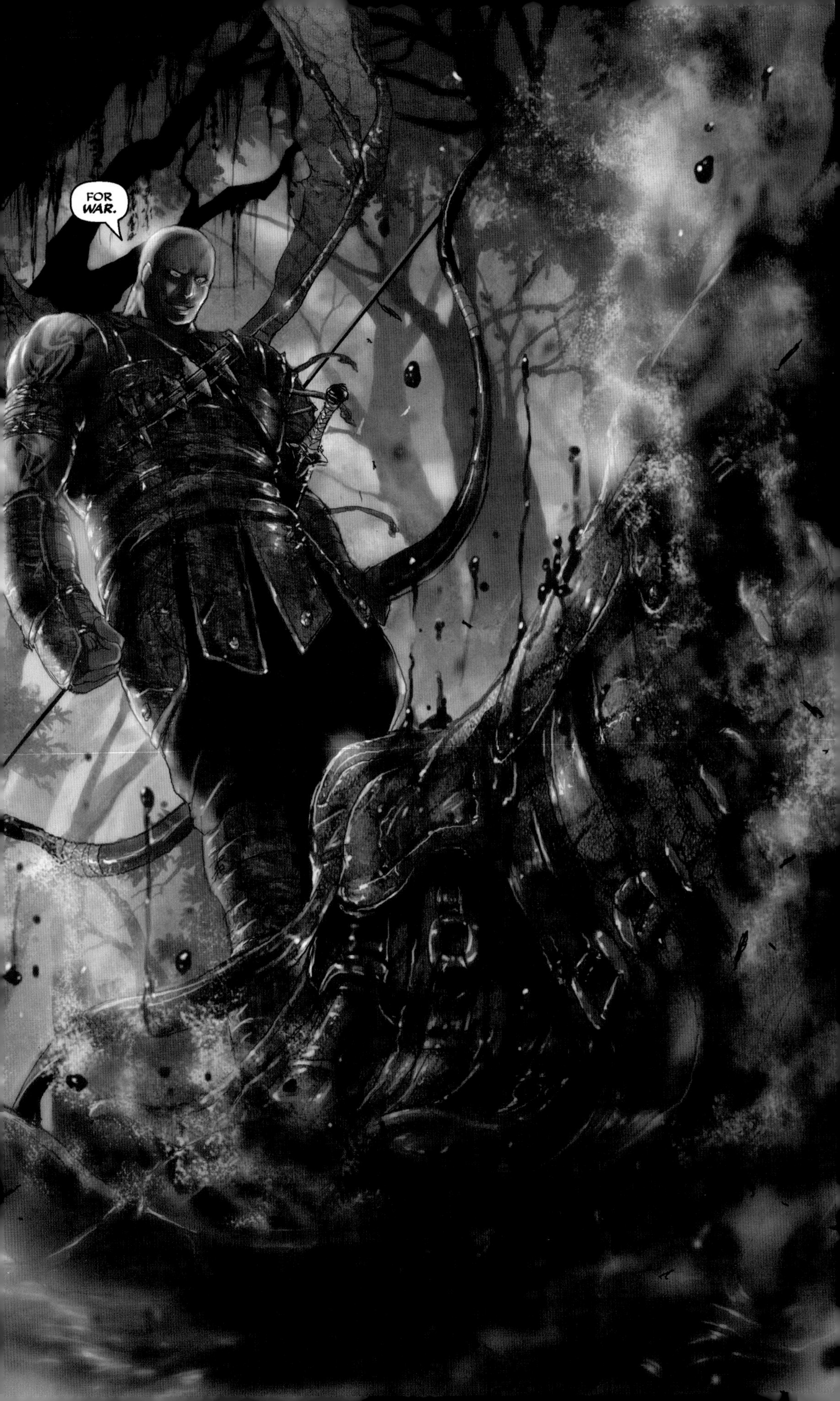
FOR WAR.

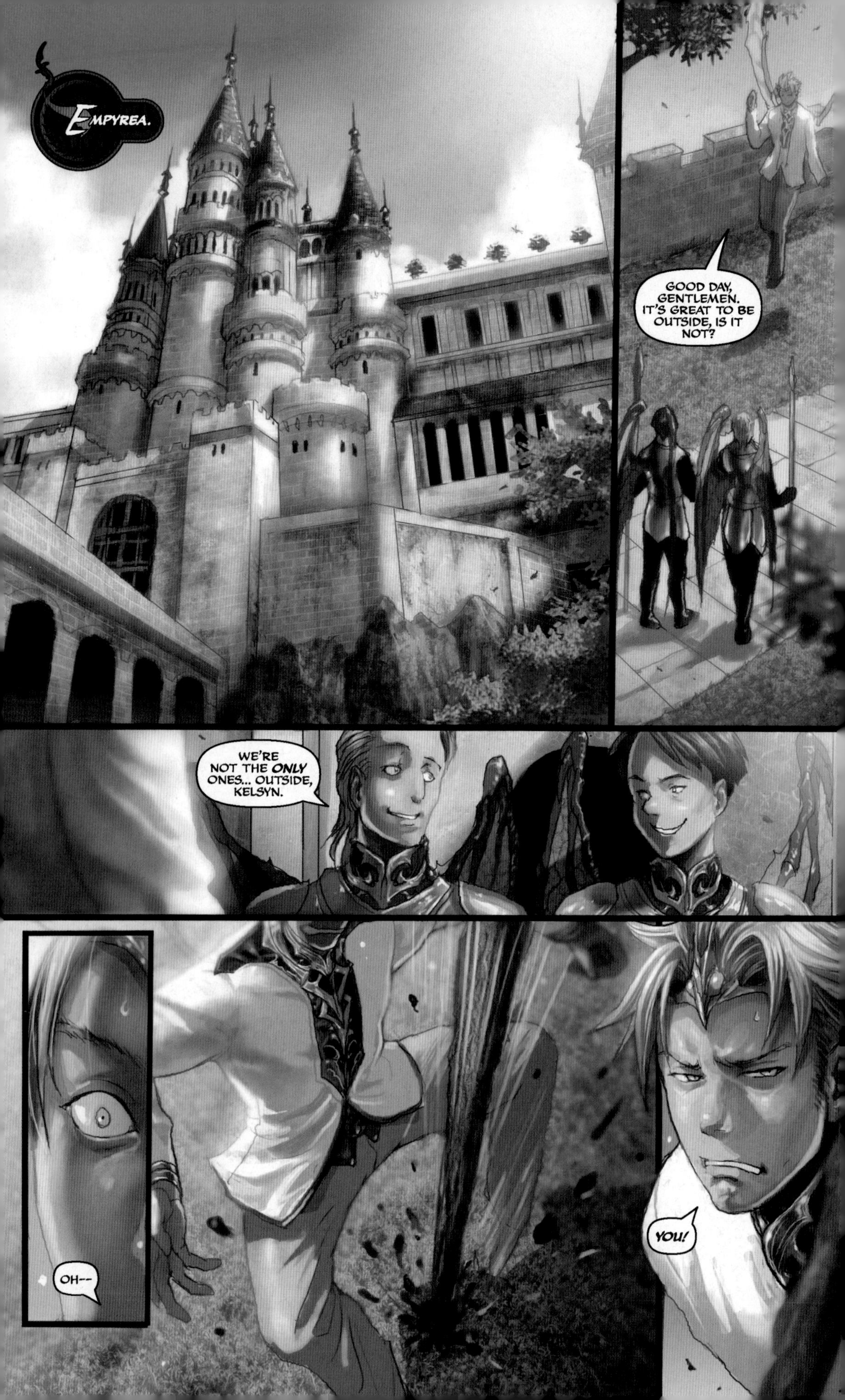
EMPYREA.
GOOD DAY, GENTLEMEN. IT'S GREAT TO BE OUTSIDE, IS IT NOT?
WE'RE NOT THE *ONLY* ONES... OUTSIDE, KELSYN.
OH--
YOU!

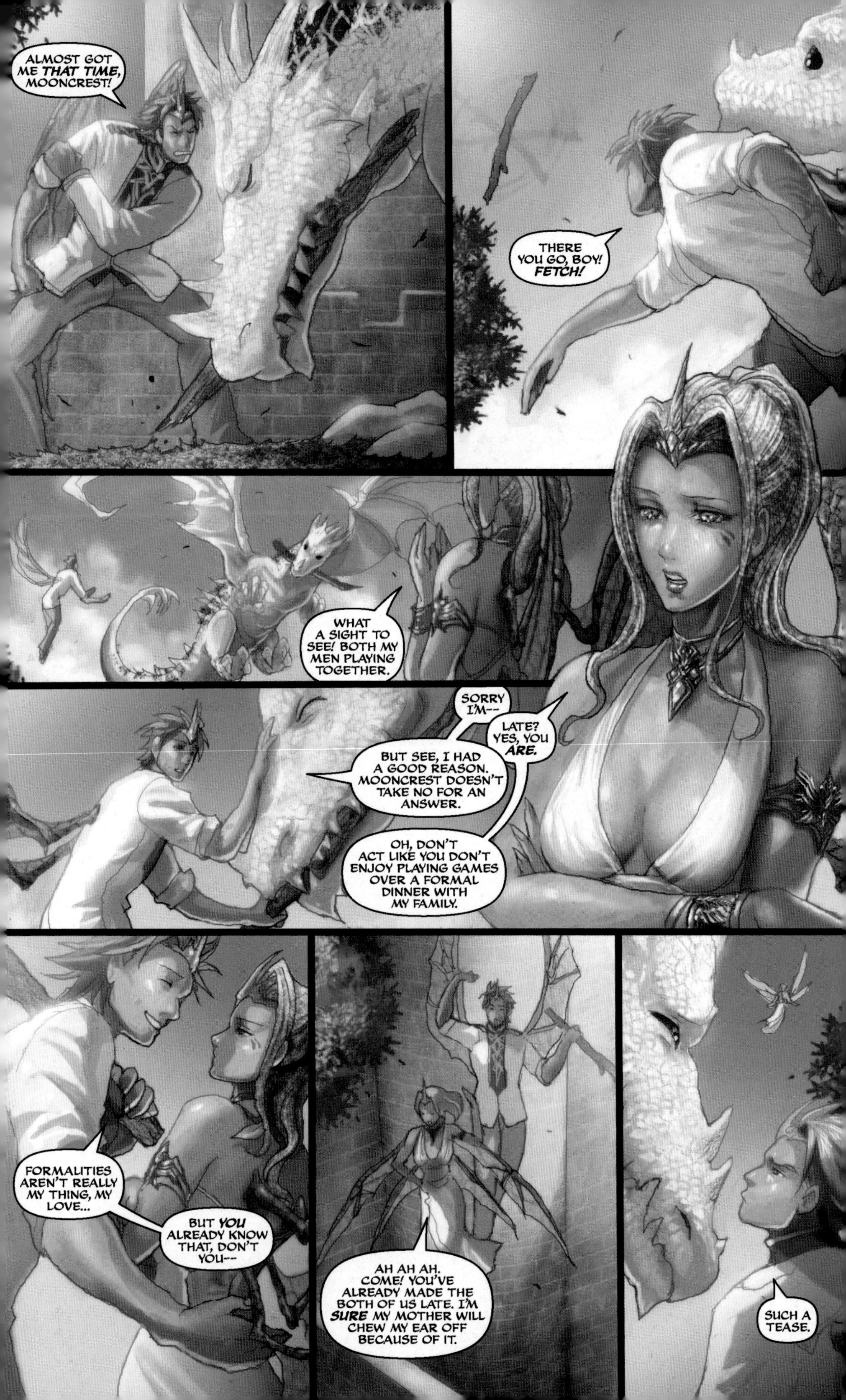

ALMOST GOT ME THAT TIME, MOONCREST!
THERE YOU GO, BOY! FETCH!
WHAT A SIGHT TO SEE! BOTH MY MEN PLAYING TOGETHER.
SORRY I'M--
LATE? YES, YOU ARE.
BUT SEE, I HAD A GOOD REASON. MOONCREST DOESN'T TAKE NO FOR AN ANSWER.
OH, DON'T ACT LIKE YOU DON'T ENJOY PLAYING GAMES OVER A FORMAL DINNER WITH MY FAMILY.
FORMALITIES AREN'T REALLY MY THING, MY LOVE...
BUT YOU ALREADY KNOW THAT, DON'T YOU--
AH AH AH. COME! YOU'VE ALREADY MADE THE BOTH OF US LATE. I'M SURE MY MOTHER WILL CHEW MY EAR OFF BECAUSE OF IT.
SUCH A TEASE.

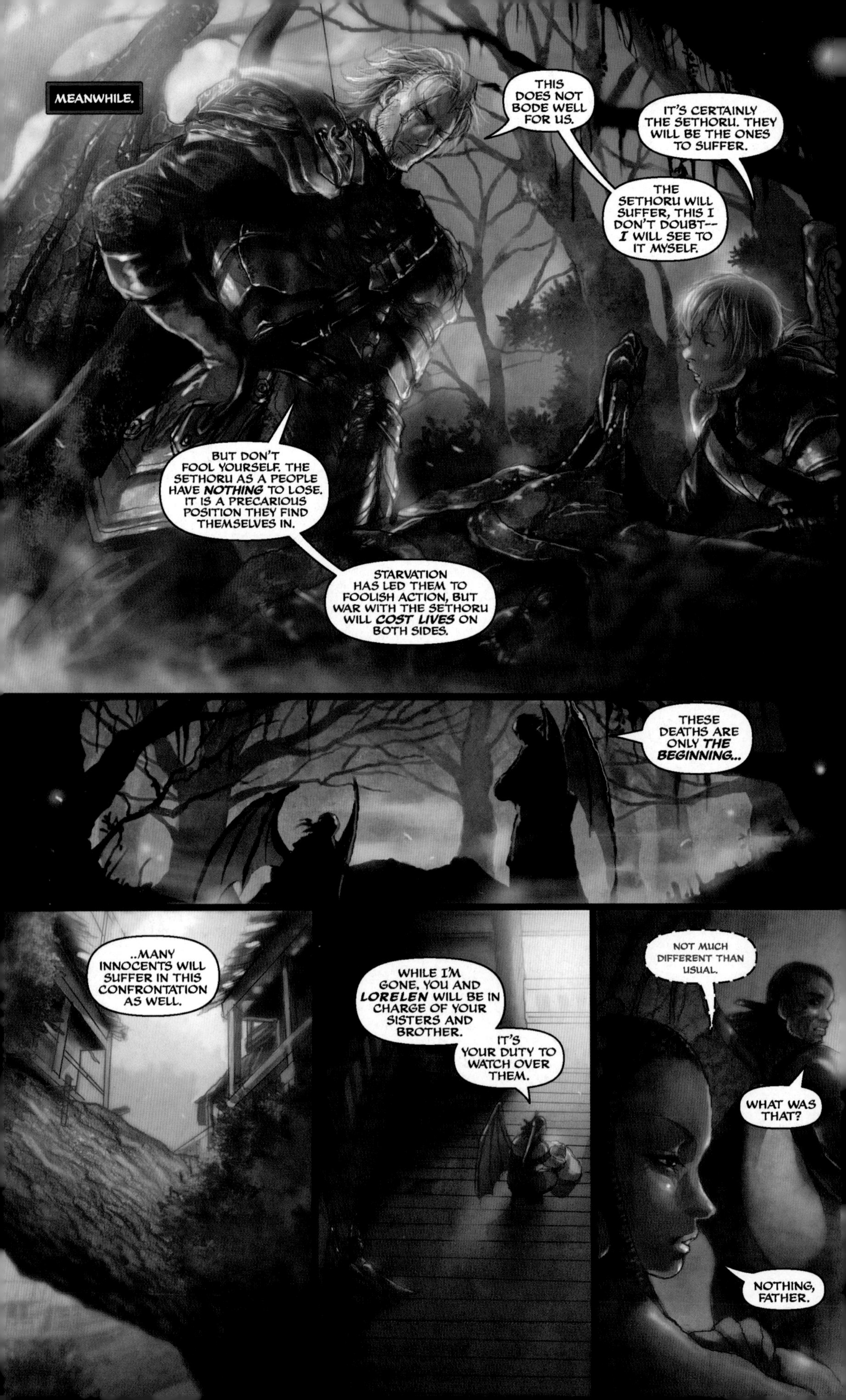
MEANWHILE.
THIS DOES NOT BODE WELL FOR US.
IT'S CERTAINLY THE SETHORU. THEY WILL BE THE ONES TO SUFFER.
THE SETHORU WILL SUFFER, THIS I DON'T DOUBT-- *I* WILL SEE TO IT MYSELF.
BUT DON'T FOOL YOURSELF. THE SETHORU AS A PEOPLE HAVE ***NOTHING*** TO LOSE. IT IS A PRECARIOUS POSITION THEY FIND THEMSELVES IN.
STARVATION HAS LED THEM TO FOOLISH ACTION, BUT WAR WITH THE SETHORU WILL ***COST LIVES*** ON BOTH SIDES.
THESE DEATHS ARE ONLY ***THE BEGINNING...***
..MANY INNOCENTS WILL SUFFER IN THIS CONFRONTATION AS WELL.
WHILE I'M GONE, YOU AND ***LORELEN*** WILL BE IN CHARGE OF YOUR SISTERS AND BROTHER.
IT'S YOUR DUTY TO WATCH OVER THEM.
NOT MUCH DIFFERENT THAN USUAL.
WHAT WAS THAT?
NOTHING, FATHER.

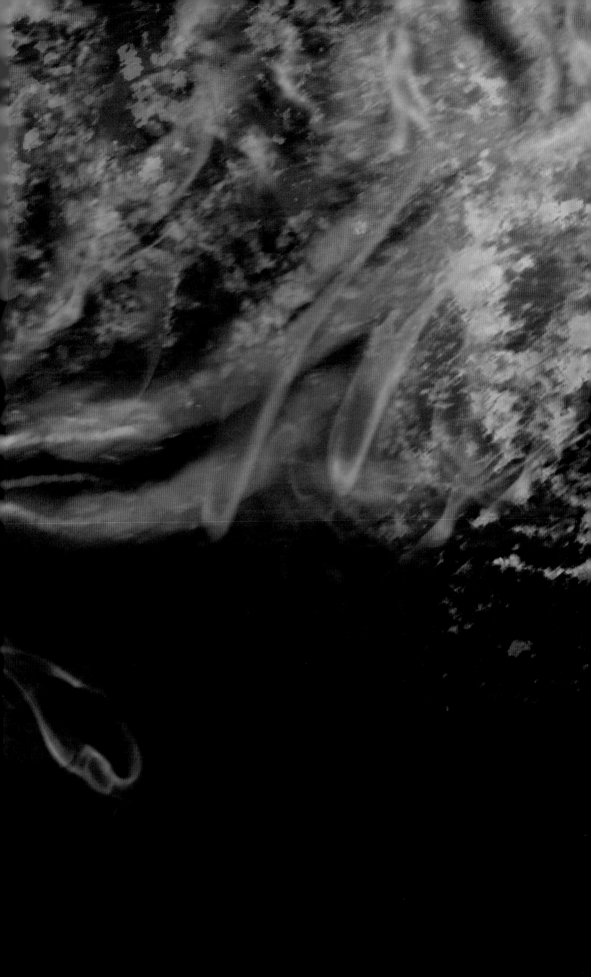

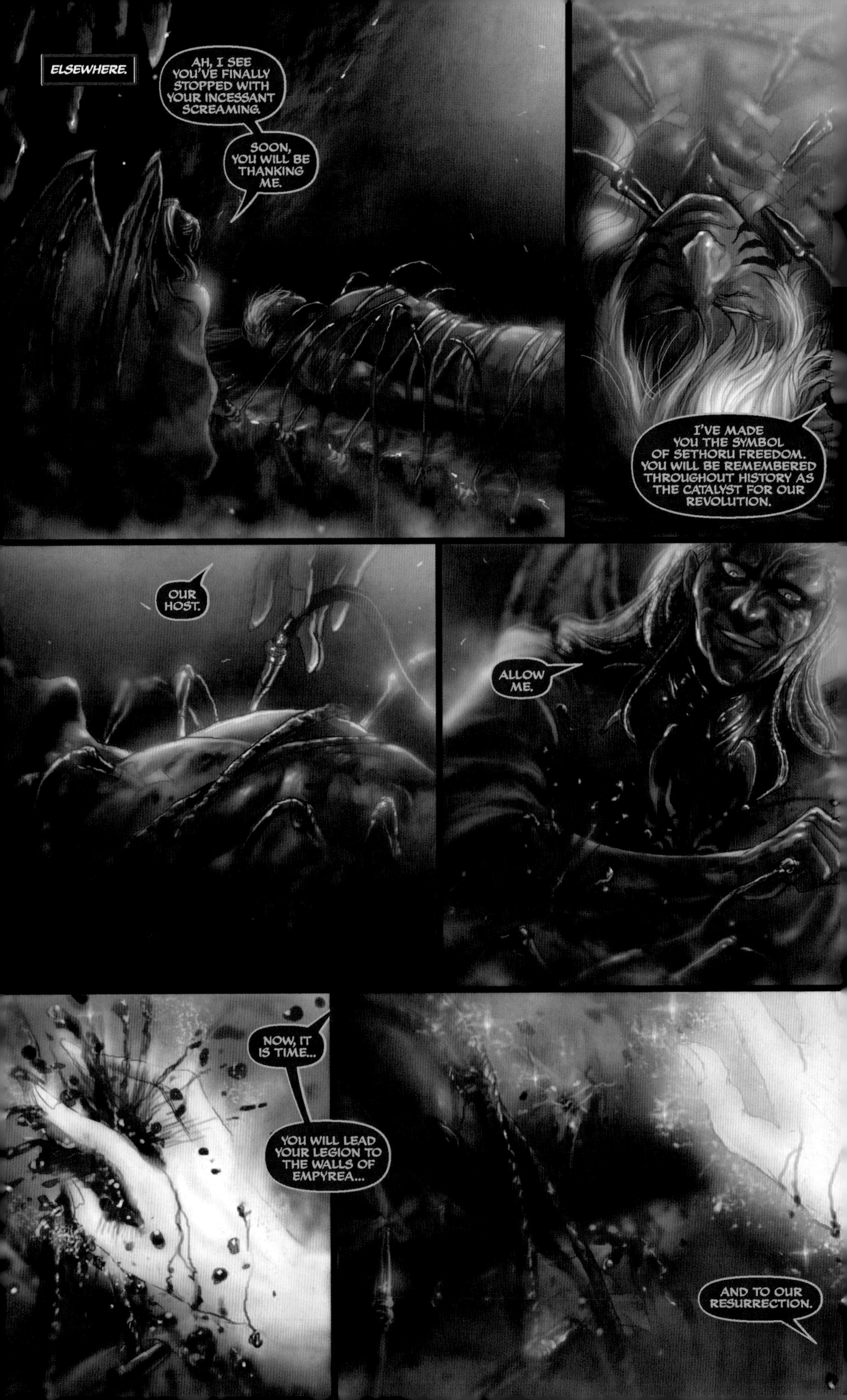
ELSEWHERE.
AH, I SEE YOU'VE FINALLY STOPPED WITH YOUR INCESSANT SCREAMING.
SOON, YOU WILL BE THANKING ME.
I'VE MADE YOU THE SYMBOL OF SETHORU FREEDOM. YOU WILL BE REMEMBERED THROUGHOUT HISTORY AS THE CATALYST FOR OUR REVOLUTION.
OUR HOST.
ALLOW ME.
NOW, IT IS TIME...
YOU WILL LEAD YOUR LEGION TO THE WALLS OF EMPYREA...
AND TO OUR RESURRECTION.

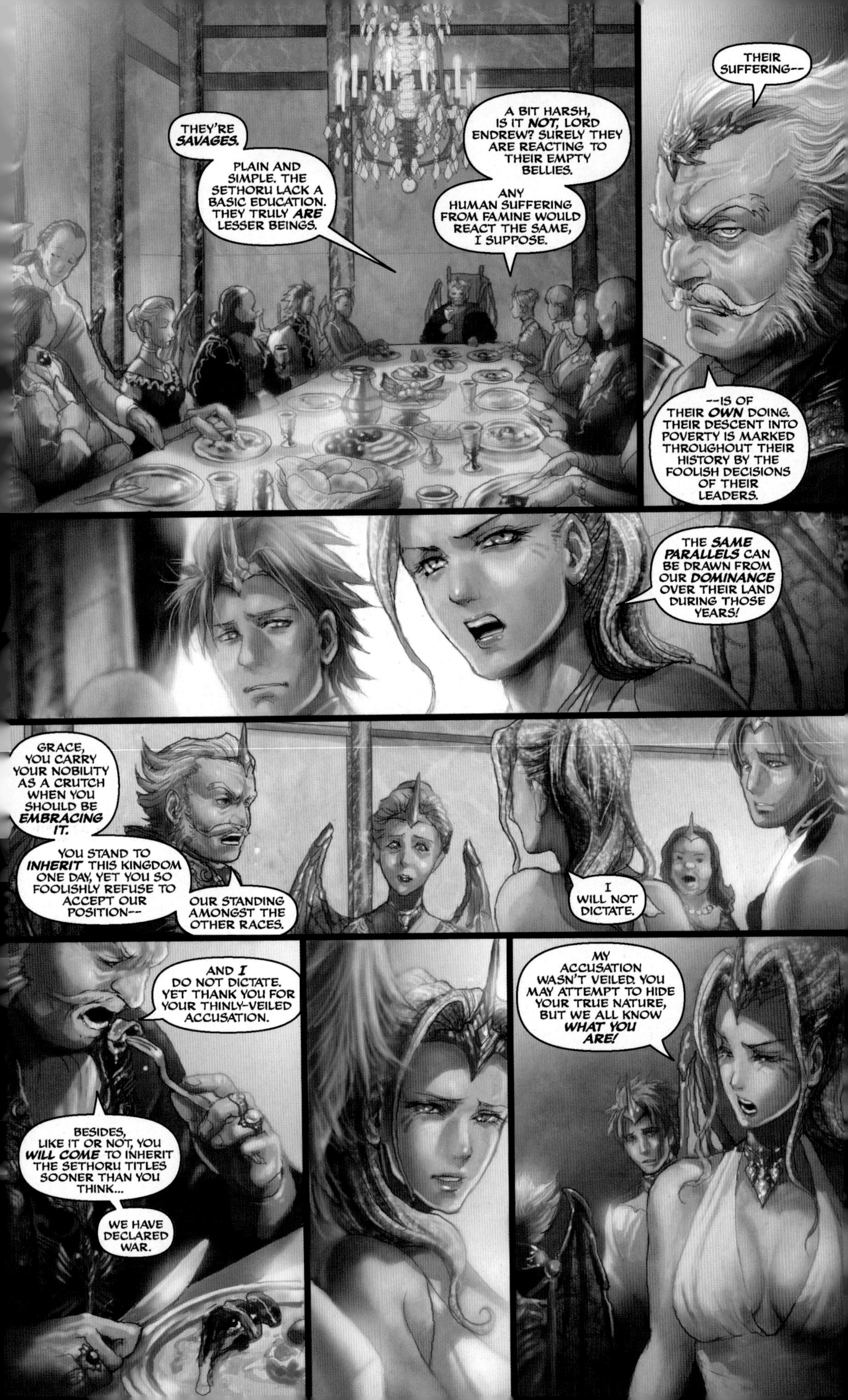
THEY'RE SAVAGES.
PLAIN AND SIMPLE. THE SETHORU LACK A BASIC EDUCATION. THEY TRULY ARE LESSER BEINGS.
A BIT HARSH, IS IT NOT, LORD ENDREW? SURELY THEY ARE REACTING TO THEIR EMPTY BELLIES.
ANY HUMAN SUFFERING FROM FAMINE WOULD REACT THE SAME, I SUPPOSE.
THEIR SUFFERING--
--IS OF THEIR OWN DOING. THEIR DESCENT INTO POVERTY IS MARKED THROUGHOUT THEIR HISTORY BY THE FOOLISH DECISIONS OF THEIR LEADERS.
THE SAME PARALLELS CAN BE DRAWN FROM OUR DOMINANCE OVER THEIR LAND DURING THOSE YEARS!
GRACE, YOU CARRY YOUR NOBILITY AS A CRUTCH WHEN YOU SHOULD BE EMBRACING IT.
YOU STAND TO INHERIT THIS KINGDOM ONE DAY, YET YOU SO FOOLISHLY REFUSE TO ACCEPT OUR POSITION--
OUR STANDING AMONGST THE OTHER RACES.
I WILL NOT DICTATE.
AND I DO NOT DICTATE. YET THANK YOU FOR YOUR THINLY-VEILED ACCUSATION.
BESIDES, LIKE IT OR NOT, YOU WILL COME TO INHERIT THE SETHORU TITLES SOONER THAN YOU THINK...
WE HAVE DECLARED WAR.
MY ACCUSATION WASN'T VEILED. YOU MAY ATTEMPT TO HIDE YOUR TRUE NATURE, BUT WE ALL KNOW WHAT YOU ARE!

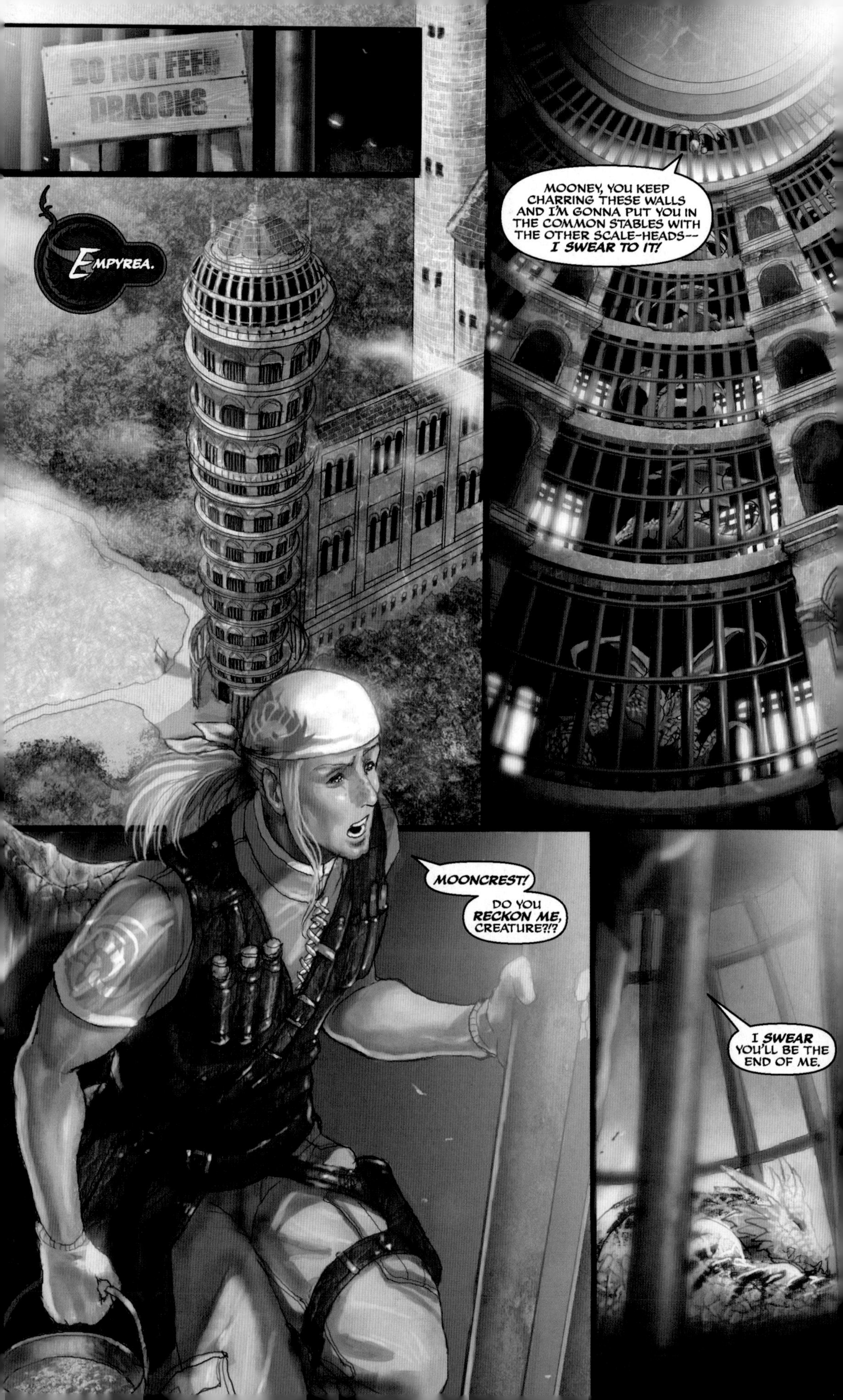
DO NOT FEED DRAGONS
EMPYREA.
MOONEY, YOU KEEP CHARRING THESE WALLS AND I'M GONNA PUT YOU IN THE COMMON STABLES WITH THE OTHER SCALE-HEADS-- I SWEAR TO IT!
MOONCREST!
DO YOU RECKON ME, CREATURE?!?
I SWEAR YOU'LL BE THE END OF ME.

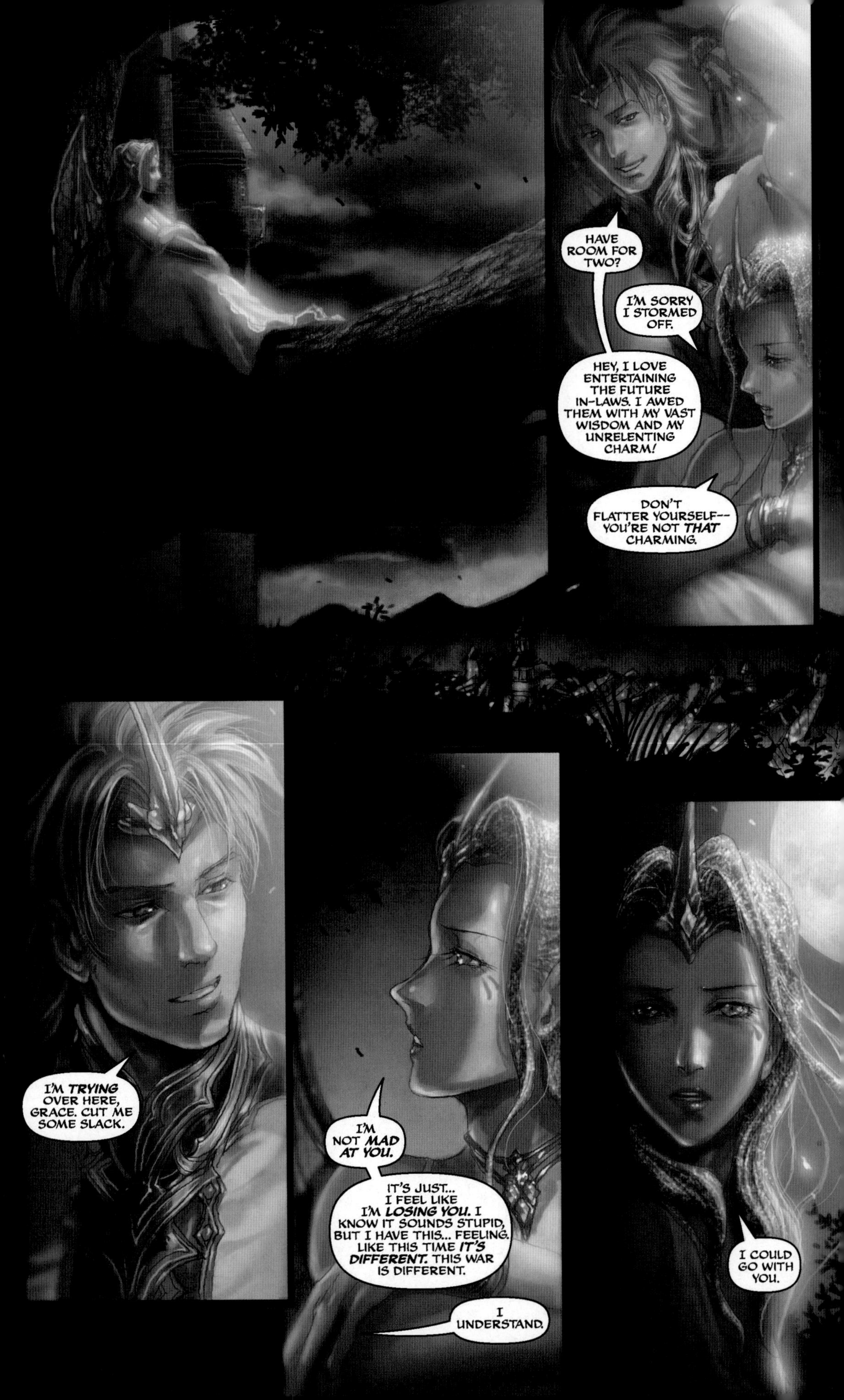
HAVE ROOM FOR TWO?
I'M SORRY I STORMED OFF.
HEY, I LOVE ENTERTAINING THE FUTURE IN-LAWS. I AWED THEM WITH MY VAST WISDOM AND MY UNRELENTING CHARM!
DON'T FLATTER YOURSELF-- YOU'RE NOT *THAT* CHARMING.
I'M *TRYING* OVER HERE, GRACE. CUT ME SOME SLACK.
I'M NOT *MAD AT YOU.*
IT'S JUST... I FEEL LIKE I'M *LOSING YOU.* I KNOW IT SOUNDS STUPID, BUT I HAVE THIS... FEELING. LIKE THIS TIME *IT'S DIFFERENT.* THIS WAR IS DIFFERENT.
I UNDERSTAND.
I COULD GO WITH YOU.

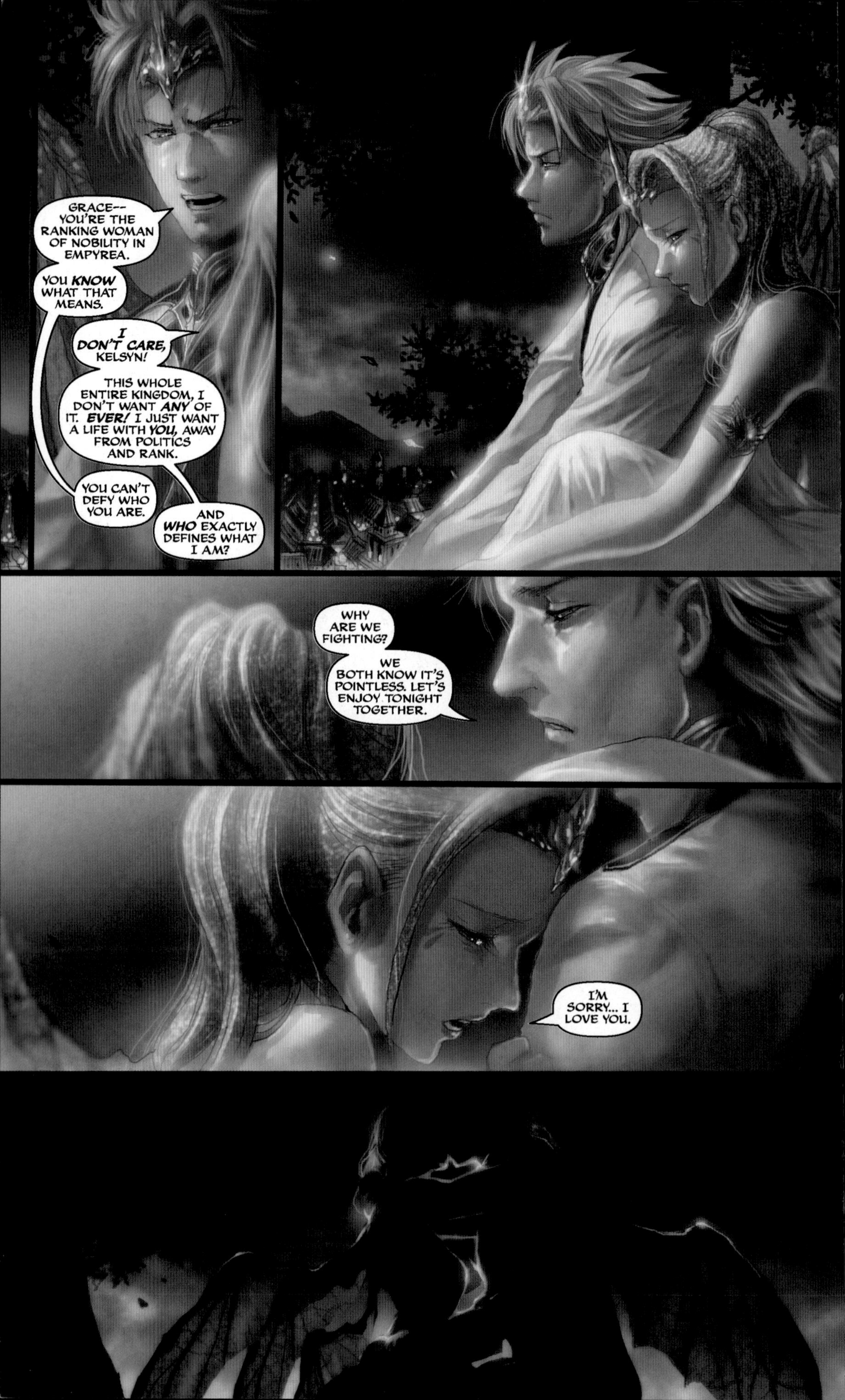
GRACE-- YOU'RE THE RANKING WOMAN OF NOBILITY IN EMPYREA.
YOU KNOW WHAT THAT MEANS.
I DON'T CARE, KELSYN!
THIS WHOLE ENTIRE KINGDOM, I DON'T WANT ANY OF IT. EVER! I JUST WANT A LIFE WITH YOU, AWAY FROM POLITICS AND RANK.
YOU CAN'T DEFY WHO YOU ARE.
AND WHO EXACTLY DEFINES WHAT I AM?
WHY ARE WE FIGHTING?
WE BOTH KNOW IT'S POINTLESS. LET'S ENJOY TONIGHT TOGETHER.
I'M SORRY... I LOVE YOU.

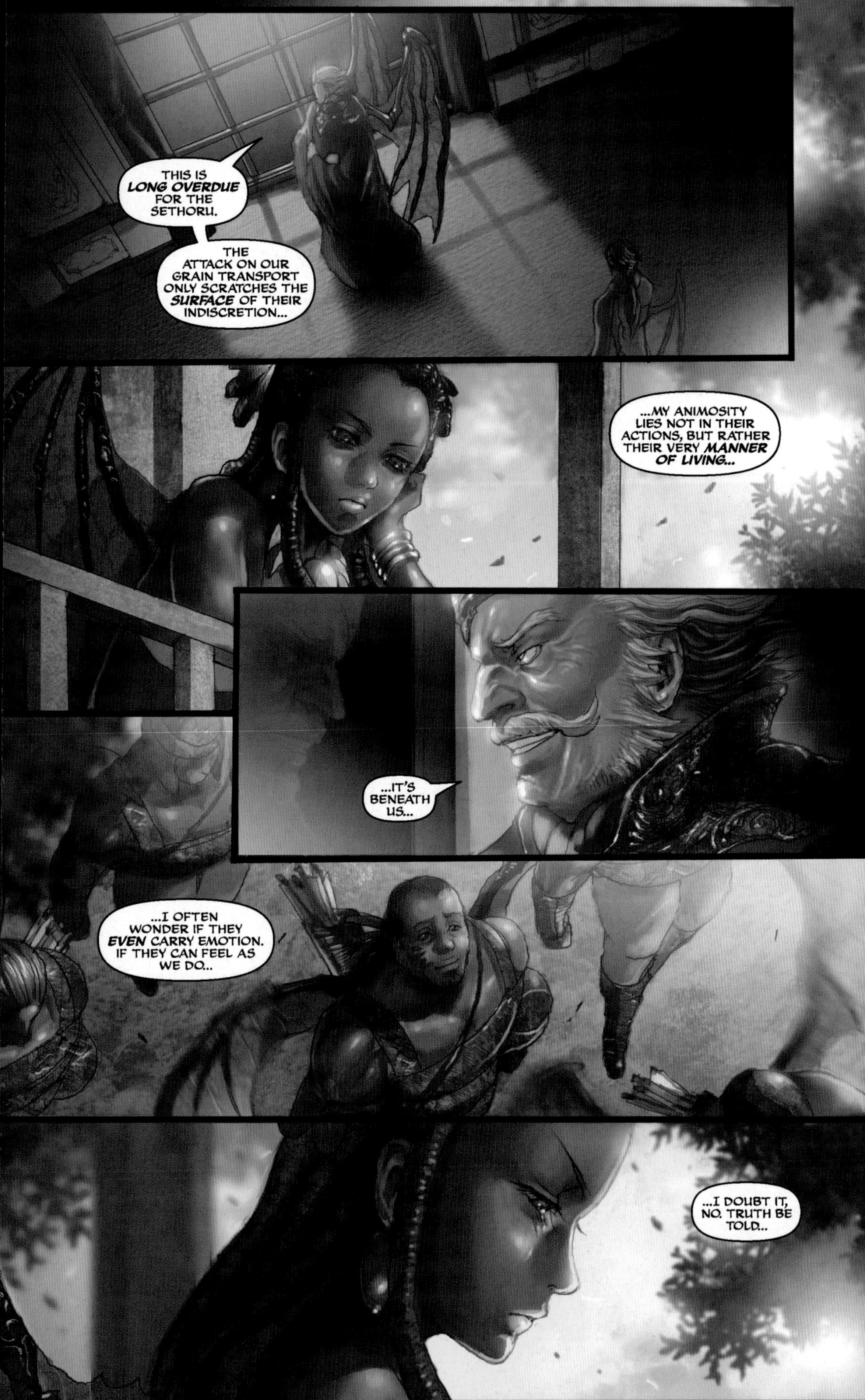

THIS IS LONG OVERDUE FOR THE SETHORU.
THE ATTACK ON OUR GRAIN TRANSPORT ONLY SCRATCHES THE SURFACE OF THEIR INDISCRETION...
...MY ANIMOSITY LIES NOT IN THEIR ACTIONS, BUT RATHER THEIR VERY MANNER OF LIVING...
...IT'S BENEATH US...
...I OFTEN WONDER IF THEY EVEN CARRY EMOTION. IF THEY CAN FEEL AS WE DO...
...I DOUBT IT, NO. TRUTH BE TOLD...

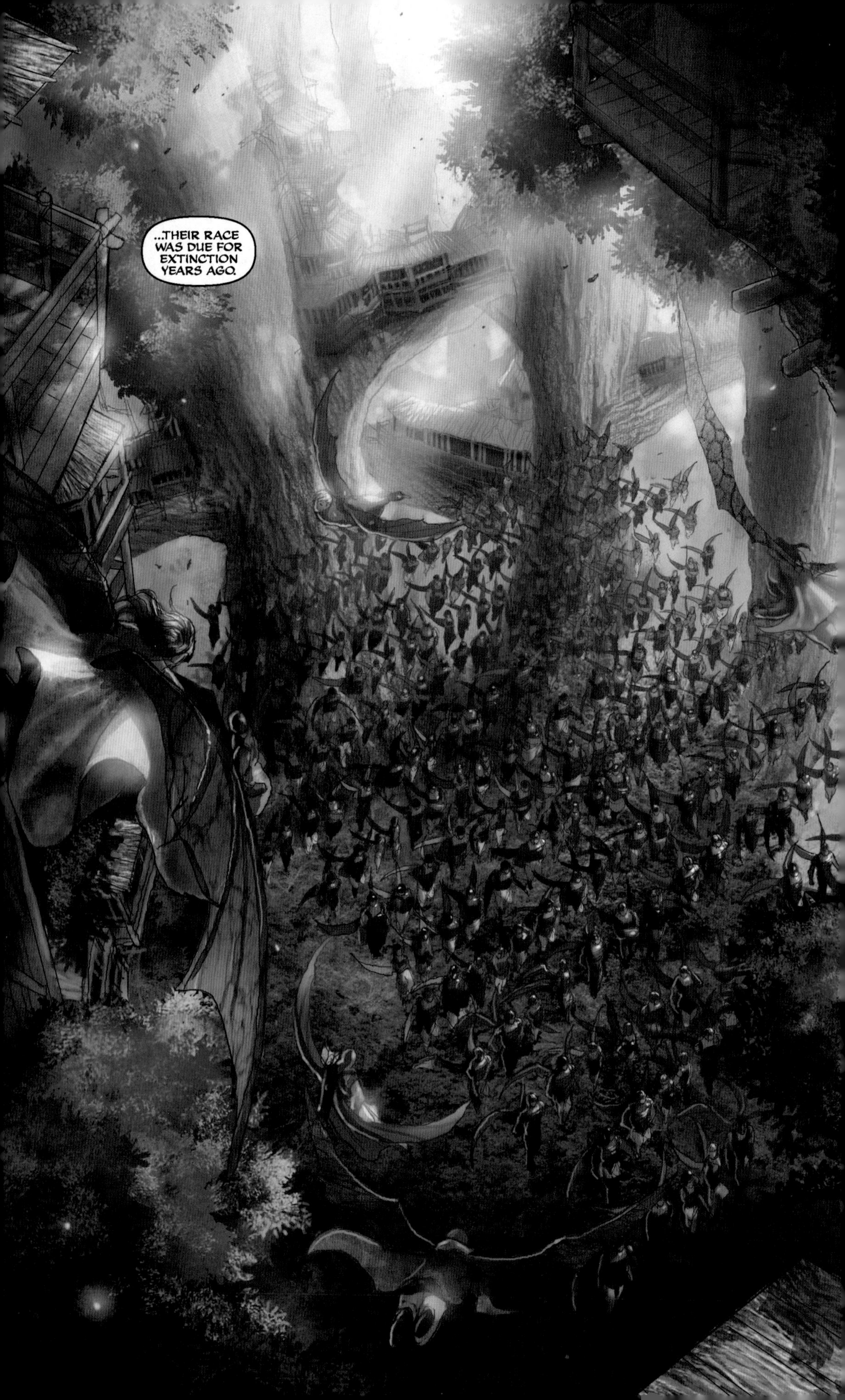
...THEIR RACE WAS DUE FOR EXTINCTION YEARS AGO.

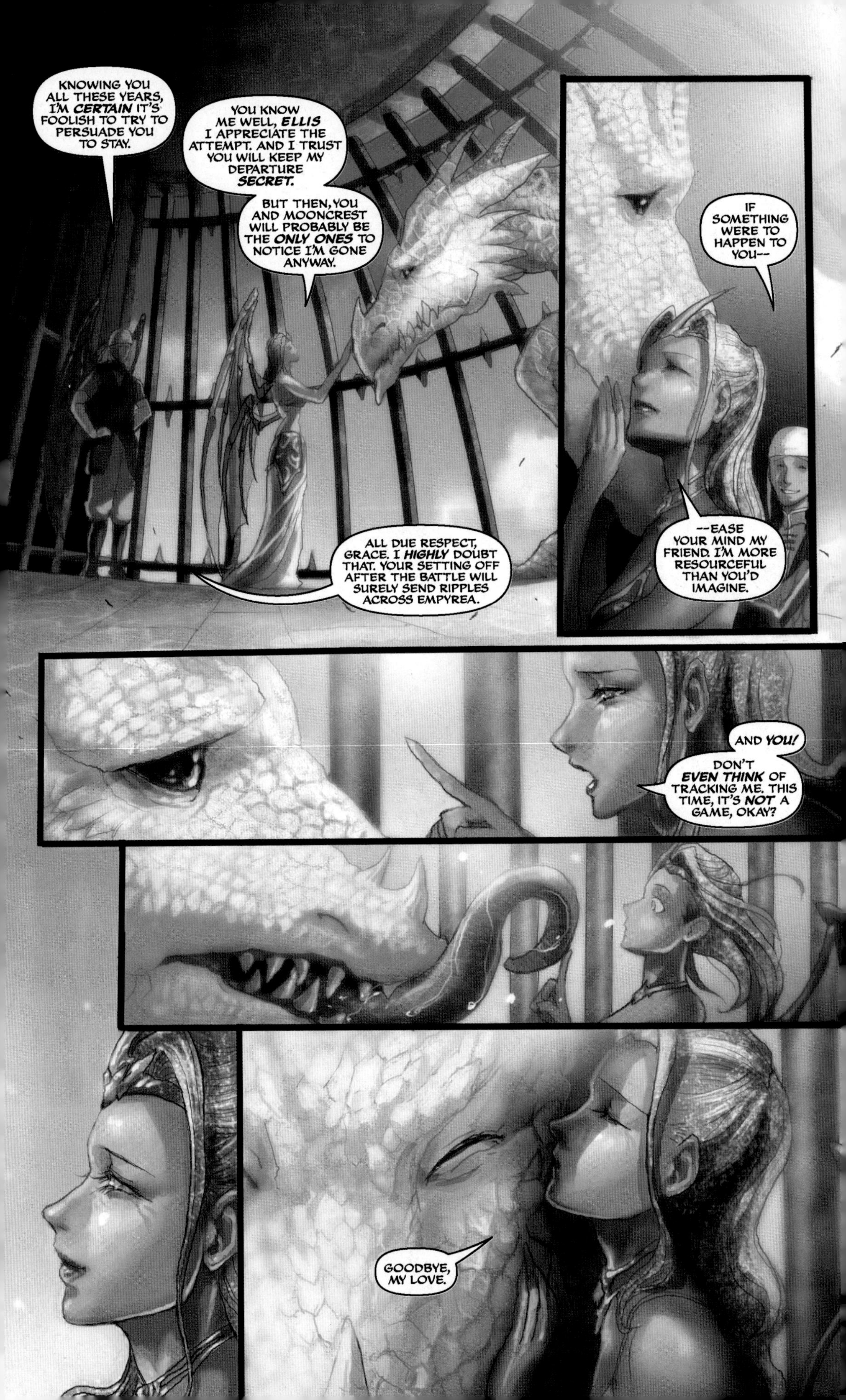
KNOWING YOU ALL THESE YEARS, I'M CERTAIN IT'S FOOLISH TO TRY TO PERSUADE YOU TO STAY.
YOU KNOW ME WELL, ELLIS I APPRECIATE THE ATTEMPT. AND I TRUST YOU WILL KEEP MY DEPARTURE SECRET.
BUT THEN, YOU AND MOONCREST WILL PROBABLY BE THE ONLY ONES TO NOTICE I'M GONE ANYWAY.
ALL DUE RESPECT, GRACE. I HIGHLY DOUBT THAT. YOUR SETTING OFF AFTER THE BATTLE WILL SURELY SEND RIPPLES ACROSS EMPYREA.
IF SOMETHING WERE TO HAPPEN TO YOU--
--EASE YOUR MIND MY FRIEND. I'M MORE RESOURCEFUL THAN YOU'D IMAGINE.
AND YOU!
DON'T EVEN THINK OF TRACKING ME. THIS TIME, IT'S NOT A GAME, OKAY?
GOODBYE, MY LOVE.

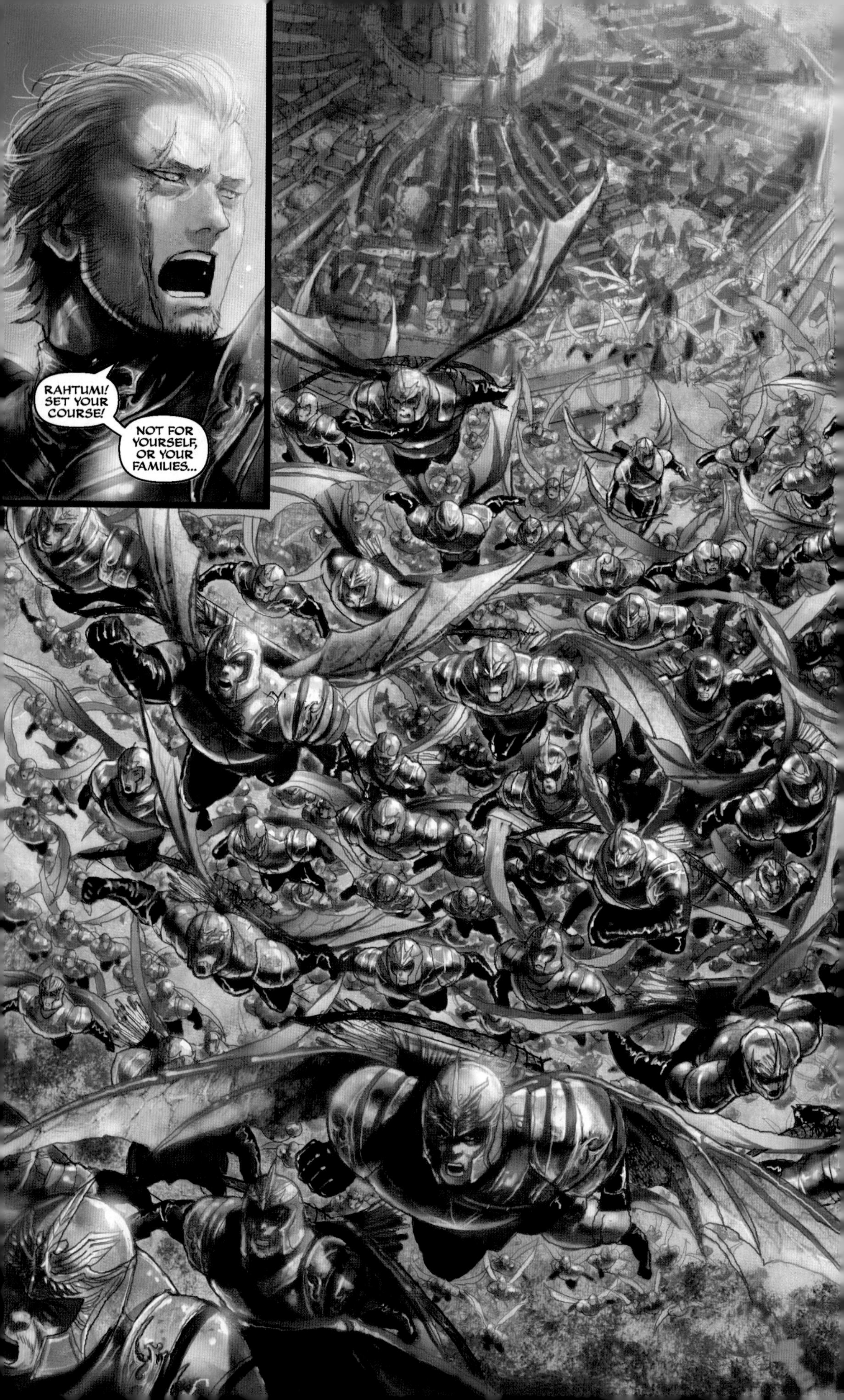
RAHTUMI! SET YOUR COURSE!
NOT FOR YOURSELF, OR YOUR FAMILIES...

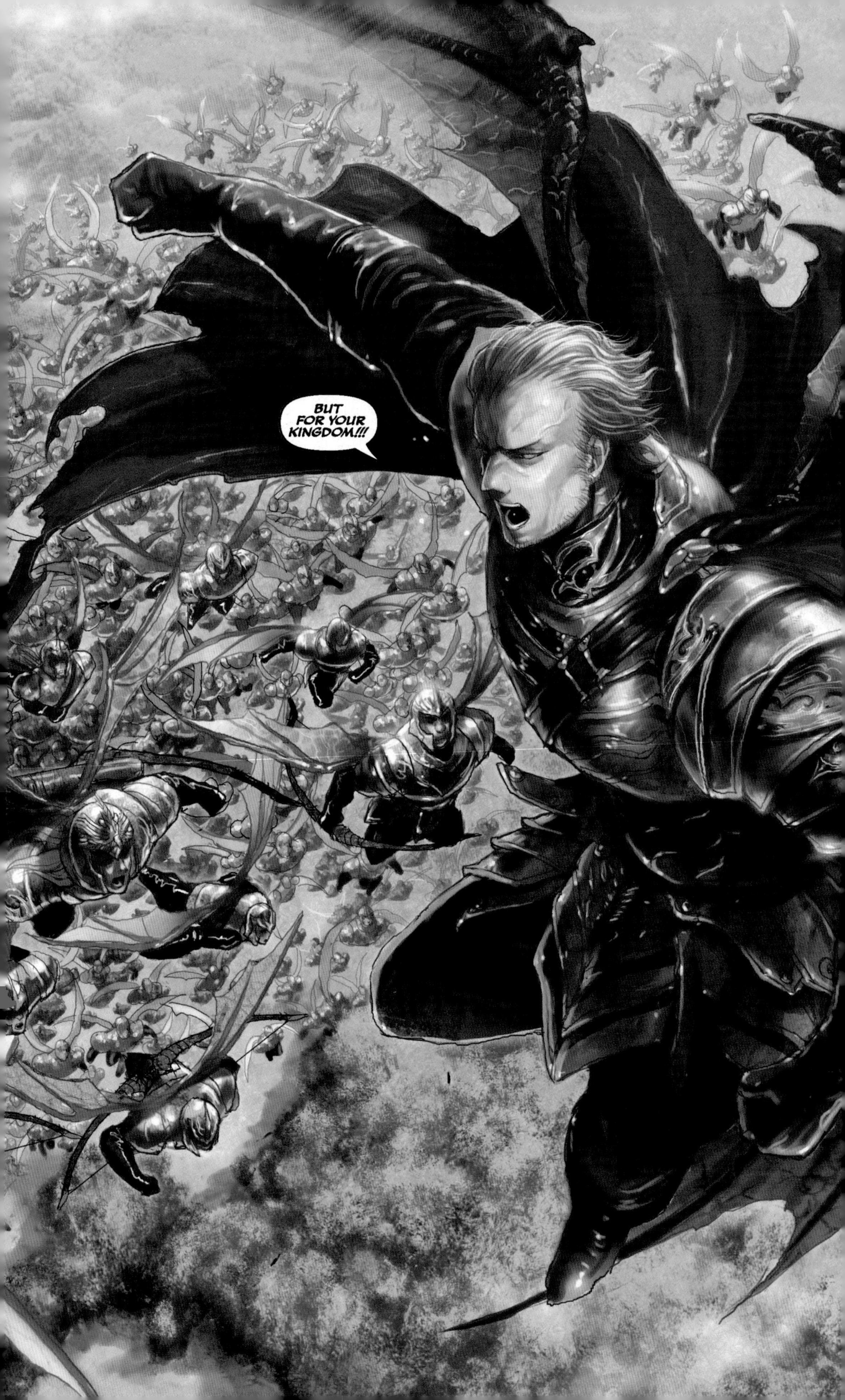
BUT FOR YOUR KINGDOM!!!

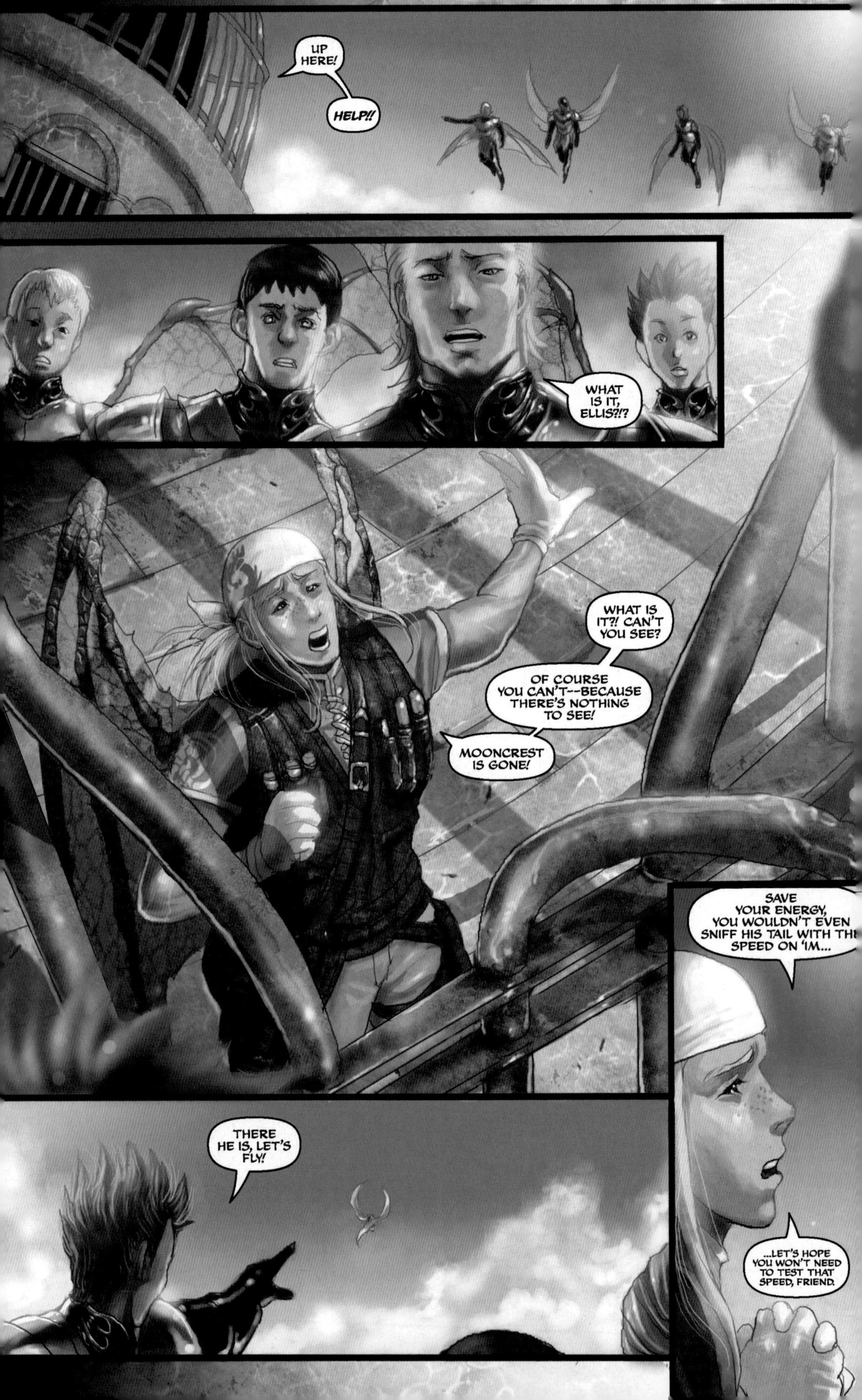
UP HERE!
HELP!!
WHAT IS IT, ELLIS?!?
WHAT IS IT?! CAN'T YOU SEE?
OF COURSE YOU CAN'T--BECAUSE THERE'S NOTHING TO SEE!
MOONCREST IS GONE!
SAVE YOUR ENERGY, YOU WOULDN'T EVEN SNIFF HIS TAIL WITH THE SPEED ON 'IM...
THERE HE IS, LET'S FLY!
...LET'S HOPE YOU WON'T NEED TO TEST THAT SPEED, FRIEND.

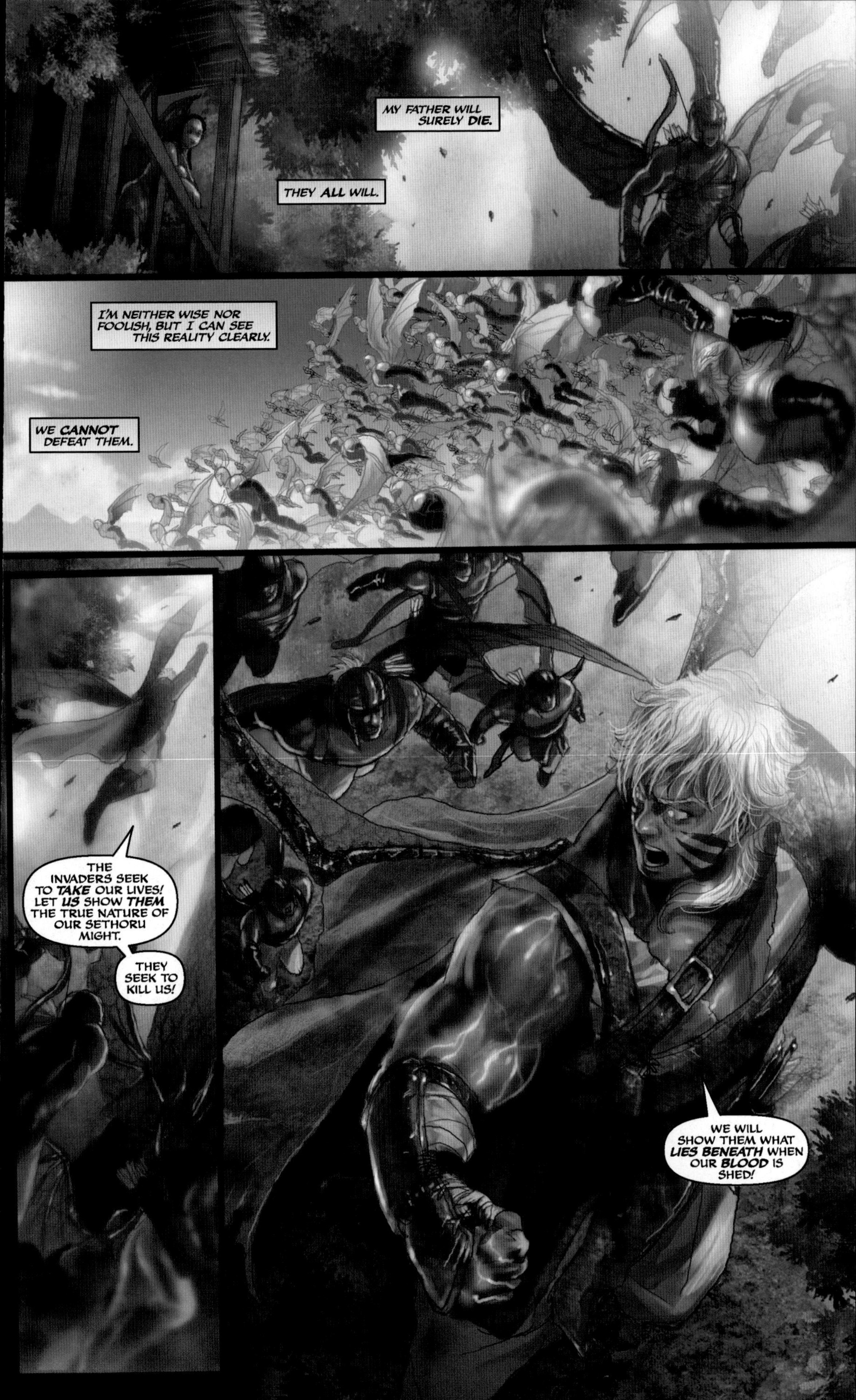
MY FATHER WILL SURELY DIE.
THEY ALL WILL.
I'M NEITHER WISE NOR FOOLISH, BUT I CAN SEE THIS REALITY CLEARLY.
WE CANNOT DEFEAT THEM.
THE INVADERS SEEK TO TAKE OUR LIVES! LET US SHOW THEM THE TRUE NATURE OF OUR SETHORU MIGHT.
THEY SEEK TO KILL US!
WE WILL SHOW THEM WHAT LIES BENEATH WHEN OUR BLOOD IS SHED!

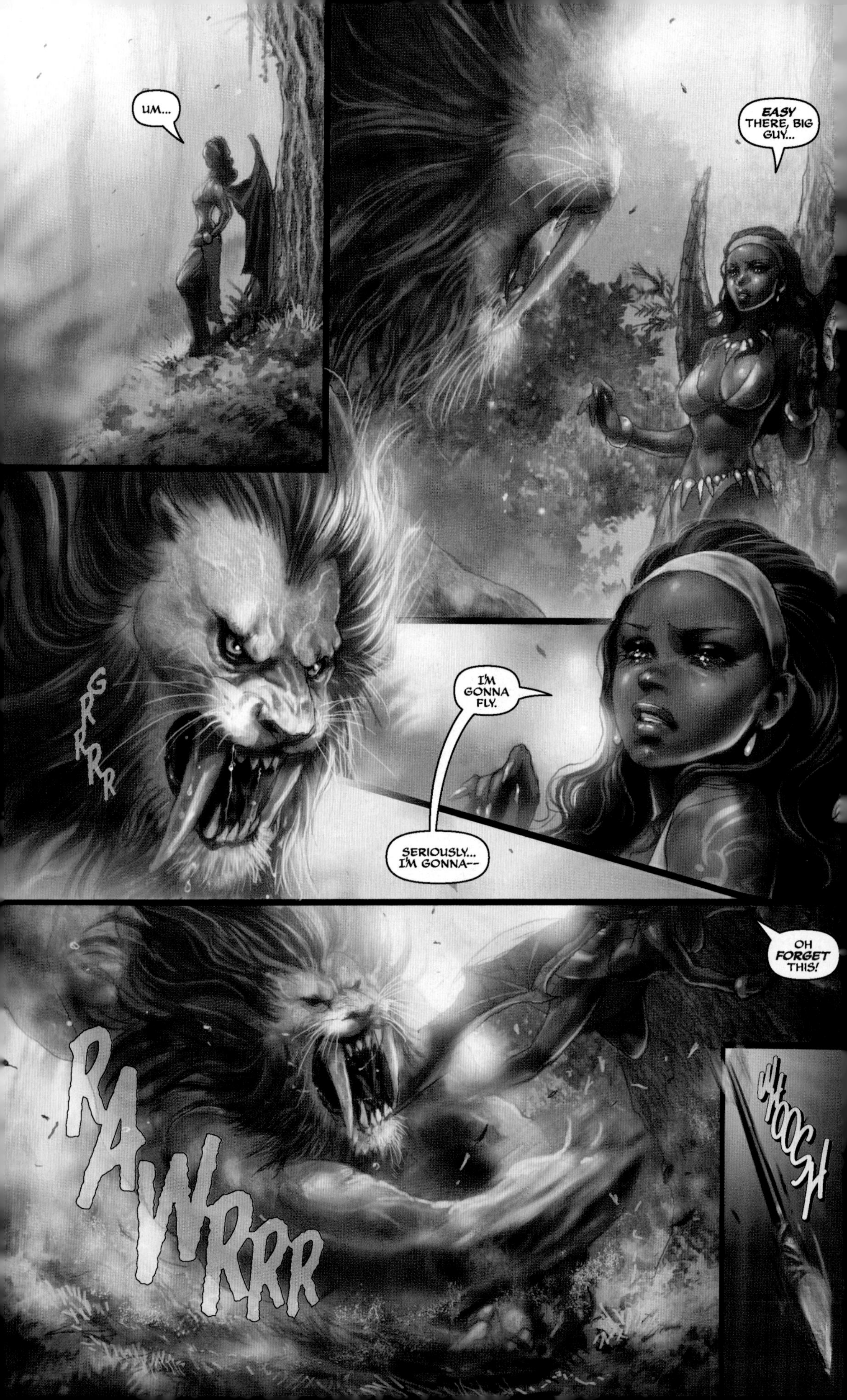
UM...
EASY THERE, BIG GUY...
GRRRR
I'M GONNA FLY.
SERIOUSLY... I'M GONNA--
OH FORGET THIS!
RAWRRR
WHOOSH

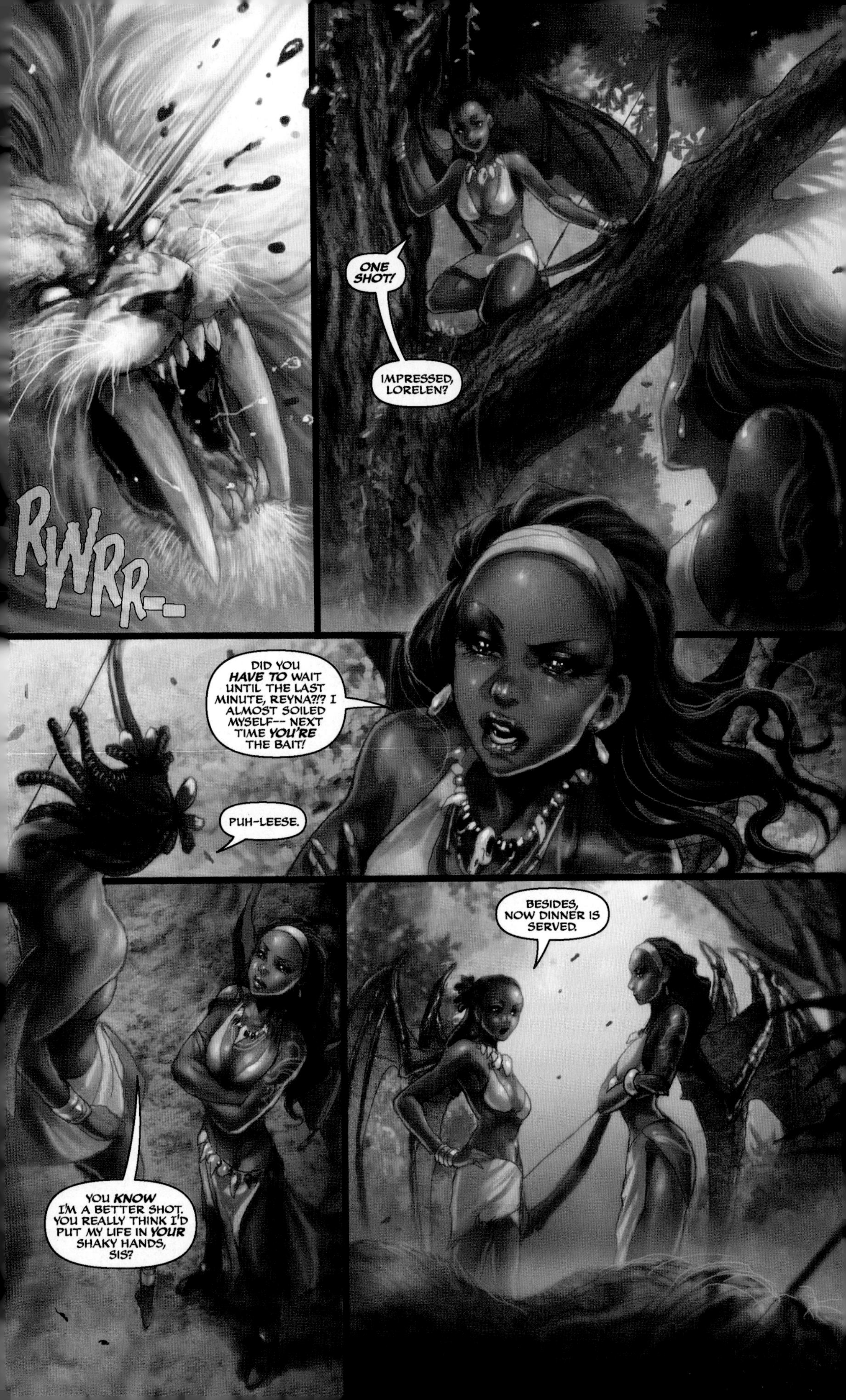
RWRR--
ONE SHOT!
IMPRESSED, LORELEN?
DID YOU HAVE TO WAIT UNTIL THE LAST MINUTE, REYNA?!? I ALMOST SOILED MYSELF-- NEXT TIME YOU'RE THE BAIT!
PUH-LEESE.
YOU KNOW I'M A BETTER SHOT. YOU REALLY THINK I'D PUT MY LIFE IN YOUR SHAKY HANDS, SIS?
BESIDES, NOW DINNER IS SERVED.

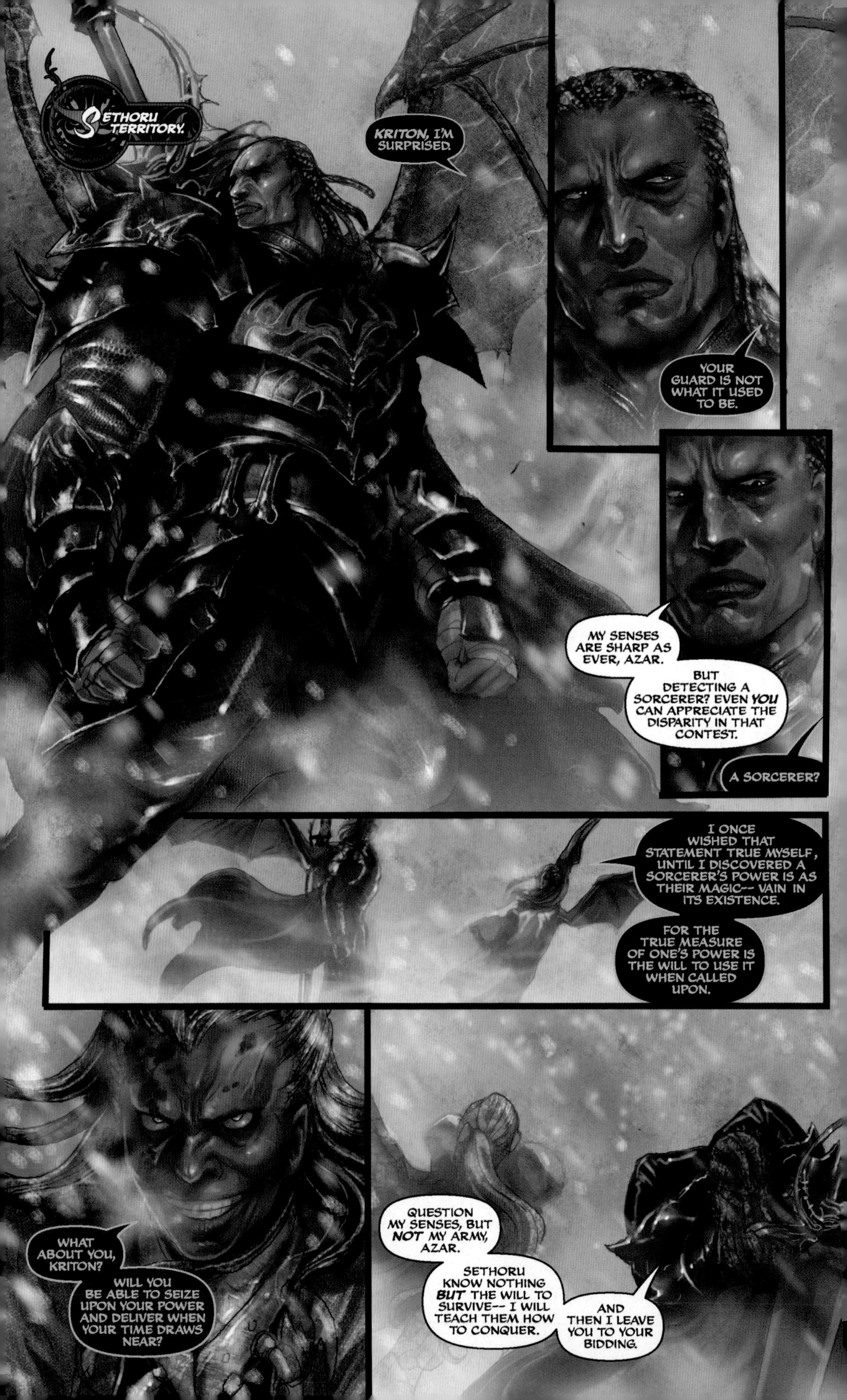

SETHORU TERRITORY.
KRITON, I'M SURPRISED.
YOUR GUARD IS NOT WHAT IT USED TO BE.
MY SENSES ARE SHARP AS EVER, AZAR.
BUT DETECTING A SORCERER? EVEN YOU CAN APPRECIATE THE DISPARITY IN THAT CONTEST.
A SORCERER?
I ONCE WISHED THAT STATEMENT TRUE MYSELF, UNTIL I DISCOVERED A SORCERER'S POWER IS AS THEIR MAGIC-- VAIN IN ITS EXISTENCE.
FOR THE TRUE MEASURE OF ONE'S POWER IS THE WILL TO USE IT WHEN CALLED UPON.
WHAT ABOUT YOU, KRITON?
WILL YOU BE ABLE TO SEIZE UPON YOUR POWER AND DELIVER WHEN YOUR TIME DRAWS NEAR?
QUESTION MY SENSES, BUT NOT MY ARMY, AZAR.
SETHORU KNOW NOTHING BUT THE WILL TO SURVIVE-- I WILL TEACH THEM HOW TO CONQUER.
AND THEN I LEAVE YOU TO YOUR BIDDING.

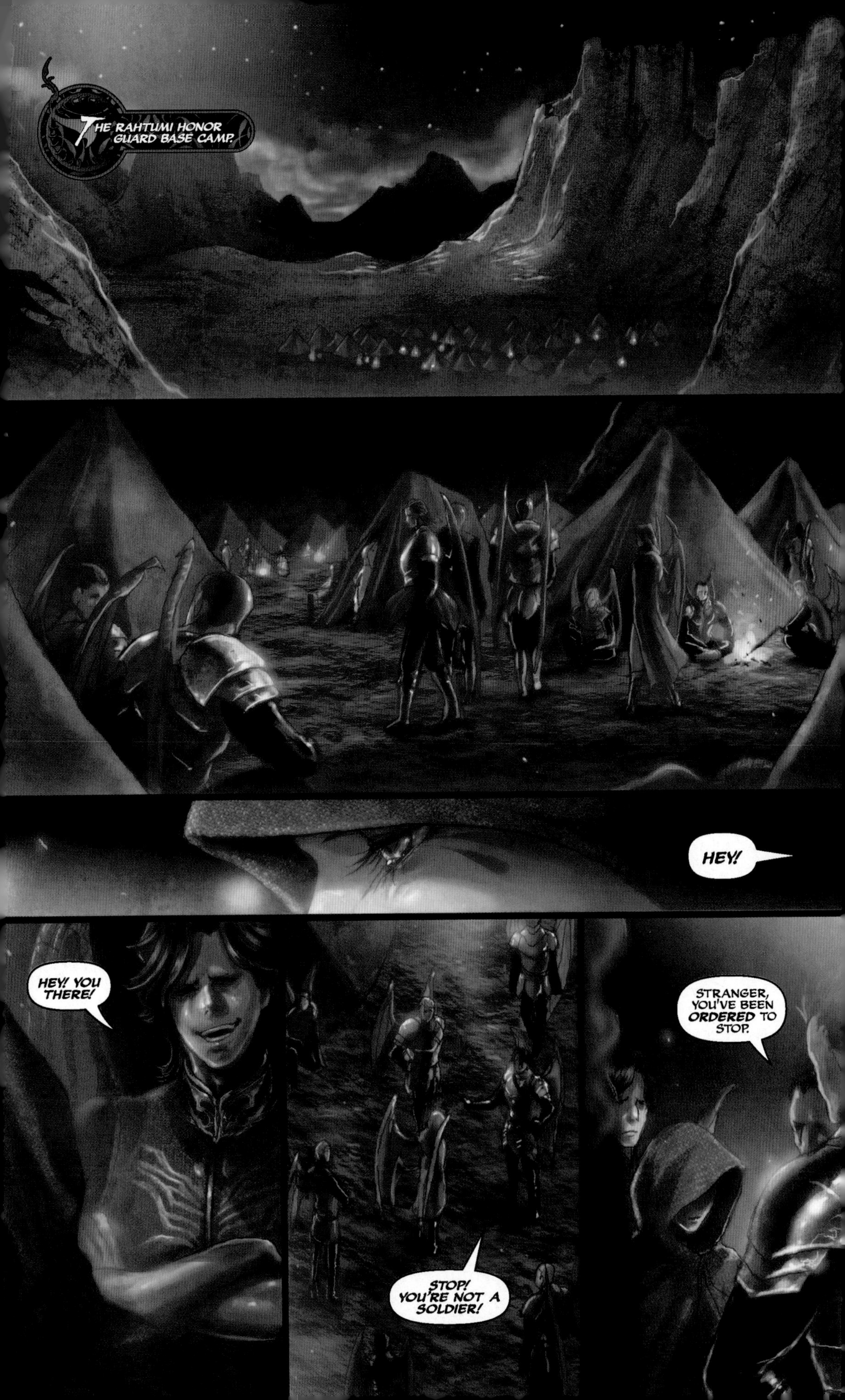
THE RAHTUMI HONOR GUARD BASE CAMP.
HEY!
HEY! YOU THERE!
STOP! YOU'RE NOT A SOLDIER!
STRANGER, YOU'VE BEEN ORDERED TO STOP.

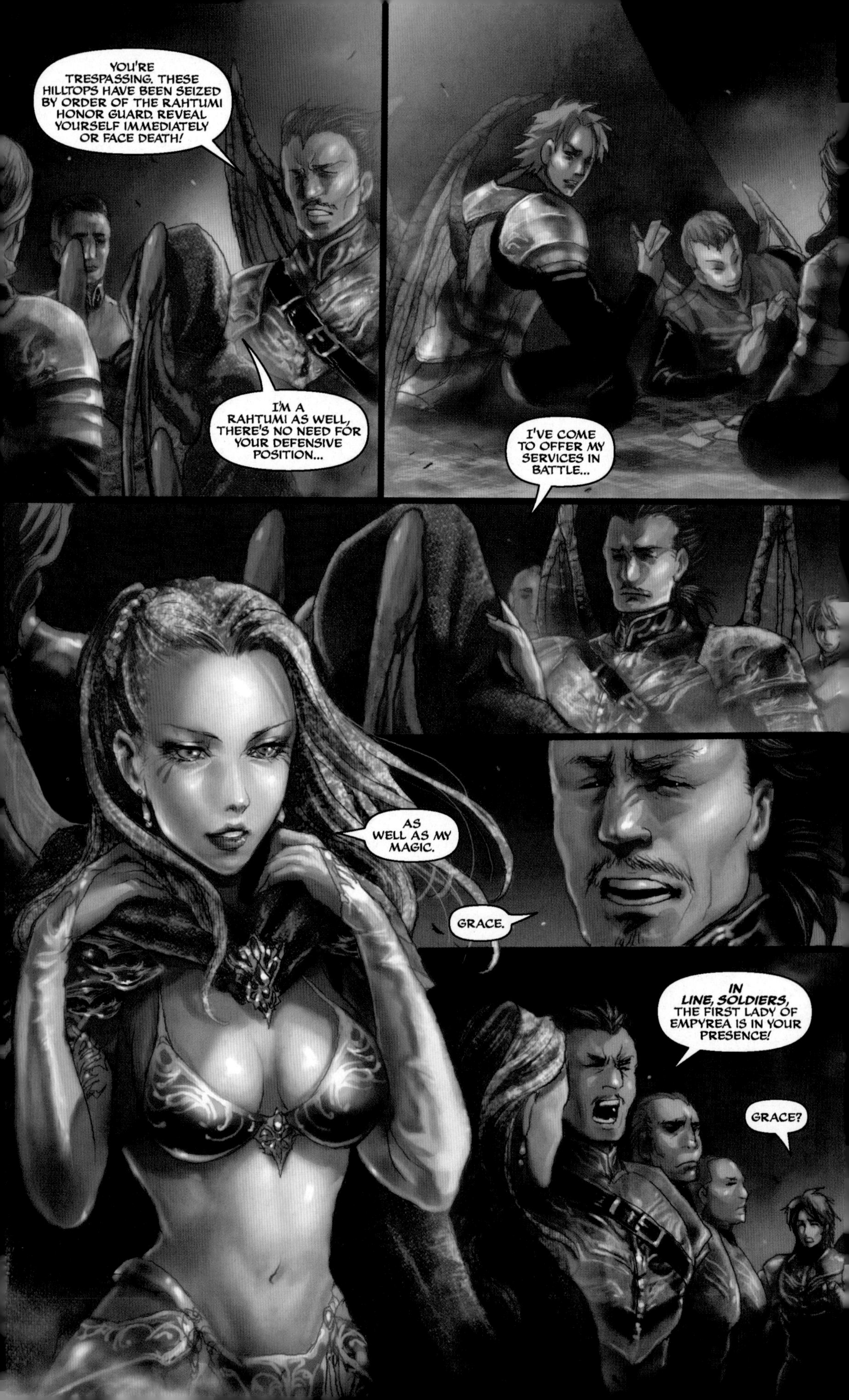
YOU'RE TRESPASSING. THESE HILLTOPS HAVE BEEN SEIZED BY ORDER OF THE RAHTUMI HONOR GUARD. REVEAL YOURSELF IMMEDIATELY OR FACE DEATH!
I'M A RAHTUMI AS WELL, THERE'S NO NEED FOR YOUR DEFENSIVE POSITION...
I'VE COME TO OFFER MY SERVICES IN BATTLE...
AS WELL AS MY MAGIC.
GRACE.
IN LINE, SOLDIERS, THE FIRST LADY OF EMPYREA IS IN YOUR PRESENCE!
GRACE?

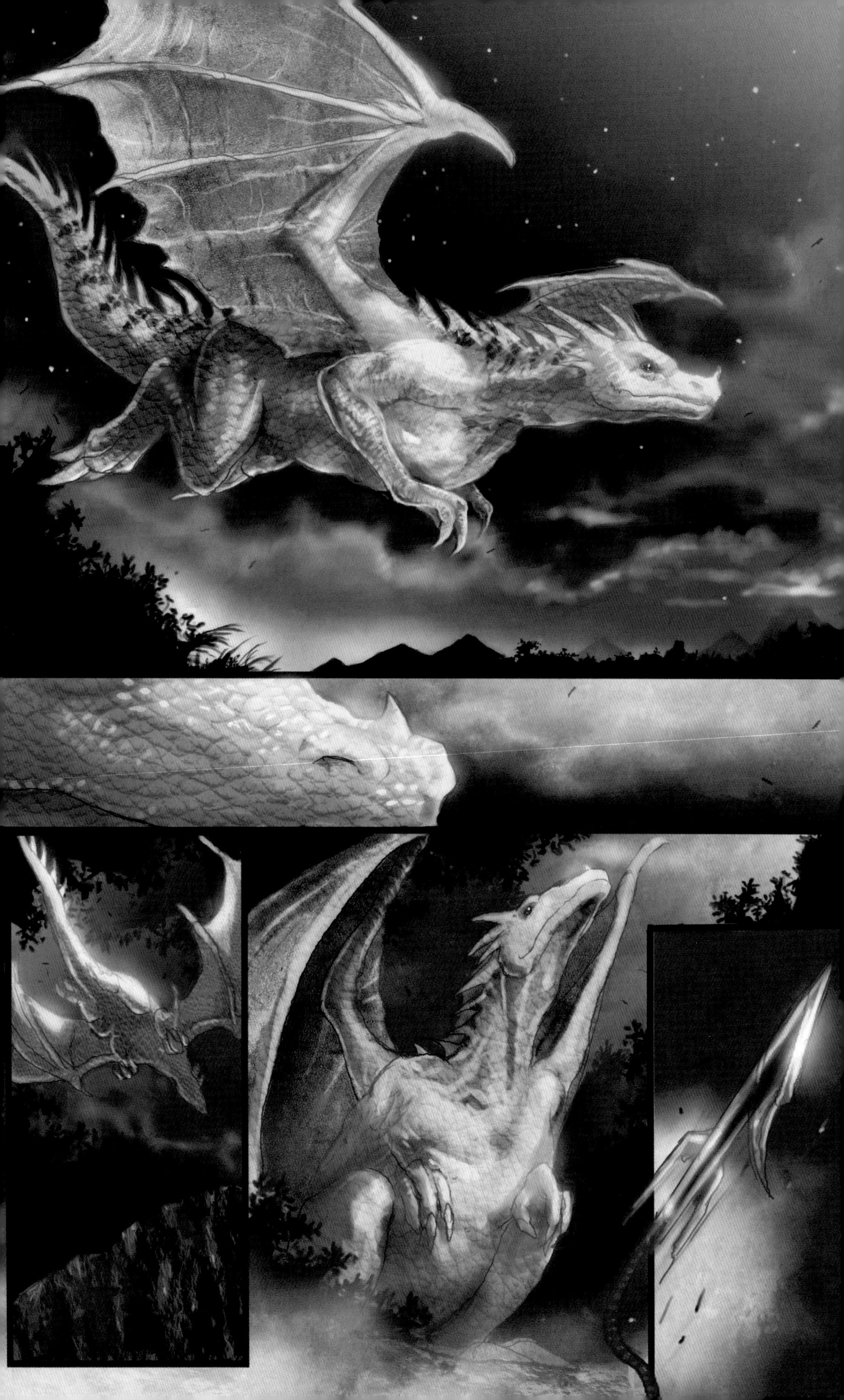

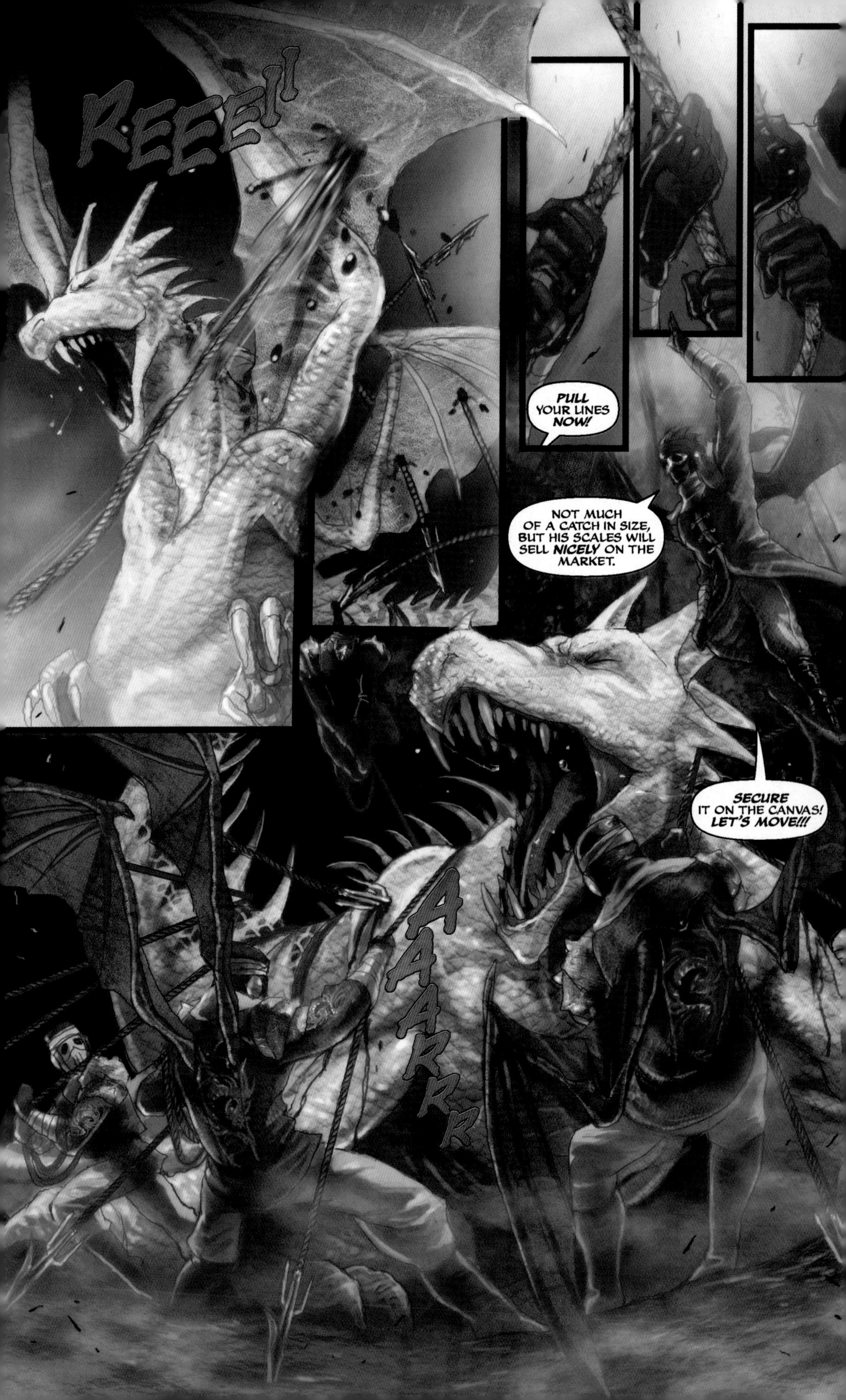
REEE!!
PULL YOUR LINES NOW!
NOT MUCH OF A CATCH IN SIZE, BUT HIS SCALES WILL SELL NICELY ON THE MARKET.
SECURE IT ON THE CANVAS! LET'S MOVE!!!
AAAARRR

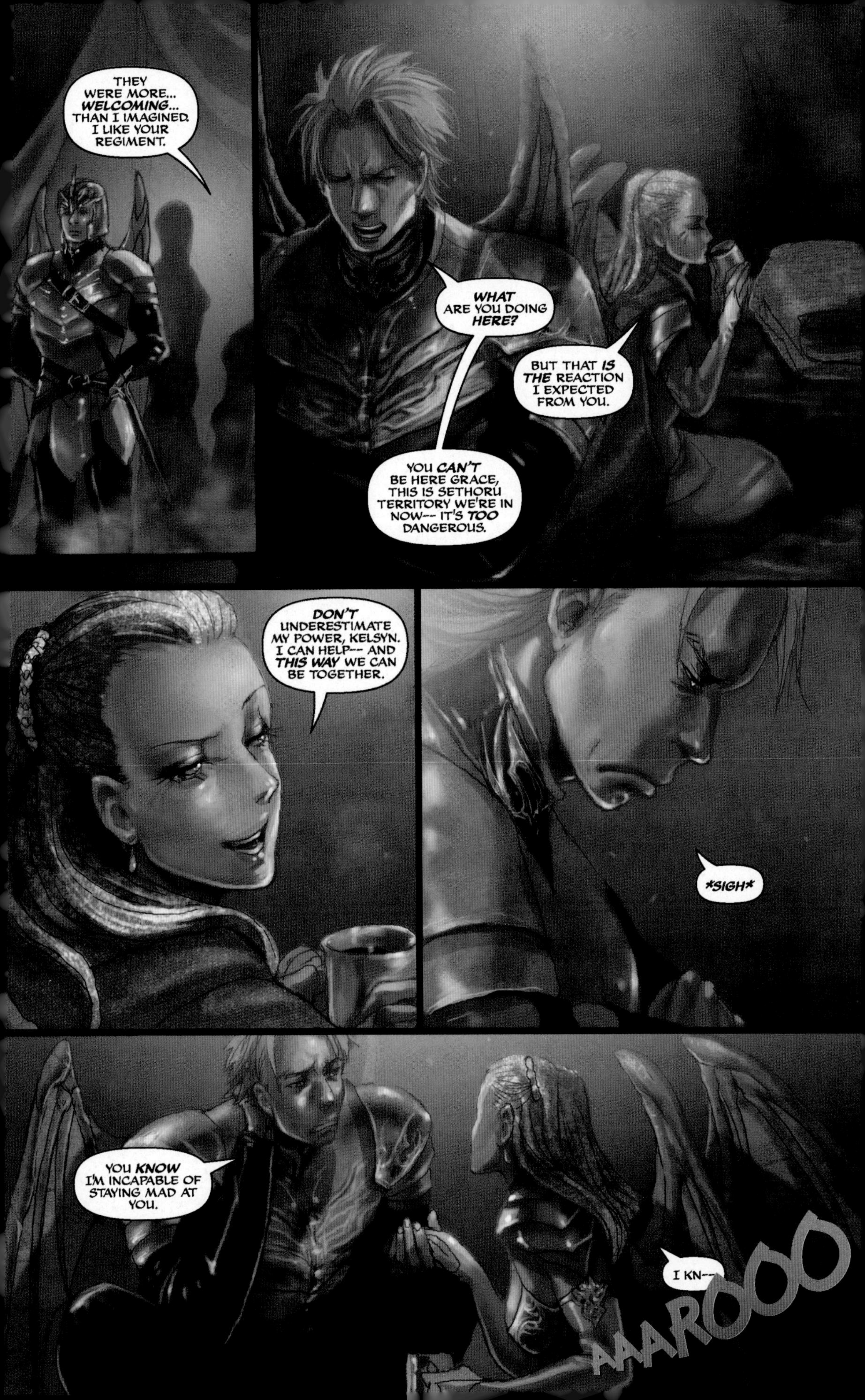
THEY WERE MORE... WELCOMING... THAN I IMAGINED. I LIKE YOUR REGIMENT.
WHAT ARE YOU DOING HERE?
BUT THAT IS THE REACTION I EXPECTED FROM YOU.
YOU CAN'T BE HERE GRACE, THIS IS SETHORU TERRITORY WE'RE IN NOW-- IT'S TOO DANGEROUS.
DON'T UNDERESTIMATE MY POWER, KELSYN. I CAN HELP-- AND THIS WAY WE CAN BE TOGETHER.
SIGH
YOU KNOW I'M INCAPABLE OF STAYING MAD AT YOU.
I KN--
AAAROOO

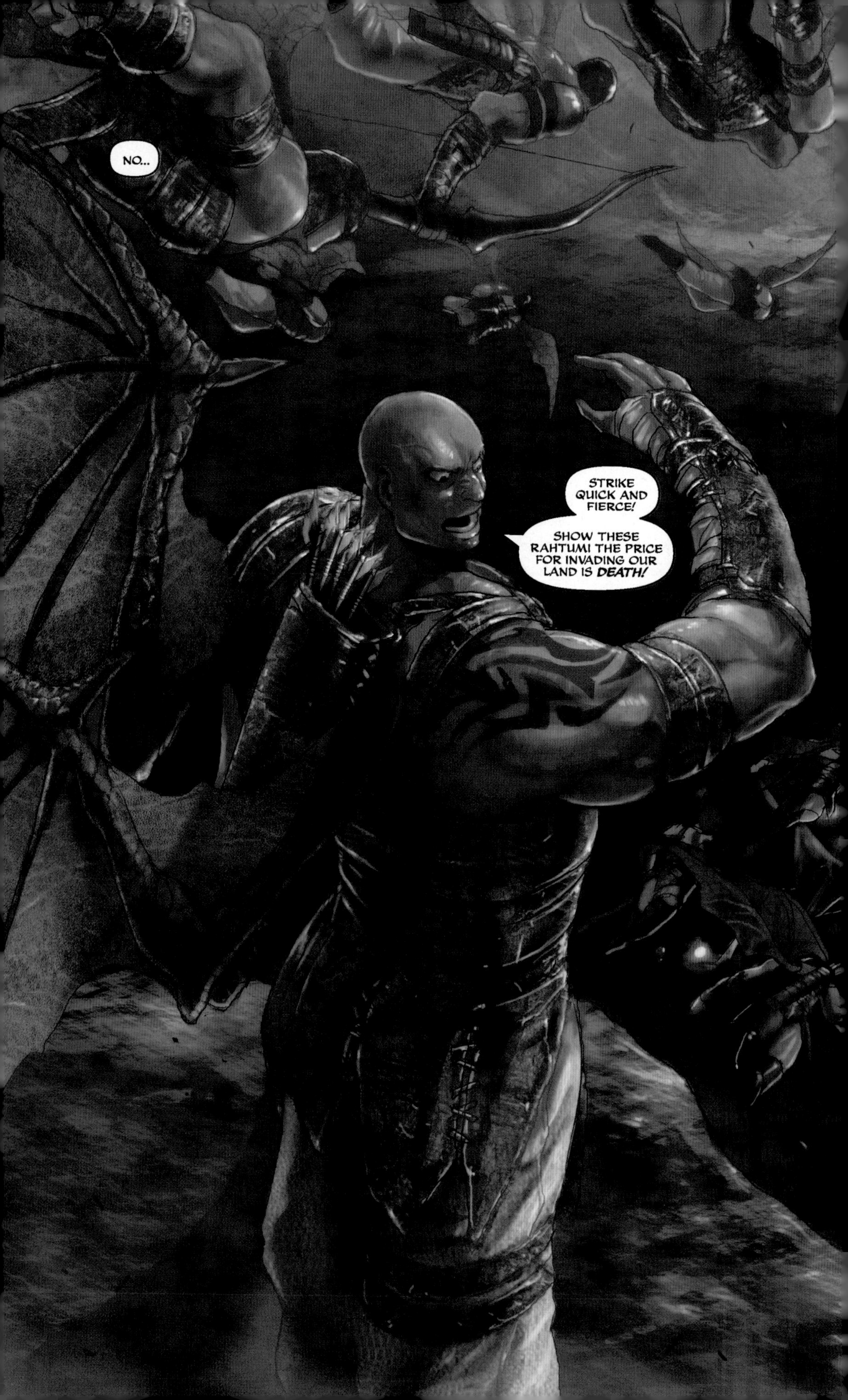
NO...
STRIKE QUICK AND FIERCE!
SHOW THESE RAHTUMI THE PRICE FOR INVADING OUR LAND IS *DEATH!*

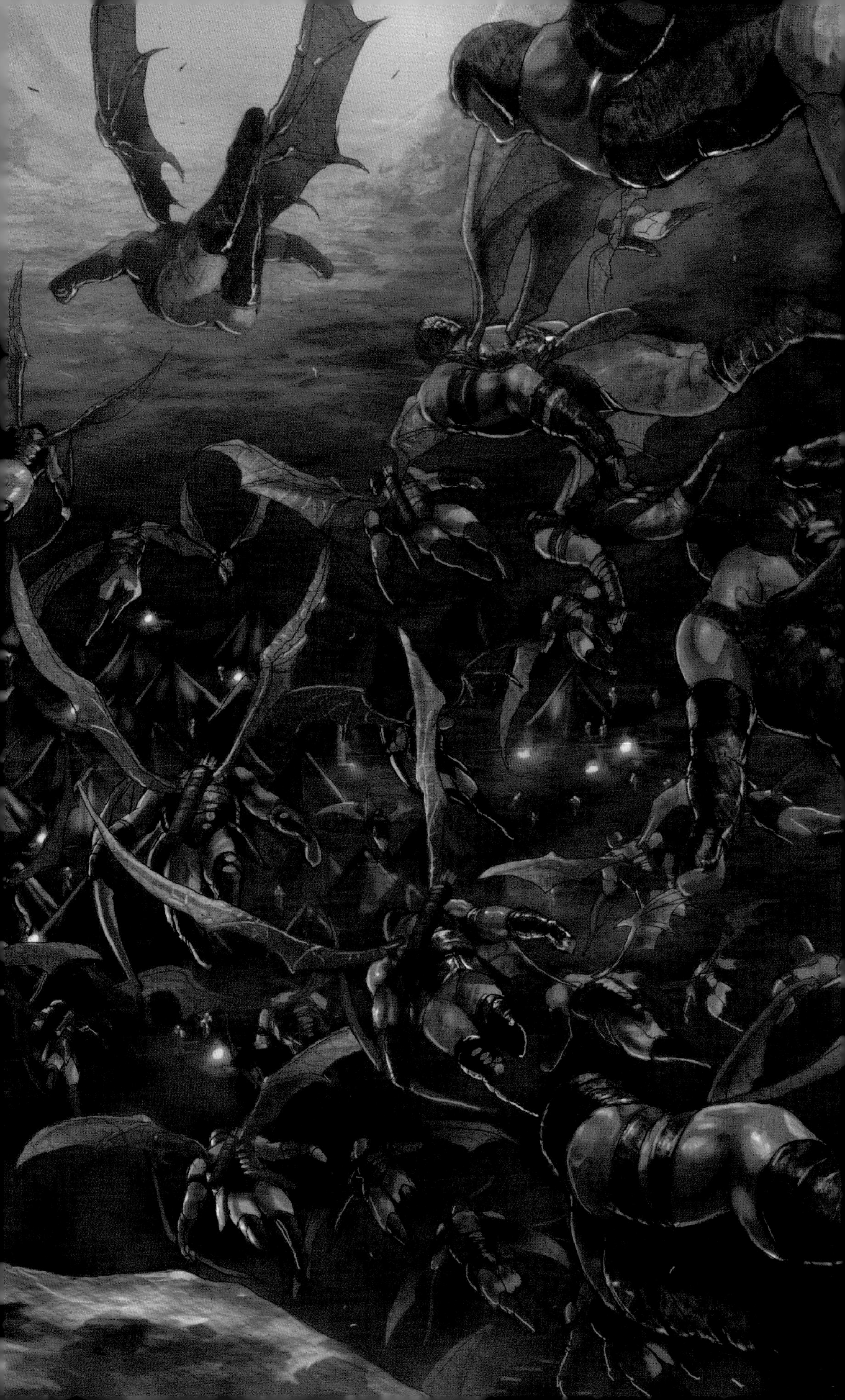

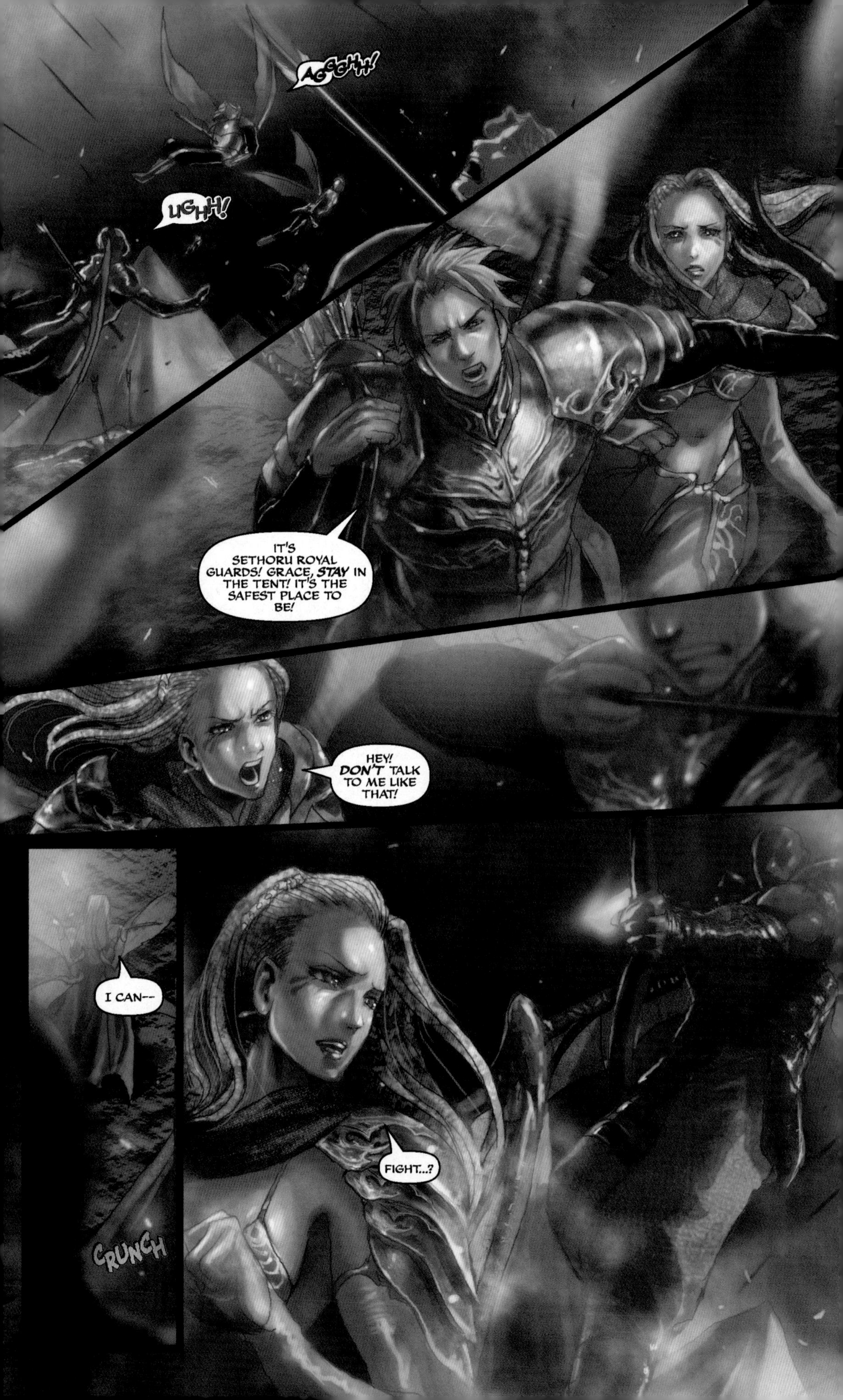
AGGGHHH!
UGHH!
IT'S SETHORU ROYAL GUARDS! GRACE, STAY IN THE TENT! IT'S THE SAFEST PLACE TO BE!
HEY! DON'T TALK TO ME LIKE THAT!
I CAN--
FIGHT...?
CRUNCH

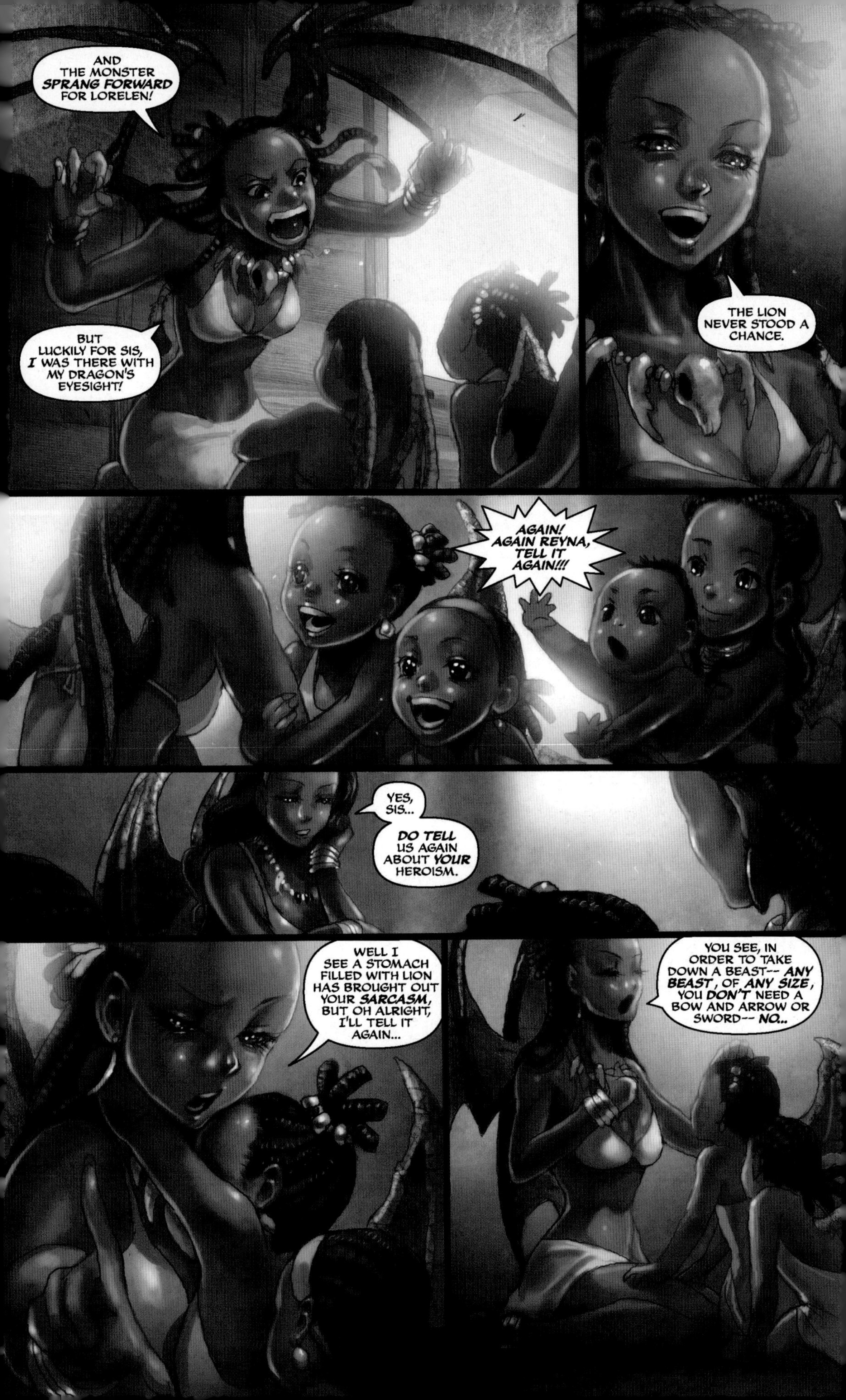
AND THE MONSTER ***SPRANG FORWARD*** FOR LORELEN!
BUT LUCKILY FOR SIS, ***I*** WAS THERE WITH MY DRAGON'S EYESIGHT!
THE LION NEVER STOOD A CHANCE.
AGAIN! AGAIN REYNA, TELL IT AGAIN!!!
YES, SIS...
DO TELL US AGAIN ABOUT ***YOUR*** HEROISM.
WELL I SEE A STOMACH FILLED WITH LION HAS BROUGHT OUT YOUR ***SARCASM***, BUT OH ALRIGHT, I'LL TELL IT AGAIN...
YOU SEE, IN ORDER TO TAKE DOWN A BEAST-- ***ANY BEAST***, OF ***ANY SIZE***, YOU ***DON'T*** NEED A BOW AND ARROW OR SWORD-- ***NO...***

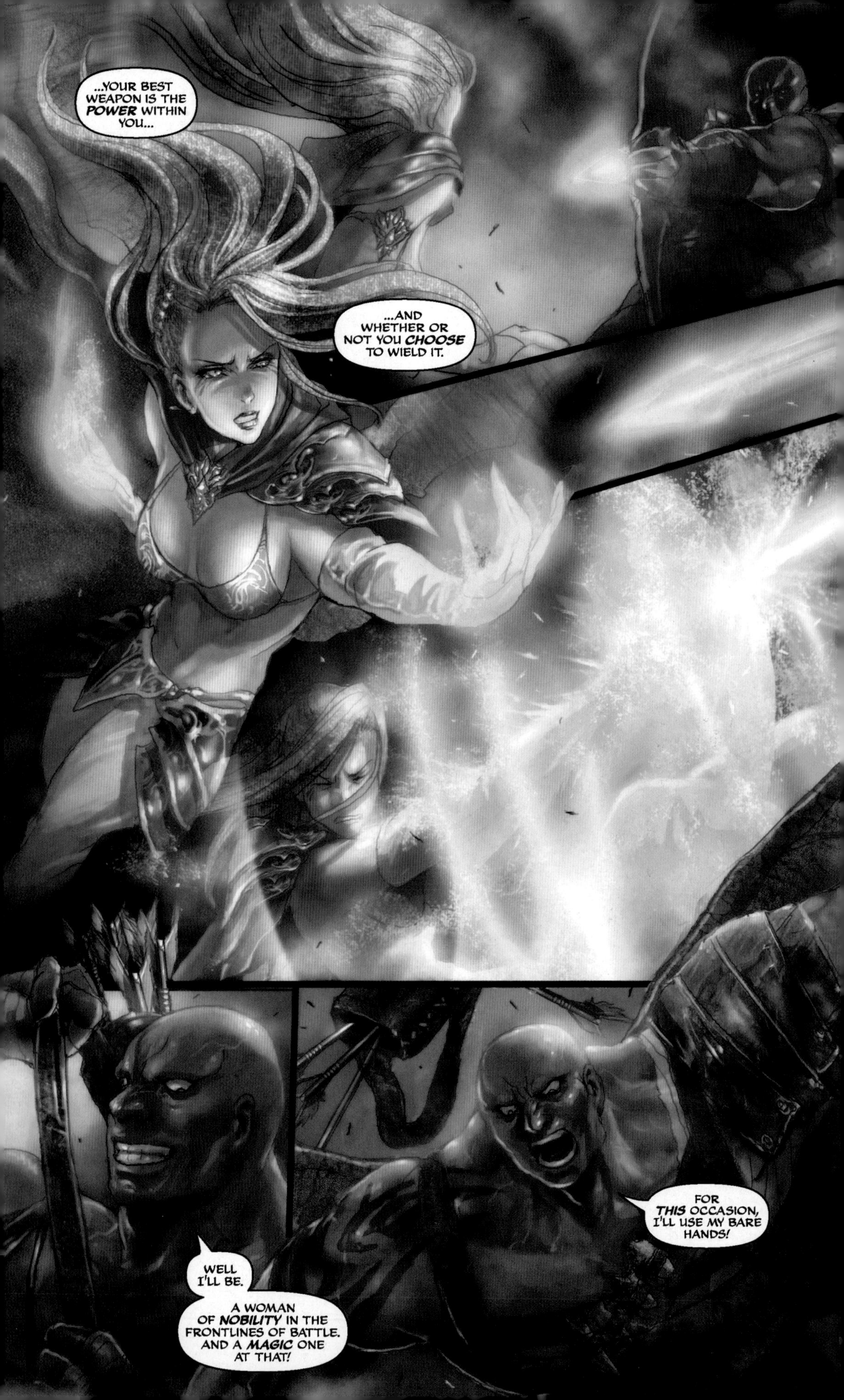
...YOUR BEST WEAPON IS THE POWER WITHIN YOU...
...AND WHETHER OR NOT YOU CHOOSE TO WIELD IT.
WELL I'LL BE.
A WOMAN OF NOBILITY IN THE FRONTLINES OF BATTLE. AND A MAGIC ONE AT THAT!
FOR THIS OCCASION, I'LL USE MY BARE HANDS!

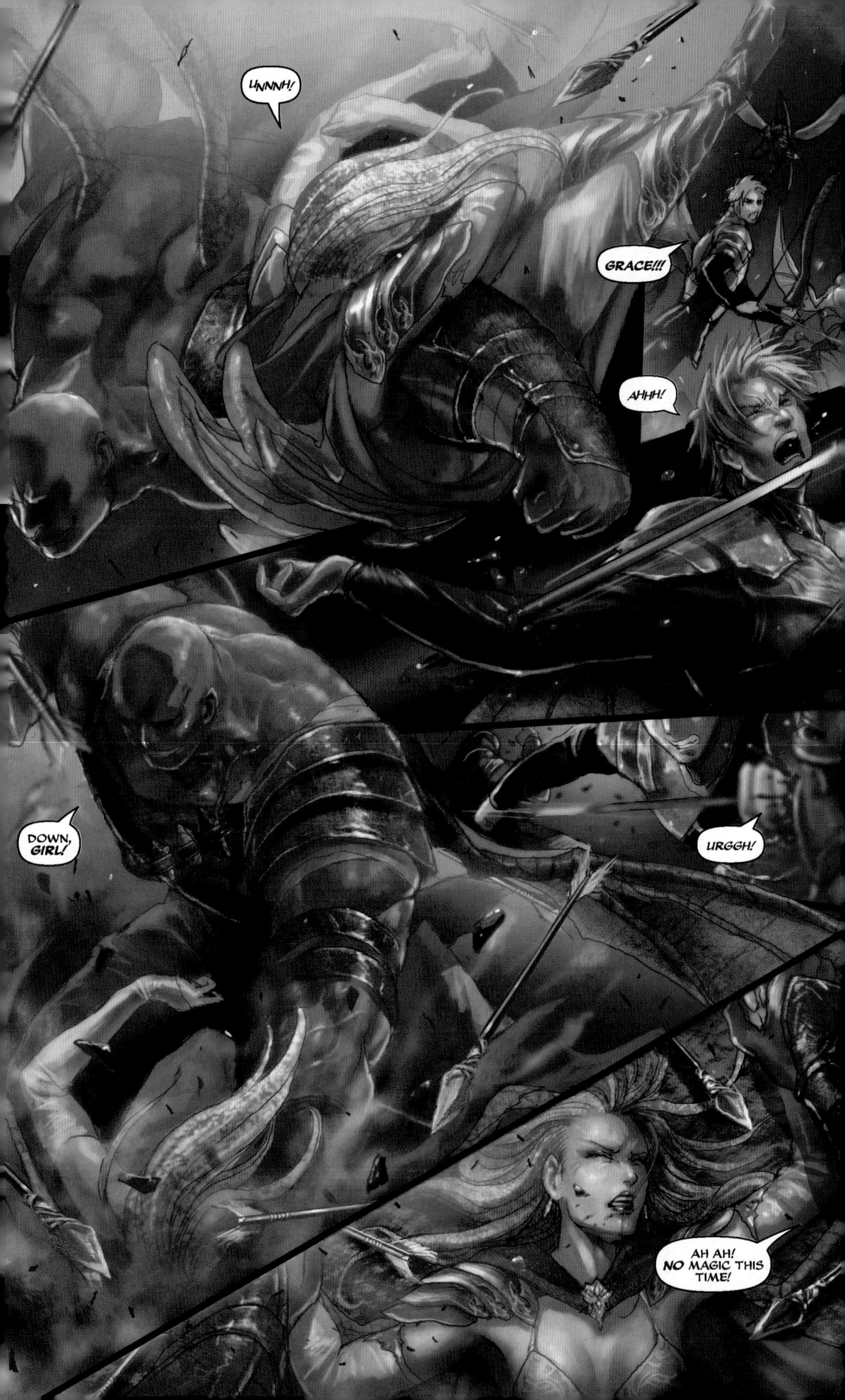
UNNNH!
GRACE!!!
AHHH!
DOWN, GIRL!
URGGH!
AH AH! NO MAGIC THIS TIME!

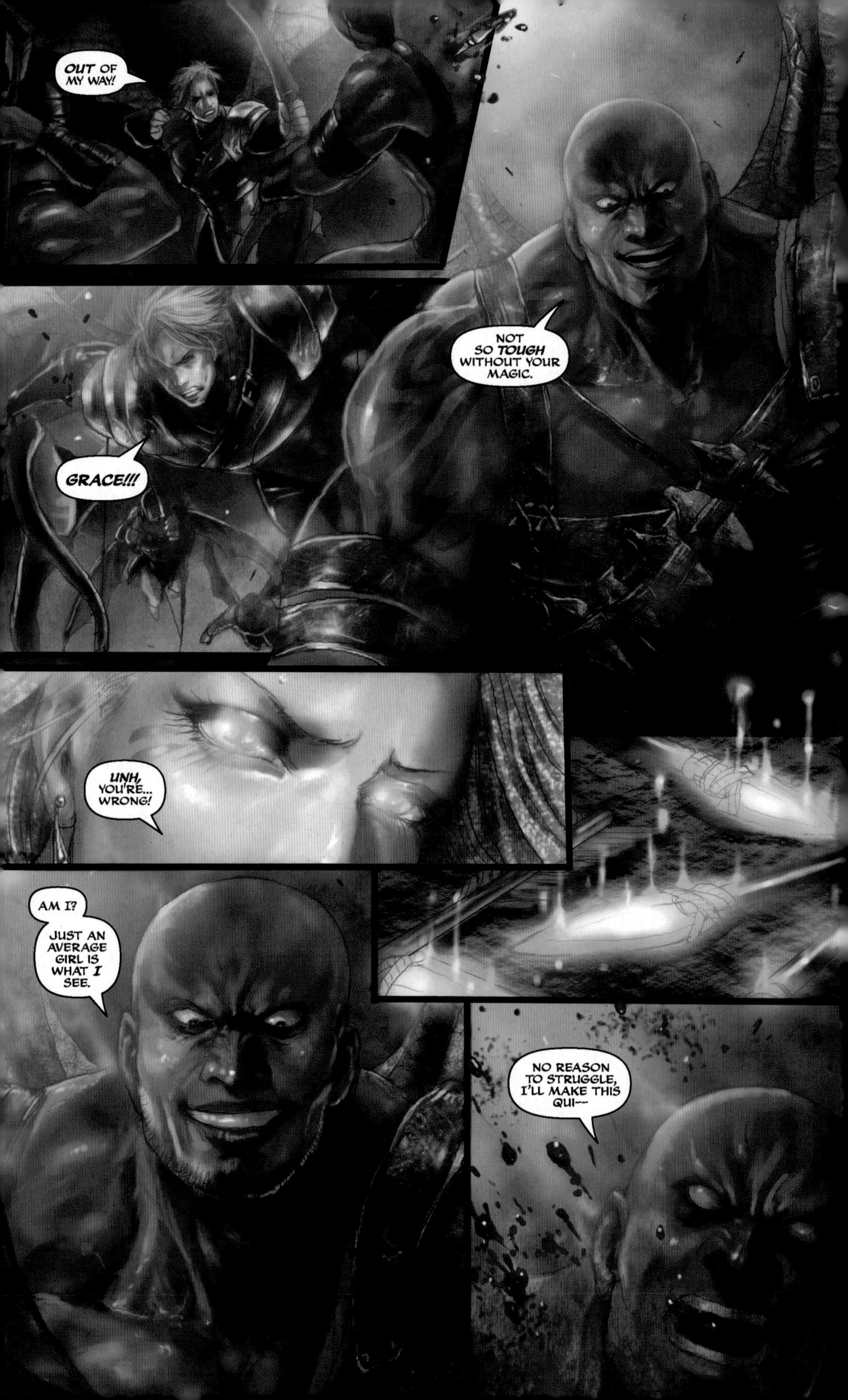
OUT OF MY WAY!
NOT SO TOUGH WITHOUT YOUR MAGIC.
GRACE!!!
UNH, YOU'RE... WRONG!
AM I?
JUST AN AVERAGE GIRL IS WHAT I SEE.
NO REASON TO STRUGGLE, I'LL MAKE THIS QUI--

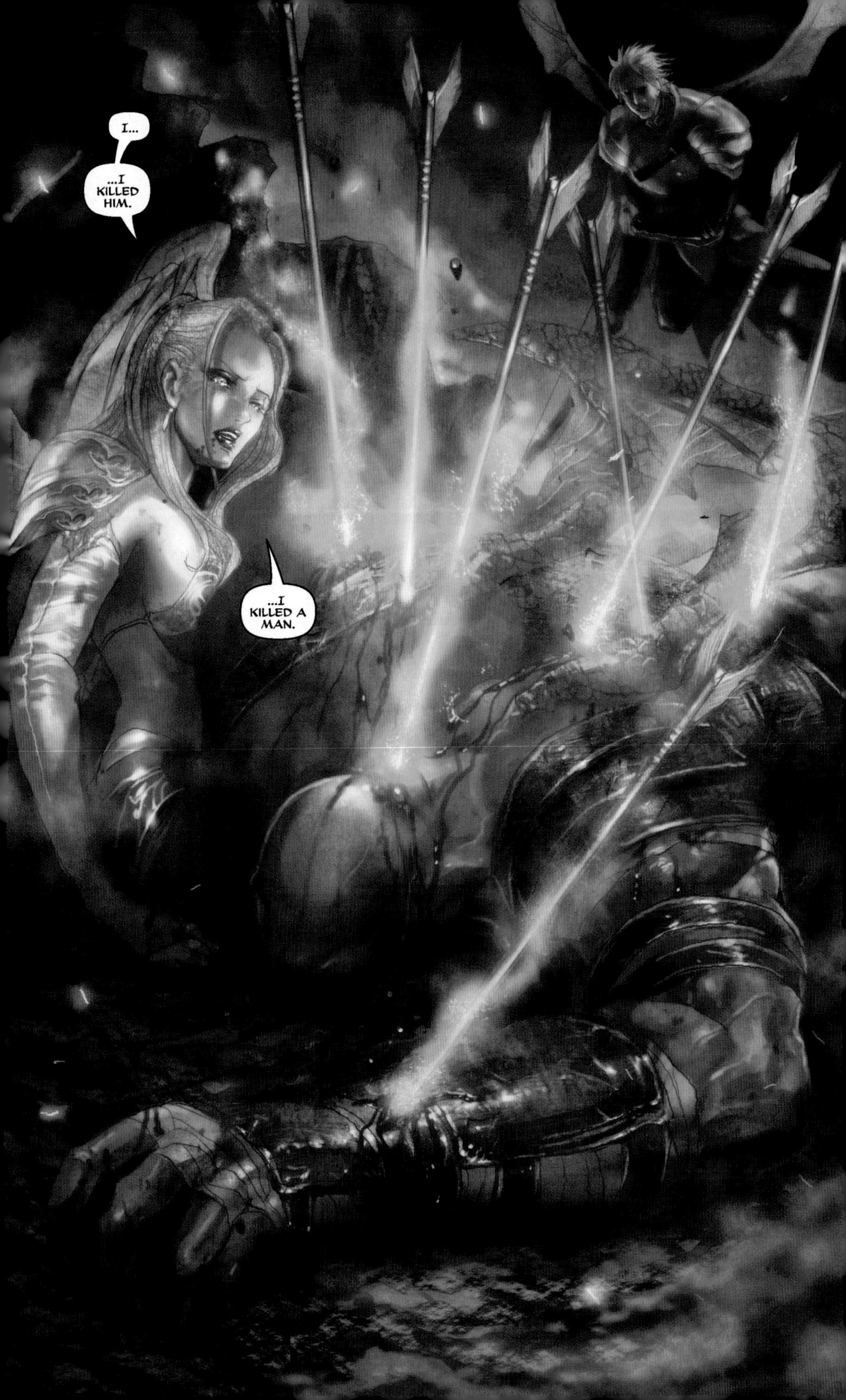
I...
...I KILLED HIM.
...I KILLED A MAN.

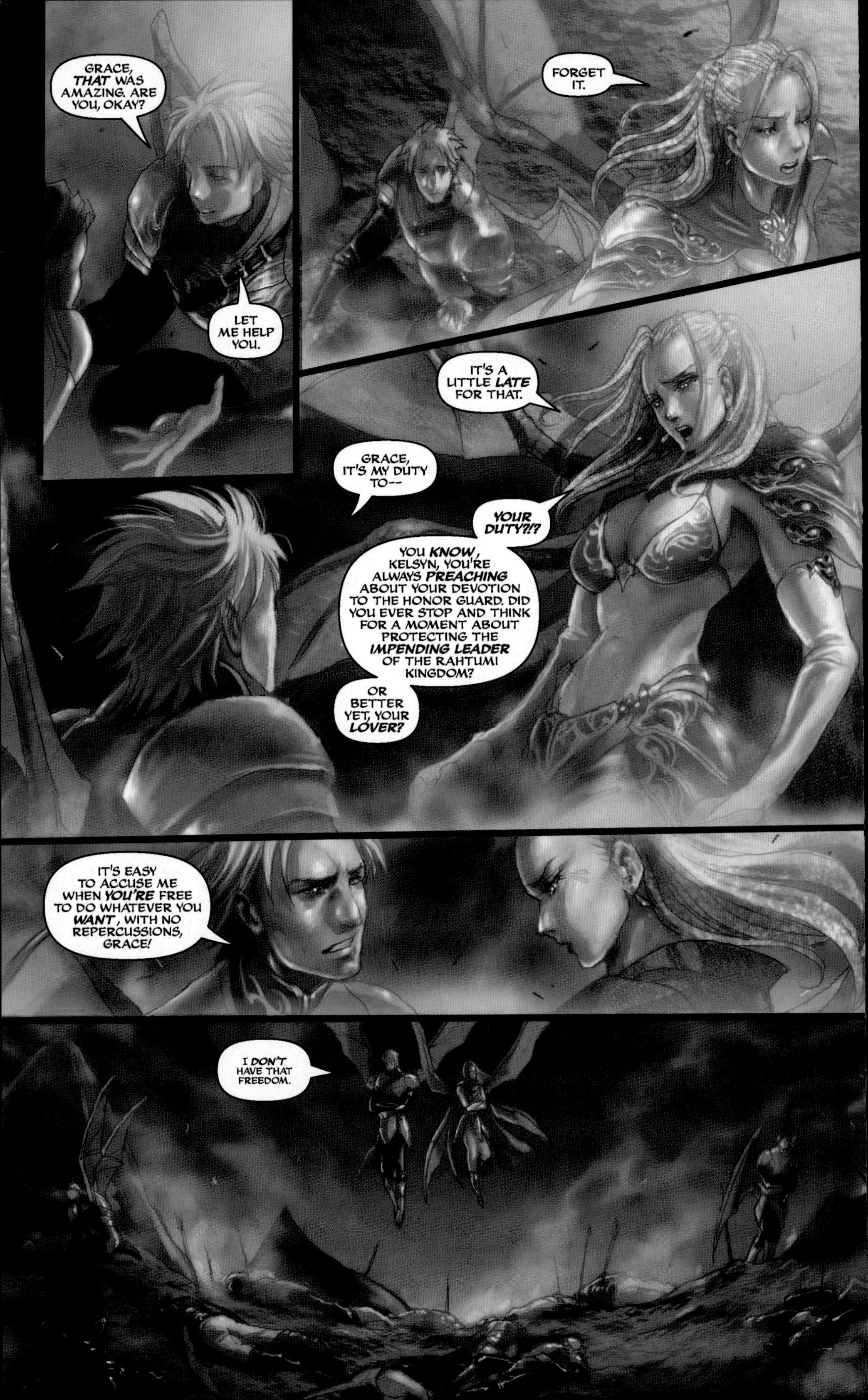
GRACE, THAT WAS AMAZING. ARE YOU, OKAY?
LET ME HELP YOU.
FORGET IT.
IT'S A LITTLE LATE FOR THAT.
GRACE, IT'S MY DUTY TO--
YOUR DUTY?!?
YOU KNOW, KELSYN, YOU'RE ALWAYS PREACHING ABOUT YOUR DEVOTION TO THE HONOR GUARD. DID YOU EVER STOP AND THINK FOR A MOMENT ABOUT PROTECTING THE IMPENDING LEADER OF THE RAHTUMI KINGDOM?
OR BETTER YET, YOUR LOVER?
IT'S EASY TO ACCUSE ME WHEN YOU'RE FREE TO DO WHATEVER YOU WANT, WITH NO REPERCUSSIONS, GRACE!
I DON'T HAVE THAT FREEDOM.

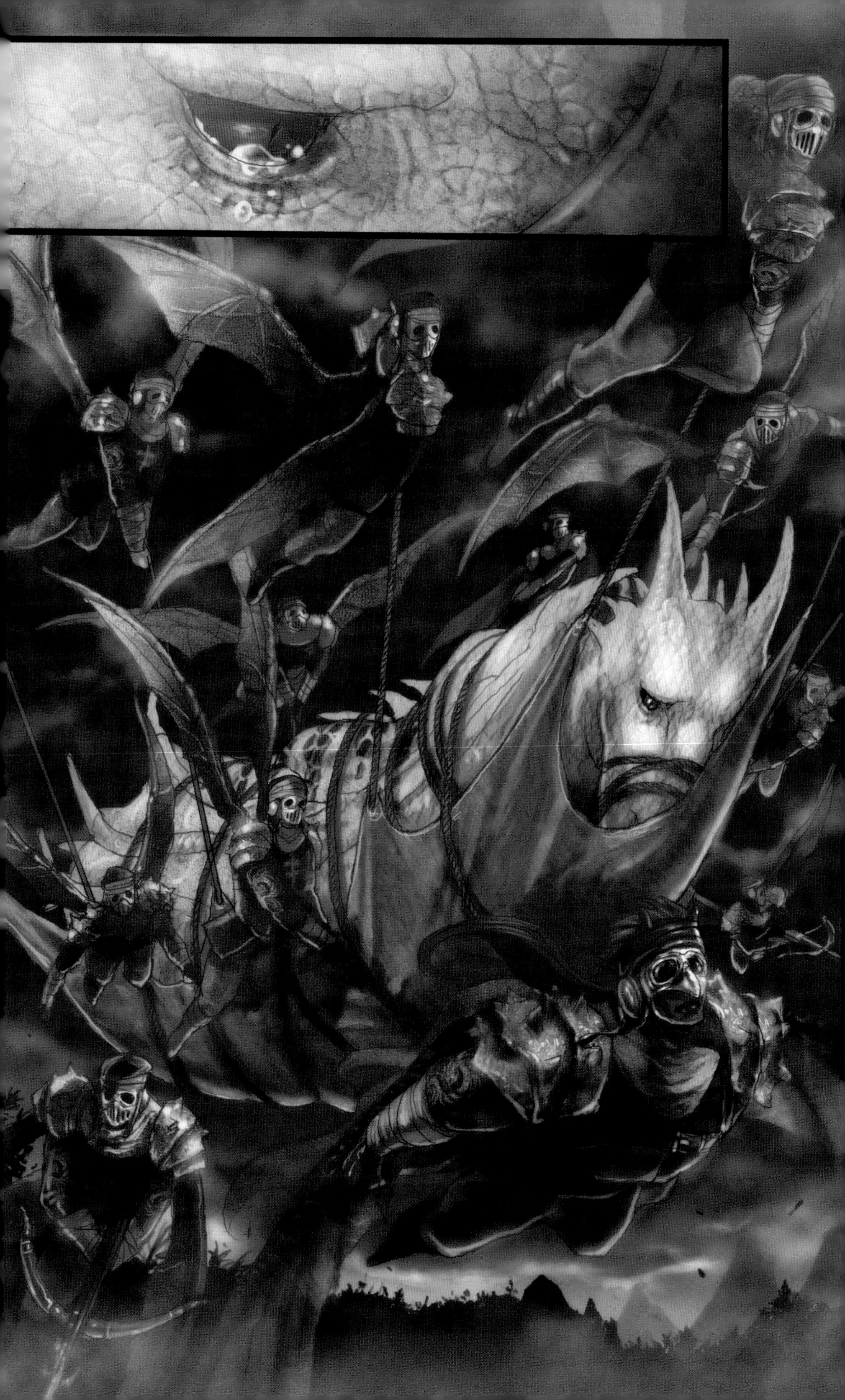

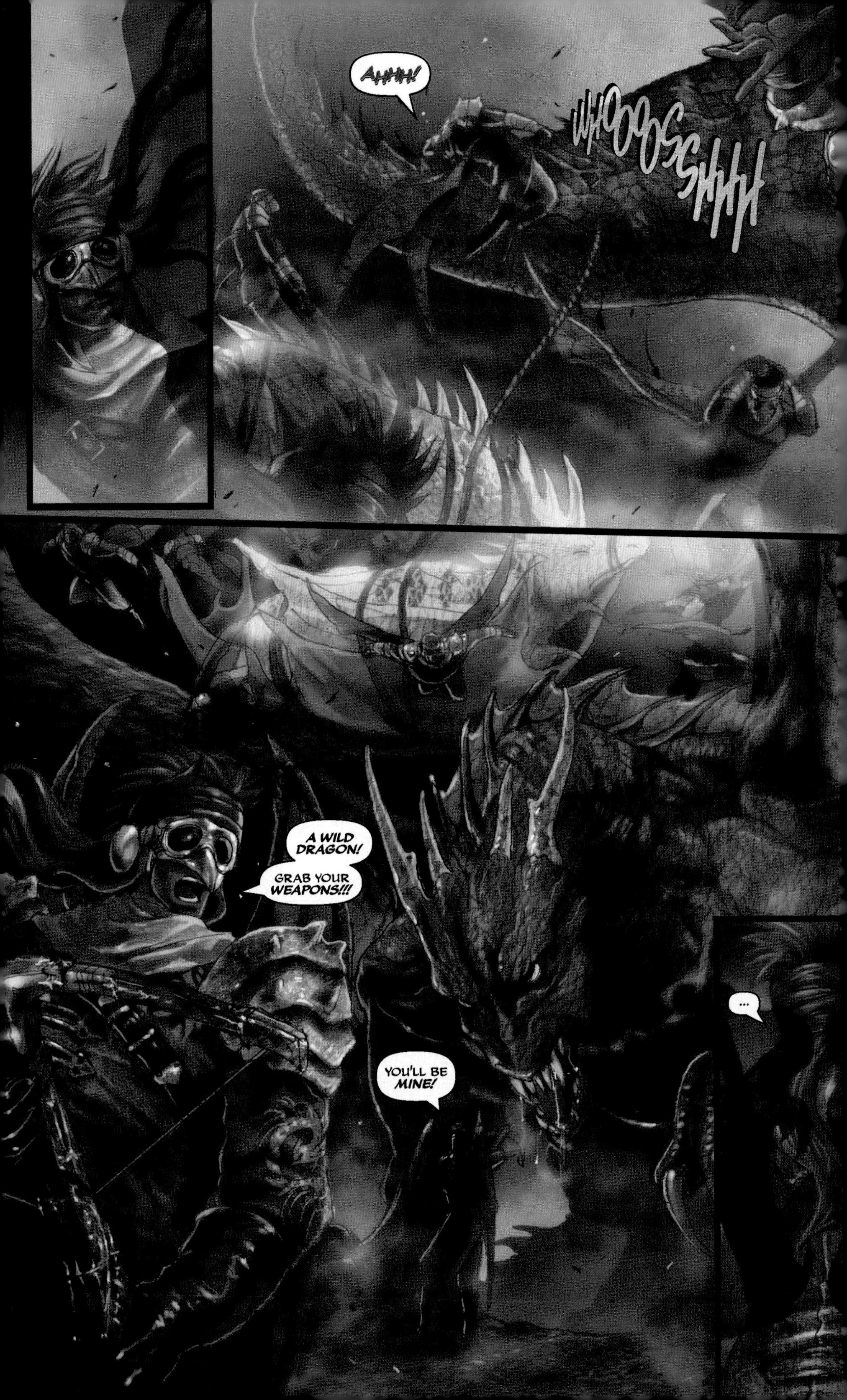
AHHH!
WHOOOOSSHHHH
A WILD DRAGON!
GRAB YOUR WEAPONS!!!
...
YOU'LL BE MINE!

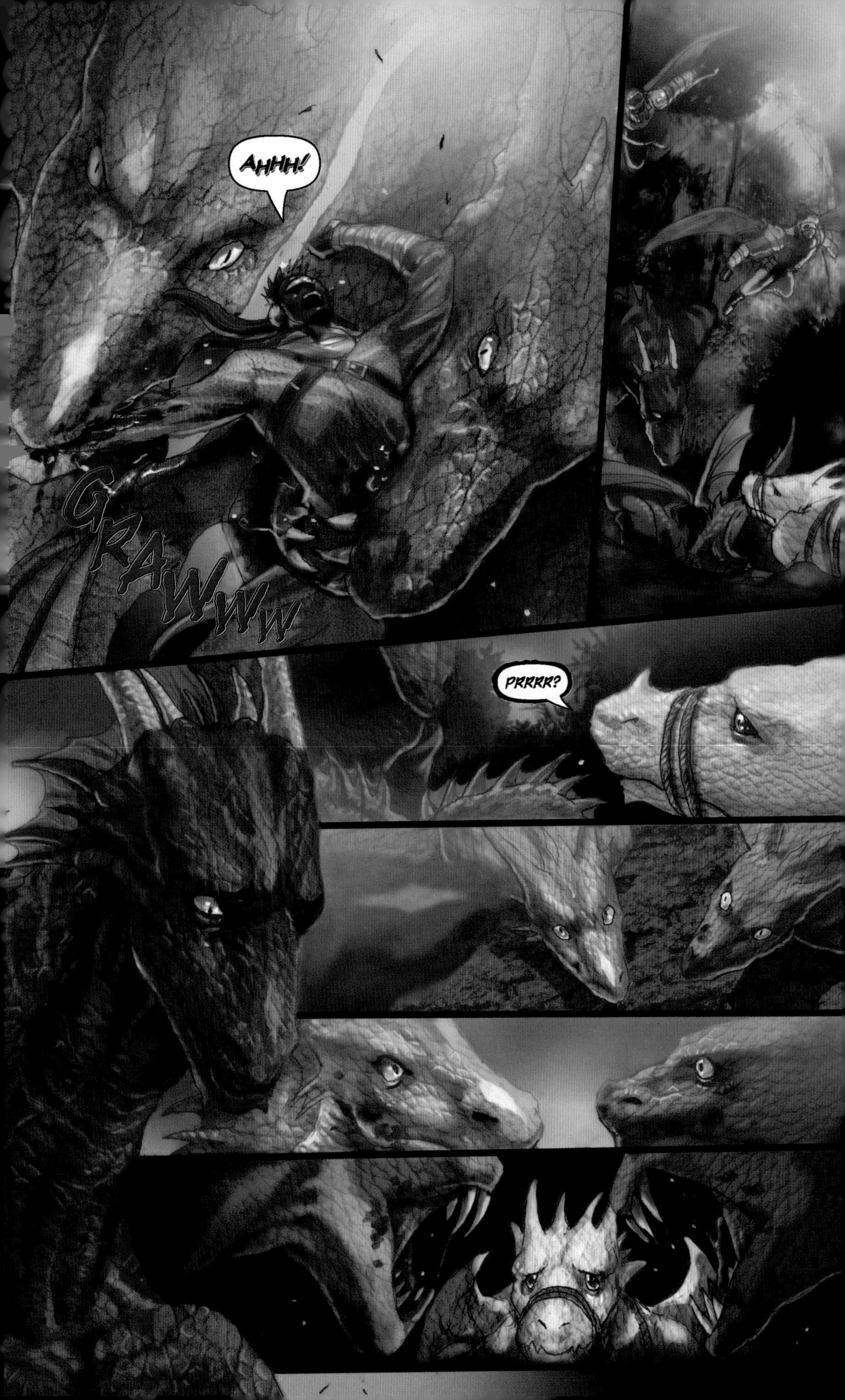
AHHH!
GRAWWW
PRRRR?

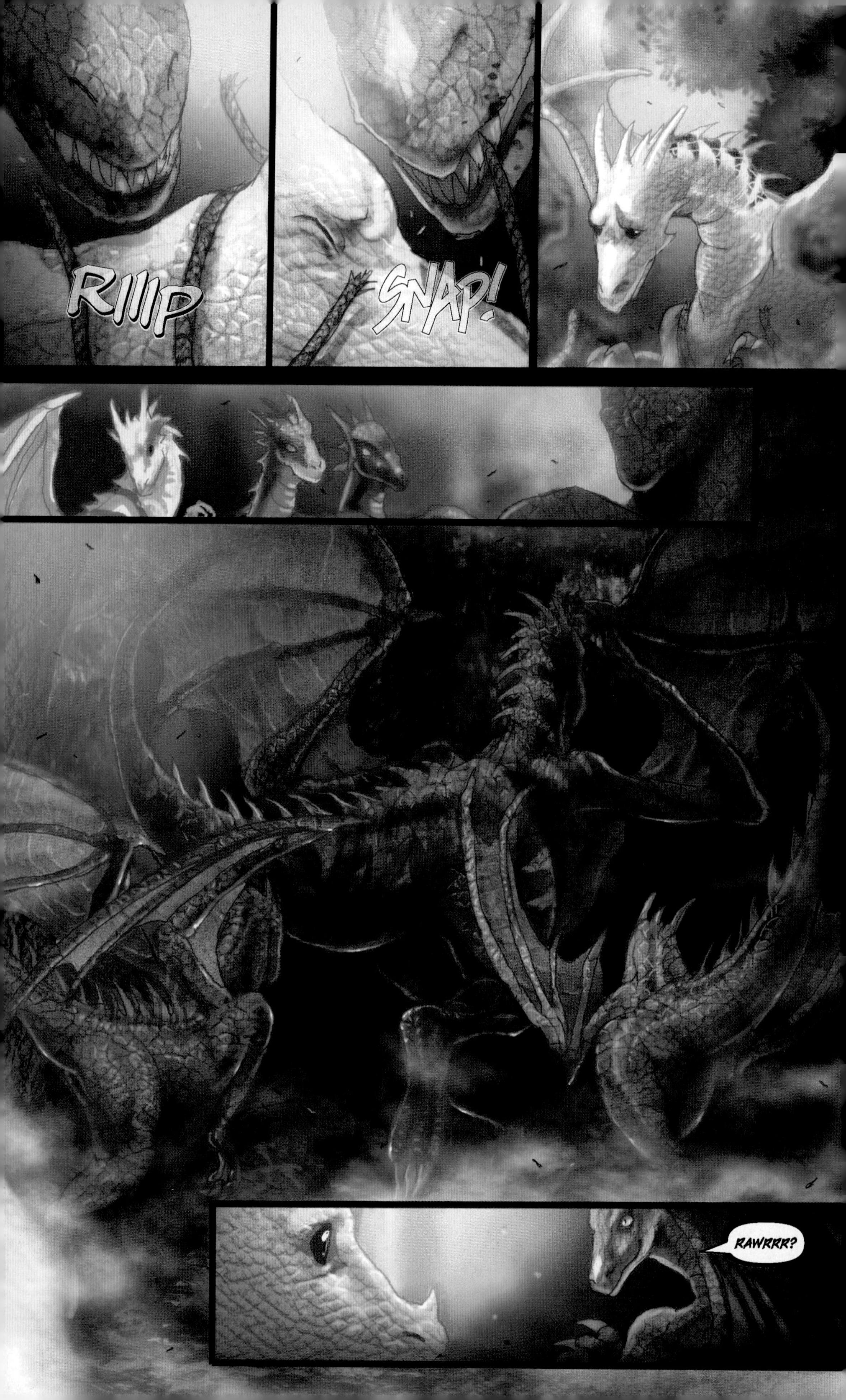
RIIIP
SNAP!
RAWRRR?

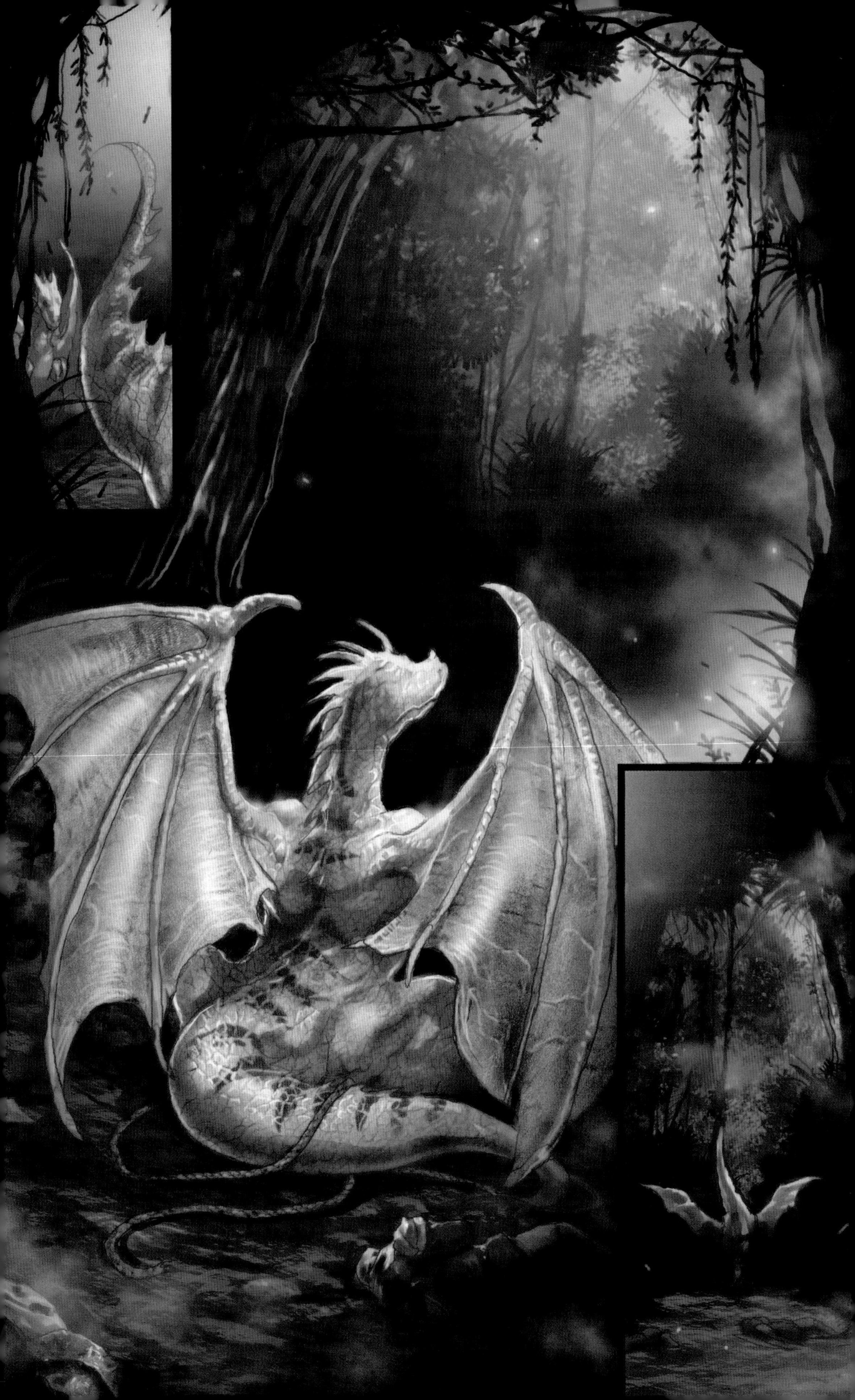

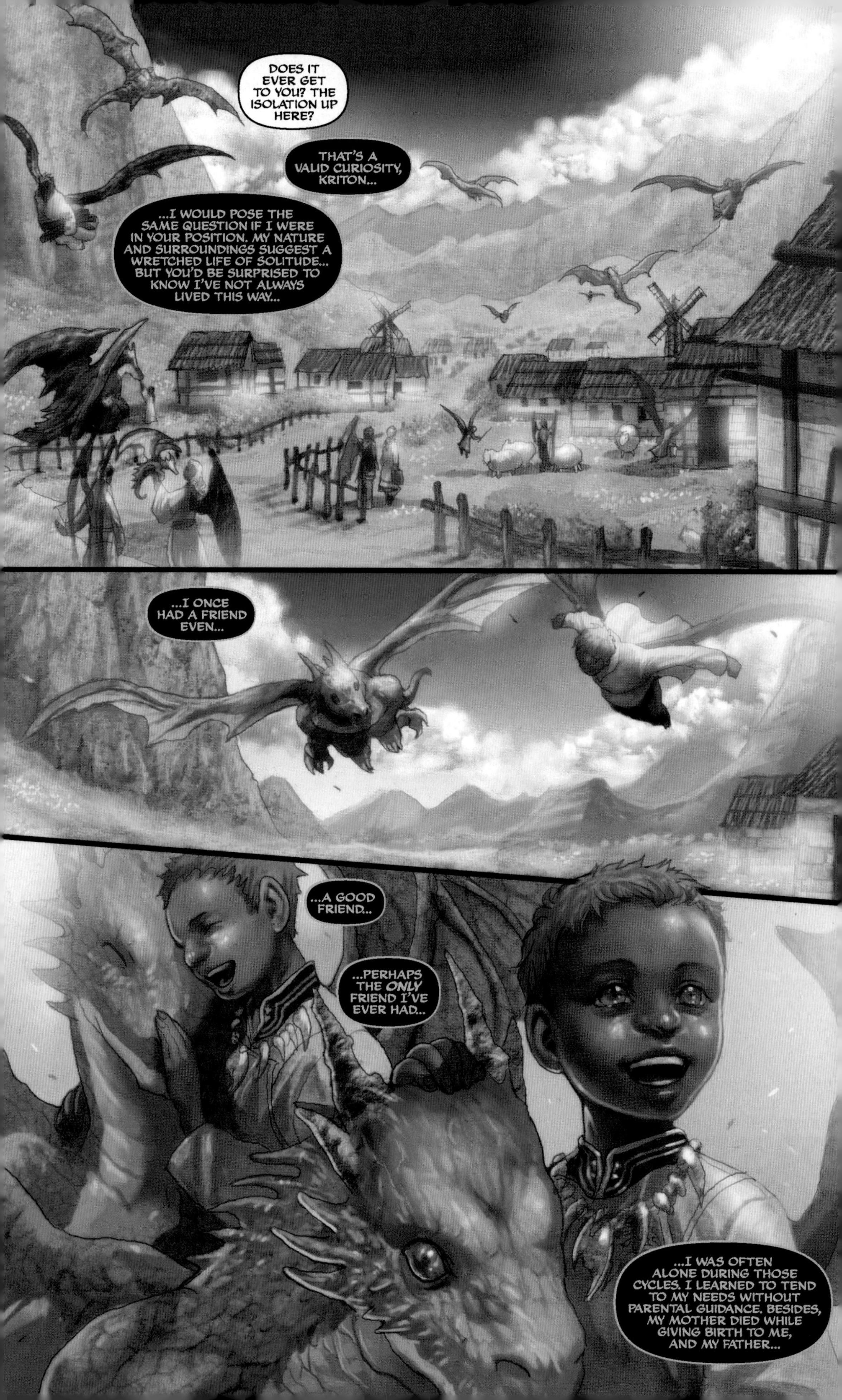
DOES IT EVER GET TO YOU? THE ISOLATION UP HERE?
THAT'S A VALID CURIOSITY, KRITON...
...I WOULD POSE THE SAME QUESTION IF I WERE IN YOUR POSITION. MY NATURE AND SURROUNDINGS SUGGEST A WRETCHED LIFE OF SOLITUDE... BUT YOU'D BE SURPRISED TO KNOW I'VE NOT ALWAYS LIVED THIS WAY...
...I ONCE HAD A FRIEND EVEN...
...A GOOD FRIEND...
...PERHAPS THE *ONLY* FRIEND I'VE EVER HAD...
...I WAS OFTEN ALONE DURING THOSE CYCLES. I LEARNED TO TEND TO MY NEEDS WITHOUT PARENTAL GUIDANCE. BESIDES, MY MOTHER DIED WHILE GIVING BIRTH TO ME, AND MY FATHER...

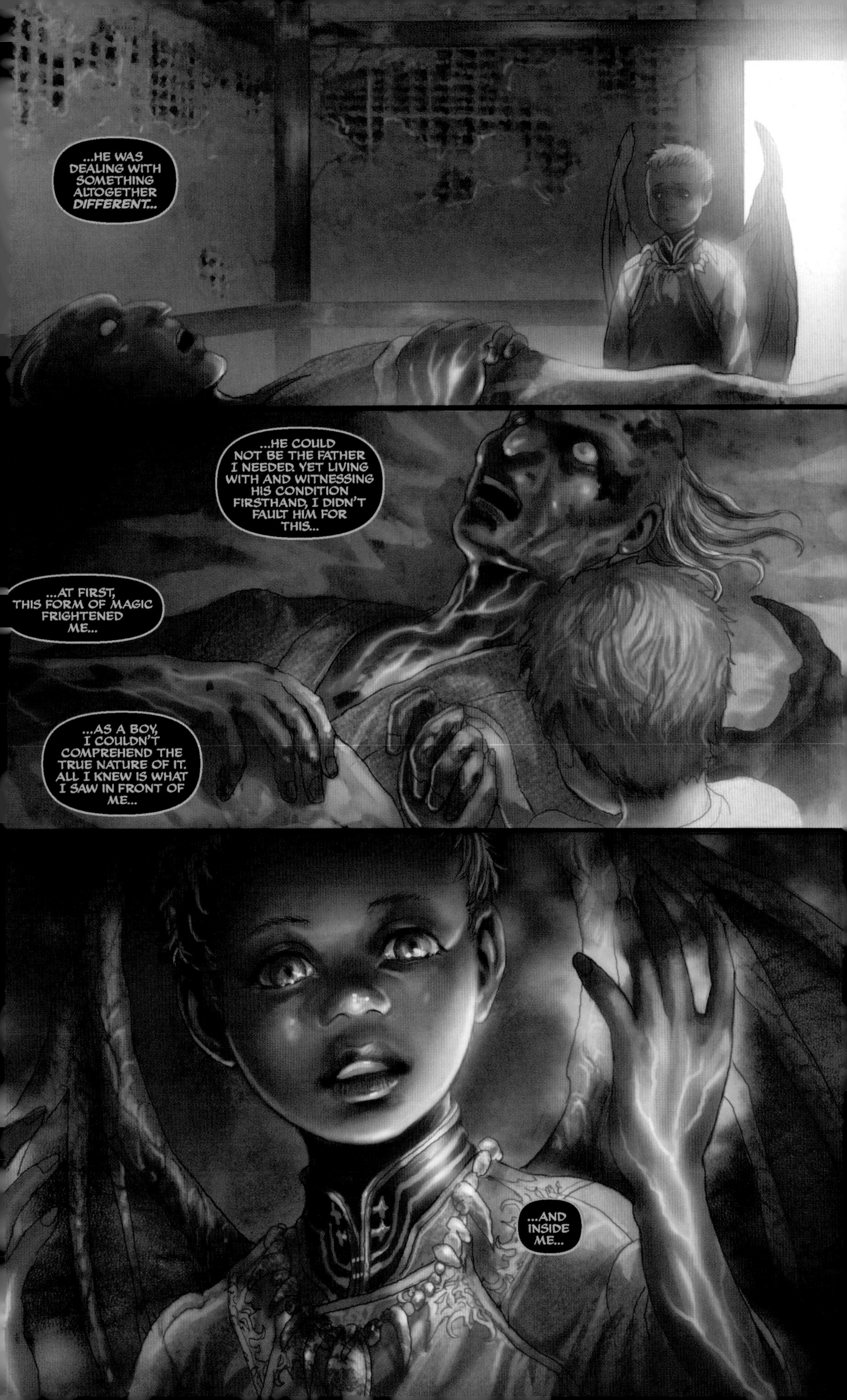

...HE WAS DEALING WITH SOMETHING ALTOGETHER *DIFFERENT*...
...HE COULD NOT BE THE FATHER I NEEDED. YET LIVING WITH AND WITNESSING HIS CONDITION FIRSTHAND, I DIDN'T FAULT HIM FOR THIS...
...AT FIRST, THIS FORM OF MAGIC FRIGHTENED ME...
...AS A BOY, I COULDN'T COMPREHEND THE TRUE NATURE OF IT. ALL I KNEW IS WHAT I SAW IN FRONT OF ME...
...AND INSIDE ME...

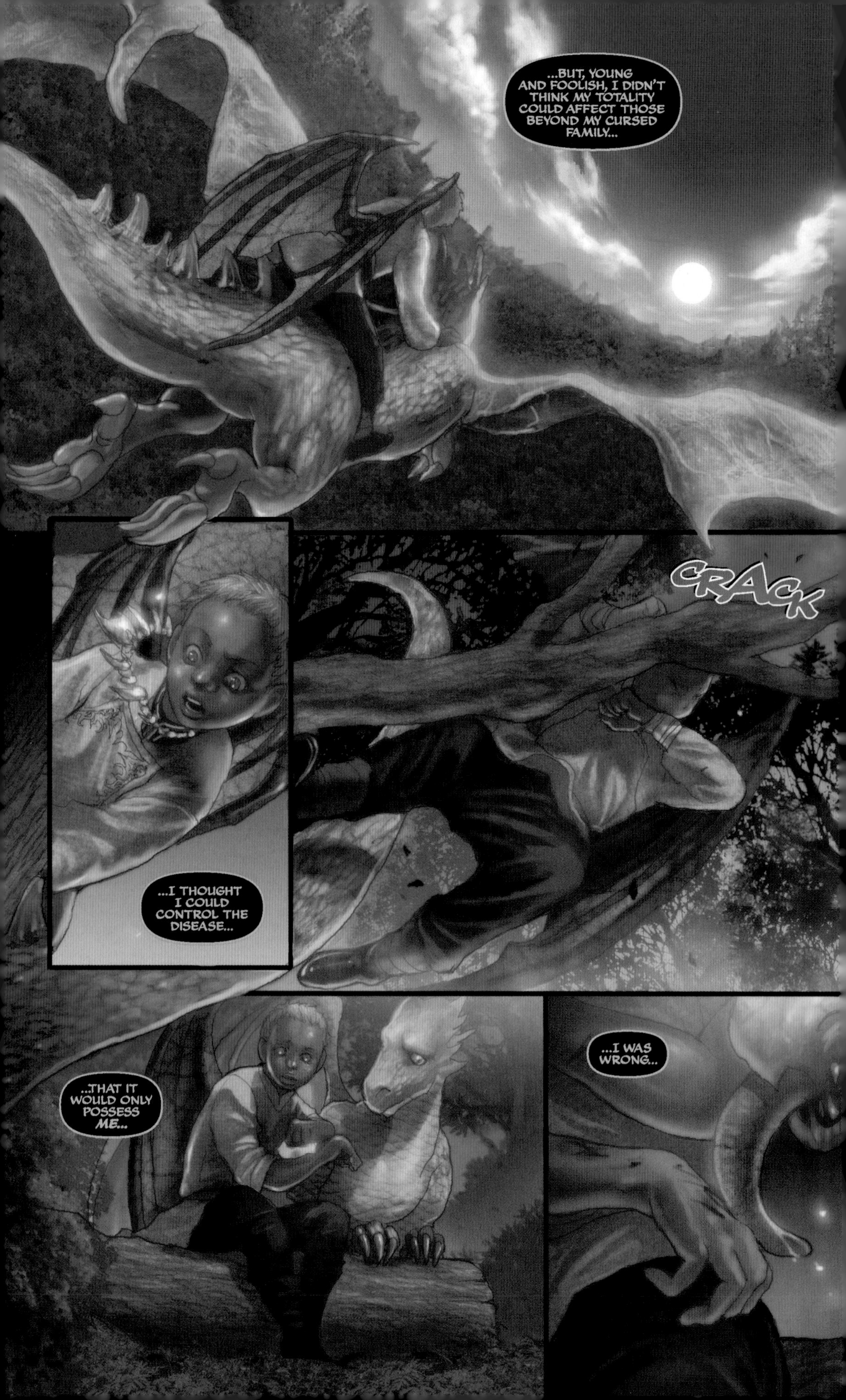
...BUT, YOUNG AND FOOLISH, I DIDN'T THINK MY TOTALITY COULD AFFECT THOSE BEYOND MY CURSED FAMILY...
CRACK
...I THOUGHT I COULD CONTROL THE DISEASE...
...THAT IT WOULD ONLY POSSESS *ME*...
...I WAS WRONG...

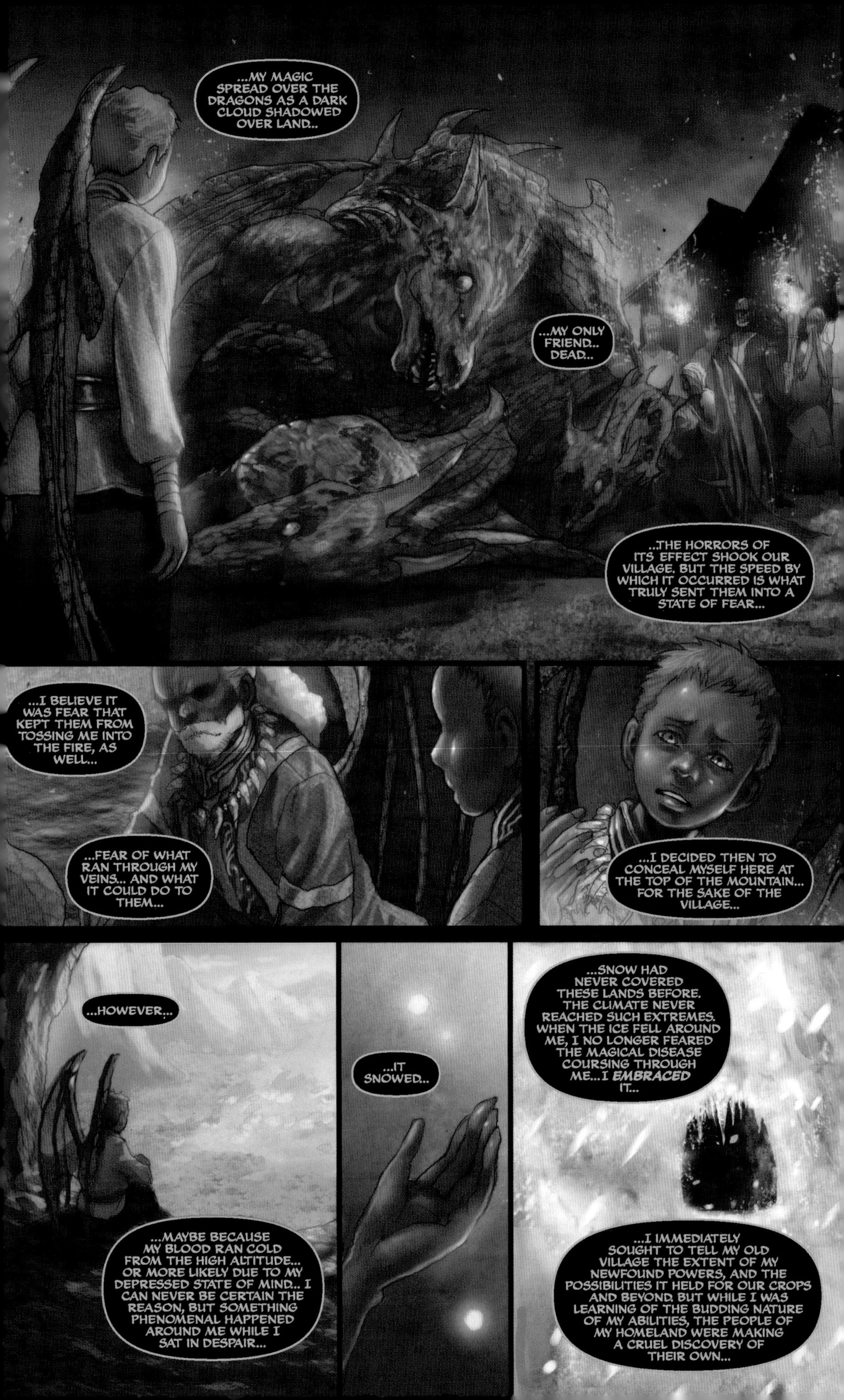
...MY MAGIC SPREAD OVER THE DRAGONS AS A DARK CLOUD SHADOWED OVER LAND...
...MY ONLY FRIEND... DEAD...
...THE HORRORS OF ITS EFFECT SHOOK OUR VILLAGE. BUT THE SPEED BY WHICH IT OCCURRED IS WHAT TRULY SENT THEM INTO A STATE OF FEAR...
...I BELIEVE IT WAS FEAR THAT KEPT THEM FROM TOSSING ME INTO THE FIRE, AS WELL...
...FEAR OF WHAT RAN THROUGH MY VEINS... AND WHAT IT COULD DO TO THEM...
...I DECIDED THEN TO CONCEAL MYSELF HERE AT THE TOP OF THE MOUNTAIN... FOR THE SAKE OF THE VILLAGE...
...HOWEVER...
...MAYBE BECAUSE MY BLOOD RAN COLD FROM THE HIGH ALTITUDE... OR MORE LIKELY DUE TO MY DEPRESSED STATE OF MIND... I CAN NEVER BE CERTAIN THE REASON, BUT SOMETHING PHENOMENAL HAPPENED AROUND ME WHILE I SAT IN DESPAIR...
...IT SNOWED...
...SNOW HAD NEVER COVERED THESE LANDS BEFORE. THE CLIMATE NEVER REACHED SUCH EXTREMES. WHEN THE ICE FELL AROUND ME, I NO LONGER FEARED THE MAGICAL DISEASE COURSING THROUGH ME...I *EMBRACED* IT...
...I IMMEDIATELY SOUGHT TO TELL MY OLD VILLAGE THE EXTENT OF MY NEWFOUND POWERS, AND THE POSSIBILITIES IT HELD FOR OUR CROPS AND BEYOND. BUT WHILE I WAS LEARNING OF THE BUDDING NATURE OF MY ABILITIES, THE PEOPLE OF MY HOMELAND WERE MAKING A CRUEL DISCOVERY OF THEIR OWN...

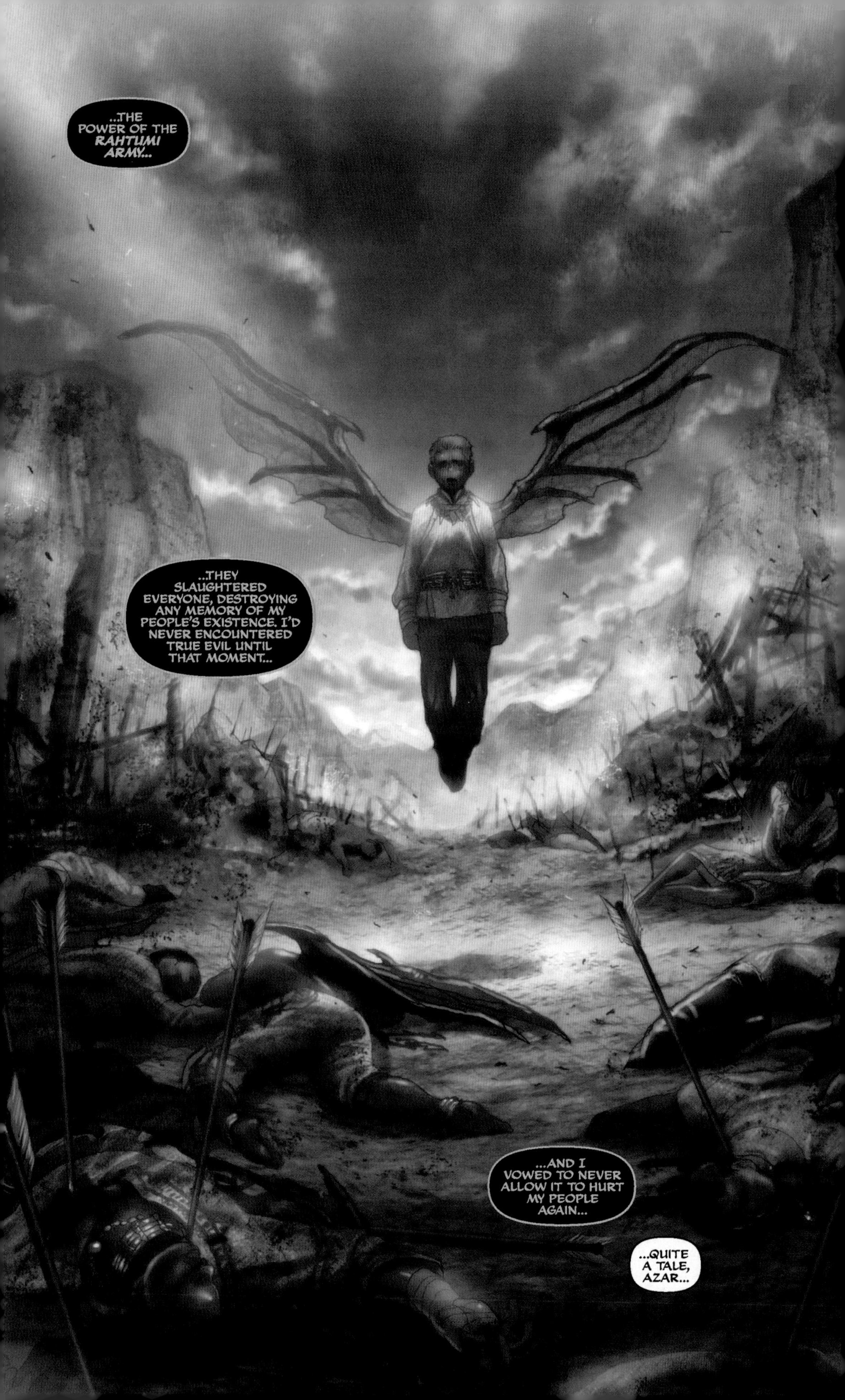
...THE POWER OF THE *RAHTUMI* ARMY...
...THEY SLAUGHTERED EVERYONE, DESTROYING ANY MEMORY OF MY PEOPLE'S EXISTENCE. I'D NEVER ENCOUNTERED TRUE EVIL UNTIL THAT MOMENT...
...AND I VOWED TO NEVER ALLOW IT TO HURT MY PEOPLE AGAIN...
...QUITE A TALE, AZAR...

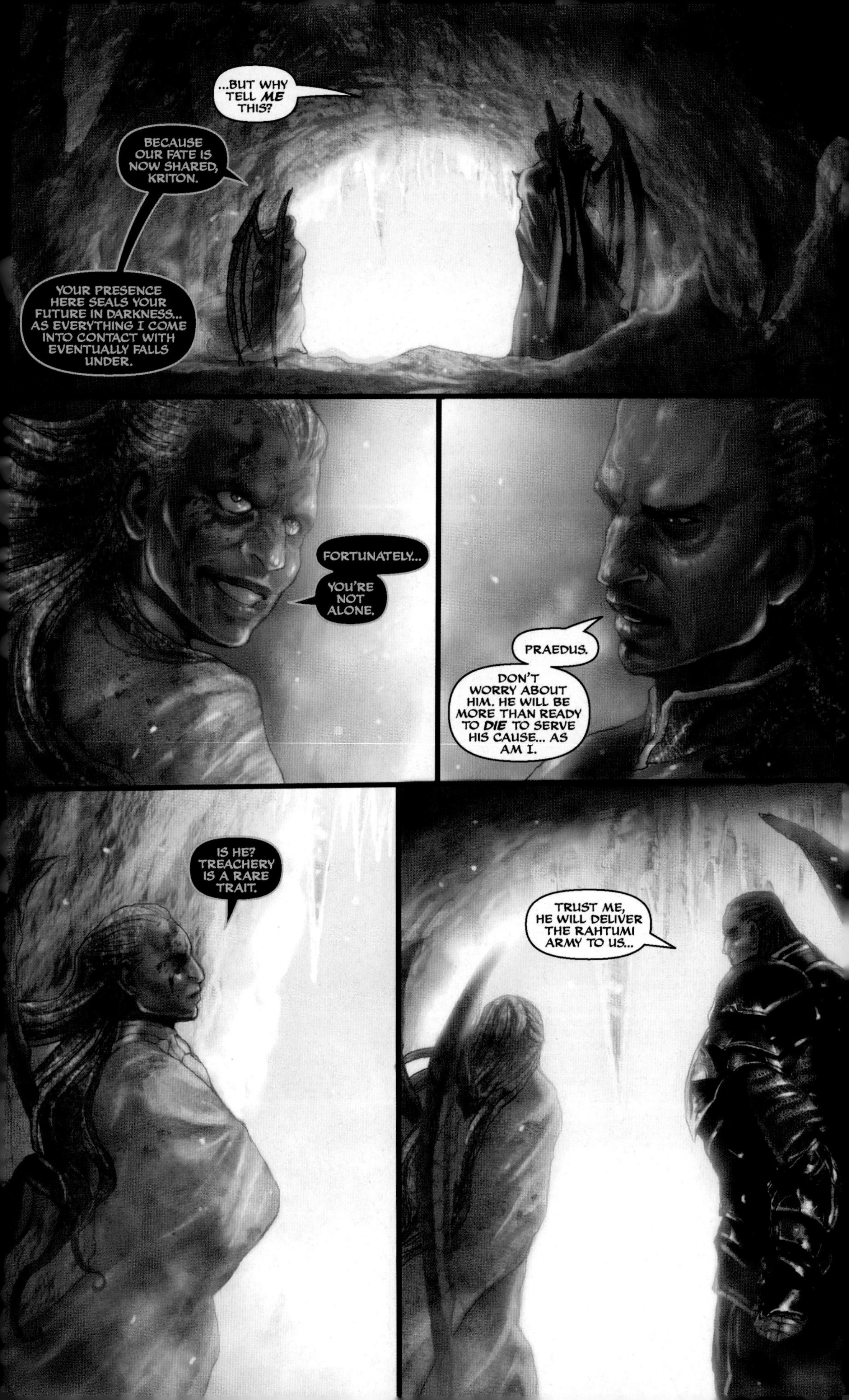
...BUT WHY TELL *ME* THIS?
BECAUSE OUR FATE IS NOW SHARED, KRITON.
YOUR PRESENCE HERE SEALS YOUR FUTURE IN DARKNESS... AS EVERYTHING I COME INTO CONTACT WITH EVENTUALLY FALLS UNDER.
FORTUNATELY...
YOU'RE NOT ALONE.
PRAEDUS.
DON'T WORRY ABOUT HIM. HE WILL BE MORE THAN READY TO *DIE* TO SERVE HIS CAUSE... AS AM I.
IS HE? TREACHERY IS A RARE TRAIT.
TRUST ME, HE WILL DELIVER THE RAHTUMI ARMY TO US...

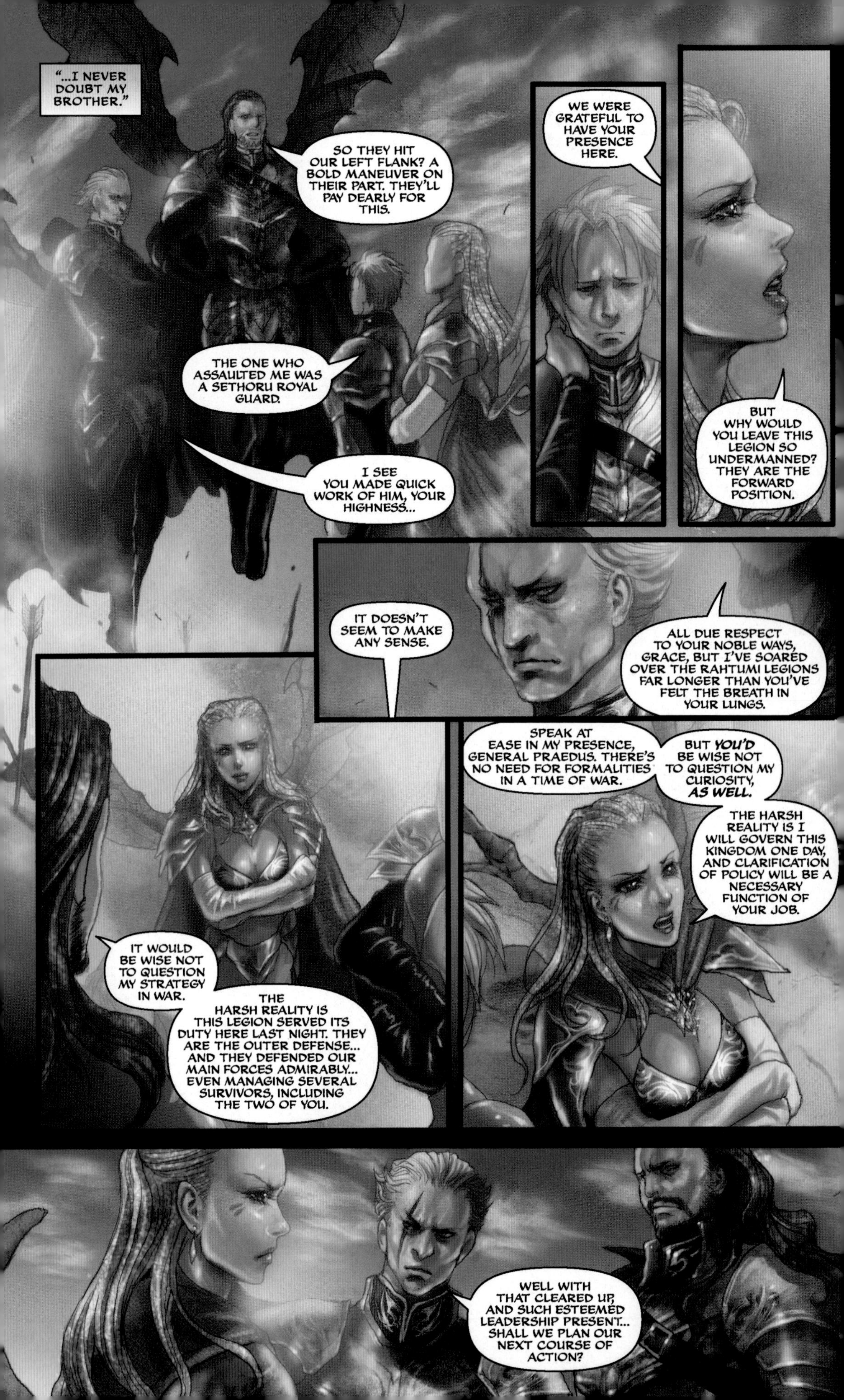
"...I NEVER DOUBT MY BROTHER."
SO THEY HIT OUR LEFT FLANK? A BOLD MANEUVER ON THEIR PART. THEY'LL PAY DEARLY FOR THIS.
THE ONE WHO ASSAULTED ME WAS A SETHORU ROYAL GUARD.
I SEE YOU MADE QUICK WORK OF HIM, YOUR HIGHNESS...
WE WERE GRATEFUL TO HAVE YOUR PRESENCE HERE.
BUT WHY WOULD YOU LEAVE THIS LEGION SO UNDERMANNED? THEY ARE THE FORWARD POSITION.
IT DOESN'T SEEM TO MAKE ANY SENSE.
ALL DUE RESPECT TO YOUR NOBLE WAYS, GRACE, BUT I'VE SOARED OVER THE RAHTUMI LEGIONS FAR LONGER THAN YOU'VE FELT THE BREATH IN YOUR LUNGS.
IT WOULD BE WISE NOT TO QUESTION MY STRATEGY IN WAR.
THE HARSH REALITY IS THIS LEGION SERVED ITS DUTY HERE LAST NIGHT. THEY ARE THE OUTER DEFENSE... AND THEY DEFENDED OUR MAIN FORCES ADMIRABLY... EVEN MANAGING SEVERAL SURVIVORS, INCLUDING THE TWO OF YOU.
SPEAK AT EASE IN MY PRESENCE, GENERAL PRAEDUS. THERE'S NO NEED FOR FORMALITIES IN A TIME OF WAR.
BUT *YOU'D* BE WISE NOT TO QUESTION MY CURIOSITY, **AS WELL.**
THE HARSH REALITY IS I WILL GOVERN THIS KINGDOM ONE DAY, AND CLARIFICATION OF POLICY WILL BE A NECESSARY FUNCTION OF YOUR JOB.
WELL WITH THAT CLEARED UP, AND SUCH ESTEEMED LEADERSHIP PRESENT... SHALL WE PLAN OUR NEXT COURSE OF ACTION?

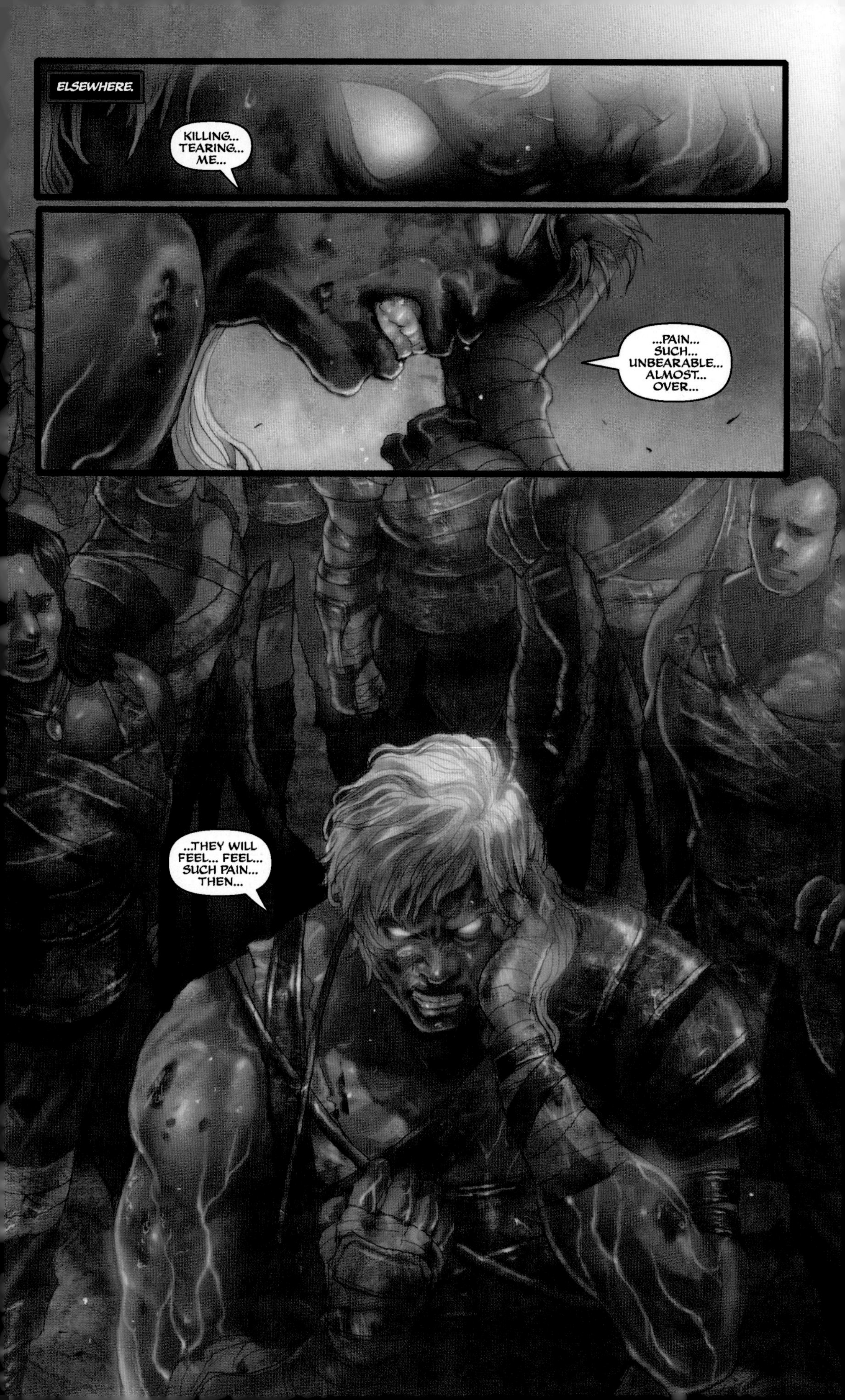
ELSEWHERE.
KILLING... TEARING... ME...
...PAIN... SUCH... UNBEARABLE... ALMOST... OVER...
...THEY WILL FEEL... FEEL... SUCH PAIN... THEN...

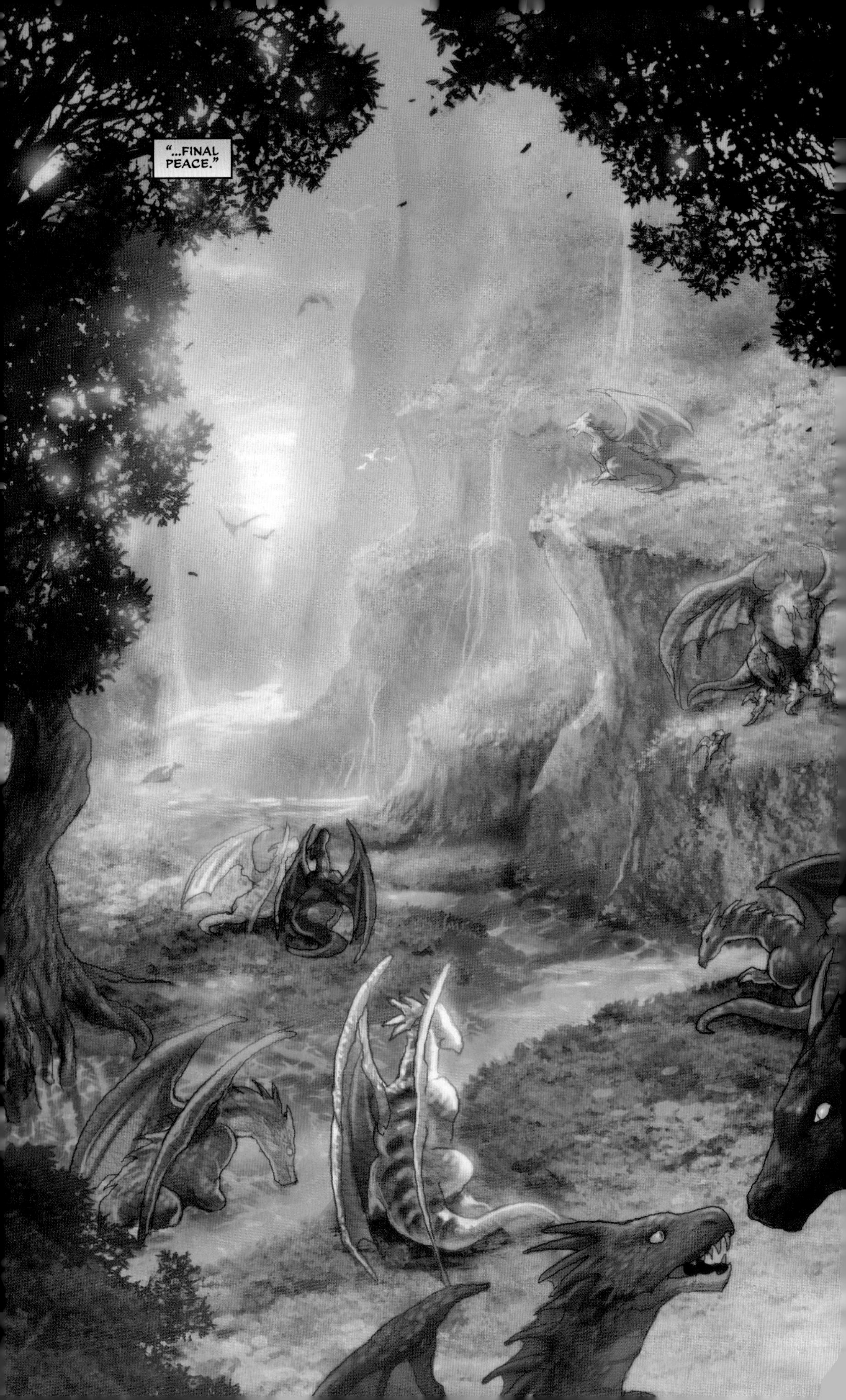
"...FINAL PEACE."

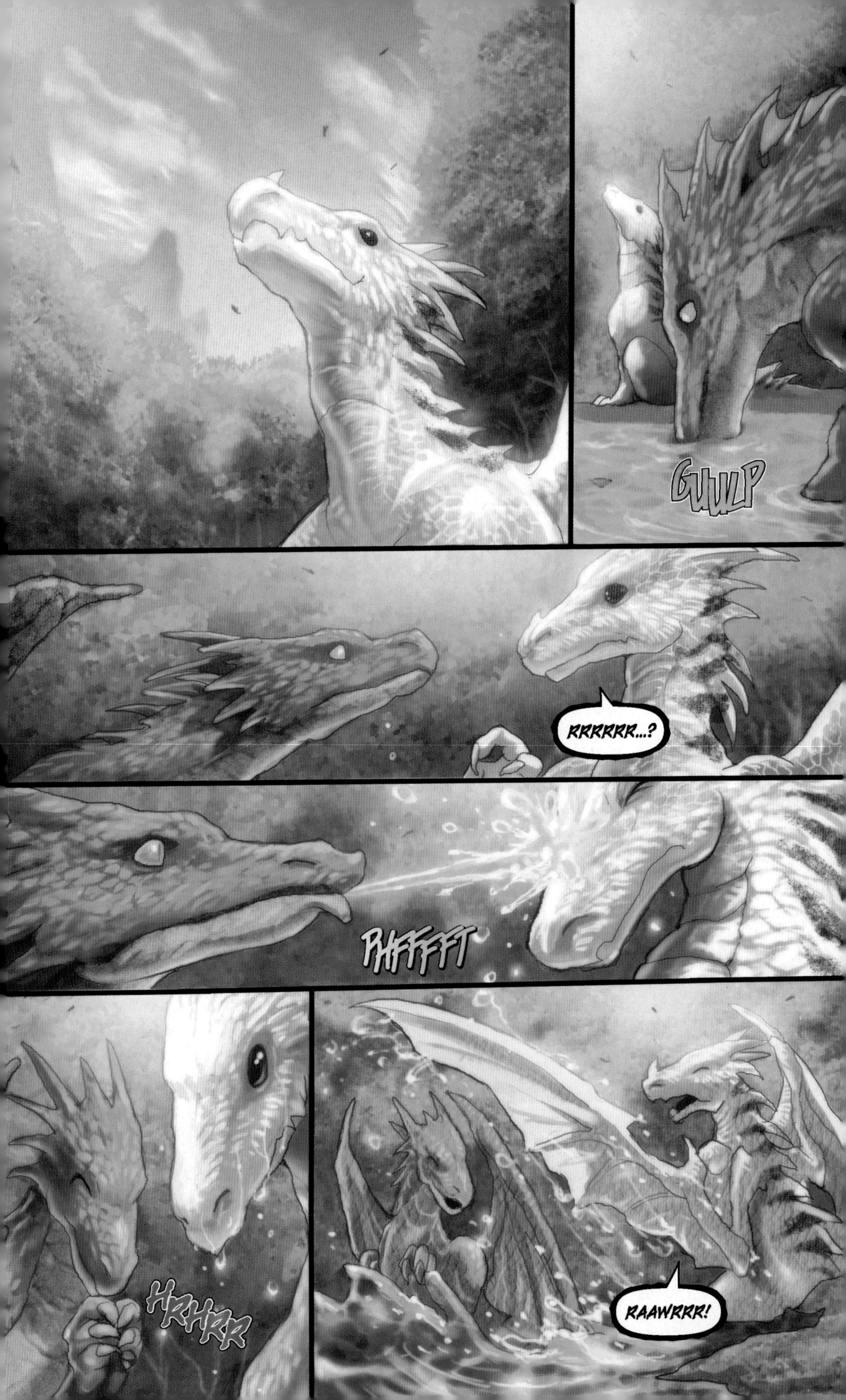
GUULP
RRRRRR...?
PHFFFFT
HRHRR
RAAWRRR!

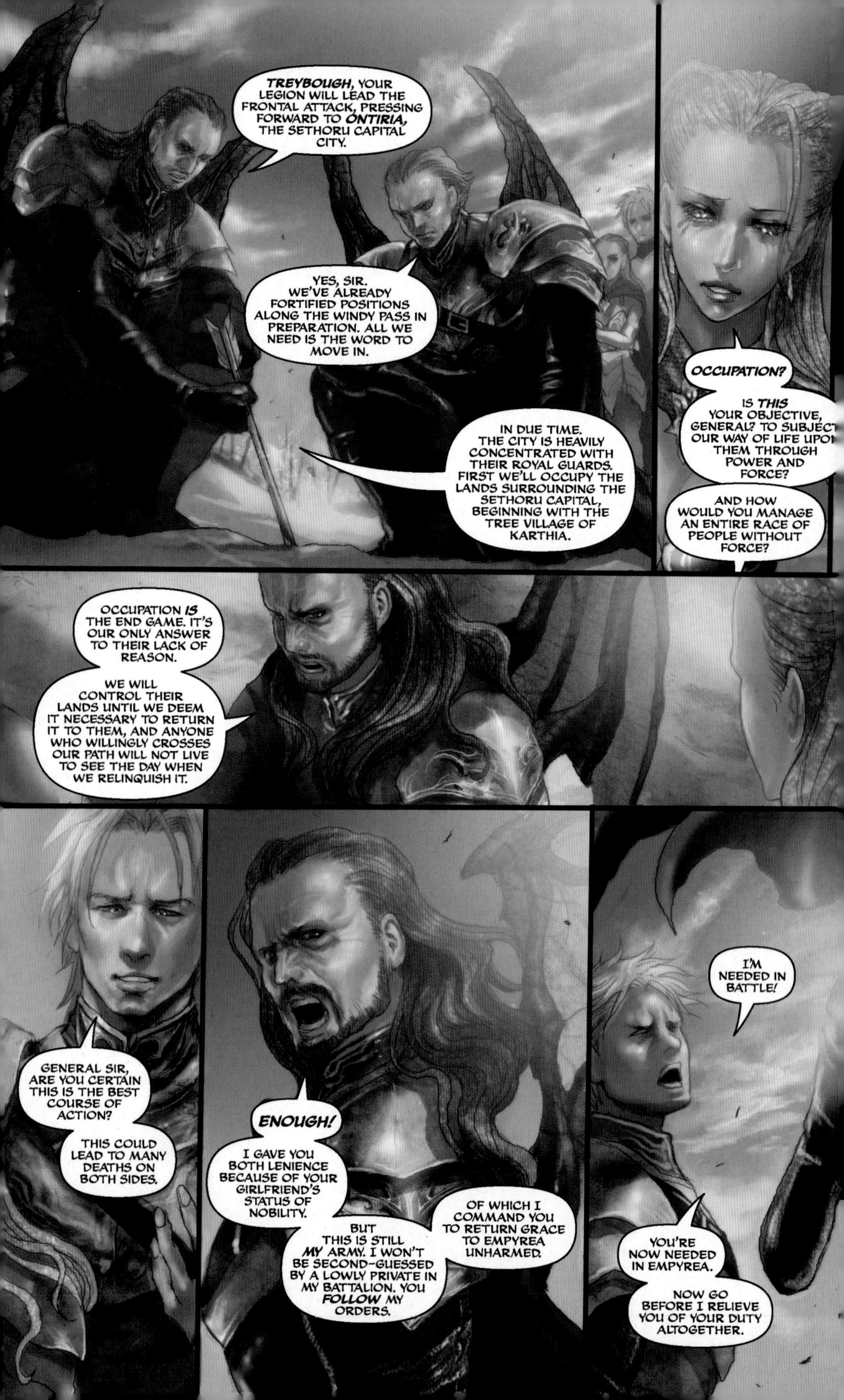
TREYBOUGH, YOUR LEGION WILL LEAD THE FRONTAL ATTACK, PRESSING FORWARD TO ONTIRIA, THE SETHORU CAPITAL CITY.
YES, SIR. WE'VE ALREADY FORTIFIED POSITIONS ALONG THE WINDY PASS IN PREPARATION. ALL WE NEED IS THE WORD TO MOVE IN.
IN DUE TIME. THE CITY IS HEAVILY CONCENTRATED WITH THEIR ROYAL GUARDS. FIRST WE'LL OCCUPY THE LANDS SURROUNDING THE SETHORU CAPITAL, BEGINNING WITH THE TREE VILLAGE OF KARTHIA.
OCCUPATION?
IS THIS YOUR OBJECTIVE, GENERAL? TO SUBJECT OUR WAY OF LIFE UPON THEM THROUGH POWER AND FORCE?
AND HOW WOULD YOU MANAGE AN ENTIRE RACE OF PEOPLE WITHOUT FORCE?
OCCUPATION IS THE END GAME. IT'S OUR ONLY ANSWER TO THEIR LACK OF REASON.
WE WILL CONTROL THEIR LANDS UNTIL WE DEEM IT NECESSARY TO RETURN IT TO THEM, AND ANYONE WHO WILLINGLY CROSSES OUR PATH WILL NOT LIVE TO SEE THE DAY WHEN WE RELINQUISH IT.
GENERAL SIR, ARE YOU CERTAIN THIS IS THE BEST COURSE OF ACTION?
THIS COULD LEAD TO MANY DEATHS ON BOTH SIDES.
ENOUGH!
I GAVE YOU BOTH LENIENCE BECAUSE OF YOUR GIRLFRIEND'S STATUS OF NOBILITY.
BUT THIS IS STILL MY ARMY. I WON'T BE SECOND-GUESSED BY A LOWLY PRIVATE IN MY BATTALION. YOU FOLLOW MY ORDERS.
OF WHICH I COMMAND YOU TO RETURN GRACE TO EMPYREA UNHARMED.
I'M NEEDED IN BATTLE!
YOU'RE NOW NEEDED IN EMPYREA.
NOW GO BEFORE I RELIEVE YOU OF YOUR DUTY ALTOGETHER.

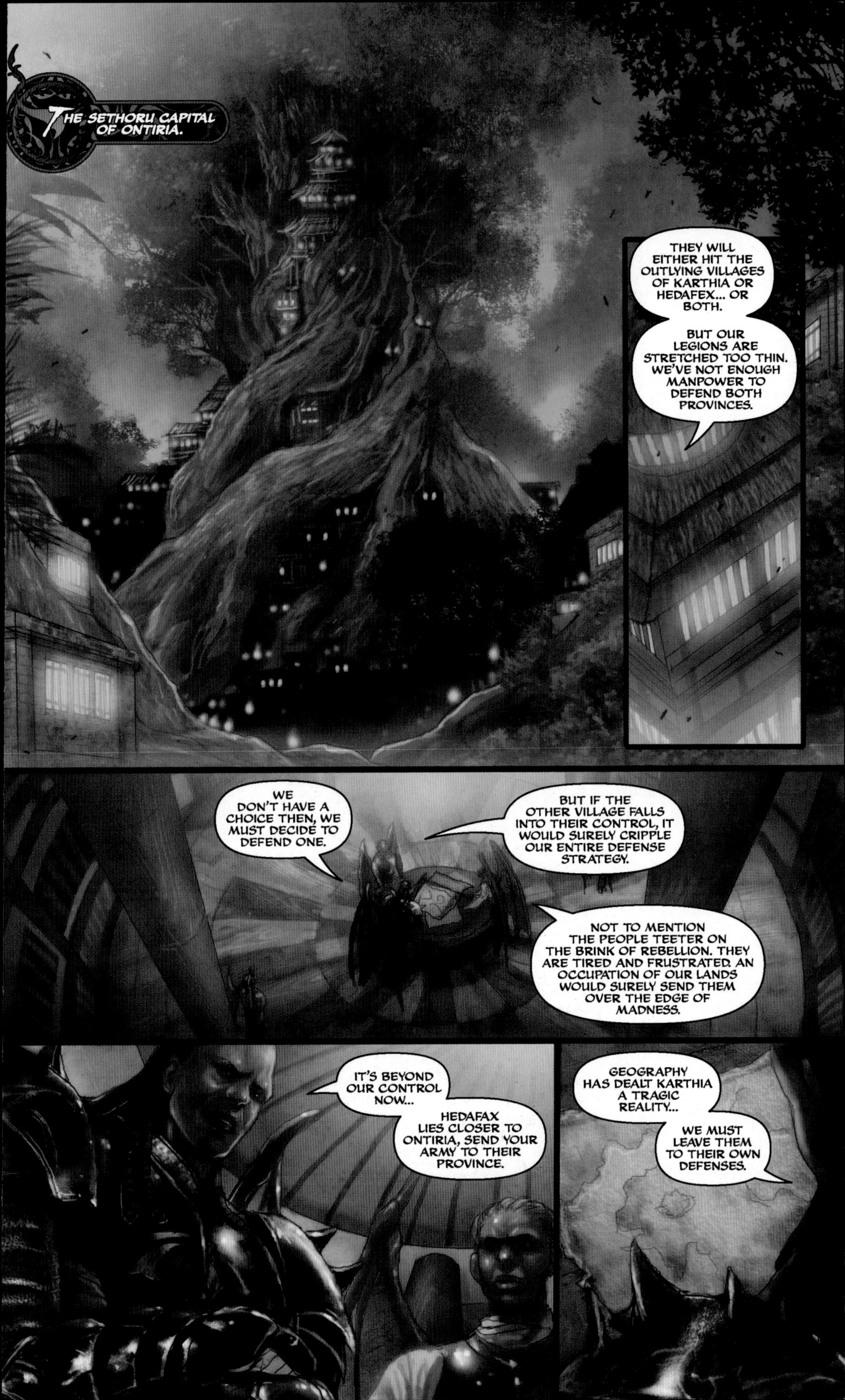
THE SETHORU CAPITAL OF ONTIRIA.
THEY WILL EITHER HIT THE OUTLYING VILLAGES OF KARTHIA OR HEDAFEX... OR BOTH.
BUT OUR LEGIONS ARE STRETCHED TOO THIN. WE'VE NOT ENOUGH MANPOWER TO DEFEND BOTH PROVINCES.
WE DON'T HAVE A CHOICE THEN, WE MUST DECIDE TO DEFEND ONE.
BUT IF THE OTHER VILLAGE FALLS INTO THEIR CONTROL, IT WOULD SURELY CRIPPLE OUR ENTIRE DEFENSE STRATEGY.
NOT TO MENTION THE PEOPLE TEETER ON THE BRINK OF REBELLION. THEY ARE TIRED AND FRUSTRATED. AN OCCUPATION OF OUR LANDS WOULD SURELY SEND THEM OVER THE EDGE OF MADNESS.
IT'S BEYOND OUR CONTROL NOW...
HEDAFAX LIES CLOSER TO ONTIRIA, SEND YOUR ARMY TO THEIR PROVINCE.
GEOGRAPHY HAS DEALT KARTHIA A TRAGIC REALITY...
WE MUST LEAVE THEM TO THEIR OWN DEFENSES.

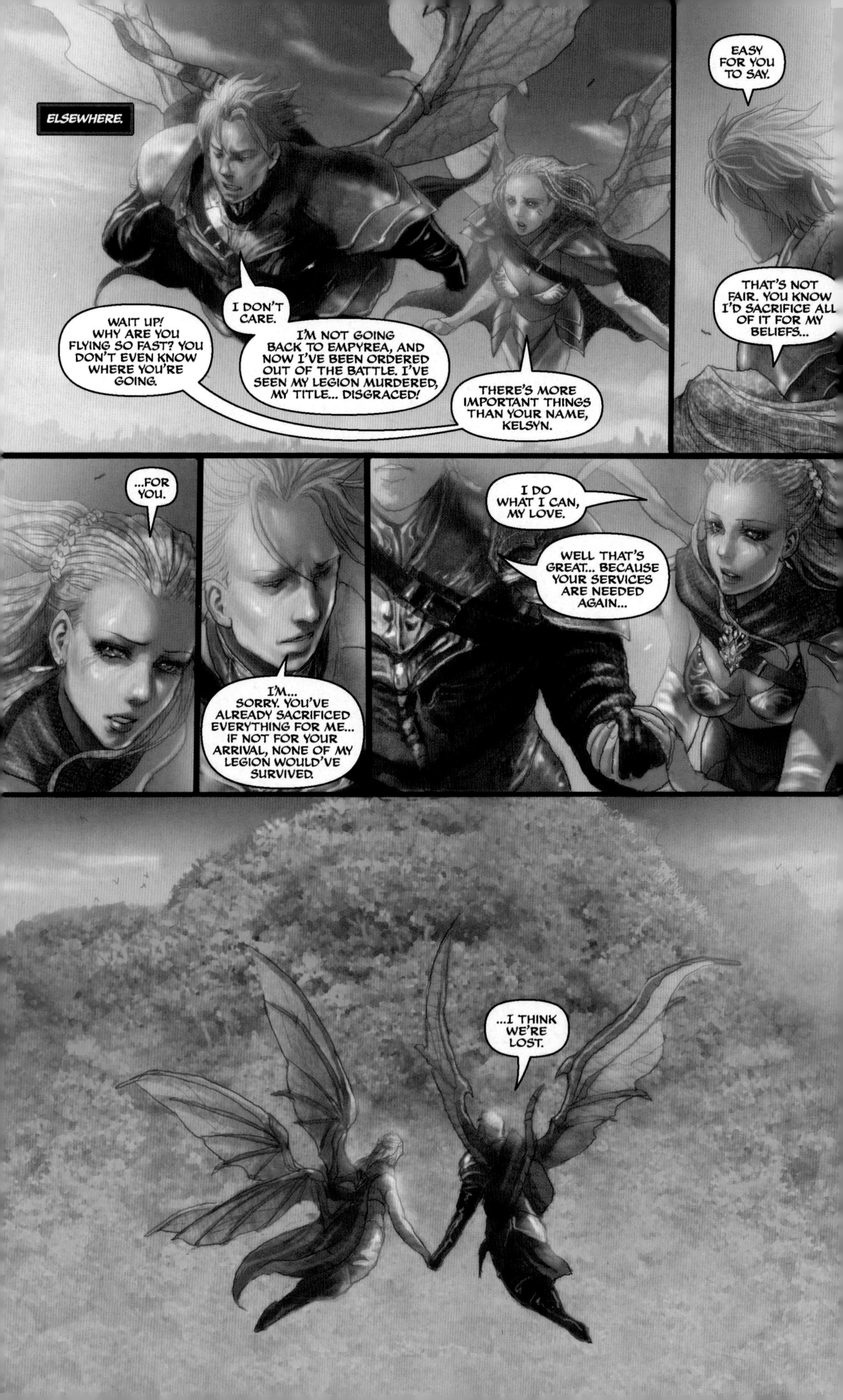
ELSEWHERE.
WAIT UP! WHY ARE YOU FLYING SO FAST? YOU DON'T EVEN KNOW WHERE YOU'RE GOING.
I DON'T CARE.
I'M NOT GOING BACK TO EMPYREA, AND NOW I'VE BEEN ORDERED OUT OF THE BATTLE. I'VE SEEN MY LEGION MURDERED, MY TITLE... DISGRACED!
THERE'S MORE IMPORTANT THINGS THAN YOUR NAME, KELSYN.
EASY FOR YOU TO SAY.
THAT'S NOT FAIR. YOU KNOW I'D SACRIFICE ALL OF IT FOR MY BELIEFS...
...FOR YOU.
I'M... SORRY. YOU'VE ALREADY SACRIFICED EVERYTHING FOR ME... IF NOT FOR YOUR ARRIVAL, NONE OF MY LEGION WOULD'VE SURVIVED.
I DO WHAT I CAN, MY LOVE.
WELL THAT'S GREAT... BECAUSE YOUR SERVICES ARE NEEDED AGAIN...
...I THINK WE'RE LOST.

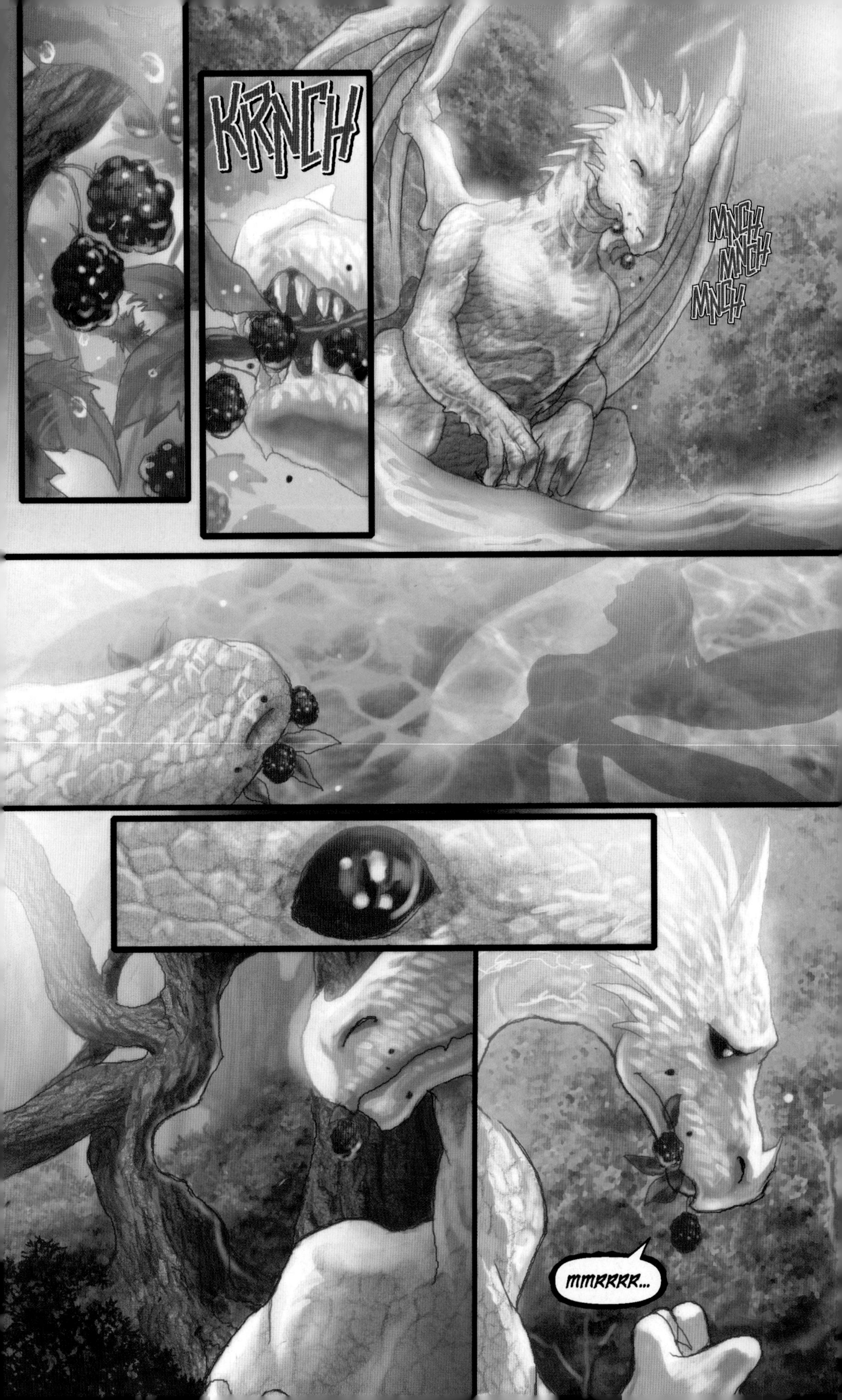
KRNCH
MNCH
MNCH
MNCH
mmRRRR...

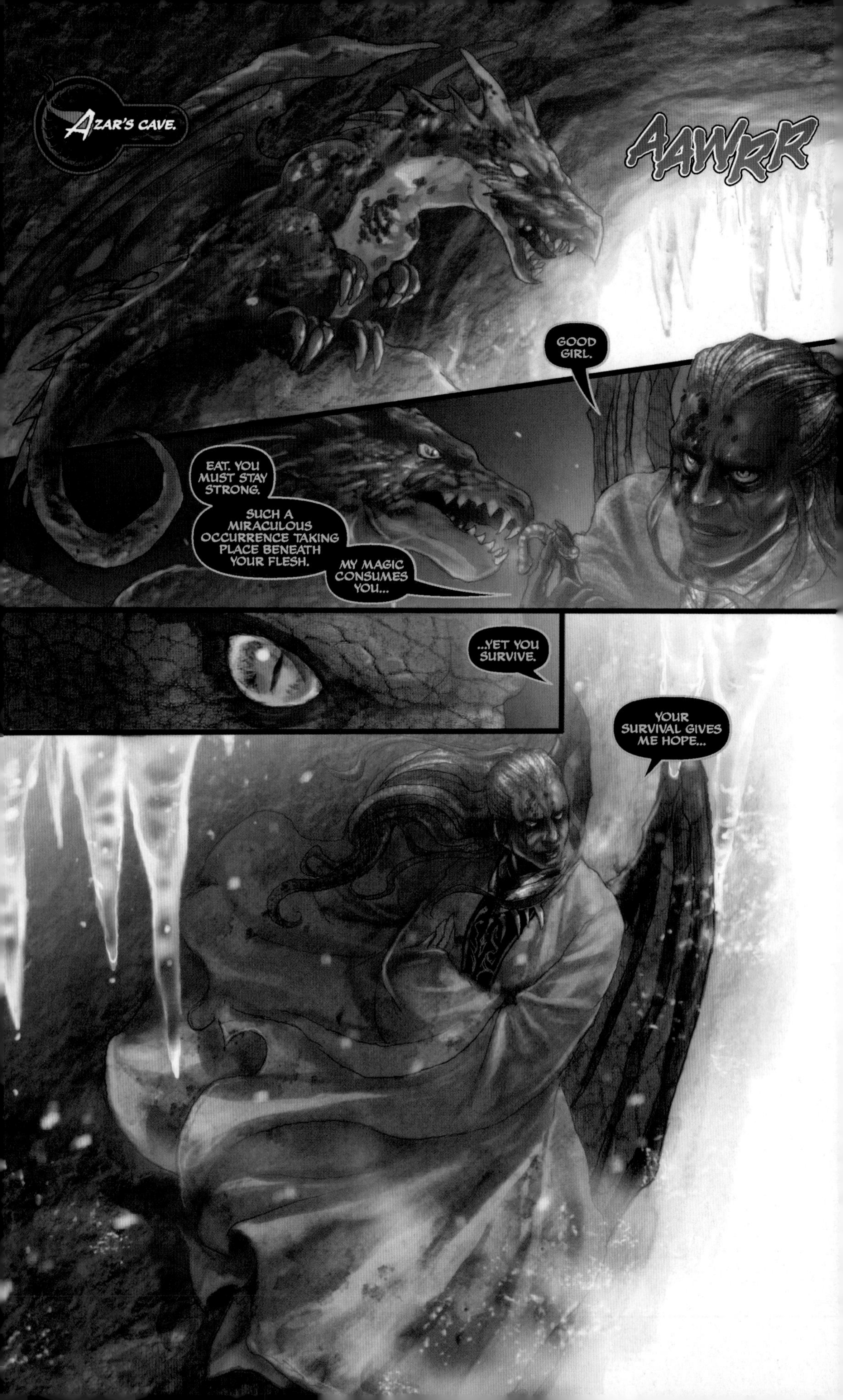
AZAR'S CAVE.
AAWRR
GOOD GIRL.
EAT. YOU MUST STAY STRONG.
SUCH A MIRACULOUS OCCURRENCE TAKING PLACE BENEATH YOUR FLESH.
MY MAGIC CONSUMES YOU...
...YET YOU SURVIVE.
YOUR SURVIVAL GIVES ME HOPE...

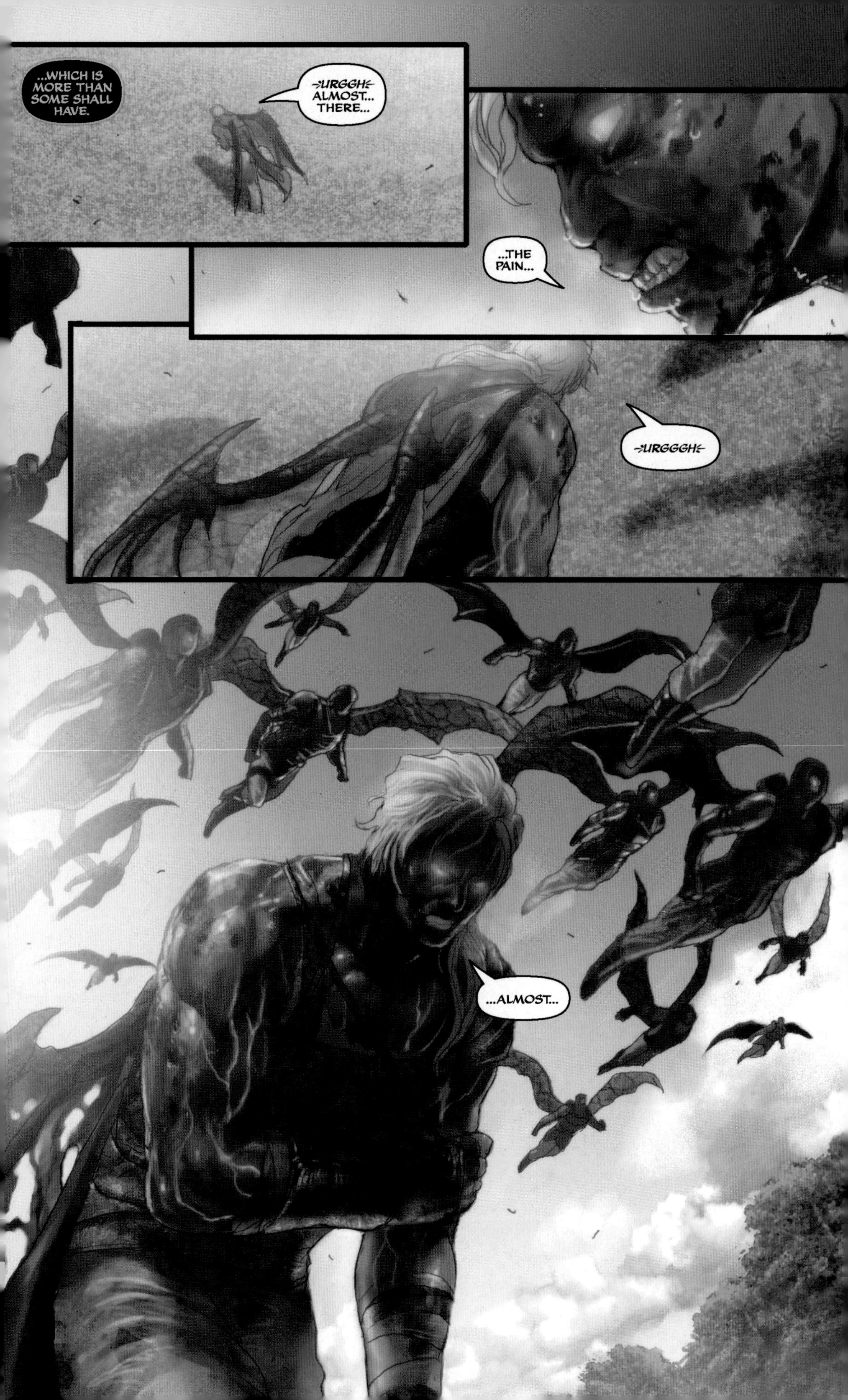
...WHICH IS MORE THAN SOME SHALL HAVE.
URGGH ALMOST... THERE...
...THE PAIN...
URGGGH
...ALMOST...

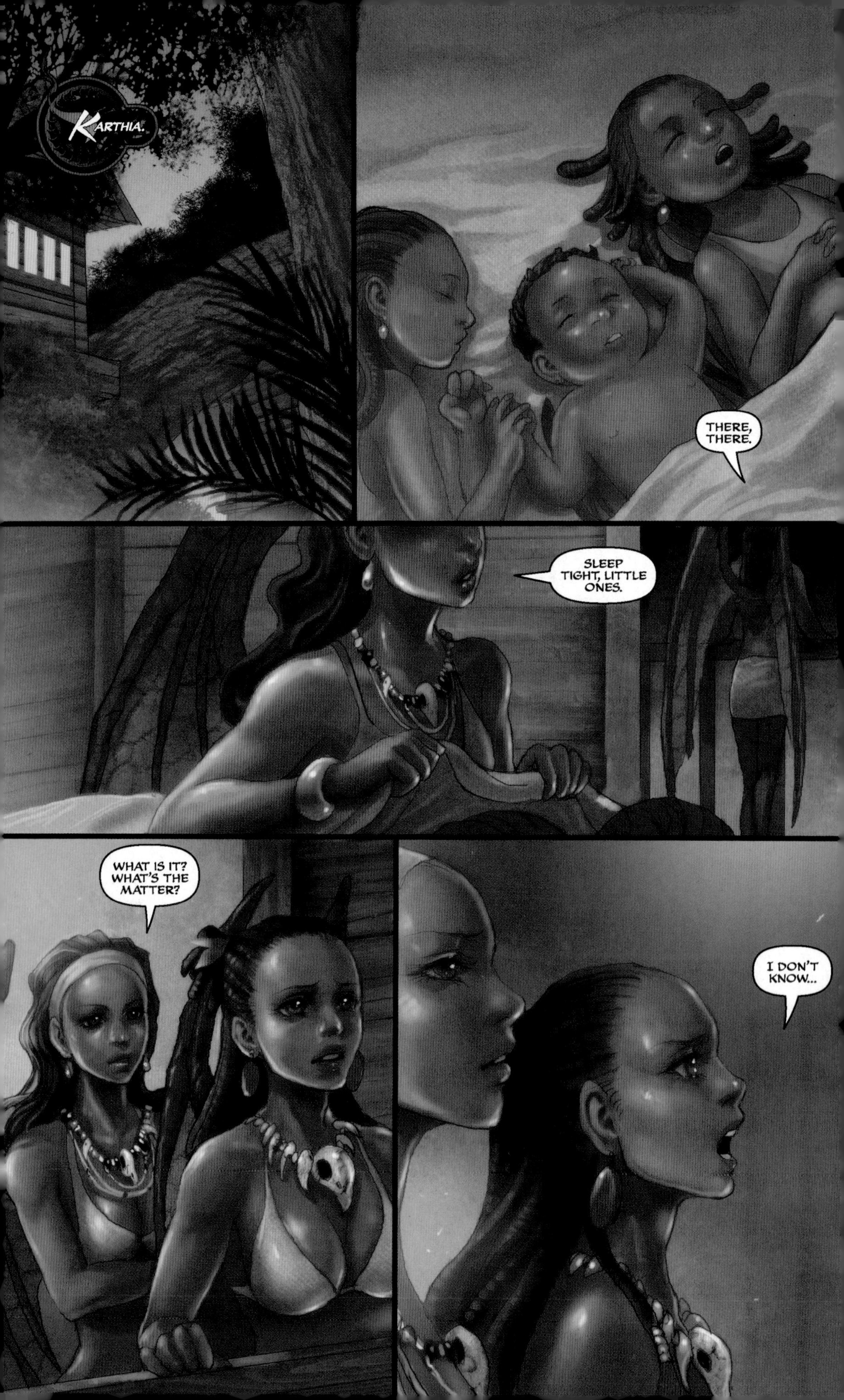
KARTHIA.
THERE, THERE.
SLEEP TIGHT, LITTLE ONES.
WHAT IS IT? WHAT'S THE MATTER?
I DON'T KNOW...

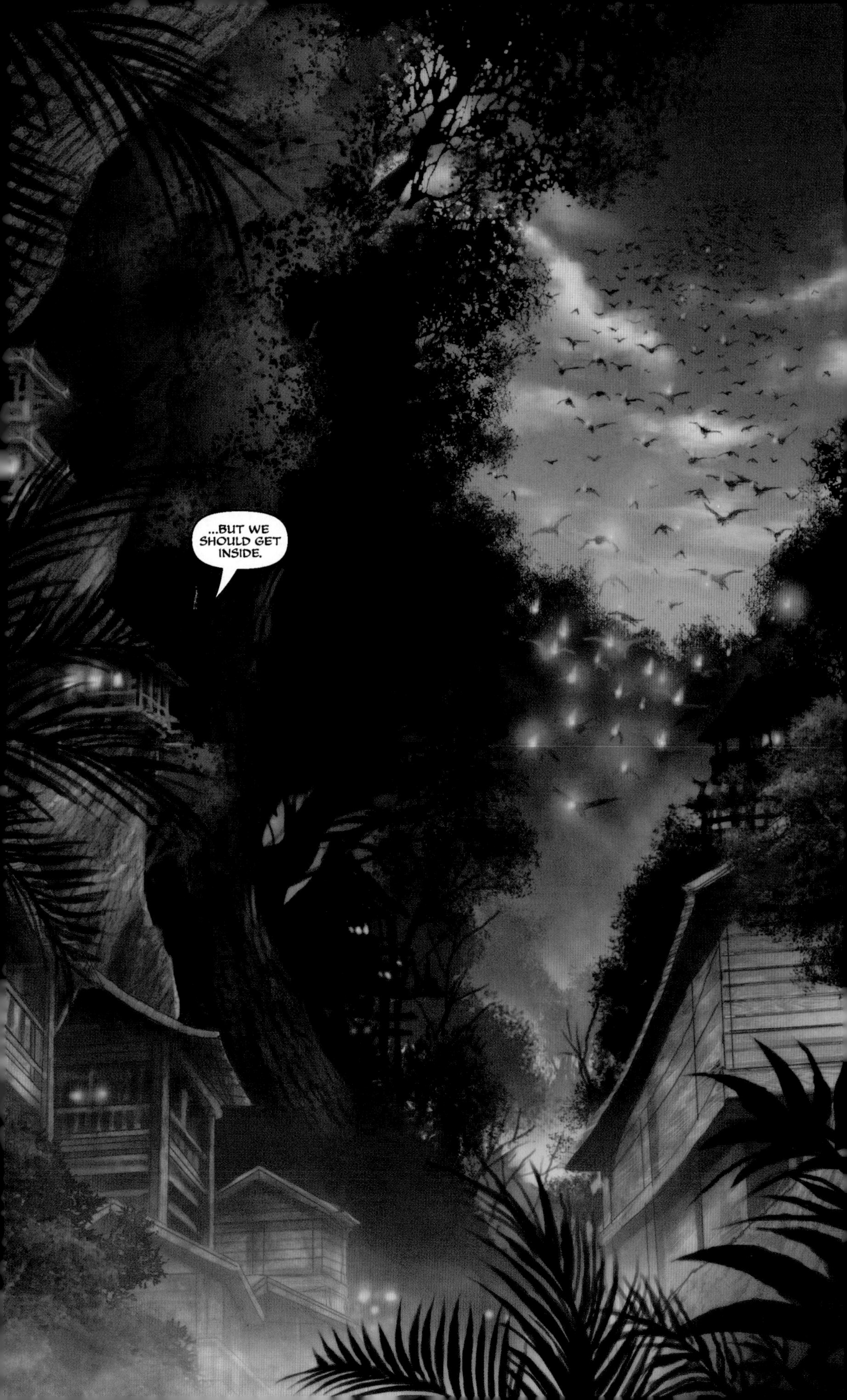
...BUT WE SHOULD GET INSIDE.

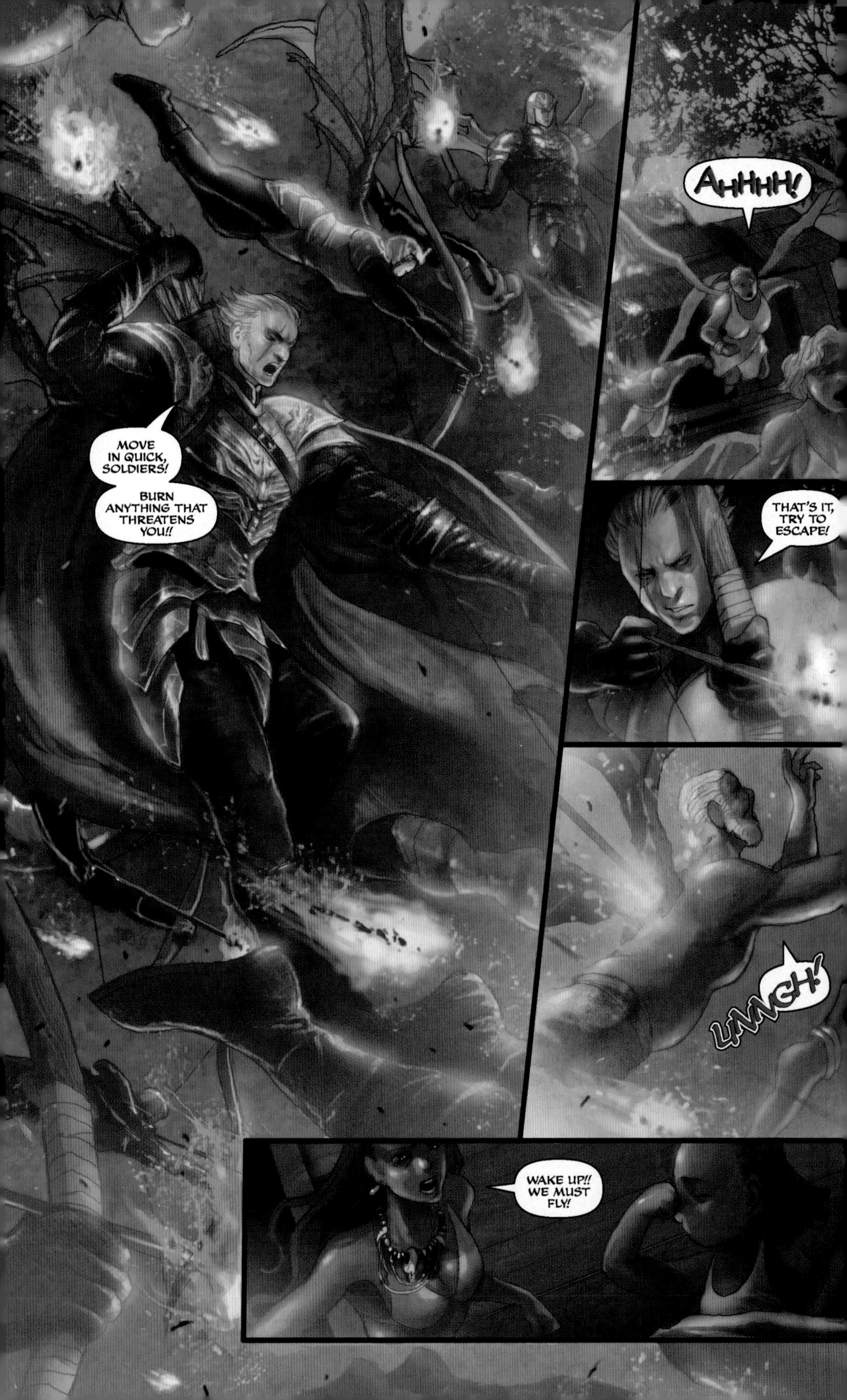
MOVE IN QUICK, SOLDIERS!
BURN ANYTHING THAT THREATENS YOU!!
AHHHH!
THAT'S IT, TRY TO ESCAPE!
UNNGH!
WAKE UP!! WE MUST FLY!

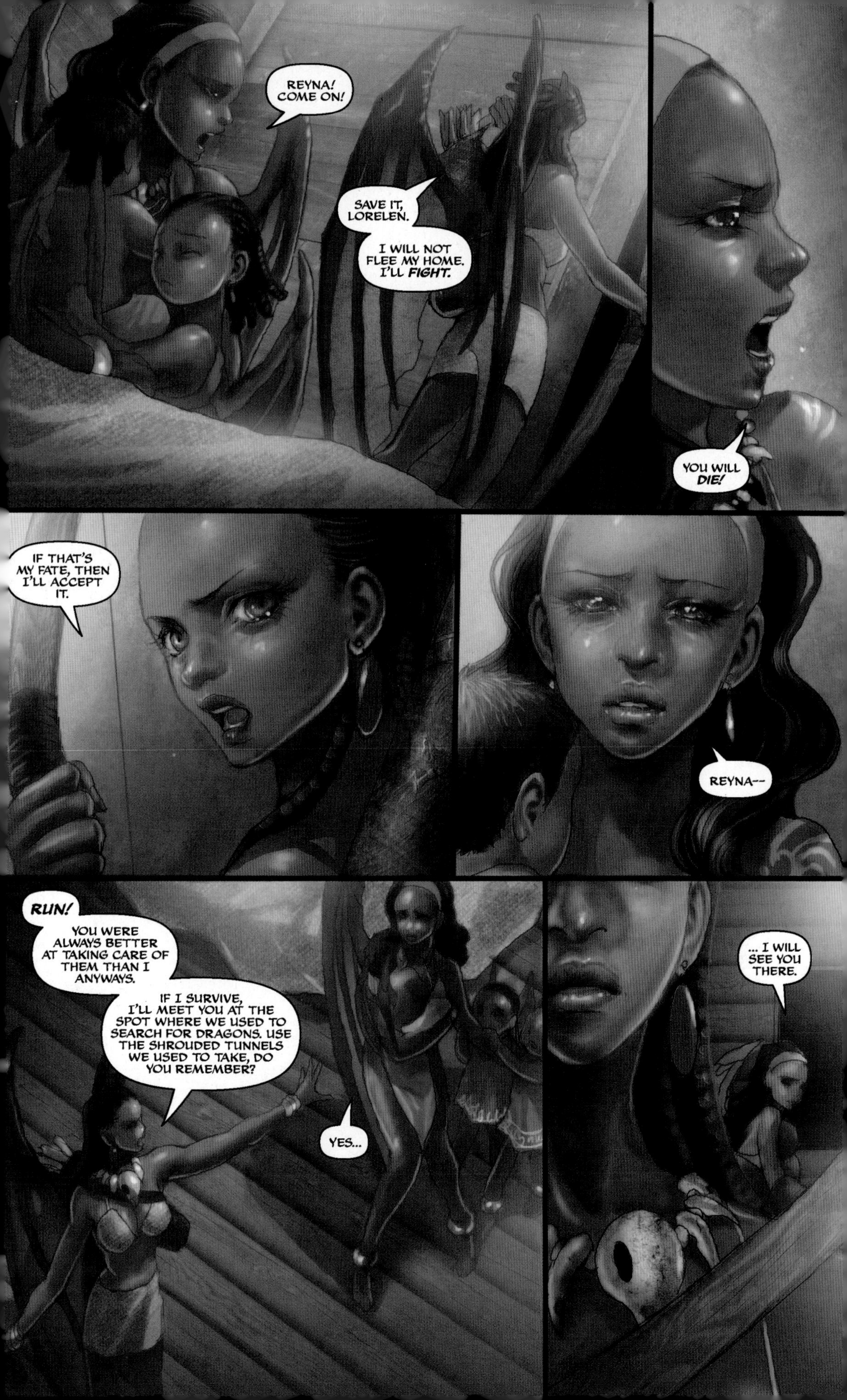
REYNA! COME ON!
SAVE IT, LORELEN.
I WILL NOT FLEE MY HOME. I'LL FIGHT.
YOU WILL DIE!
IF THAT'S MY FATE, THEN I'LL ACCEPT IT.
REYNA--
RUN!
YOU WERE ALWAYS BETTER AT TAKING CARE OF THEM THAN I ANYWAYS.
IF I SURVIVE, I'LL MEET YOU AT THE SPOT WHERE WE USED TO SEARCH FOR DRAGONS. USE THE SHROUDED TUNNELS WE USED TO TAKE, DO YOU REMEMBER?
YES...
... I WILL SEE YOU THERE.

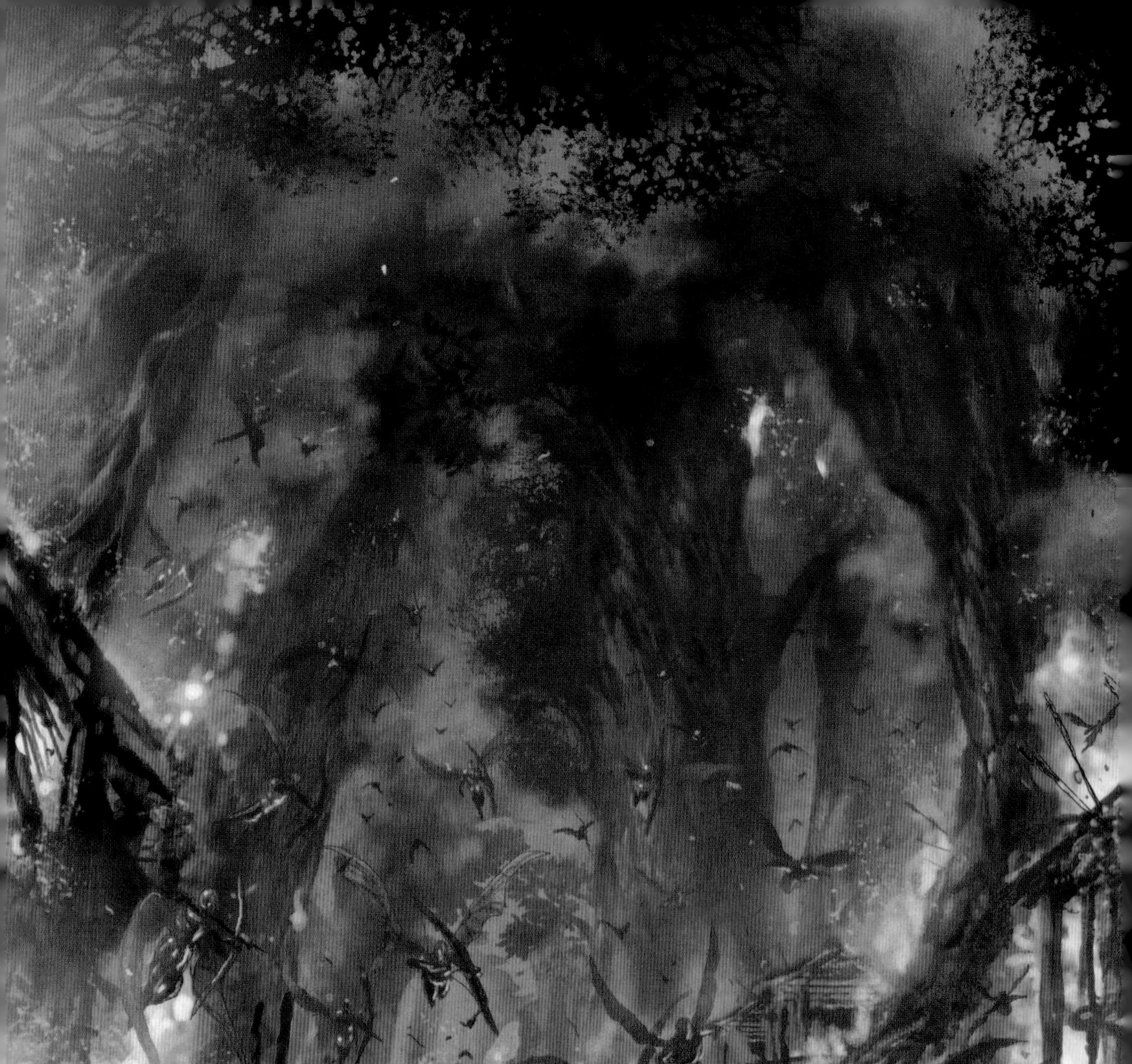

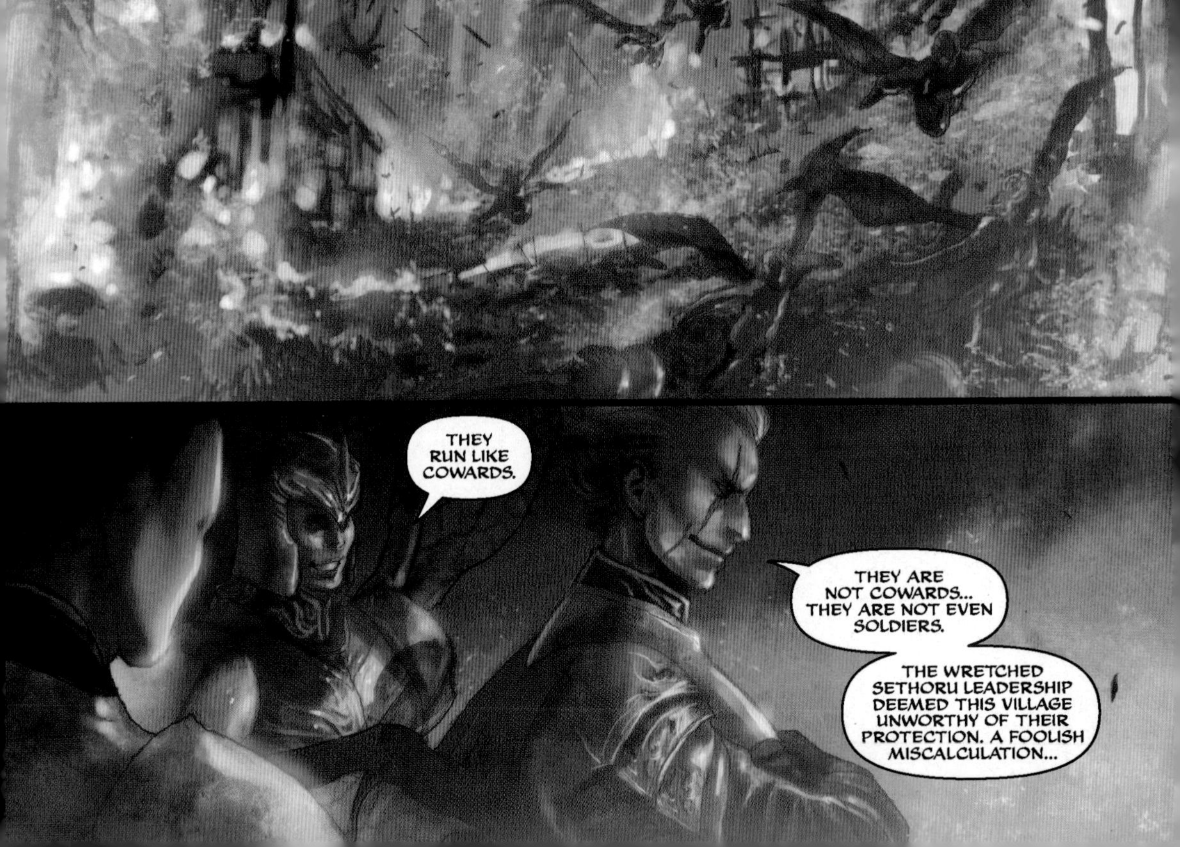
THEY RUN LIKE COWARDS.
THEY ARE NOT COWARDS... THEY ARE NOT EVEN SOLDIERS.
THE WRETCHED SETHORU LEADERSHIP DEEMED THIS VILLAGE UNWORTHY OF THEIR PROTECTION. A FOOLISH MISCALCULATION...

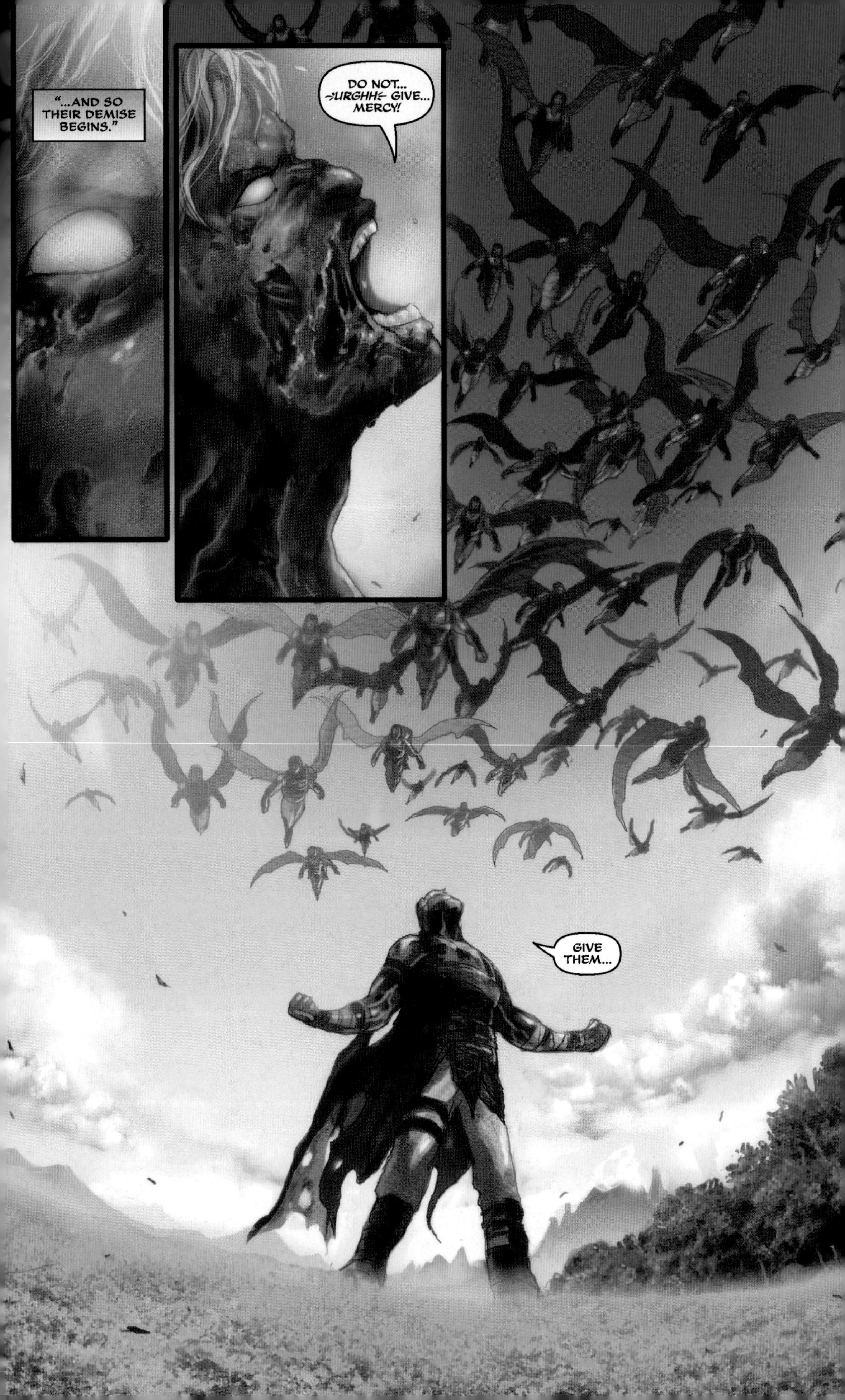
"...AND SO THEIR DEMISE BEGINS."
DO NOT... -URGHH- GIVE... MERCY!
GIVE THEM...

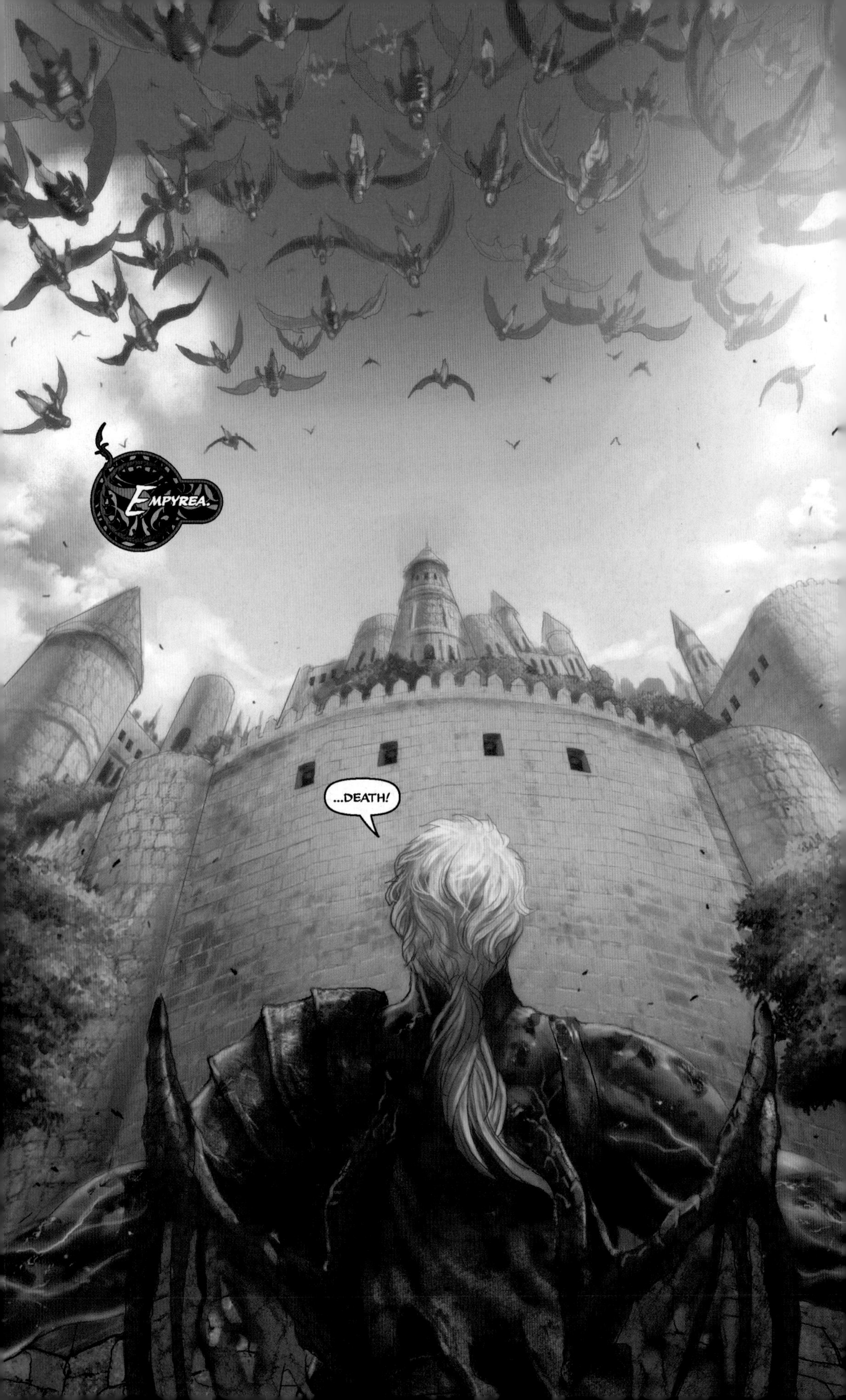
EMPYREA.
...DEATH!

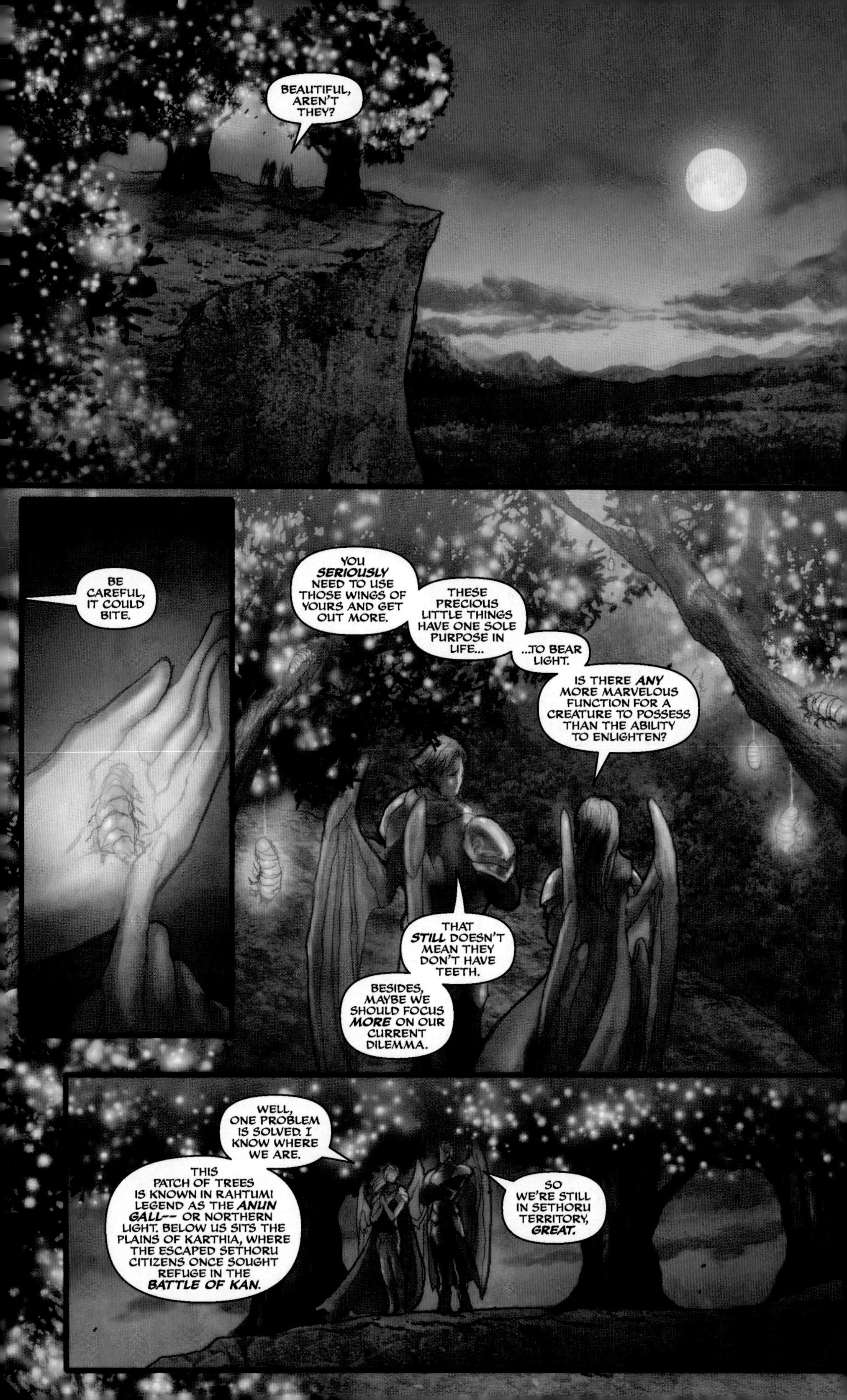
BEAUTIFUL, AREN'T THEY?
BE CAREFUL, IT COULD BITE.
YOU SERIOUSLY NEED TO USE THOSE WINGS OF YOURS AND GET OUT MORE.
THESE PRECIOUS LITTLE THINGS HAVE ONE SOLE PURPOSE IN LIFE...
...TO BEAR LIGHT.
IS THERE ANY MORE MARVELOUS FUNCTION FOR A CREATURE TO POSSESS THAN THE ABILITY TO ENLIGHTEN?
THAT STILL DOESN'T MEAN THEY DON'T HAVE TEETH.
BESIDES, MAYBE WE SHOULD FOCUS MORE ON OUR CURRENT DILEMMA.
WELL, ONE PROBLEM IS SOLVED. I KNOW WHERE WE ARE.
THIS PATCH OF TREES IS KNOWN IN RAHTUMI LEGEND AS THE ANUN GALL-- OR NORTHERN LIGHT. BELOW US SITS THE PLAINS OF KARTHIA, WHERE THE ESCAPED SETHORU CITIZENS ONCE SOUGHT REFUGE IN THE BATTLE OF KAN.
SO WE'RE STILL IN SETHORU TERRITORY, GREAT.

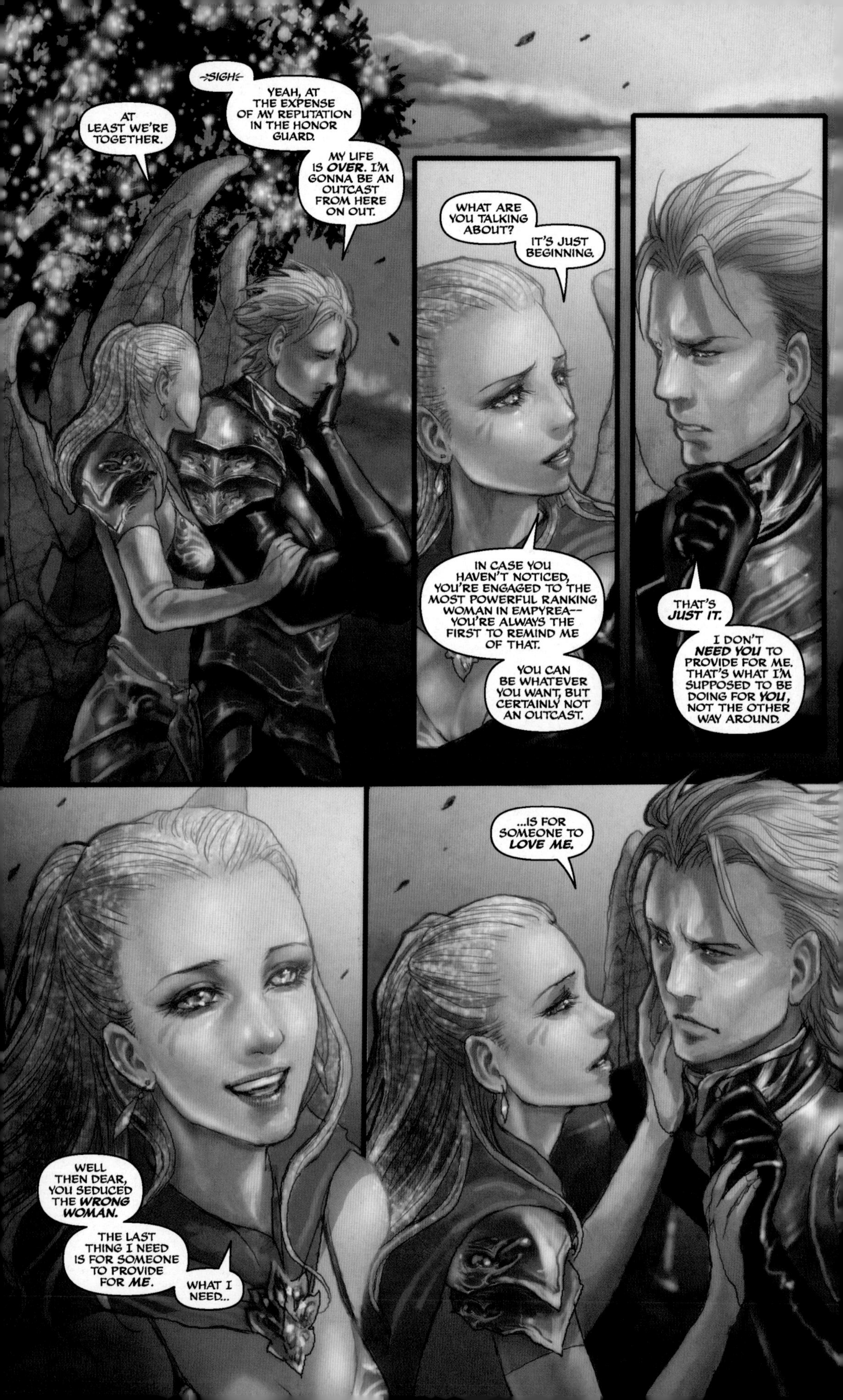

AT LEAST WE'RE TOGETHER.
-SIGH-
YEAH, AT THE EXPENSE OF MY REPUTATION IN THE HONOR GUARD.
MY LIFE IS OVER. I'M GONNA BE AN OUTCAST FROM HERE ON OUT.
WHAT ARE YOU TALKING ABOUT?
IT'S JUST BEGINNING.
IN CASE YOU HAVEN'T NOTICED, YOU'RE ENGAGED TO THE MOST POWERFUL RANKING WOMAN IN EMPYREA-- YOU'RE ALWAYS THE FIRST TO REMIND ME OF THAT.
YOU CAN BE WHATEVER YOU WANT, BUT CERTAINLY NOT AN OUTCAST.
THAT'S JUST IT.
I DON'T NEED YOU TO PROVIDE FOR ME. THAT'S WHAT I'M SUPPOSED TO BE DOING FOR YOU, NOT THE OTHER WAY AROUND.
WELL THEN DEAR, YOU SEDUCED THE WRONG WOMAN.
THE LAST THING I NEED IS FOR SOMEONE TO PROVIDE FOR ME.
WHAT I NEED...
...IS FOR SOMEONE TO LOVE ME.

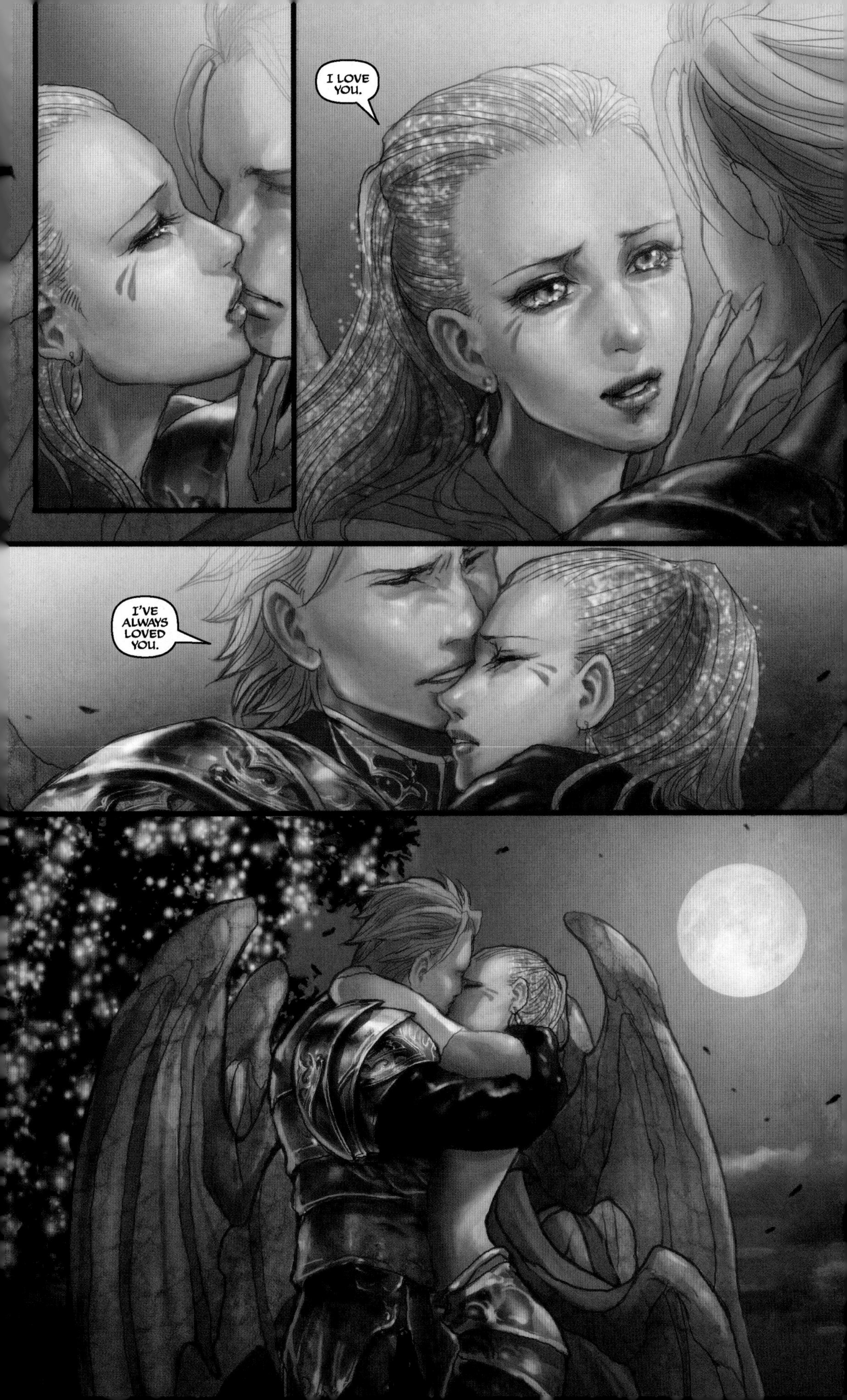
I LOVE YOU.
I'VE ALWAYS LOVED YOU.

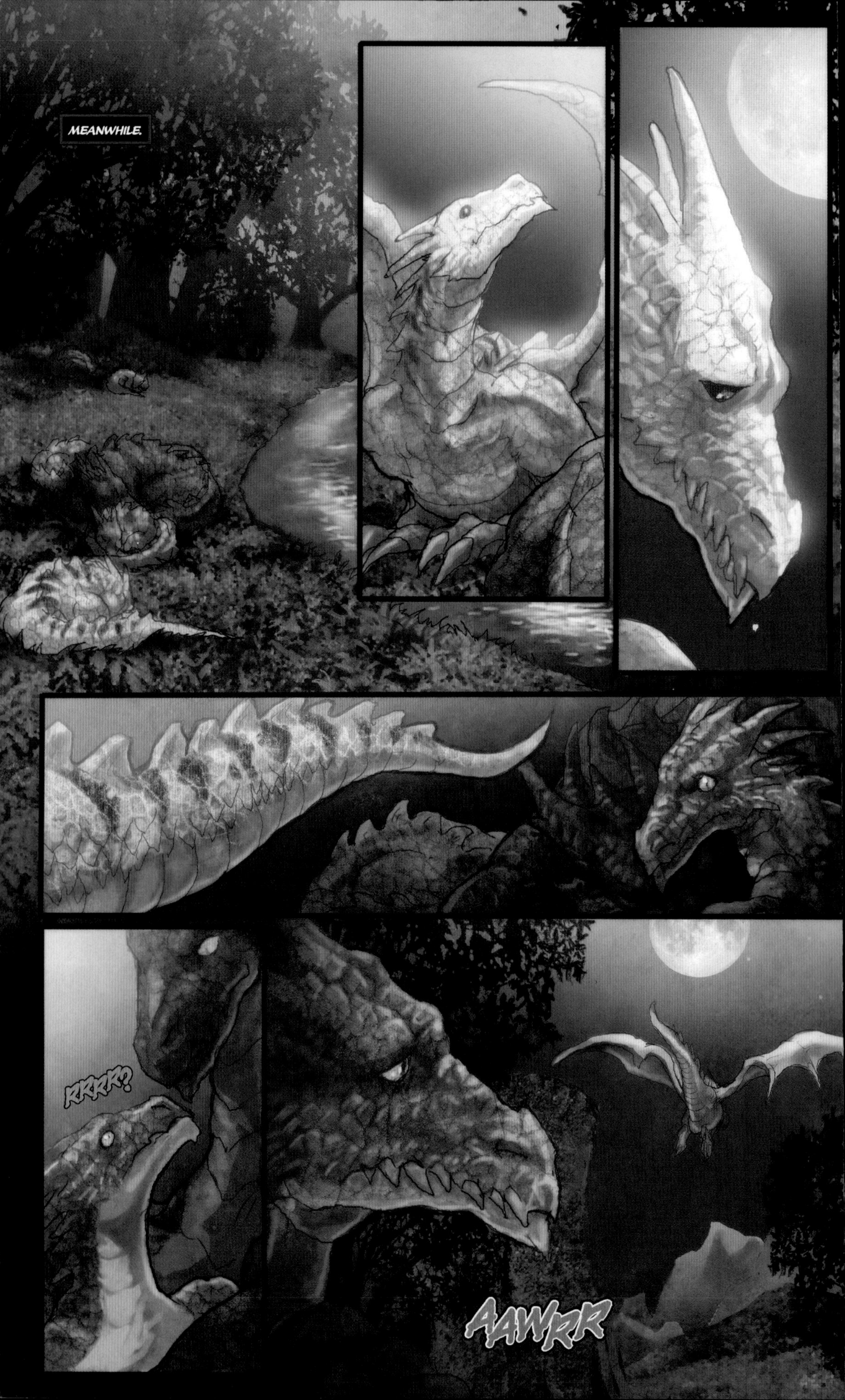
MEANWHILE.
KRRRR?
AAWRR

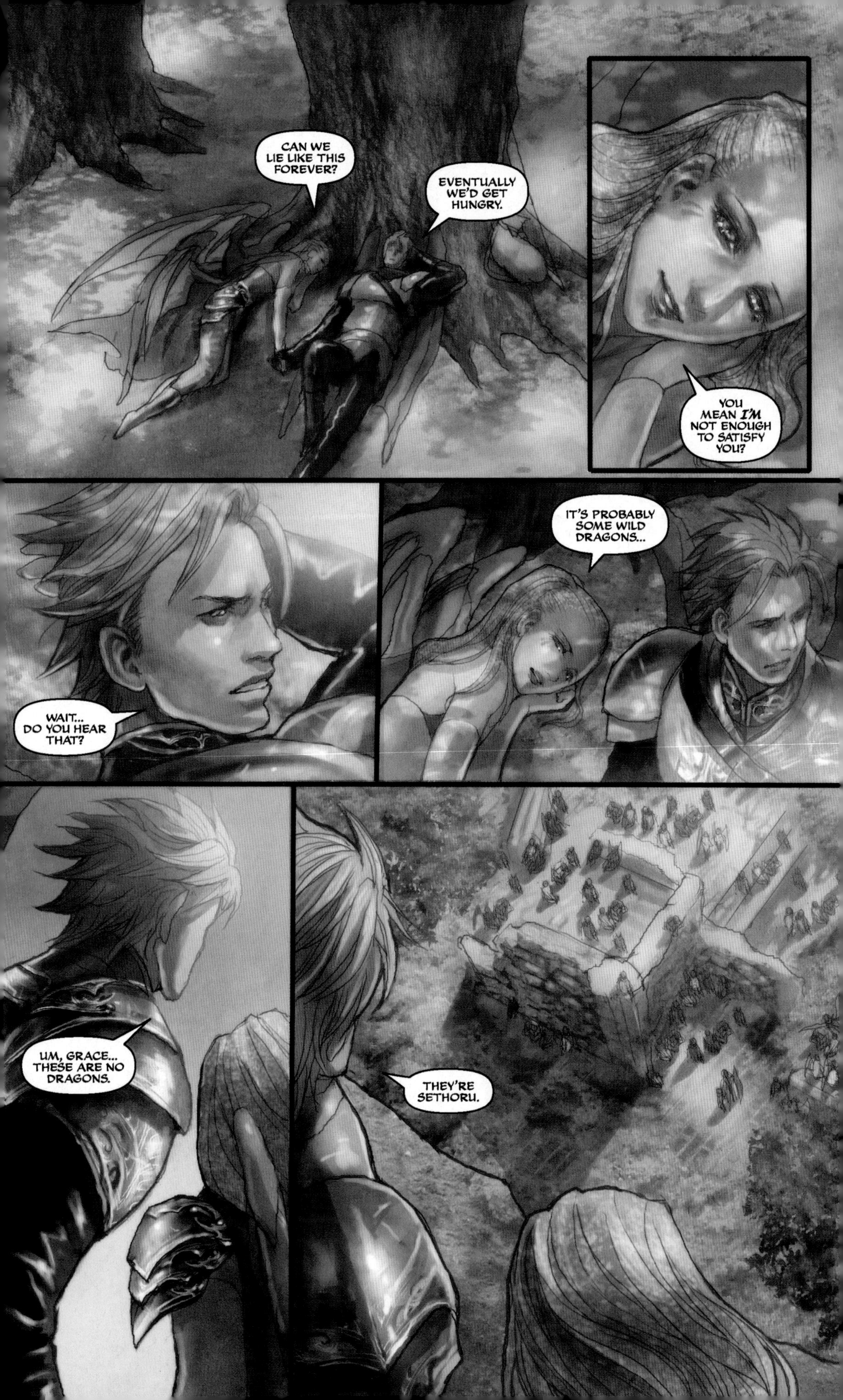
CAN WE LIE LIKE THIS FOREVER?
EVENTUALLY WE'D GET HUNGRY.
YOU MEAN *I'M* NOT ENOUGH TO SATISFY YOU?
WAIT... DO YOU HEAR THAT?
IT'S PROBABLY SOME WILD DRAGONS...
UM, GRACE... THESE ARE NO DRAGONS.
THEY'RE SETHORU.

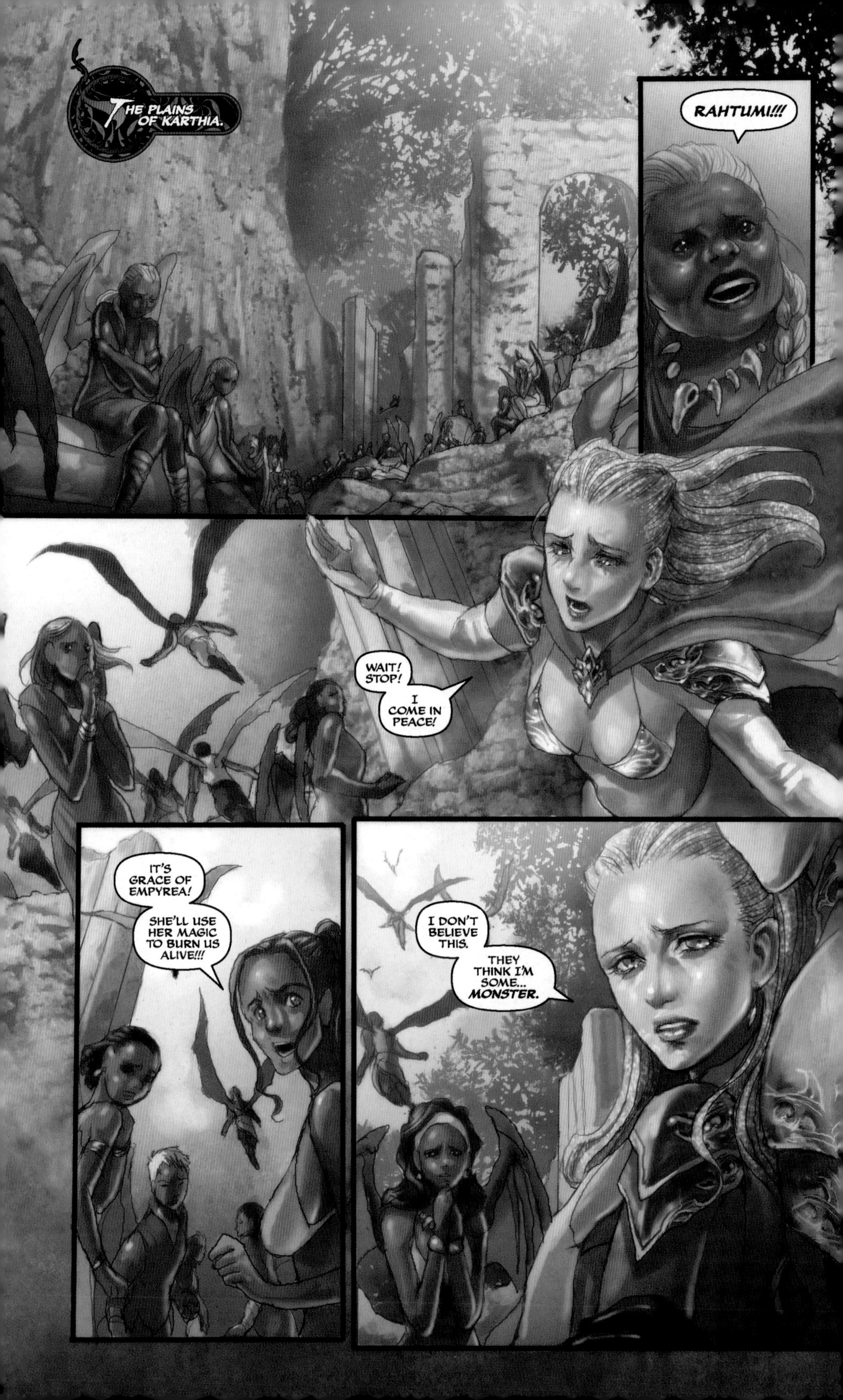
THE PLAINS OF KARTHIA.
RAHTUMI!!!
WAIT! STOP!
I COME IN PEACE!
IT'S GRACE OF EMPYREA!
SHE'LL USE HER MAGIC TO BURN US ALIVE!!!
I DON'T BELIEVE THIS.
THEY THINK I'M SOME... MONSTER.

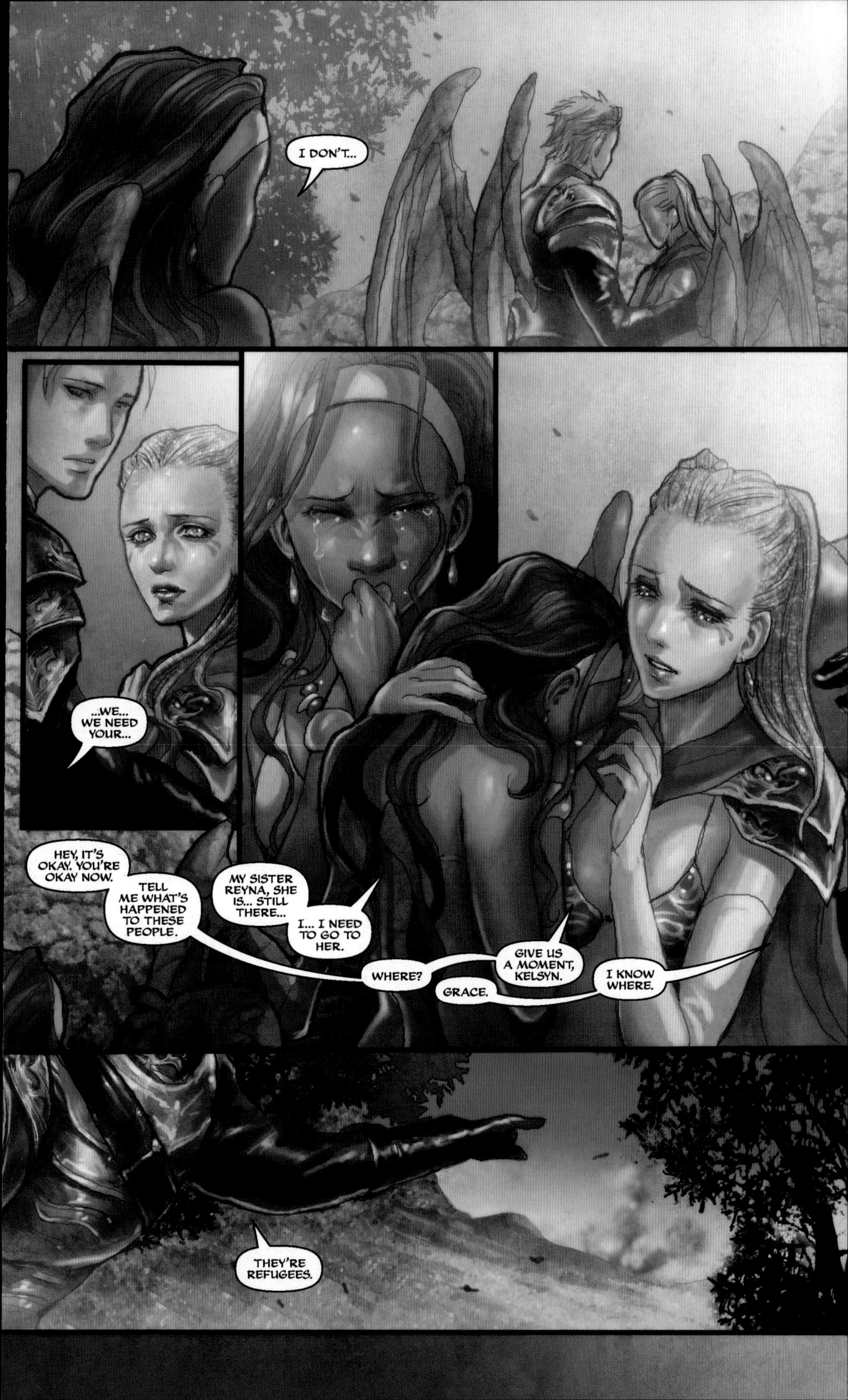
I DON'T...
...WE... WE NEED YOUR...
HEY, IT'S OKAY. YOU'RE OKAY NOW.
TELL ME WHAT'S HAPPENED TO THESE PEOPLE.
MY SISTER REYNA, SHE IS... STILL THERE...
I... I NEED TO GO TO HER.
WHERE?
GIVE US A MOMENT, KELSYN.
GRACE.
I KNOW WHERE.
THEY'RE REFUGEES.

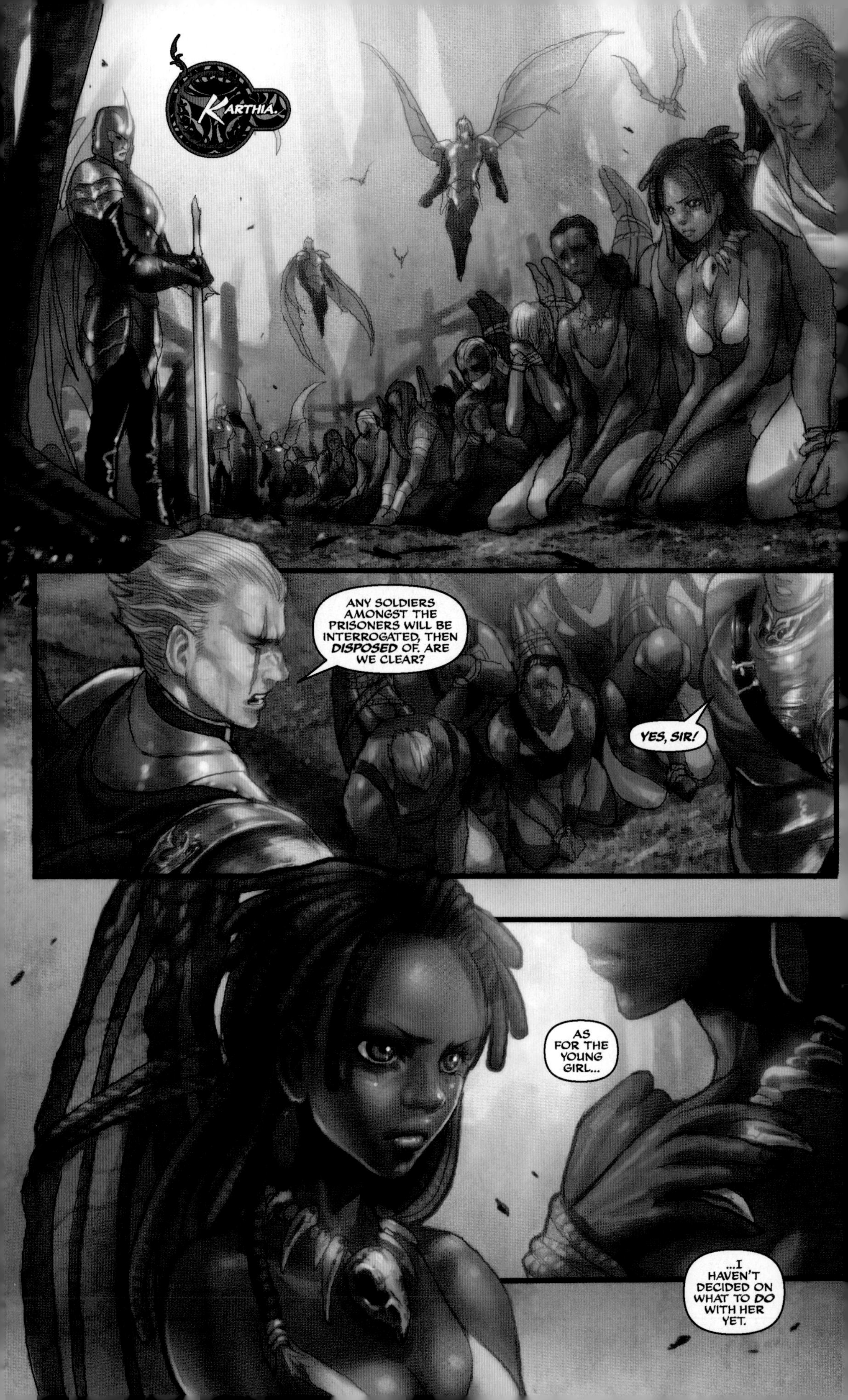
KARTHIA.
ANY SOLDIERS AMONGST THE PRISONERS WILL BE INTERROGATED, THEN DISPOSED OF. ARE WE CLEAR?
YES, SIR!
AS FOR THE YOUNG GIRL...
...I HAVEN'T DECIDED ON WHAT TO DO WITH HER YET.

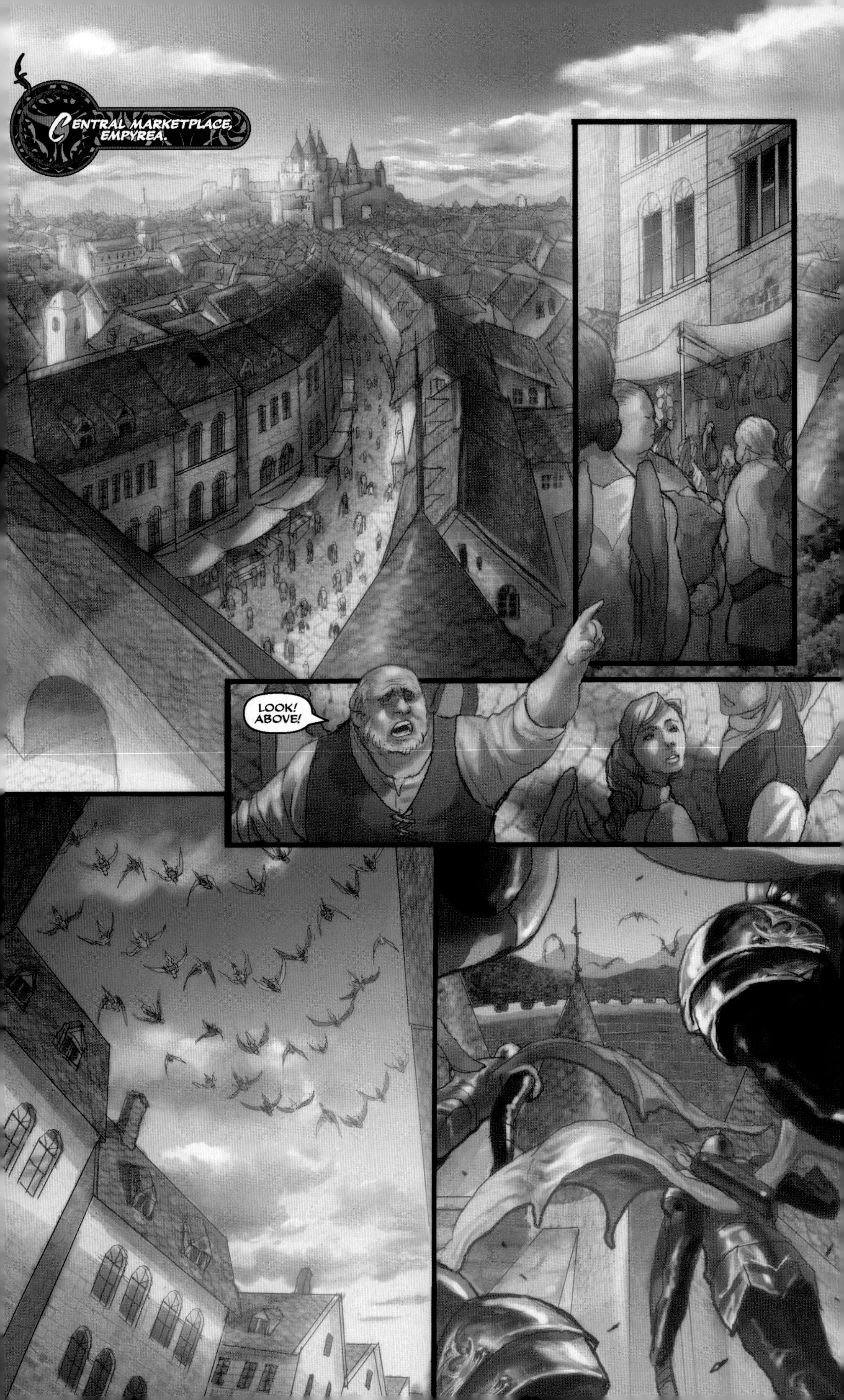
CENTRAL MARKETPLACE, EMPYREA.
LOOK! ABOVE!

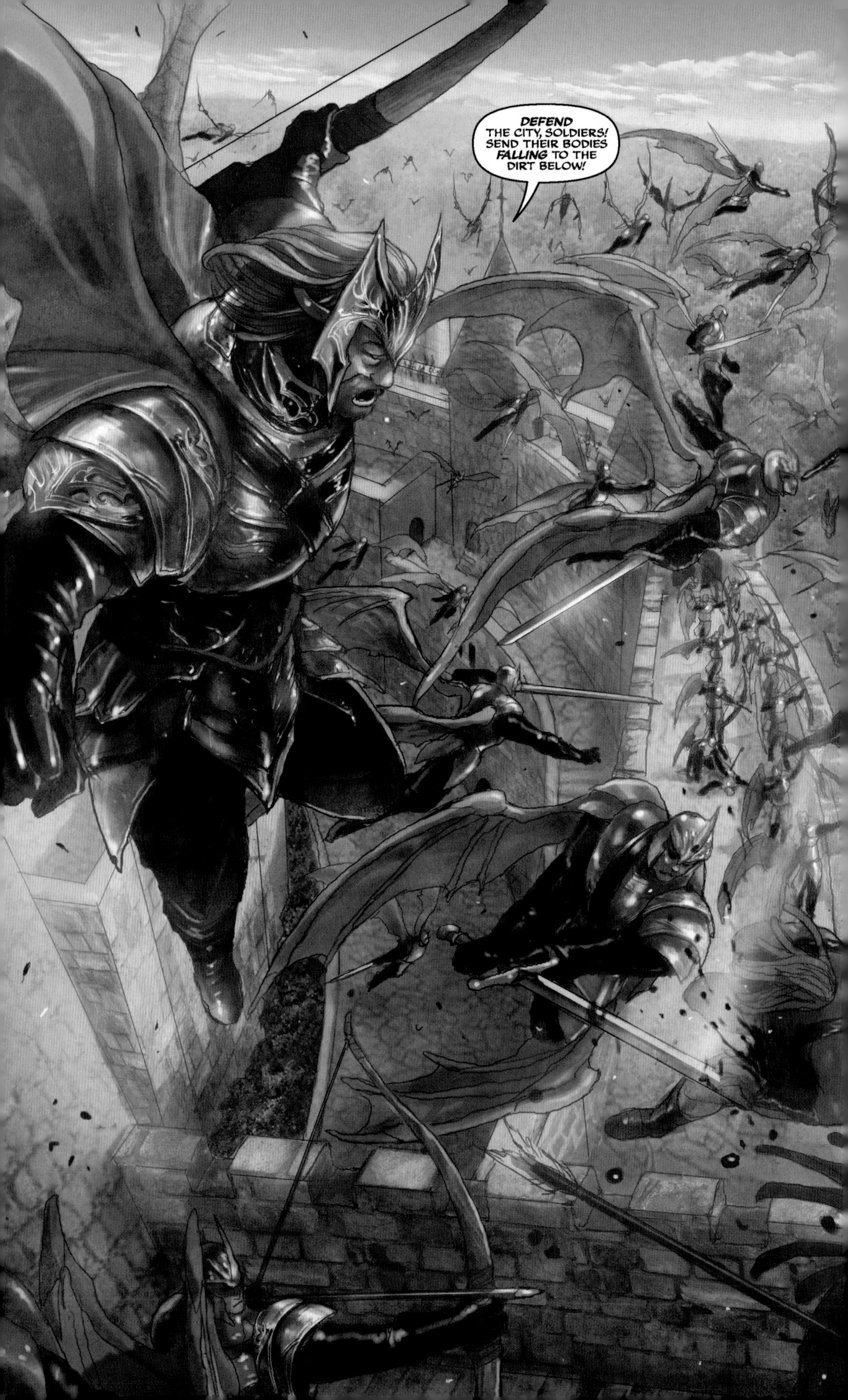
DEFEND THE CITY, SOLDIERS! SEND THEIR BODIES FALLING TO THE DIRT BELOW!

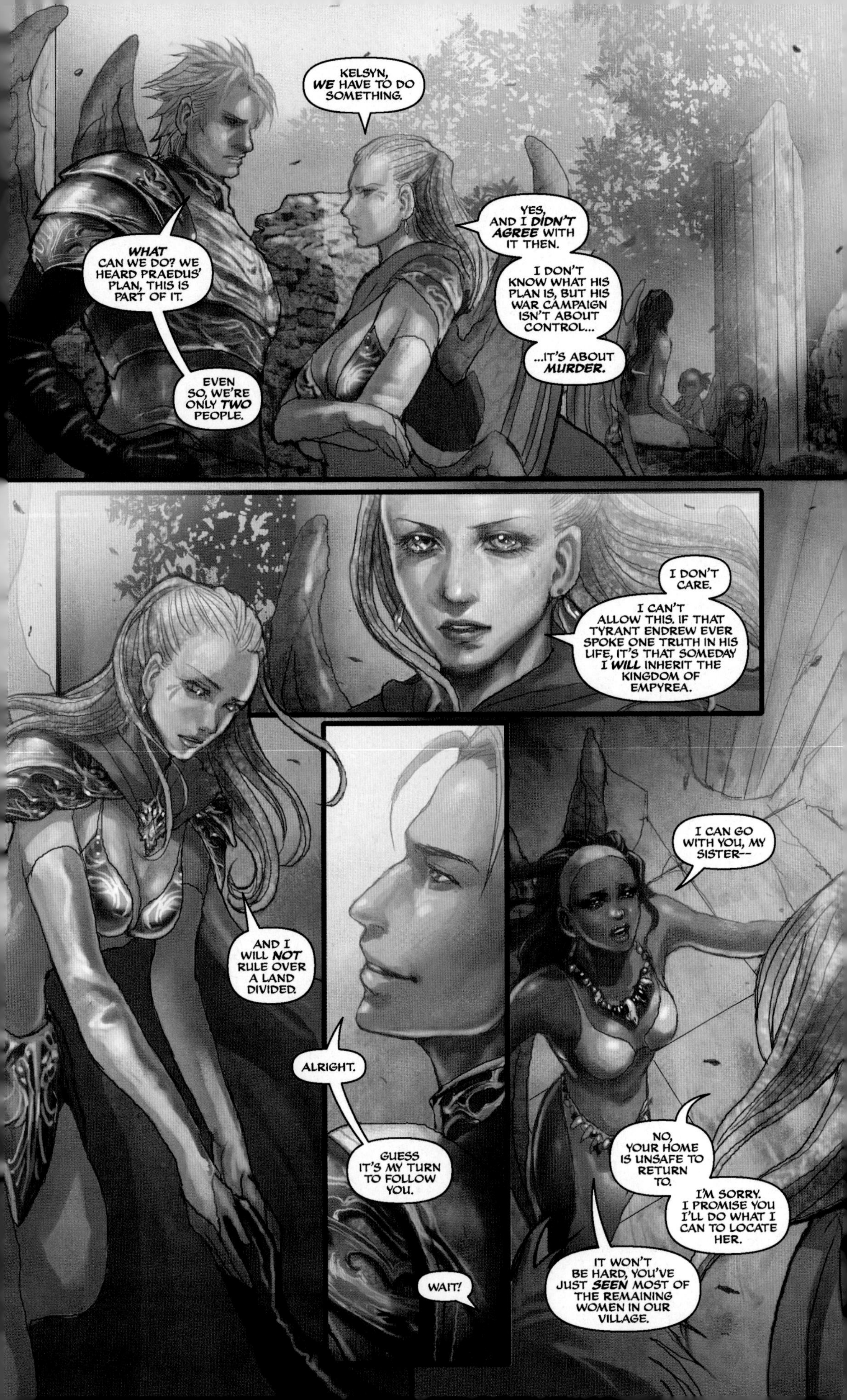
KELSYN, WE HAVE TO DO SOMETHING.
WHAT CAN WE DO? WE HEARD PRAEDUS' PLAN, THIS IS PART OF IT.
EVEN SO, WE'RE ONLY TWO PEOPLE.
YES, AND I DIDN'T AGREE WITH IT THEN.
I DON'T KNOW WHAT HIS PLAN IS, BUT HIS WAR CAMPAIGN ISN'T ABOUT CONTROL...
...IT'S ABOUT MURDER.
I DON'T CARE.
I CAN'T ALLOW THIS. IF THAT TYRANT ENDREW EVER SPOKE ONE TRUTH IN HIS LIFE, IT'S THAT SOMEDAY I WILL INHERIT THE KINGDOM OF EMPYREA.
AND I WILL NOT RULE OVER A LAND DIVIDED.
ALRIGHT.
GUESS IT'S MY TURN TO FOLLOW YOU.
WAIT!
I CAN GO WITH YOU, MY SISTER--
NO, YOUR HOME IS UNSAFE TO RETURN TO.
I'M SORRY. I PROMISE YOU I'LL DO WHAT I CAN TO LOCATE HER.
IT WON'T BE HARD, YOU'VE JUST SEEN MOST OF THE REMAINING WOMEN IN OUR VILLAGE.

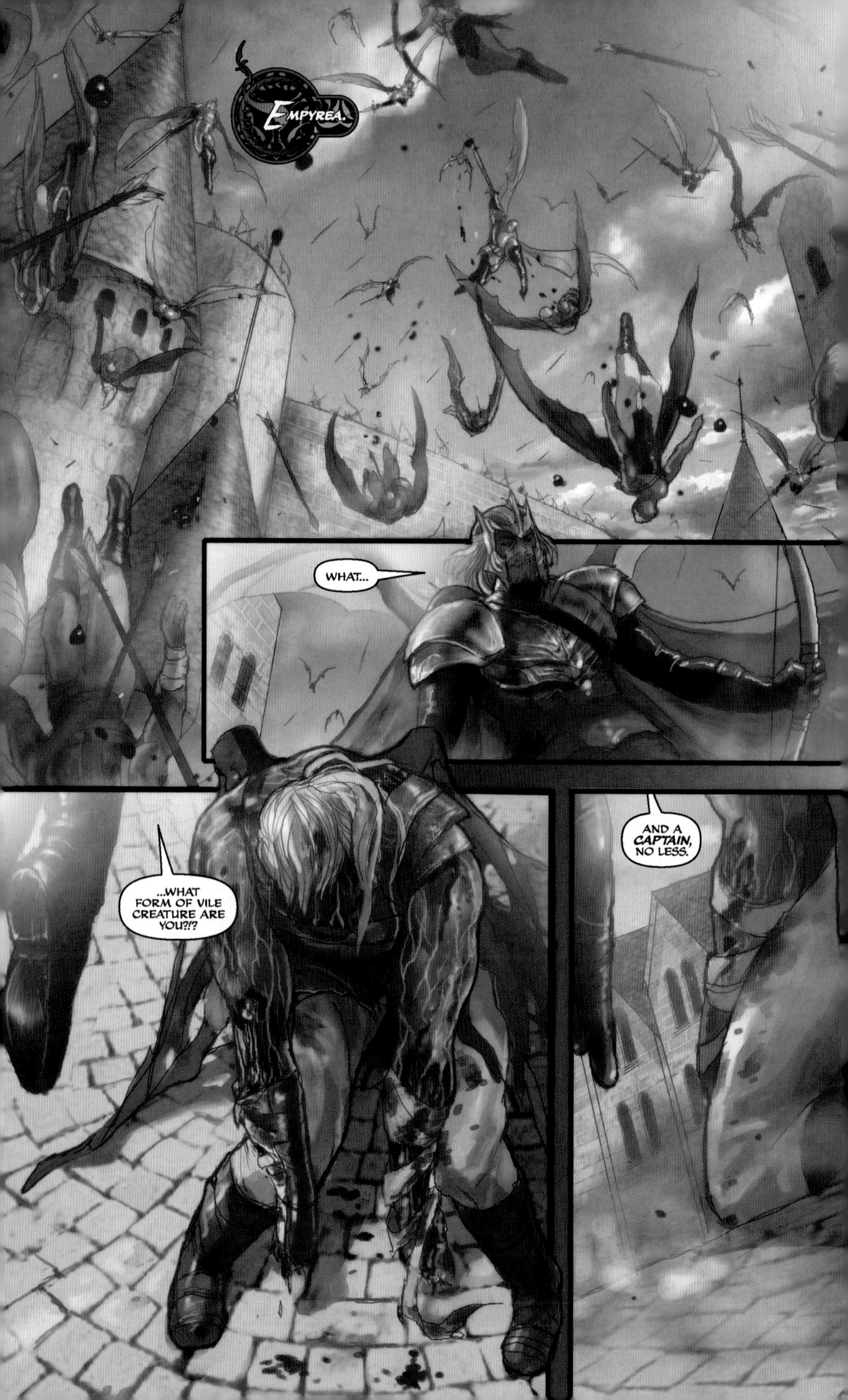
EMPYREA.
WHAT...
...WHAT FORM OF VILE CREATURE ARE YOU?!?
AND A CAPTAIN, NO LESS.

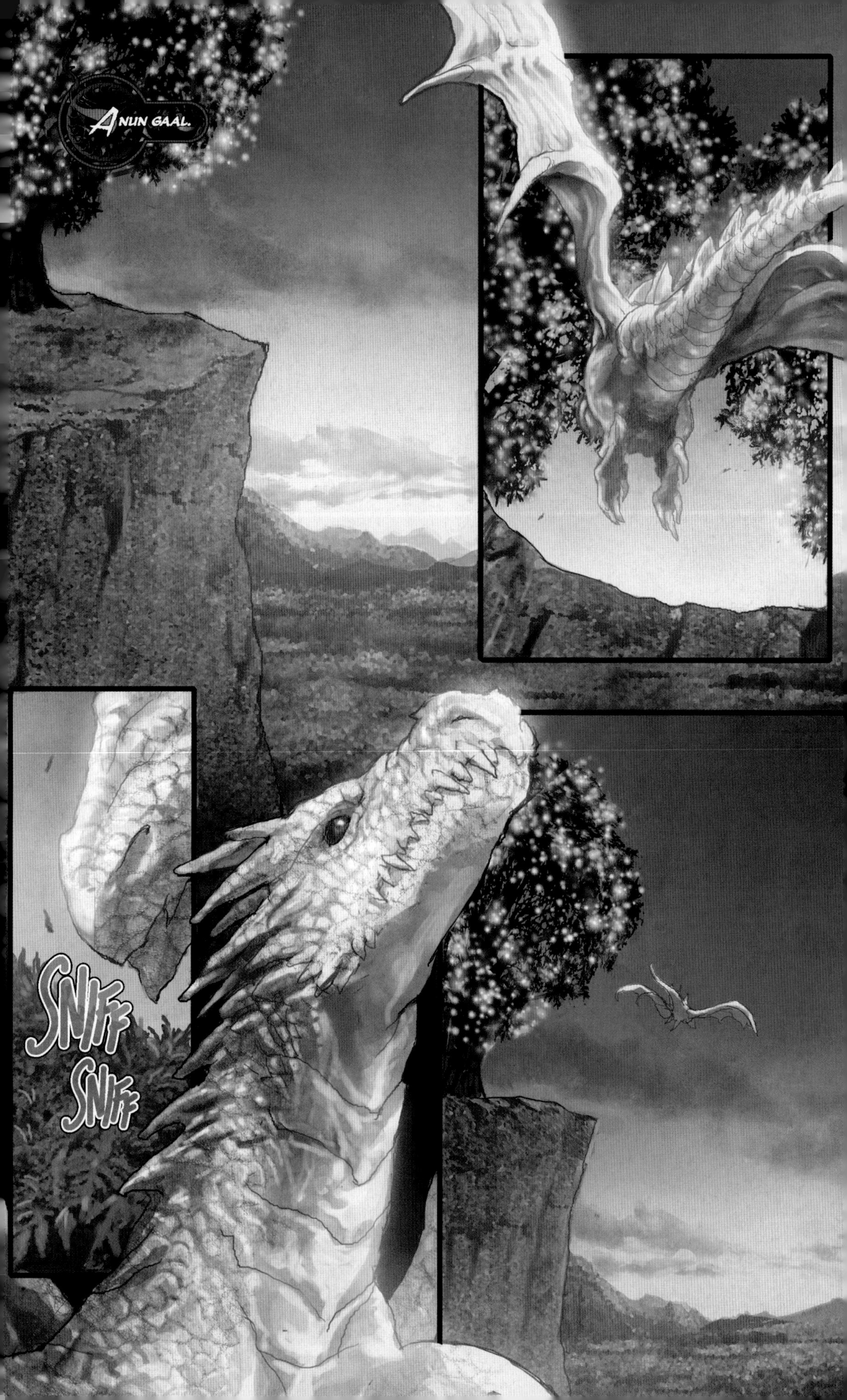
ANUN GAAL.
SNIFF
SNIFF

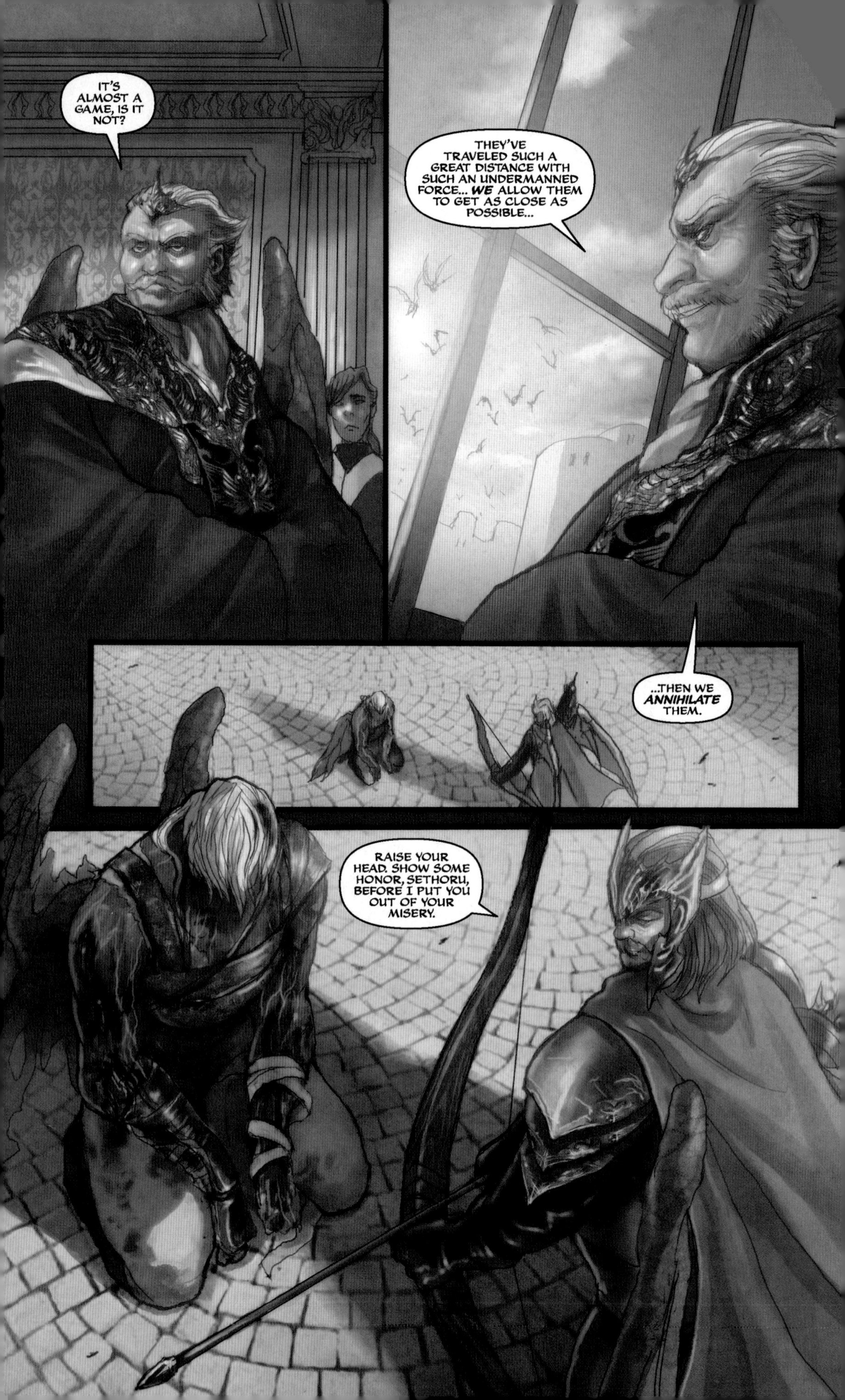
IT'S ALMOST A GAME, IS IT NOT?
THEY'VE TRAVELED SUCH A GREAT DISTANCE WITH SUCH AN UNDERMANNED FORCE... *WE* ALLOW THEM TO GET AS CLOSE AS POSSIBLE...
...THEN WE ***ANNIHILATE*** THEM.
RAISE YOUR HEAD. SHOW SOME HONOR, SETHORU, BEFORE I PUT YOU OUT OF YOUR MISERY.

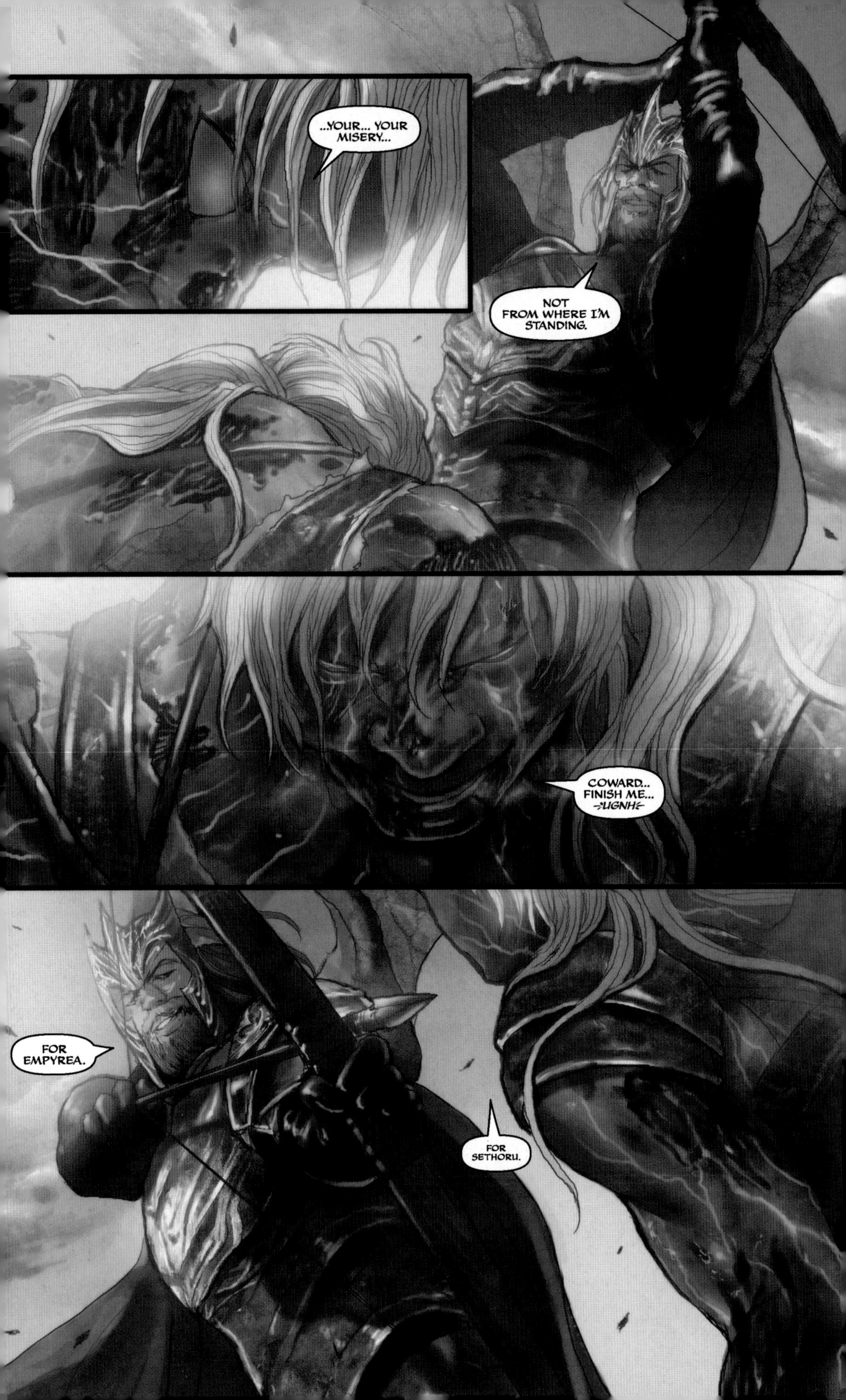

...YOUR... YOUR MISERY...
NOT FROM WHERE I'M STANDING.
COWARD... FINISH ME... -UGNH-
FOR EMPYREA.
FOR SETHORU.

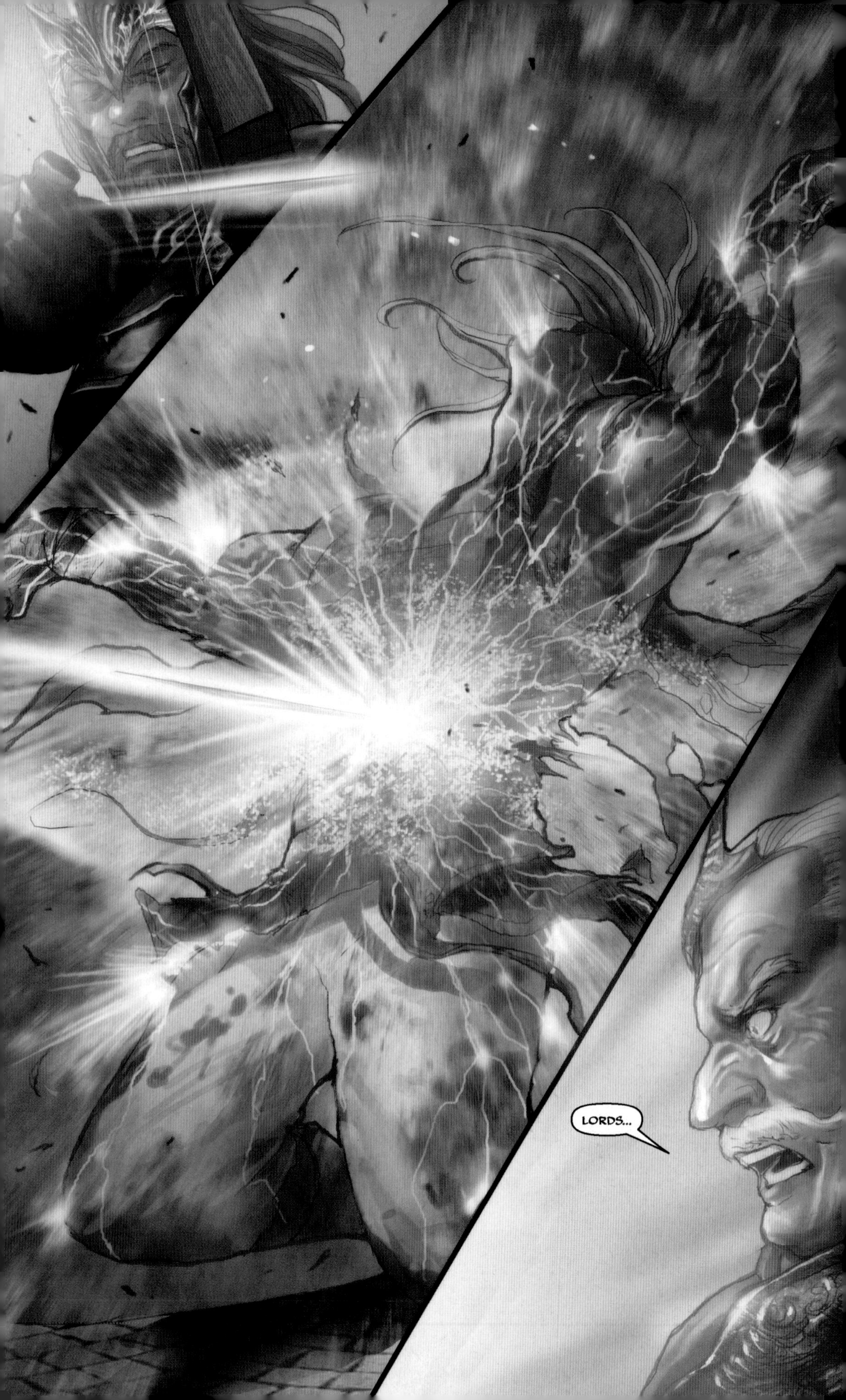
LORDS...

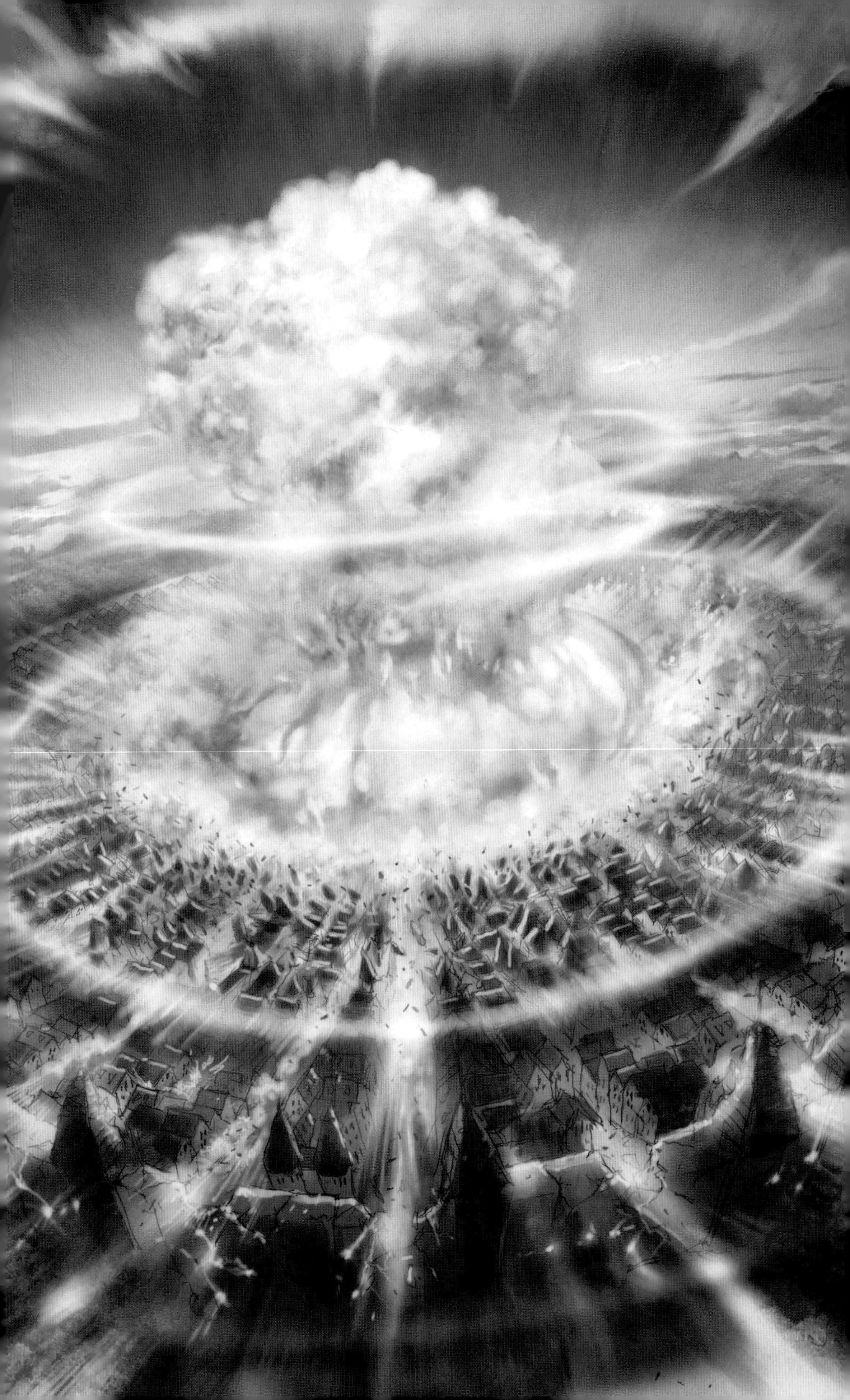

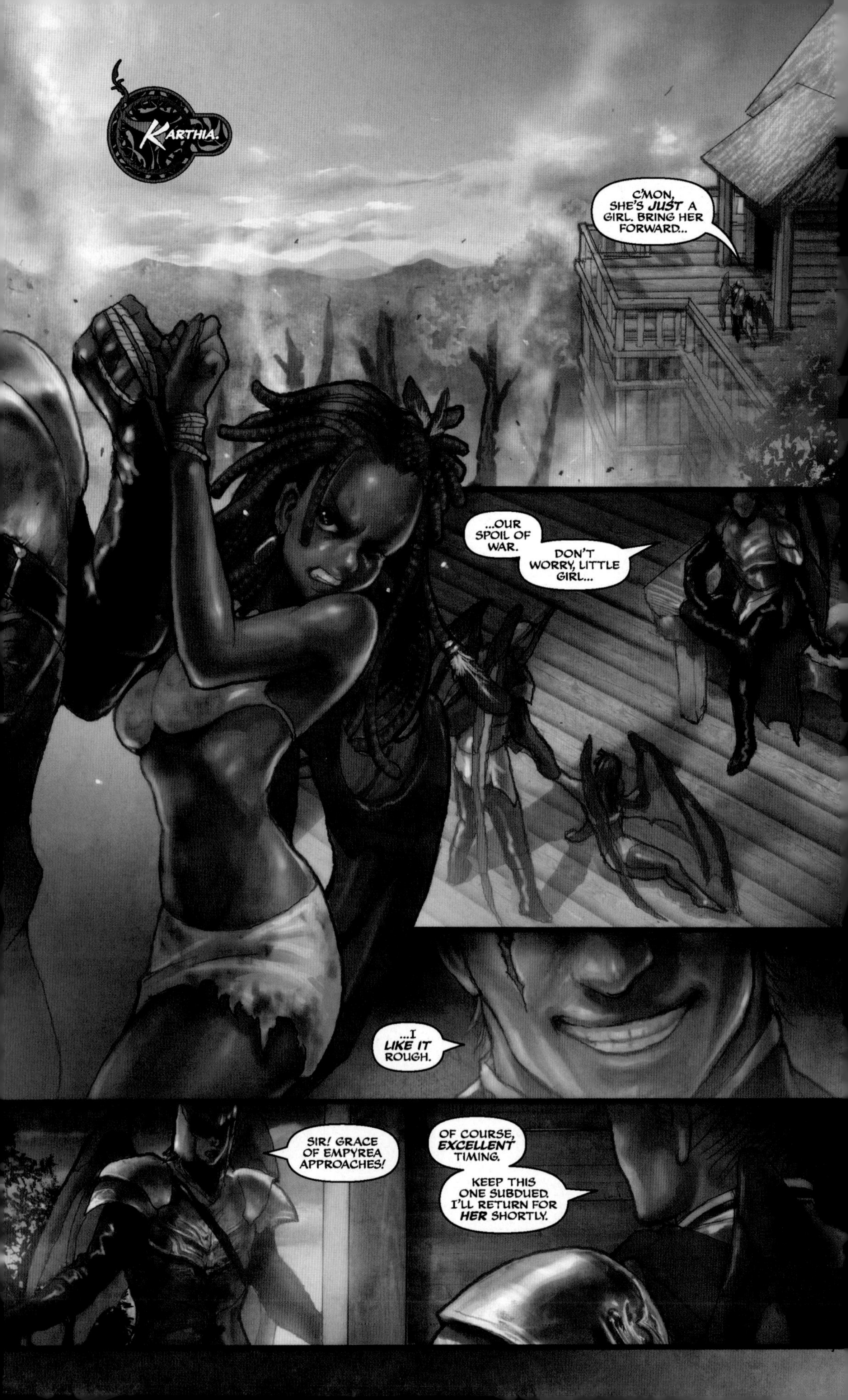
KARTHIA.
C'MON, SHE'S JUST A GIRL. BRING HER FORWARD...
...OUR SPOIL OF WAR.
DON'T WORRY, LITTLE GIRL...
...I LIKE IT ROUGH.
SIR! GRACE OF EMPYREA APPROACHES!
OF COURSE, EXCELLENT TIMING.
KEEP THIS ONE SUBDUED. I'LL RETURN FOR HER SHORTLY.

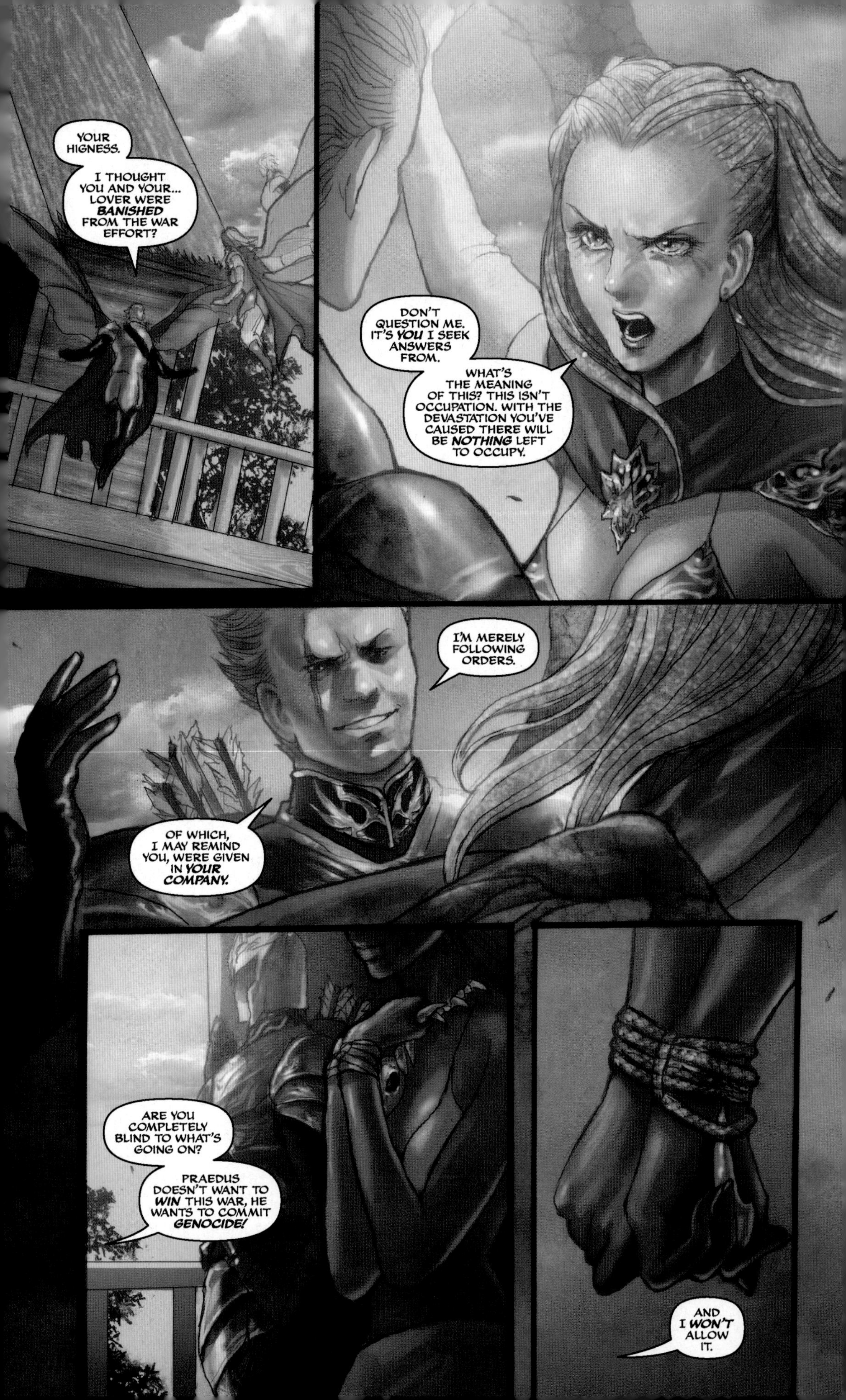
YOUR HIGNESS.
I THOUGHT YOU AND YOUR... LOVER WERE BANISHED FROM THE WAR EFFORT?
DON'T QUESTION ME. IT'S YOU I SEEK ANSWERS FROM.
WHAT'S THE MEANING OF THIS? THIS ISN'T OCCUPATION. WITH THE DEVASTATION YOU'VE CAUSED THERE WILL BE NOTHING LEFT TO OCCUPY.
I'M MERELY FOLLOWING ORDERS.
OF WHICH, I MAY REMIND YOU, WERE GIVEN IN YOUR COMPANY.
ARE YOU COMPLETELY BLIND TO WHAT'S GOING ON?
PRAEDUS DOESN'T WANT TO WIN THIS WAR, HE WANTS TO COMMIT GENOCIDE!
AND I WON'T ALLOW IT.

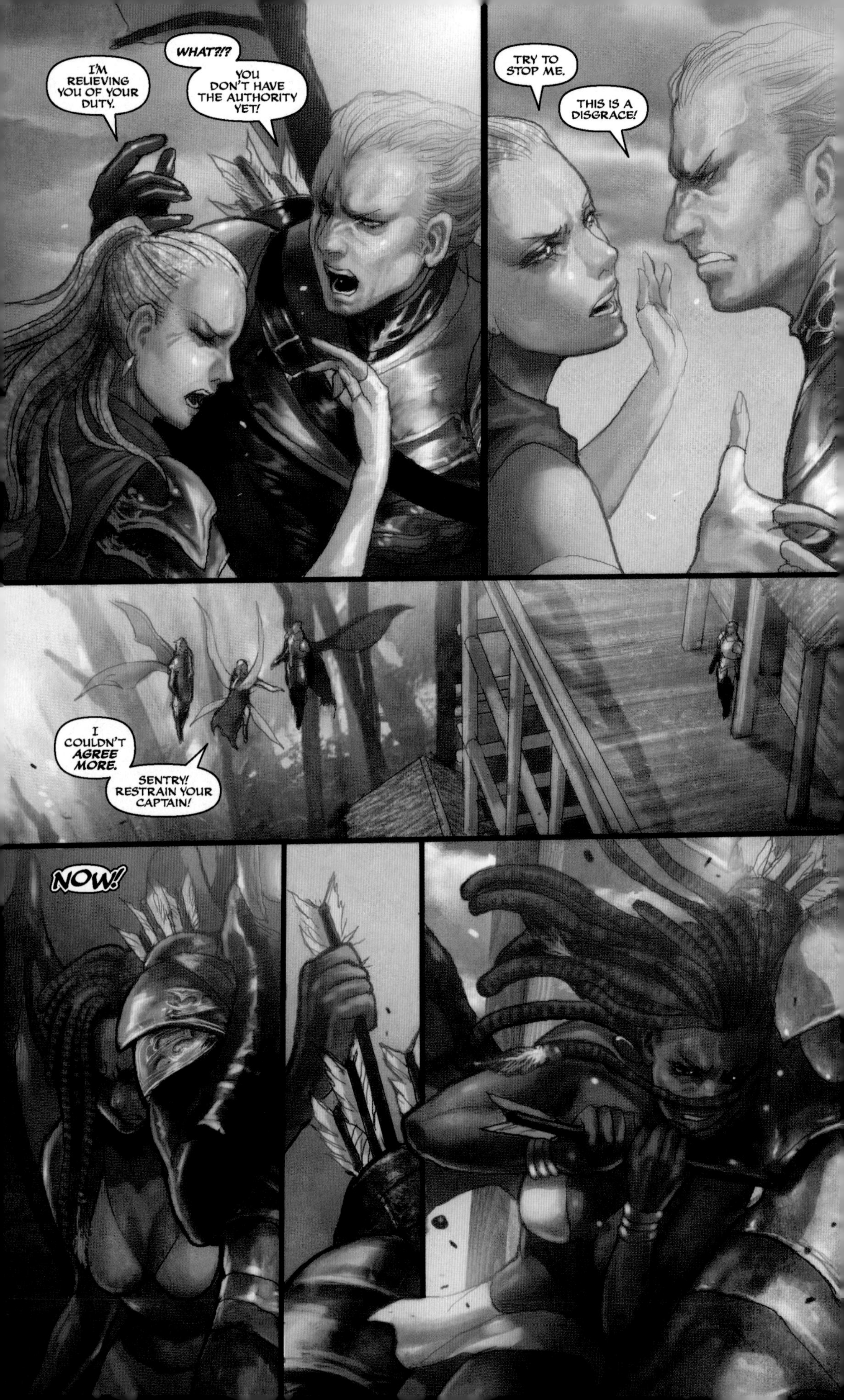
I'M RELIEVING YOU OF YOUR DUTY.
WHAT?!?
YOU DON'T HAVE THE AUTHORITY YET!
TRY TO STOP ME.
THIS IS A DISGRACE!
I COULDN'T AGREE MORE.
SENTRY! RESTRAIN YOUR CAPTAIN!
NOW!

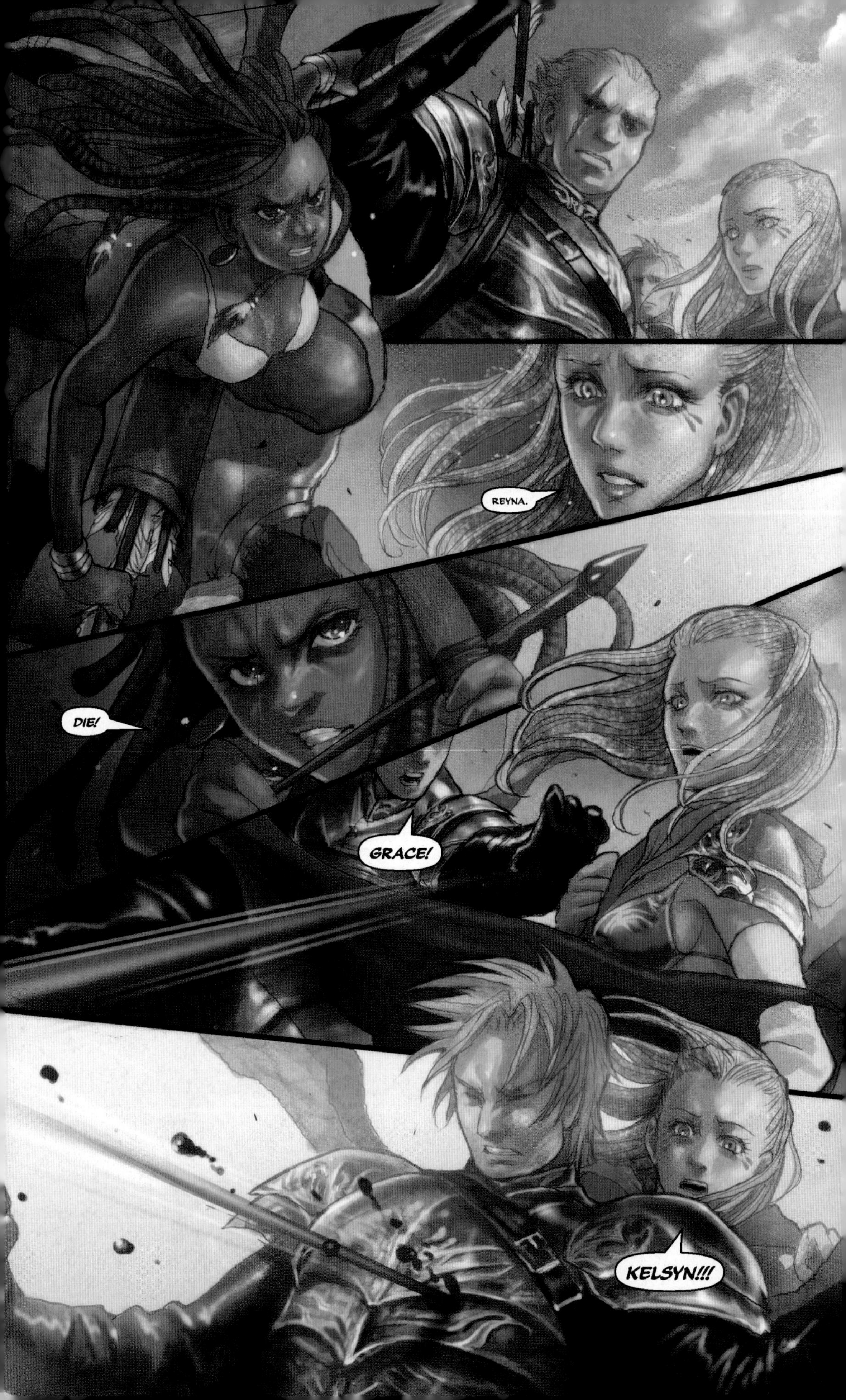
REYNA.
DIE!
GRACE!
KELSYN!!!

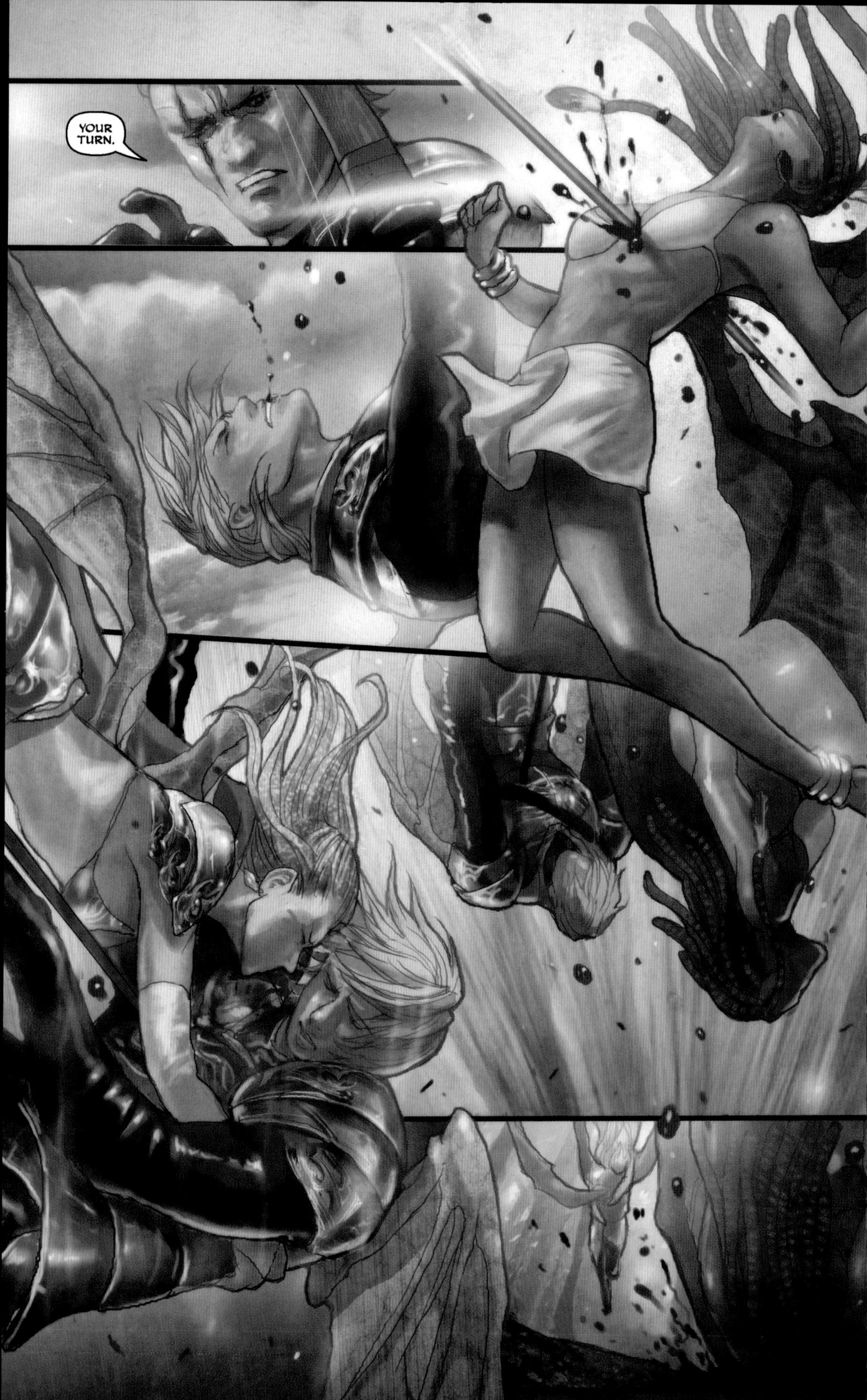
YOUR TURN.

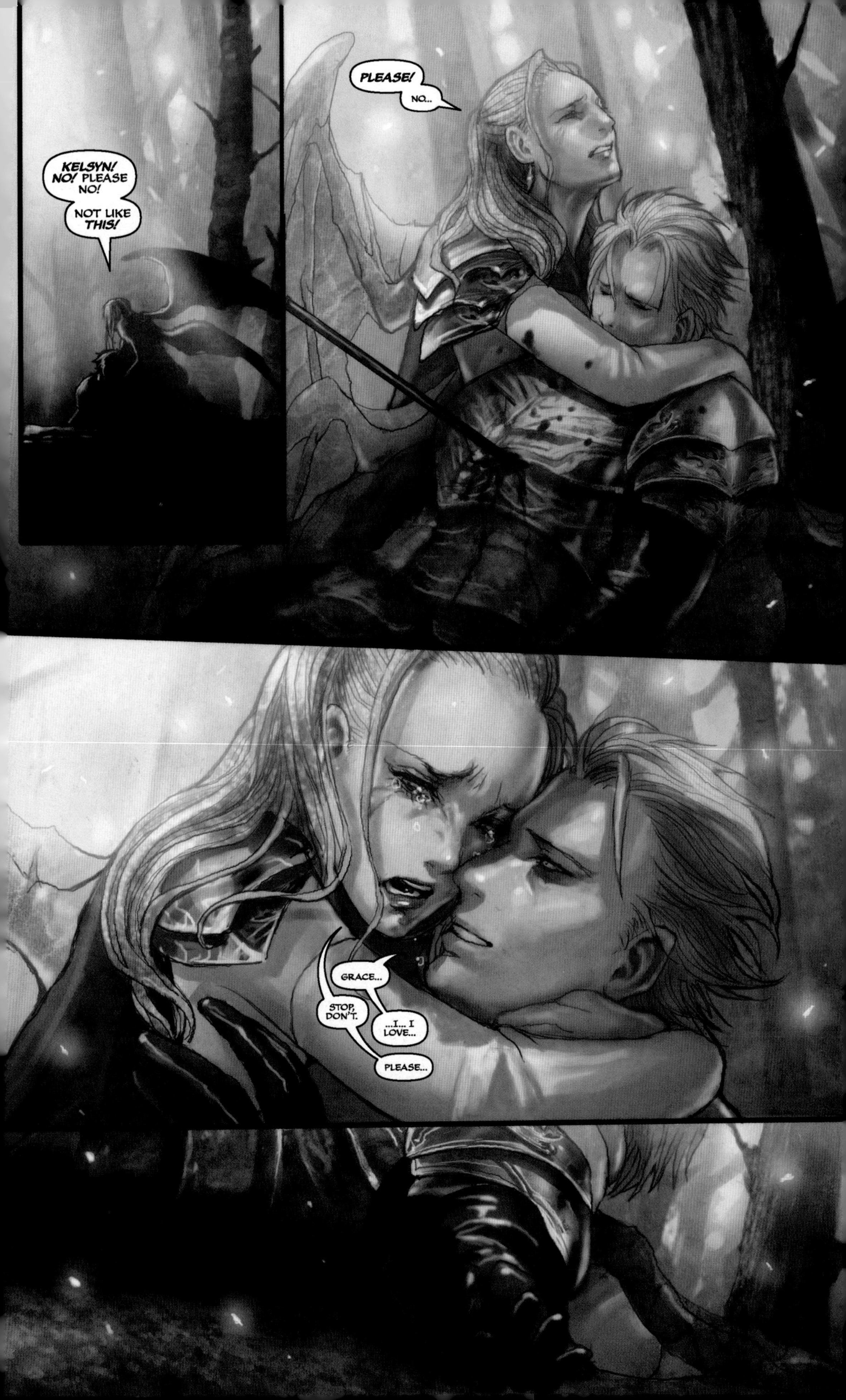
KELSYN! NO! PLEASE NO!
NOT LIKE THIS!
PLEASE!
NO...
GRACE...
STOP, DON'T.
...I... I LOVE...
PLEASE...

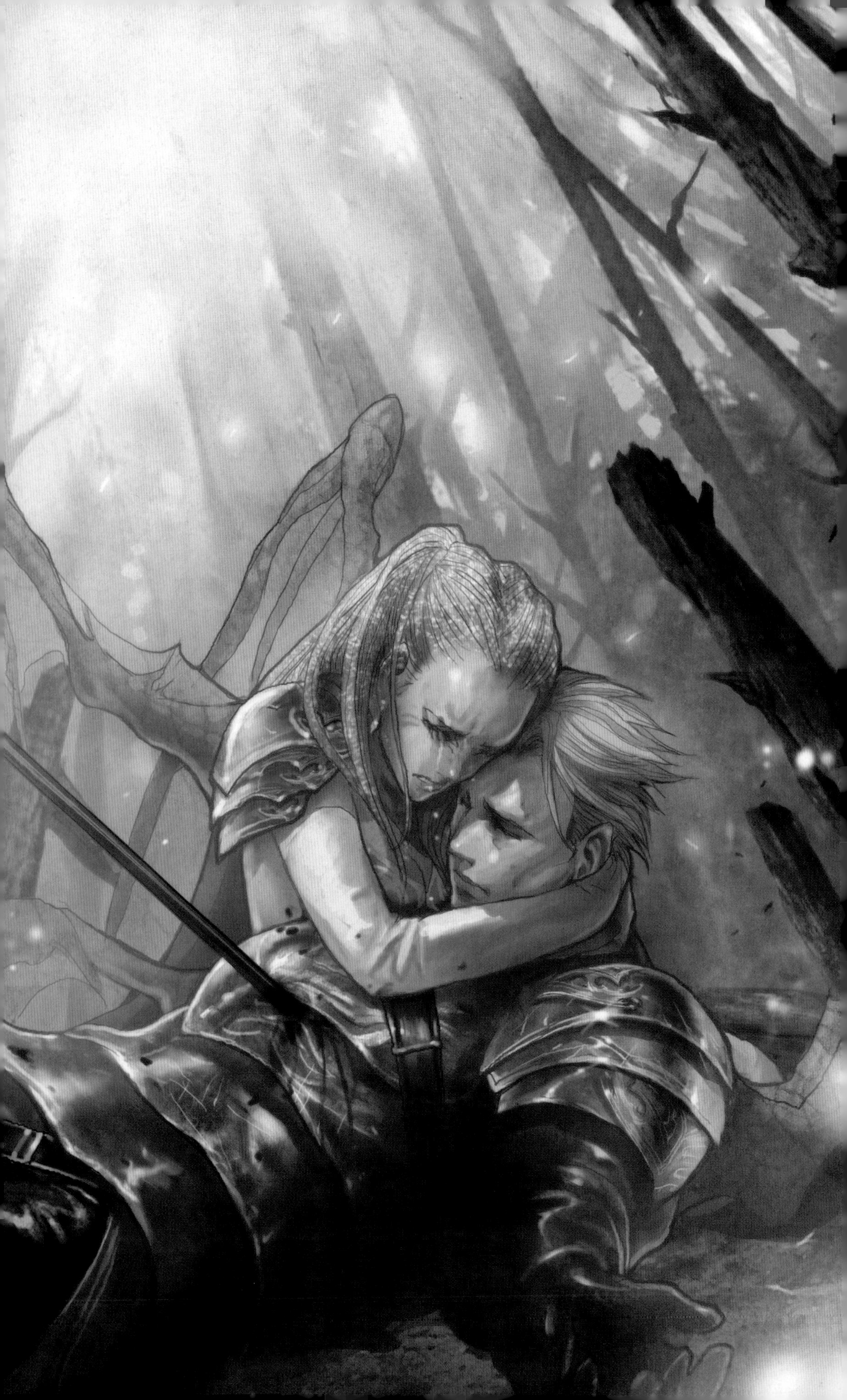

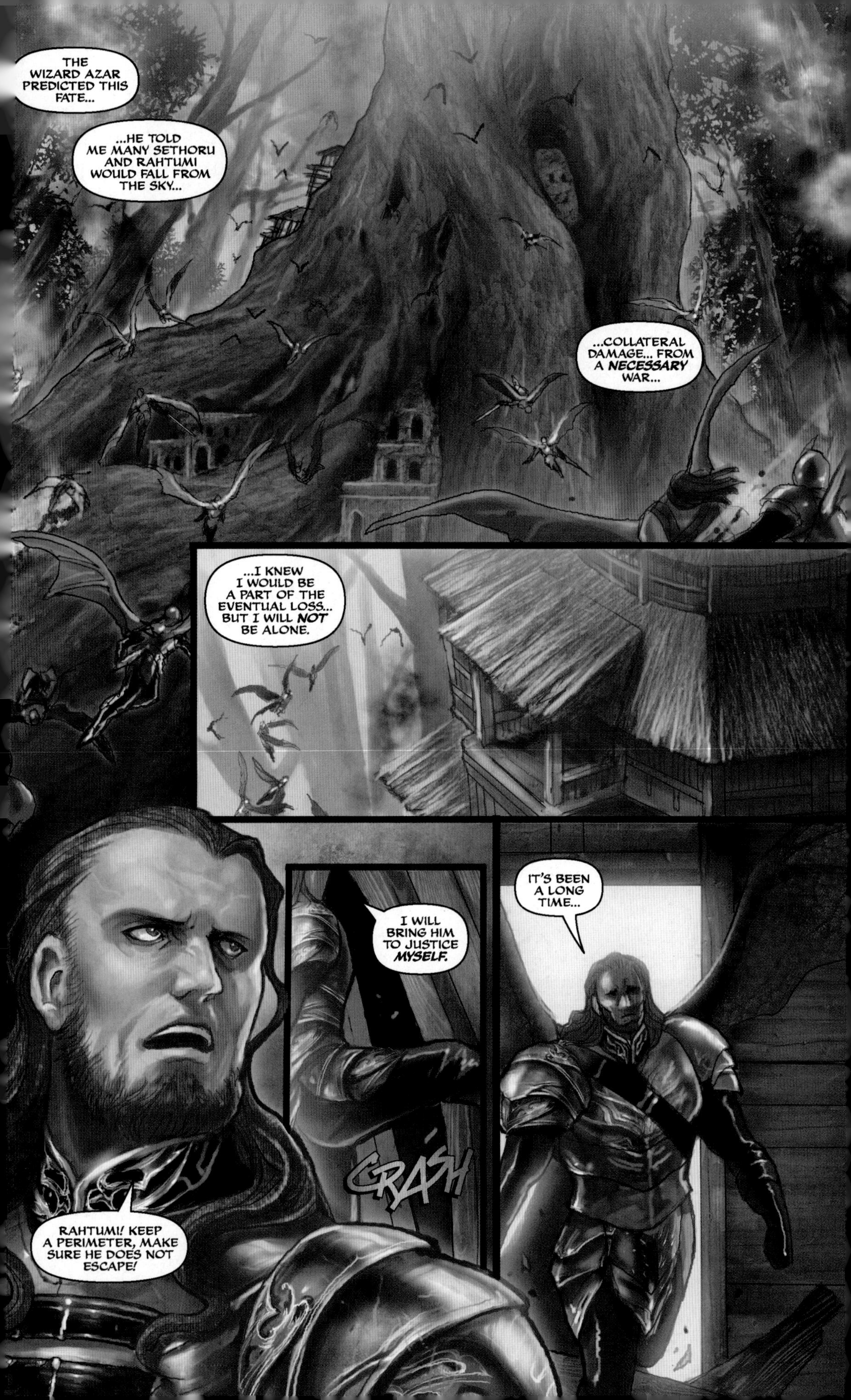
THE WIZARD AZAR PREDICTED THIS FATE...
...HE TOLD ME MANY SETHORU AND RAHTUMI WOULD FALL FROM THE SKY...
...COLLATERAL DAMAGE... FROM A NECESSARY WAR...
...I KNEW I WOULD BE A PART OF THE EVENTUAL LOSS... BUT I WILL NOT BE ALONE.
I WILL BRING HIM TO JUSTICE MYSELF.
IT'S BEEN A LONG TIME...
CRASH
RAHTUMI! KEEP A PERIMETER, MAKE SURE HE DOES NOT ESCAPE!

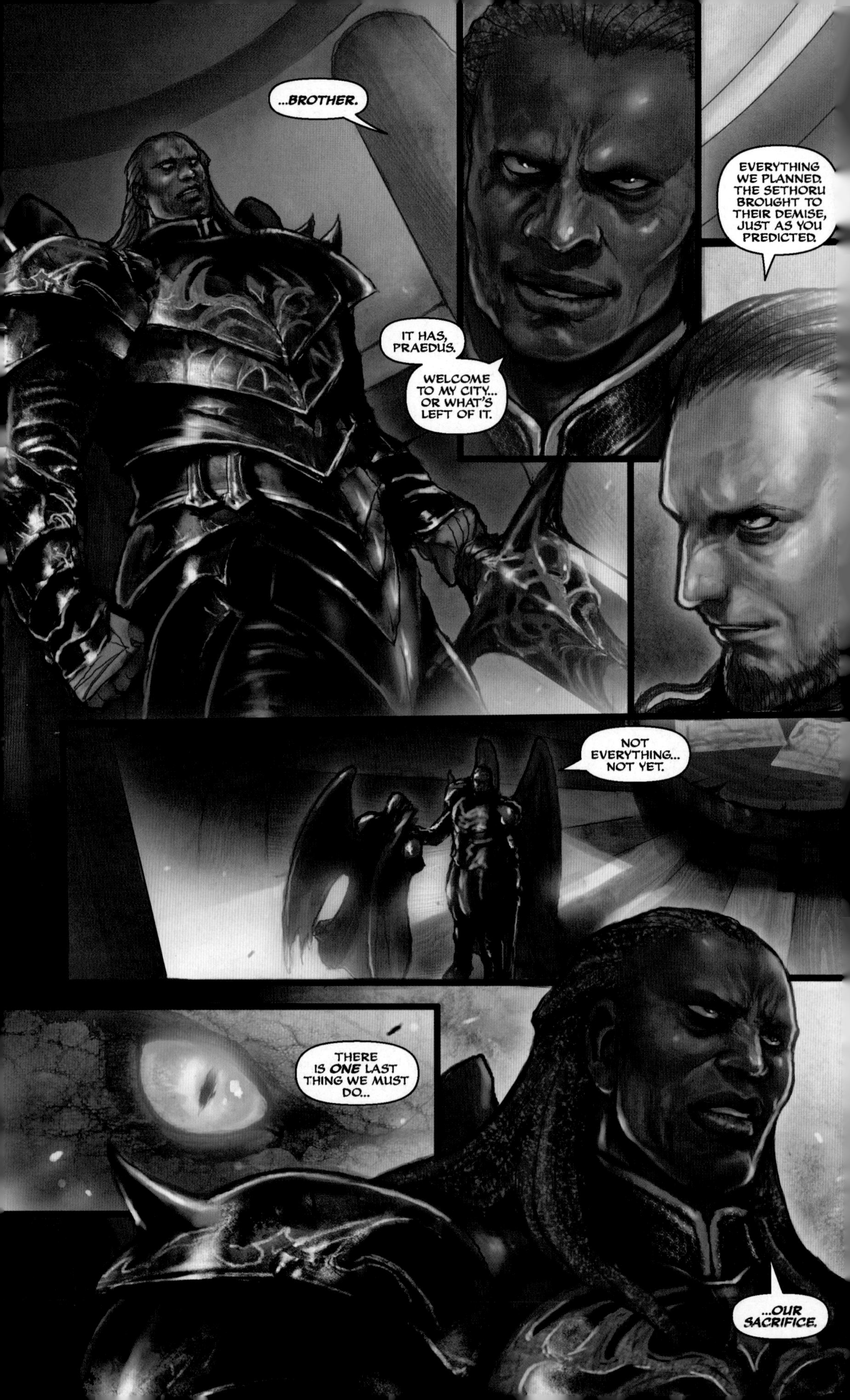
...BROTHER.
EVERYTHING WE PLANNED. THE SETHORU BROUGHT TO THEIR DEMISE, JUST AS YOU PREDICTED.
IT HAS, PRAEDUS.
WELCOME TO MY CITY... OR WHAT'S LEFT OF IT.
NOT EVERYTHING... NOT YET.
THERE IS ONE LAST THING WE MUST DO...
...OUR SACRIFICE.

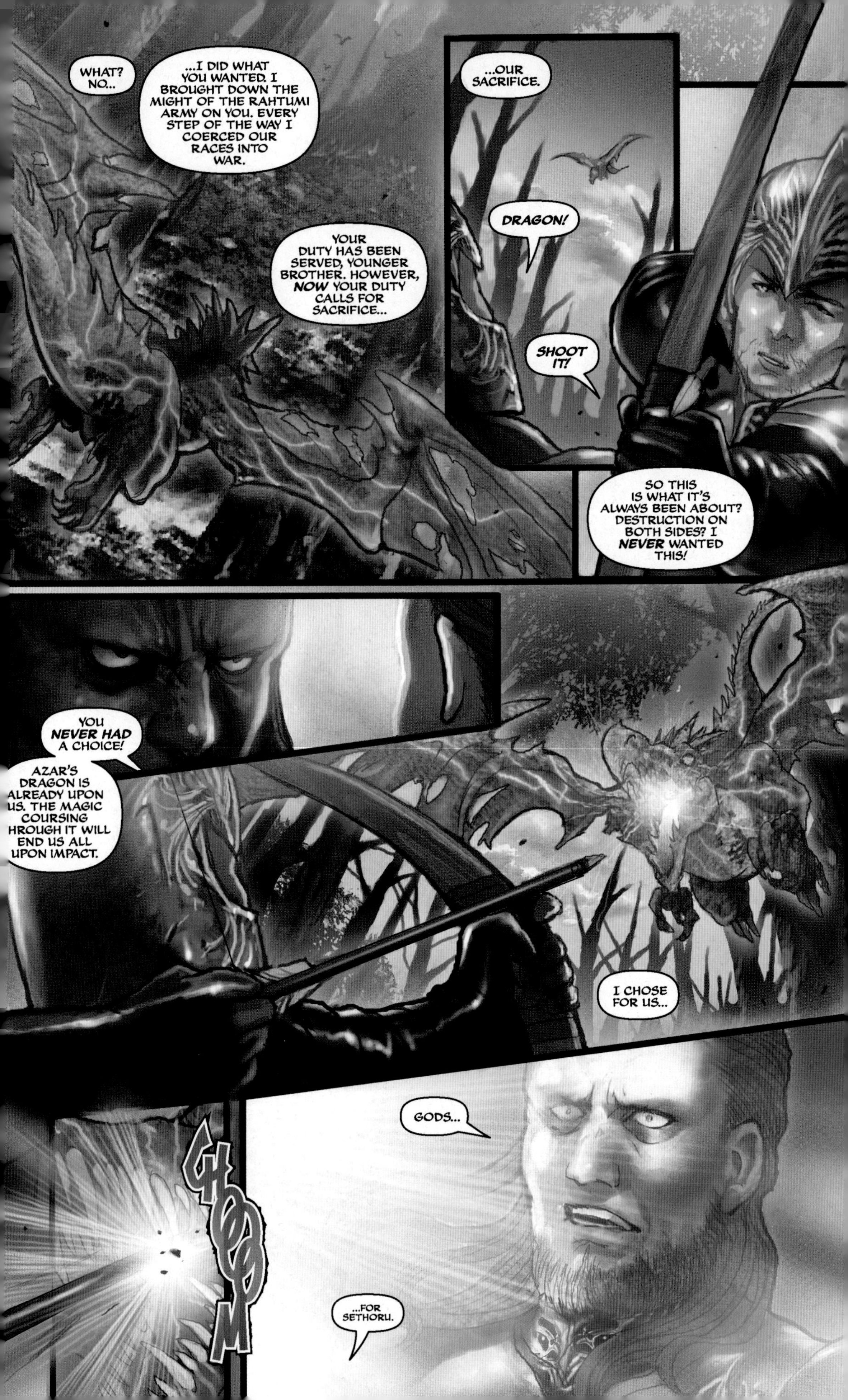
WHAT? NO...
...I DID WHAT YOU WANTED. I BROUGHT DOWN THE MIGHT OF THE RAHTUMI ARMY ON YOU. EVERY STEP OF THE WAY I COERCED OUR RACES INTO WAR.
YOUR DUTY HAS BEEN SERVED, YOUNGER BROTHER. HOWEVER, NOW YOUR DUTY CALLS FOR SACRIFICE...
...OUR SACRIFICE.
DRAGON!
SHOOT IT!
SO THIS IS WHAT IT'S ALWAYS BEEN ABOUT? DESTRUCTION ON BOTH SIDES? I NEVER WANTED THIS!
YOU NEVER HAD A CHOICE!
AZAR'S DRAGON IS ALREADY UPON US. THE MAGIC COURSING HROUGH IT WILL END US ALL UPON IMPACT.
I CHOSE FOR US...
GODS...
CHOOOM
...FOR SETHORU.

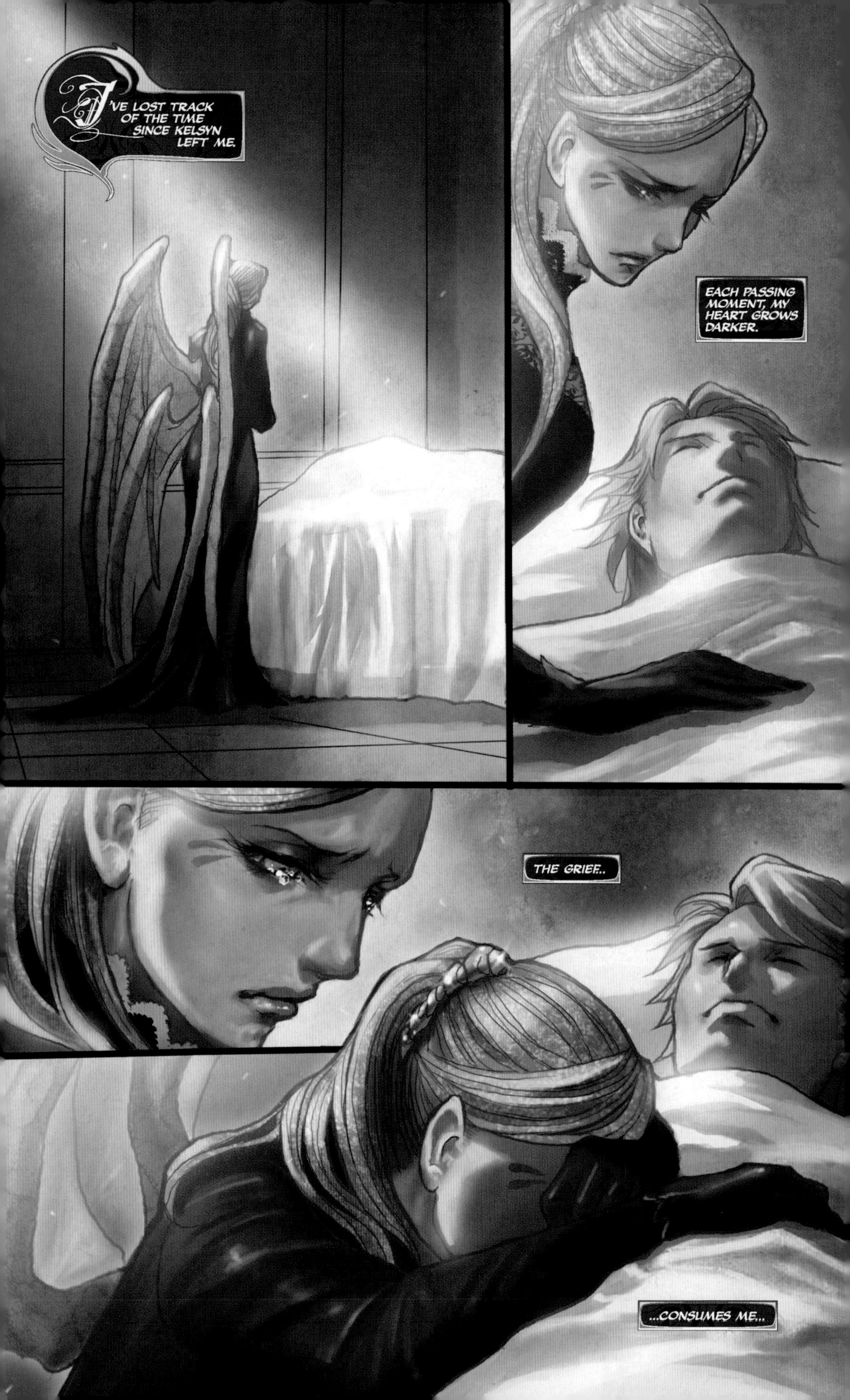
I'VE LOST TRACK OF THE TIME SINCE KELSYN LEFT ME.
EACH PASSING MOMENT, MY HEART GROWS DARKER.
THE GRIEF..
...CONSUMES ME...

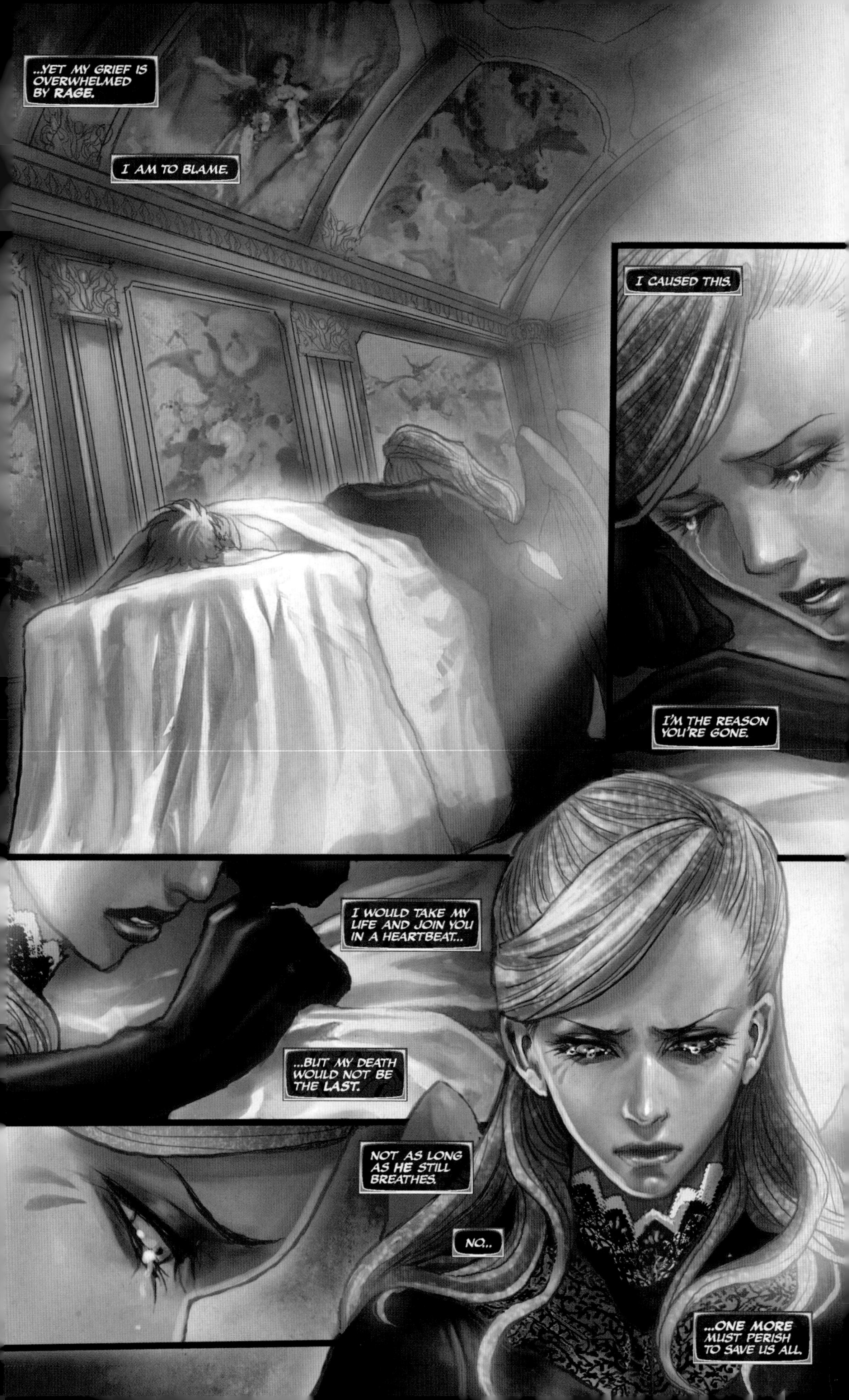

...YET MY GRIEF IS OVERWHELMED BY RAGE.
I AM TO BLAME.
I CAUSED THIS.
I'M THE REASON YOU'RE GONE.
I WOULD TAKE MY LIFE AND JOIN YOU IN A HEARTBEAT...
...BUT MY DEATH WOULD NOT BE THE LAST.
NOT AS LONG AS HE STILL BREATHES.
NO...
...ONE MORE MUST PERISH TO SAVE US ALL.

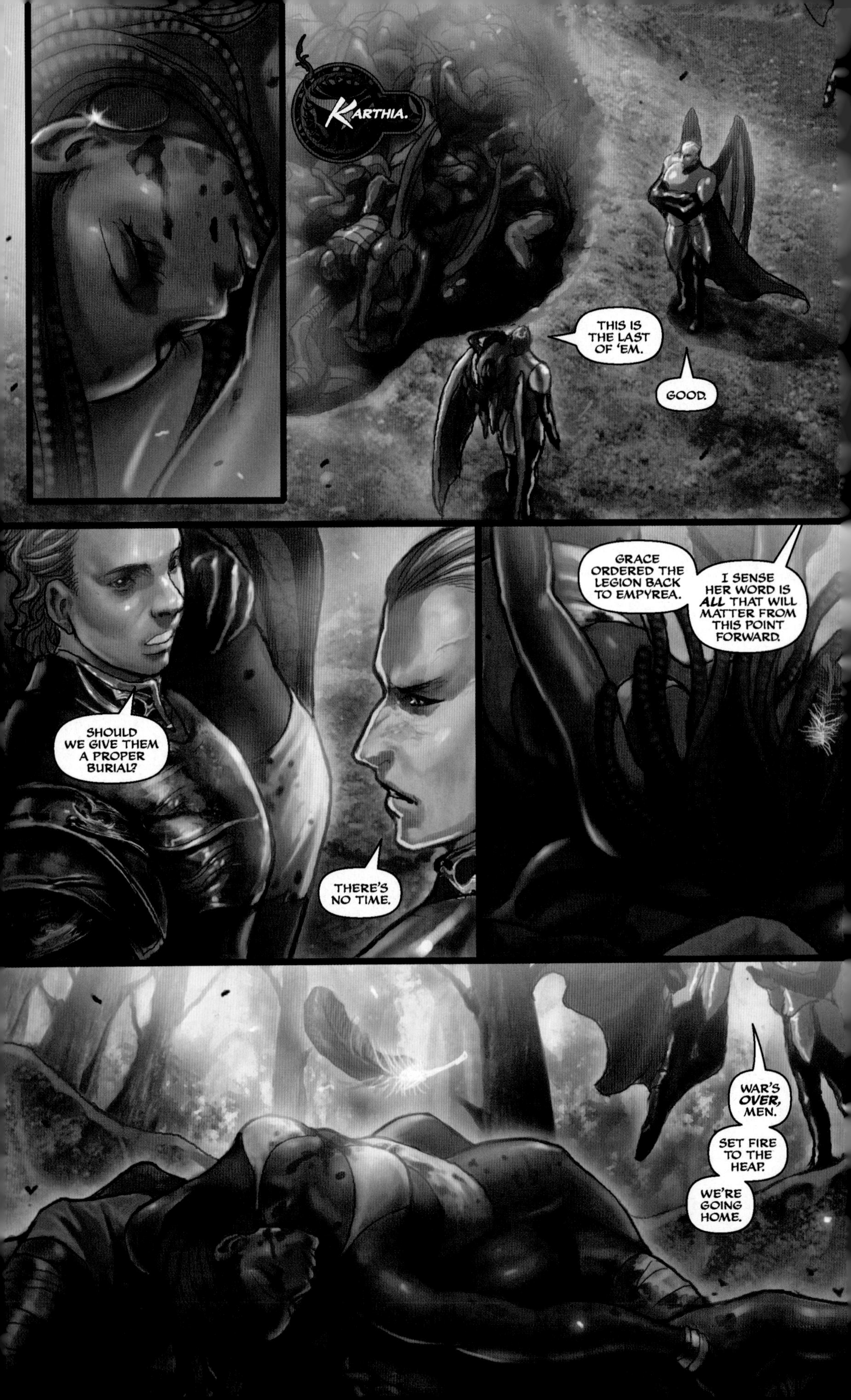
KARTHIA.
THIS IS THE LAST OF 'EM.
GOOD.
SHOULD WE GIVE THEM A PROPER BURIAL?
THERE'S NO TIME.
GRACE ORDERED THE LEGION BACK TO EMPYREA.
I SENSE HER WORD IS ALL THAT WILL MATTER FROM THIS POINT FORWARD.
WAR'S OVER, MEN.
SET FIRE TO THE HEAP.
WE'RE GOING HOME.

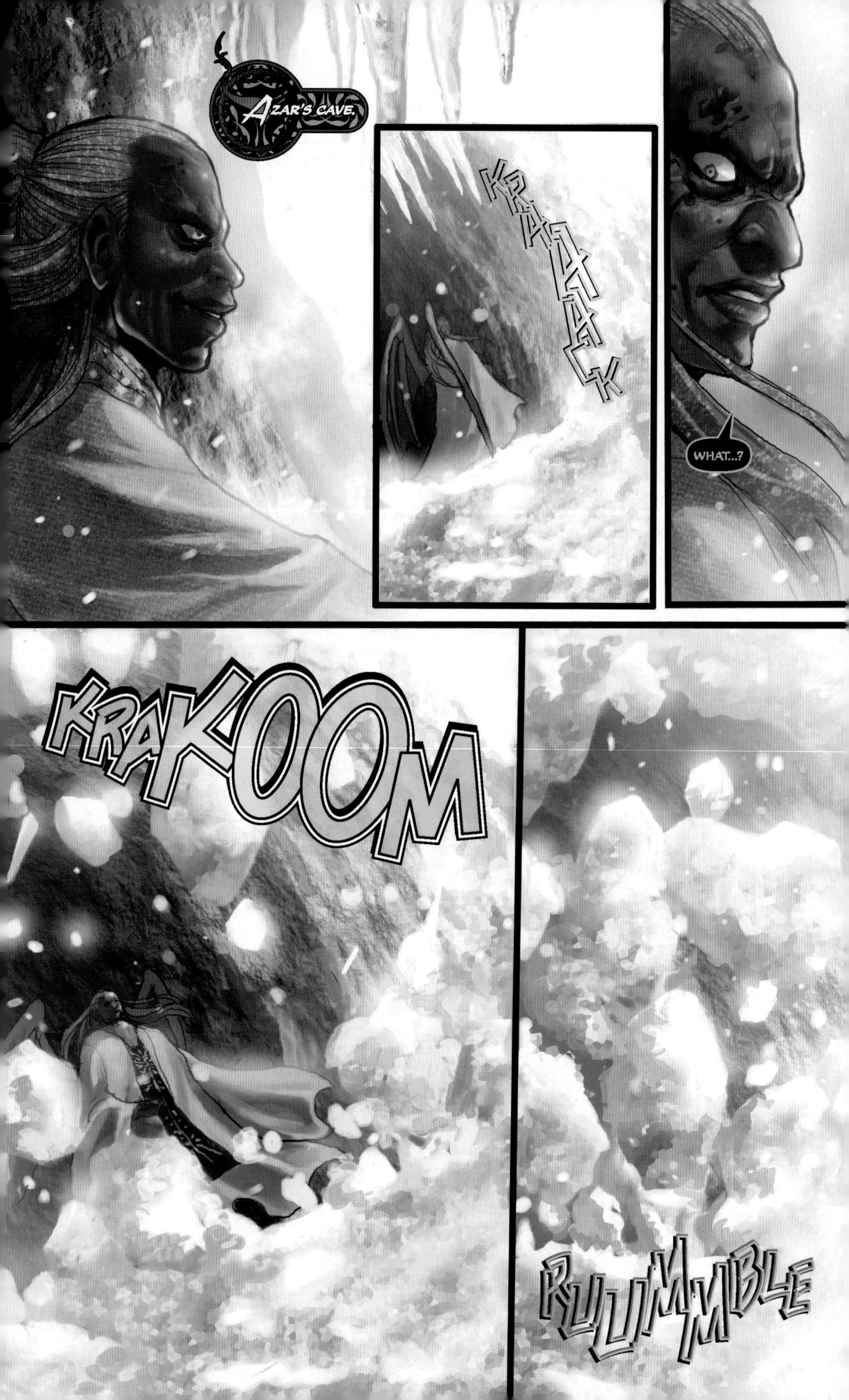
AZAR'S CAVE.
KRAKKKACK
WHAT...?
KRAKOOM
RUUMMMBLE

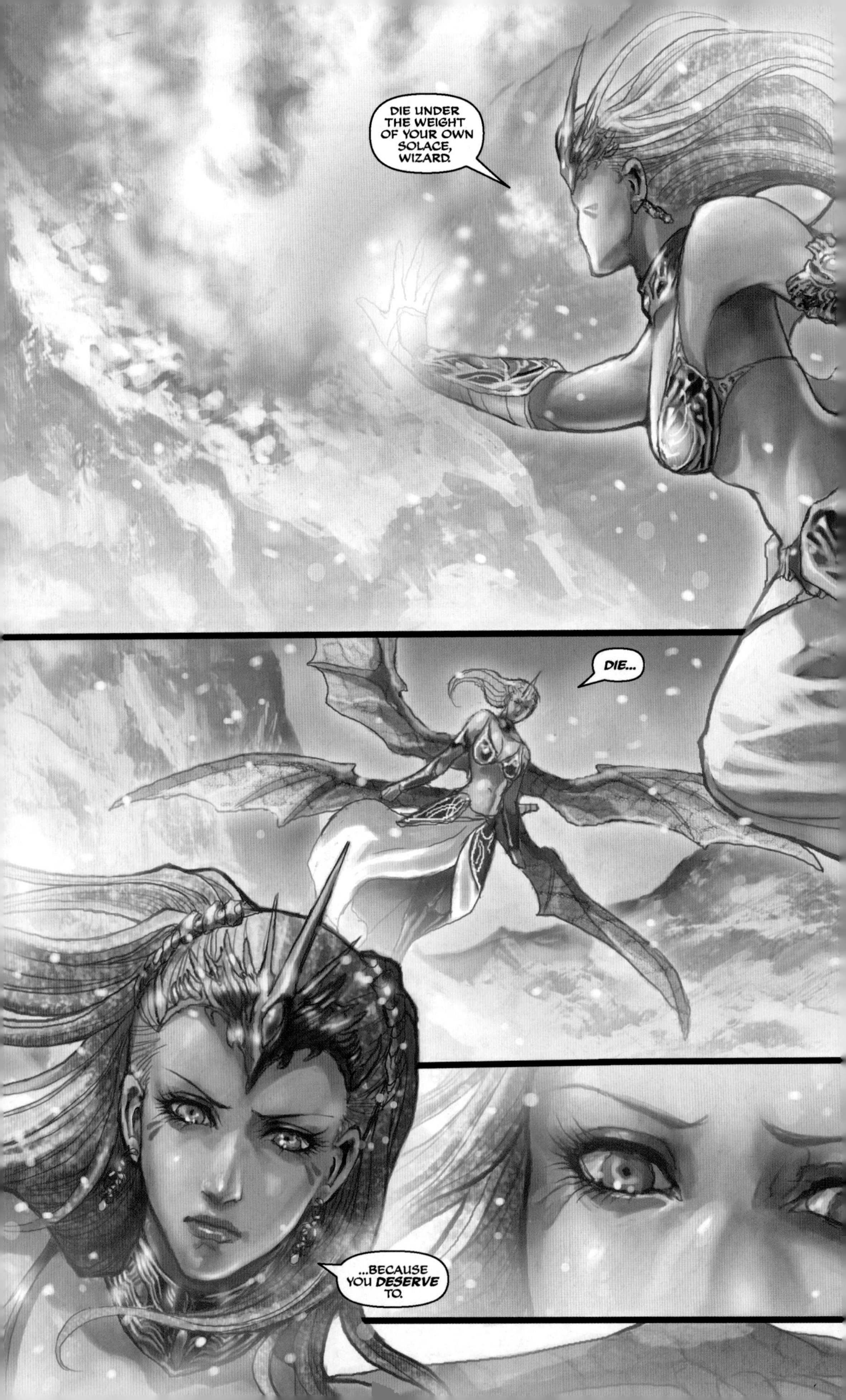
DIE UNDER THE WEIGHT OF YOUR OWN SOLACE, WIZARD.
DIE...
...BECAUSE YOU **DESERVE** TO.

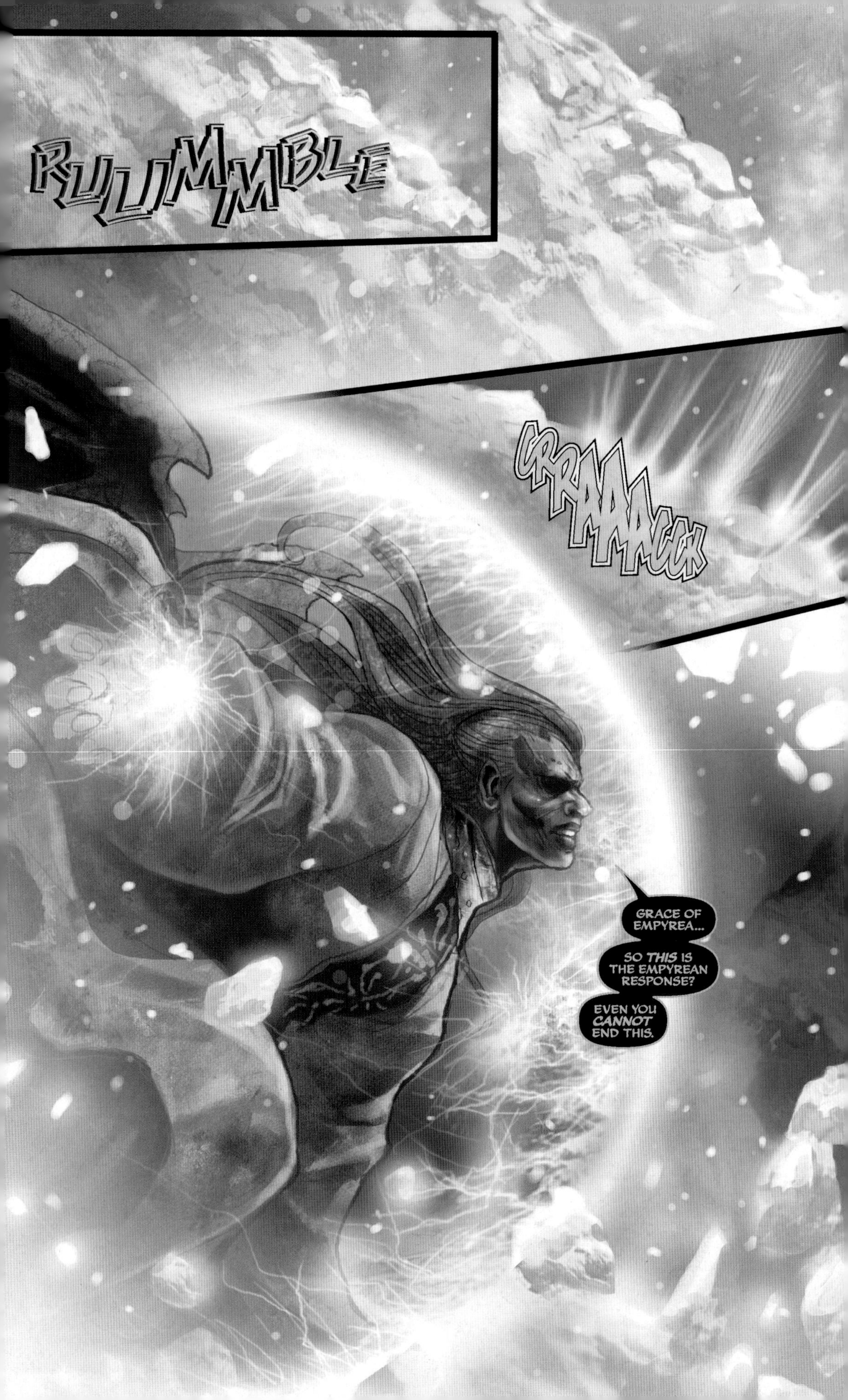
RUUMMBLE
CRRAAACCK
GRACE OF EMPYREA...
SO THIS IS THE EMPYREAN RESPONSE?
EVEN YOU CANNOT END THIS.

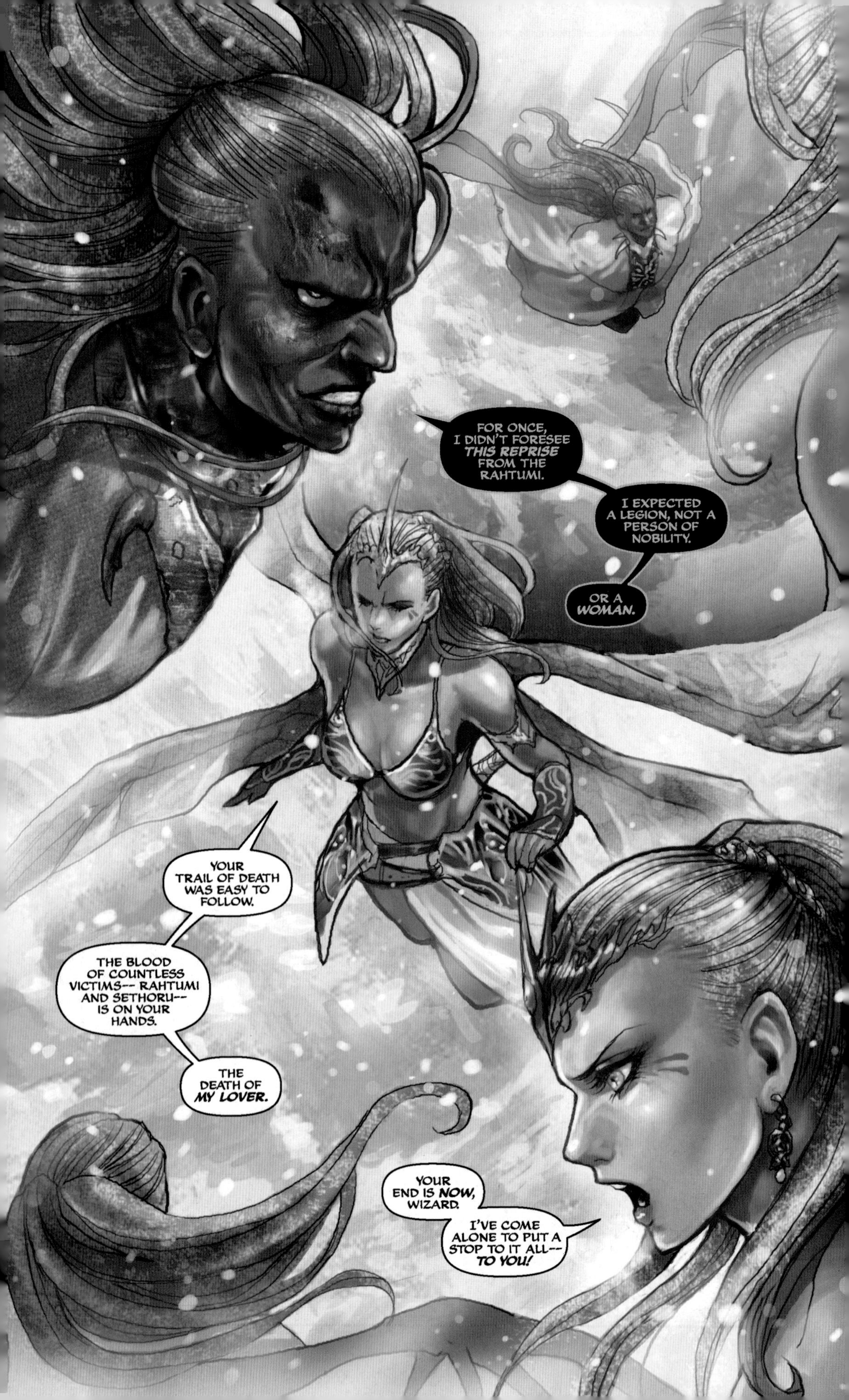

FOR ONCE, I DIDN'T FORESEE *THIS REPRISE* FROM THE RAHTUMI.
I EXPECTED A LEGION, NOT A PERSON OF NOBILITY.
OR A *WOMAN.*
YOUR TRAIL OF DEATH WAS EASY TO FOLLOW.
THE BLOOD OF COUNTLESS VICTIMS-- RAHTUMI AND SETHORU-- IS ON YOUR HANDS.
THE DEATH OF *MY LOVER.*
YOUR END IS *NOW,* WIZARD.
I'VE COME ALONE TO PUT A STOP TO IT ALL-- *TO YOU!*

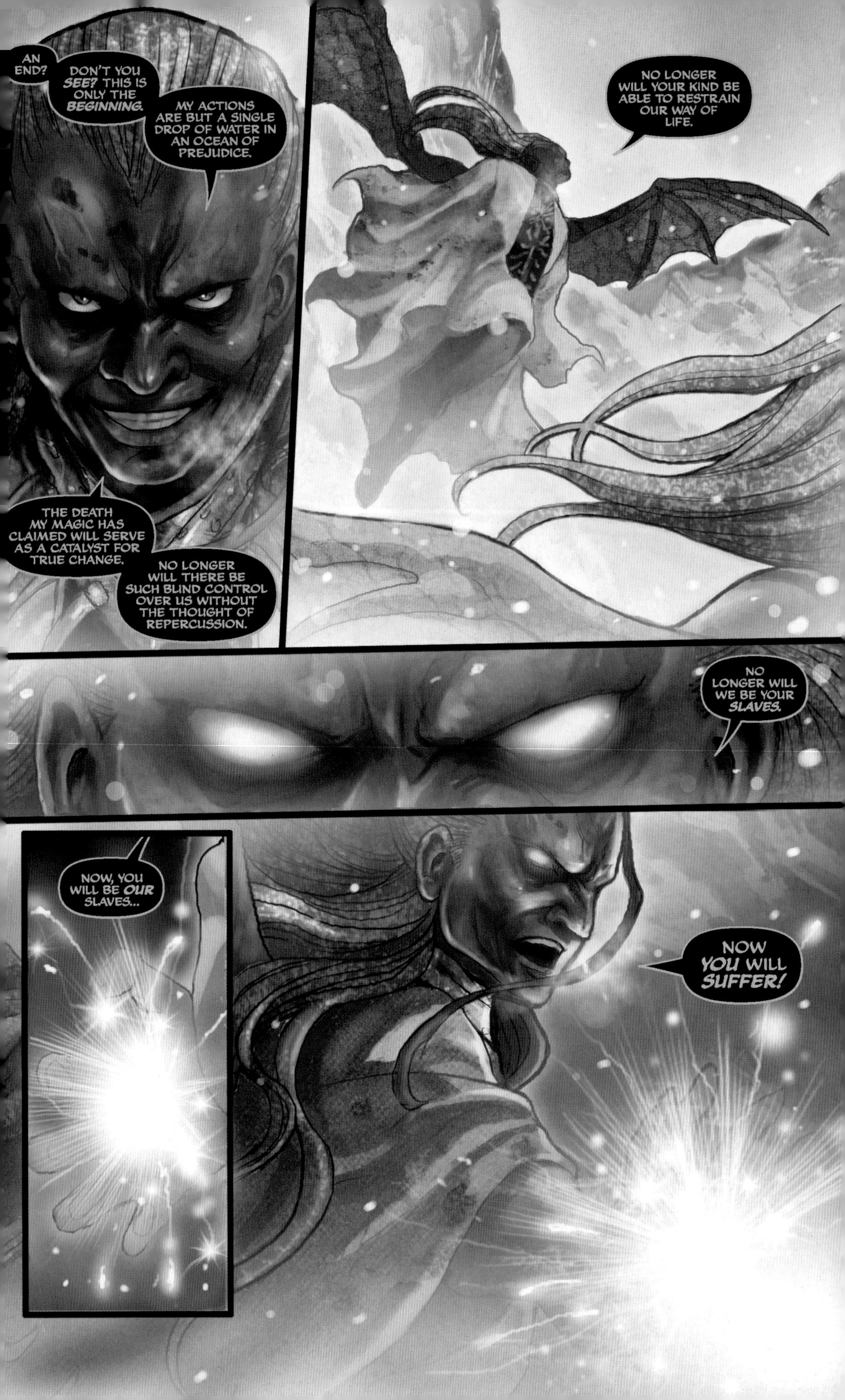
AN END?
DON'T YOU *SEE?* THIS IS ONLY THE *BEGINNING.*
MY ACTIONS ARE BUT A SINGLE DROP OF WATER IN AN OCEAN OF PREJUDICE.
THE DEATH MY MAGIC HAS CLAIMED WILL SERVE AS A CATALYST FOR TRUE CHANGE.
NO LONGER WILL THERE BE SUCH BLIND CONTROL OVER US WITHOUT THE THOUGHT OF REPERCUSSION.
NO LONGER WILL YOUR KIND BE ABLE TO RESTRAIN OUR WAY OF LIFE.
NO LONGER WILL WE BE YOUR *SLAVES.*
NOW, YOU WILL BE *OUR* SLAVES...
NOW *YOU* WILL *SUFFER!*

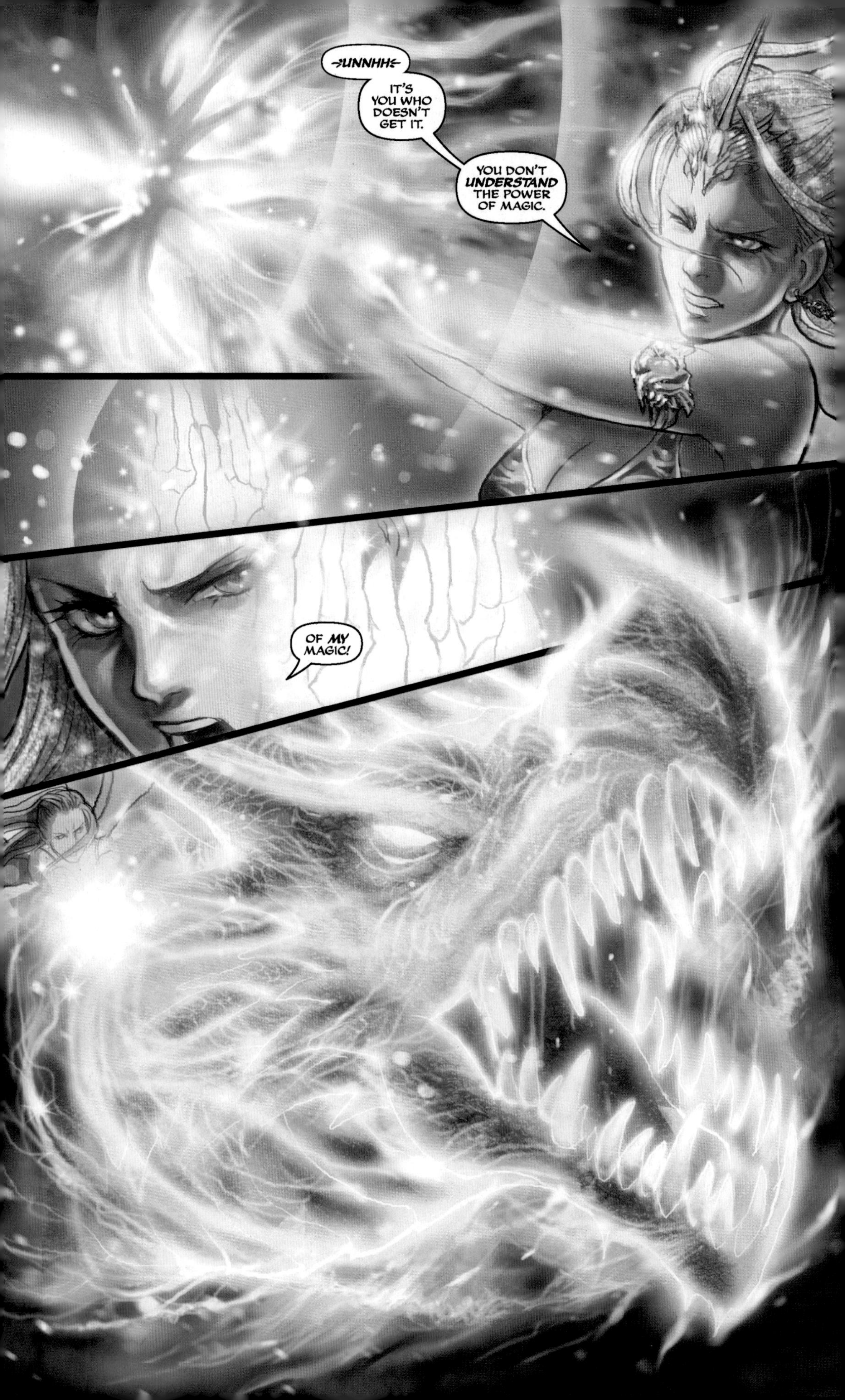
-UNNHH-
IT'S YOU WHO DOESN'T GET IT.
YOU DON'T UNDERSTAND THE POWER OF MAGIC.
OF MY MAGIC!

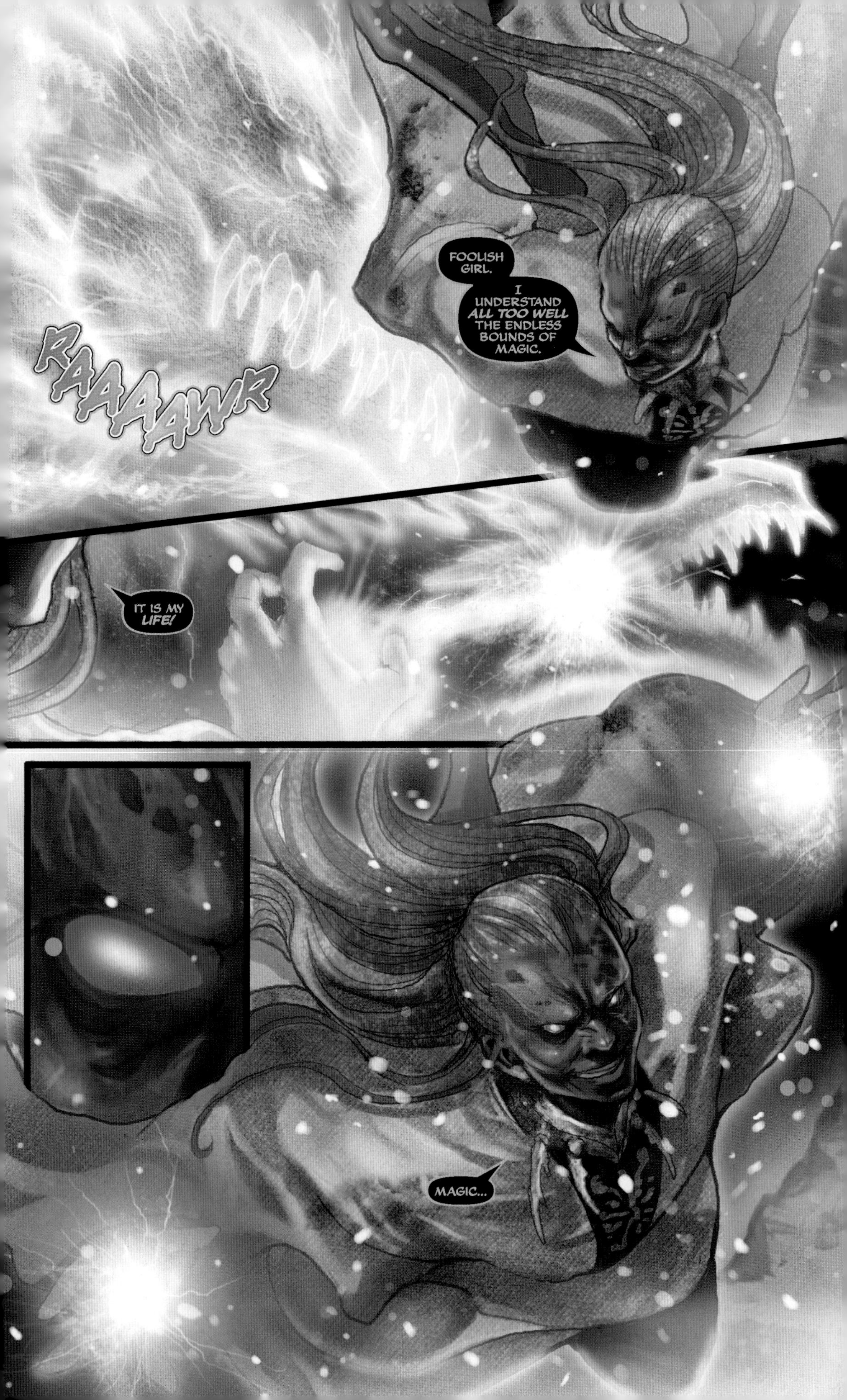
FOOLISH GIRL.
I UNDERSTAND ALL TOO WELL THE ENDLESS BOUNDS OF MAGIC.
RAAAAAWR
IT IS MY LIFE!
MAGIC...

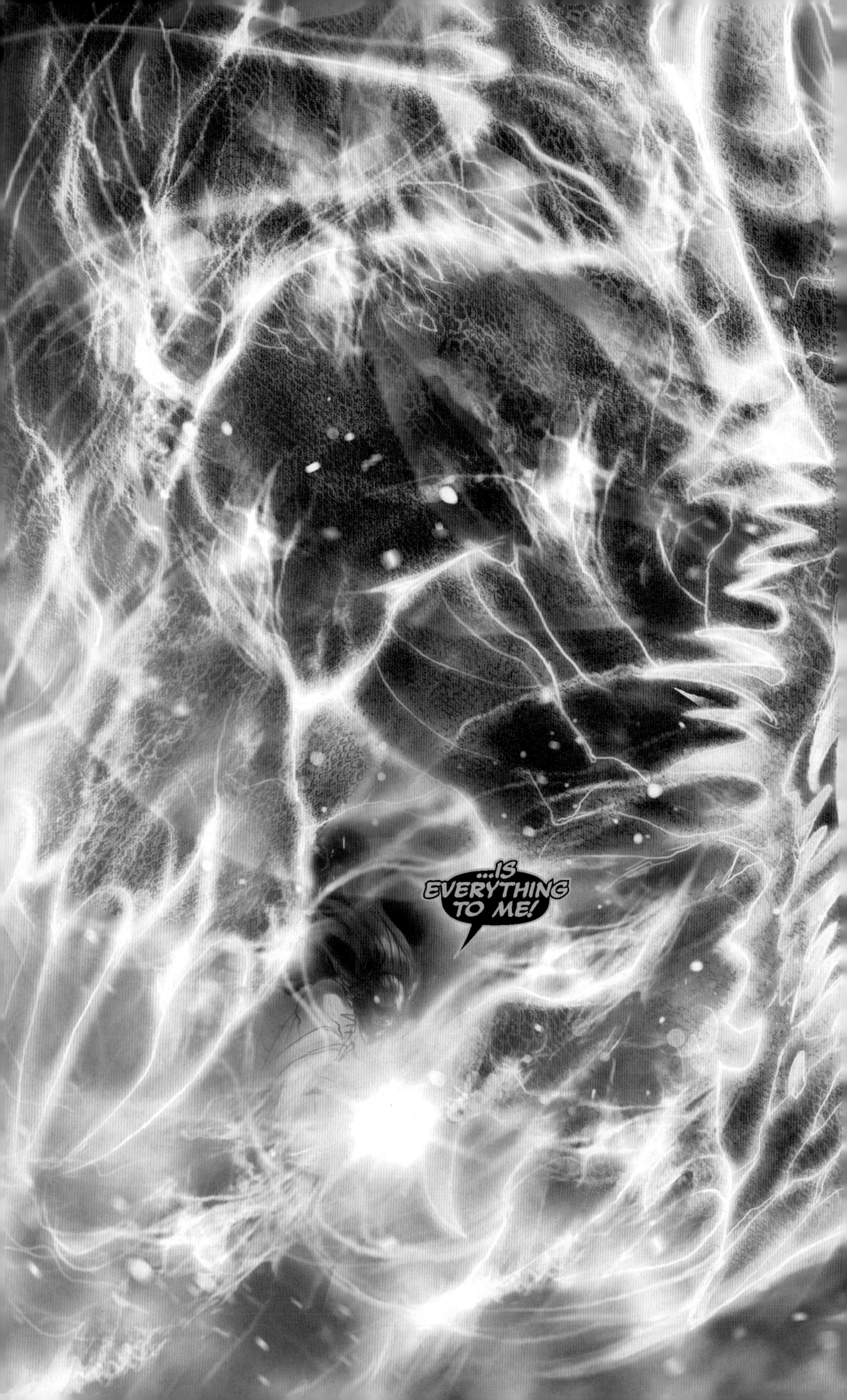
...IS EVERYTHING TO ME!

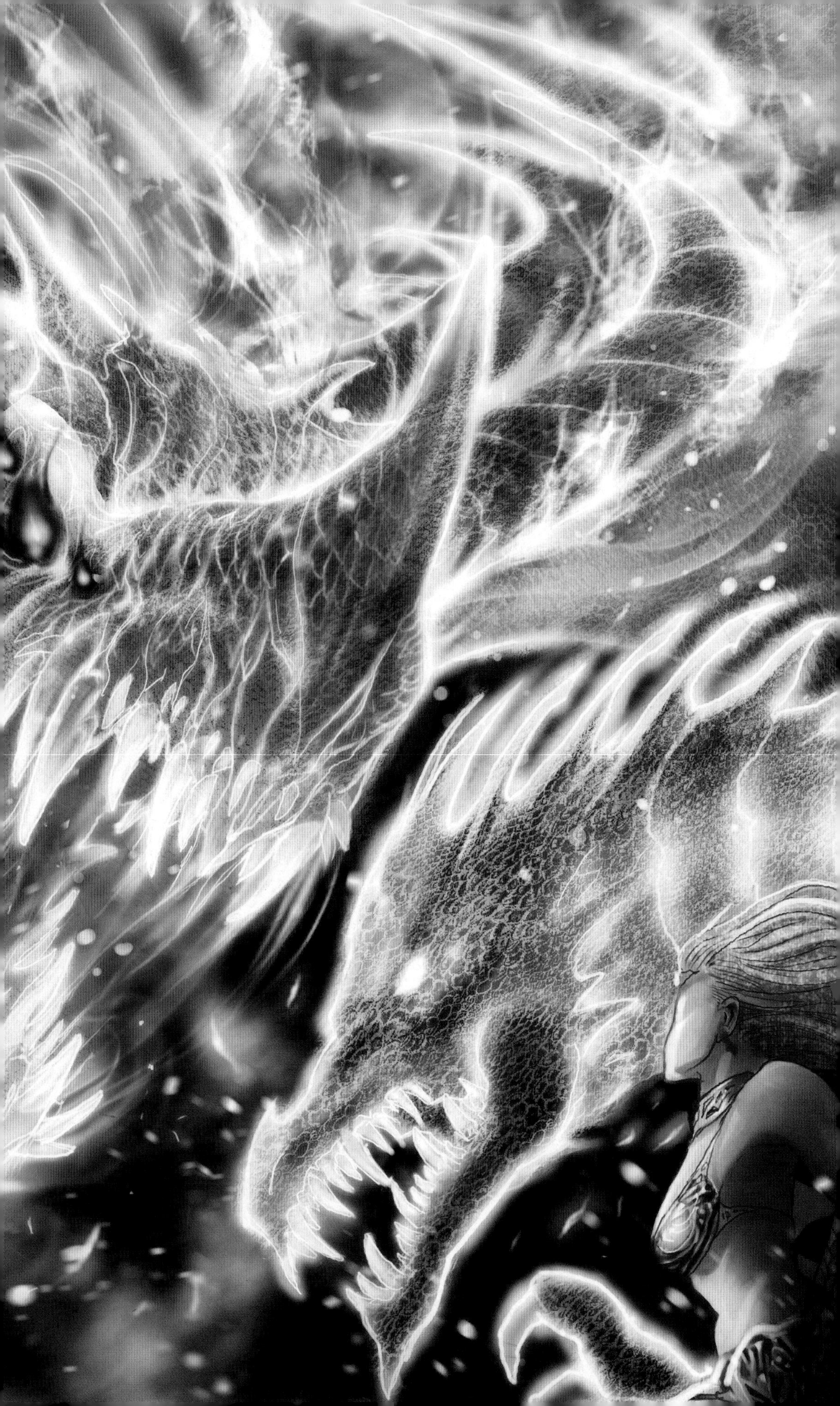

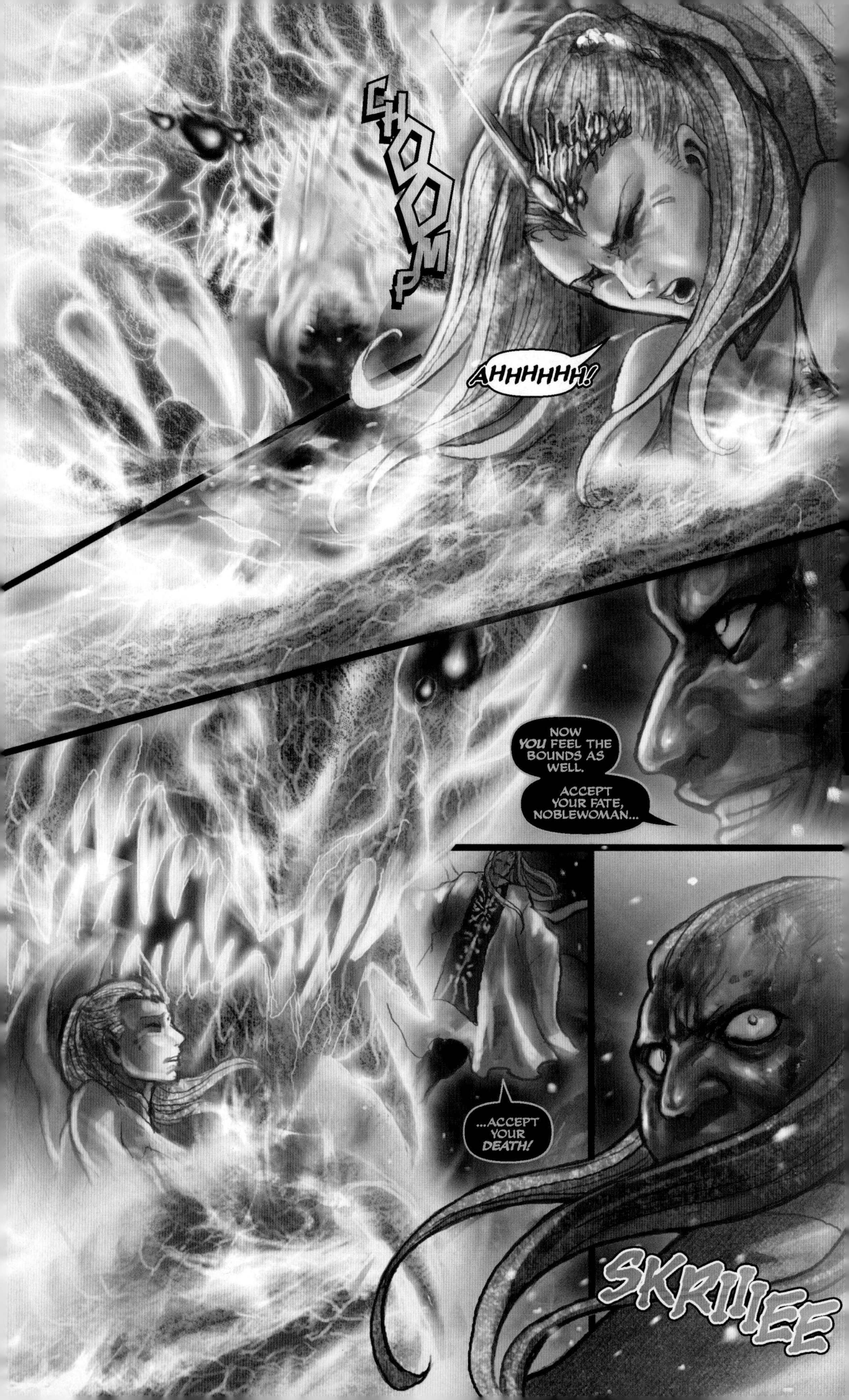
CHOOOMP
AHHHHHH!
NOW YOU FEEL THE BOUNDS AS WELL.
ACCEPT YOUR FATE, NOBLEWOMAN...
...ACCEPT YOUR DEATH!
SKRIIIEE

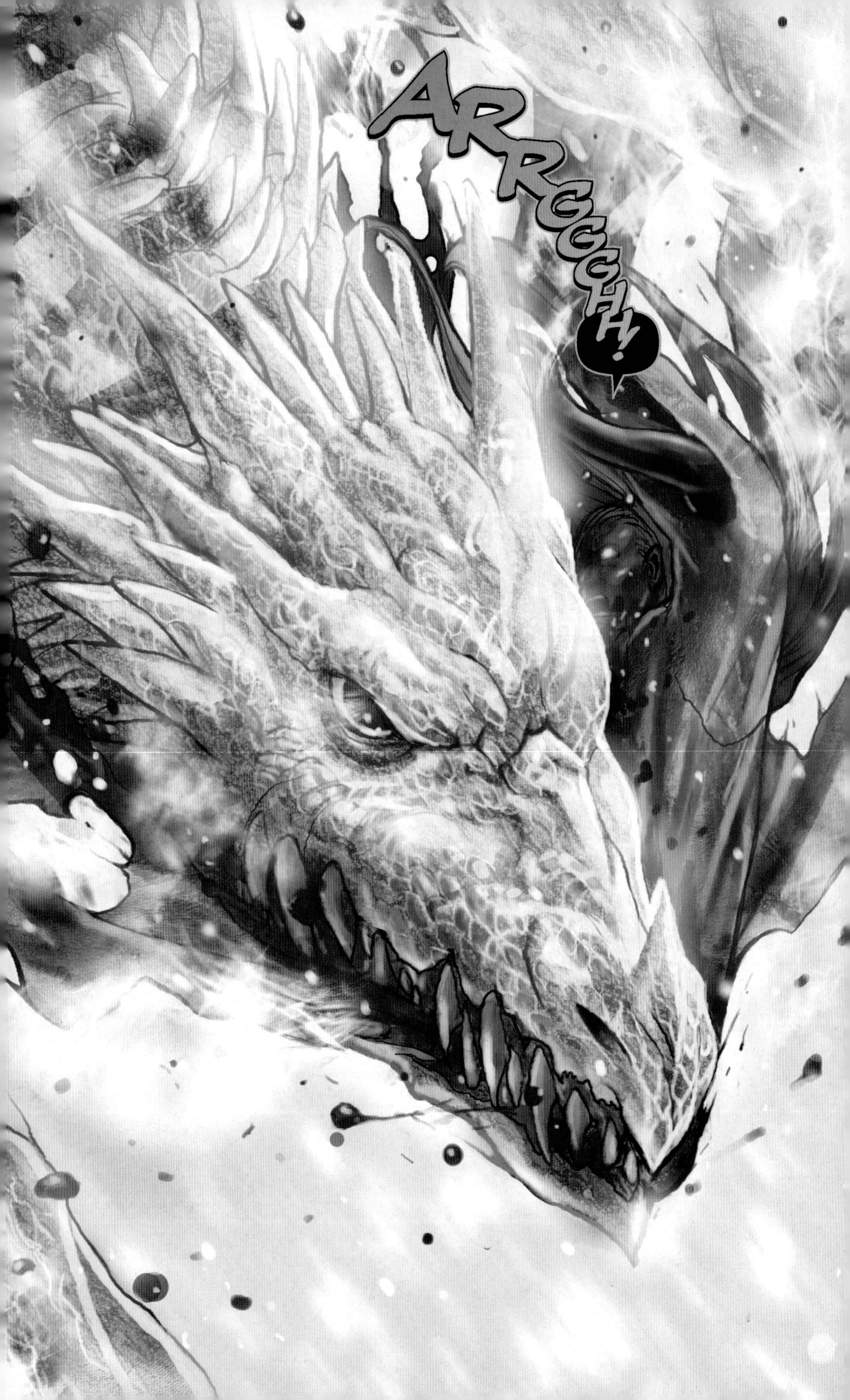
ARRGGGH!

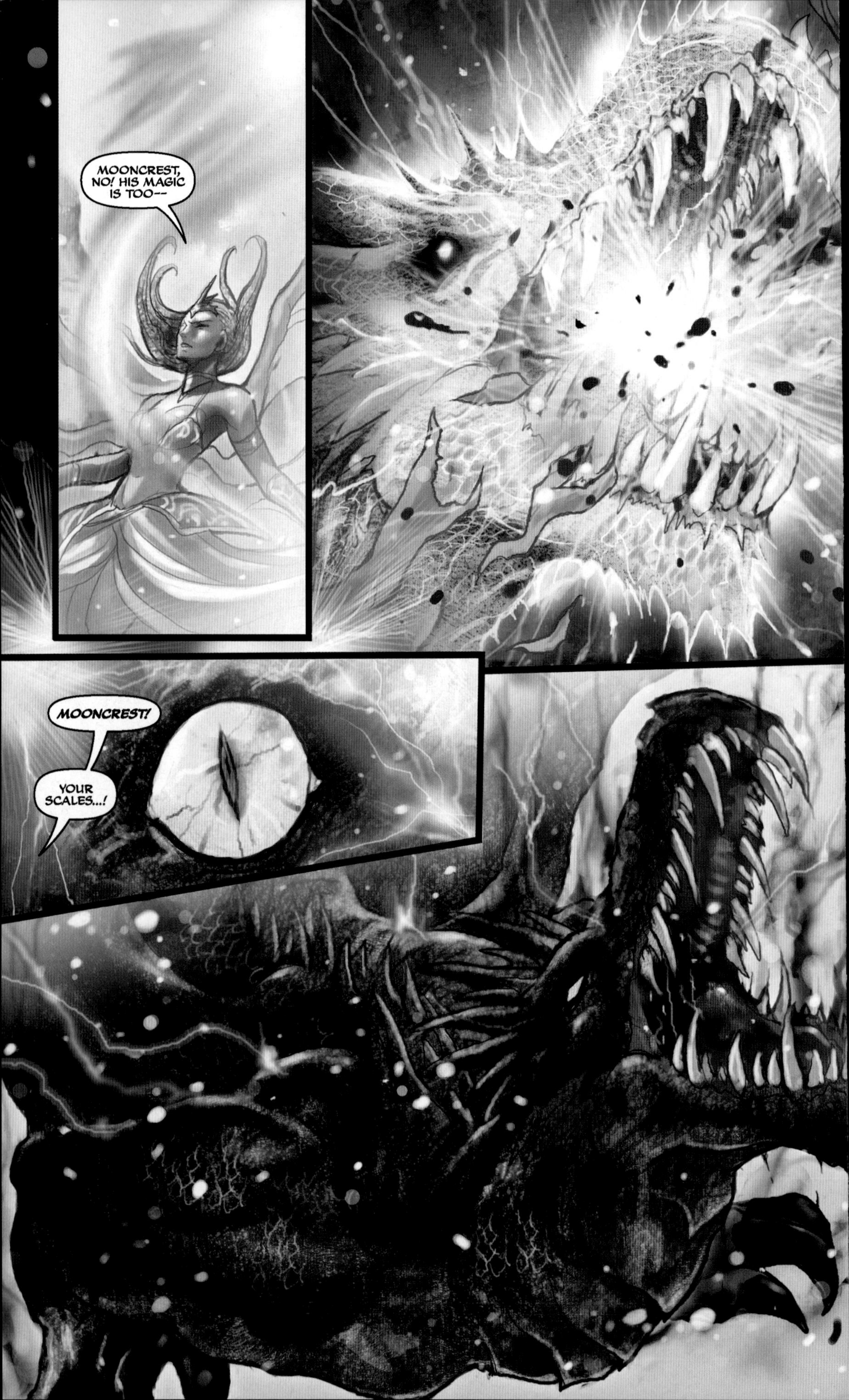
MOONCREST, NO! HIS MAGIC IS TOO--
MOONCREST!
YOUR SCALES...!

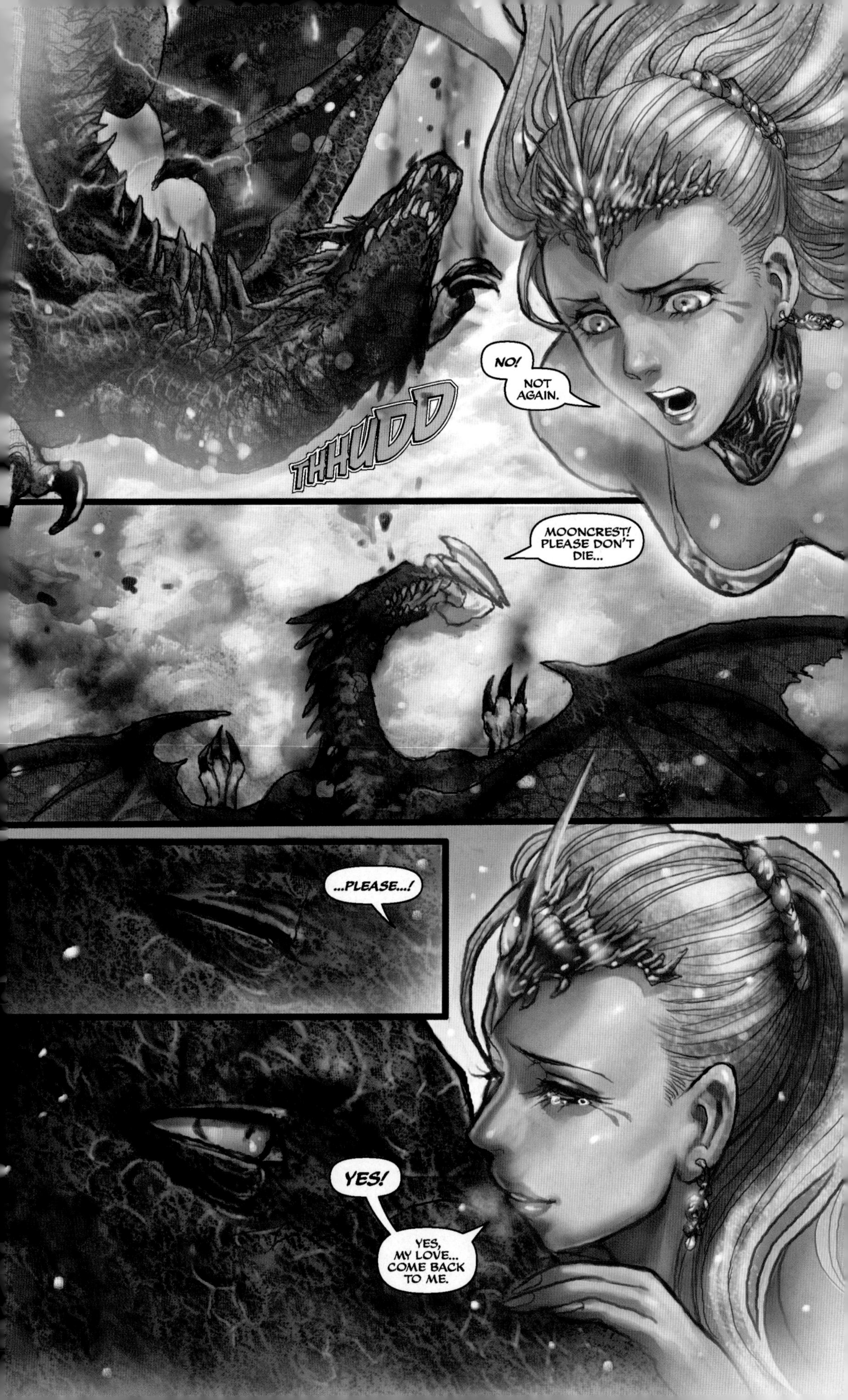
NO!
NOT AGAIN.
THHUDD
MOONCREST! PLEASE DON'T DIE...
...PLEASE...!
YES!
YES, MY LOVE... COME BACK TO ME.

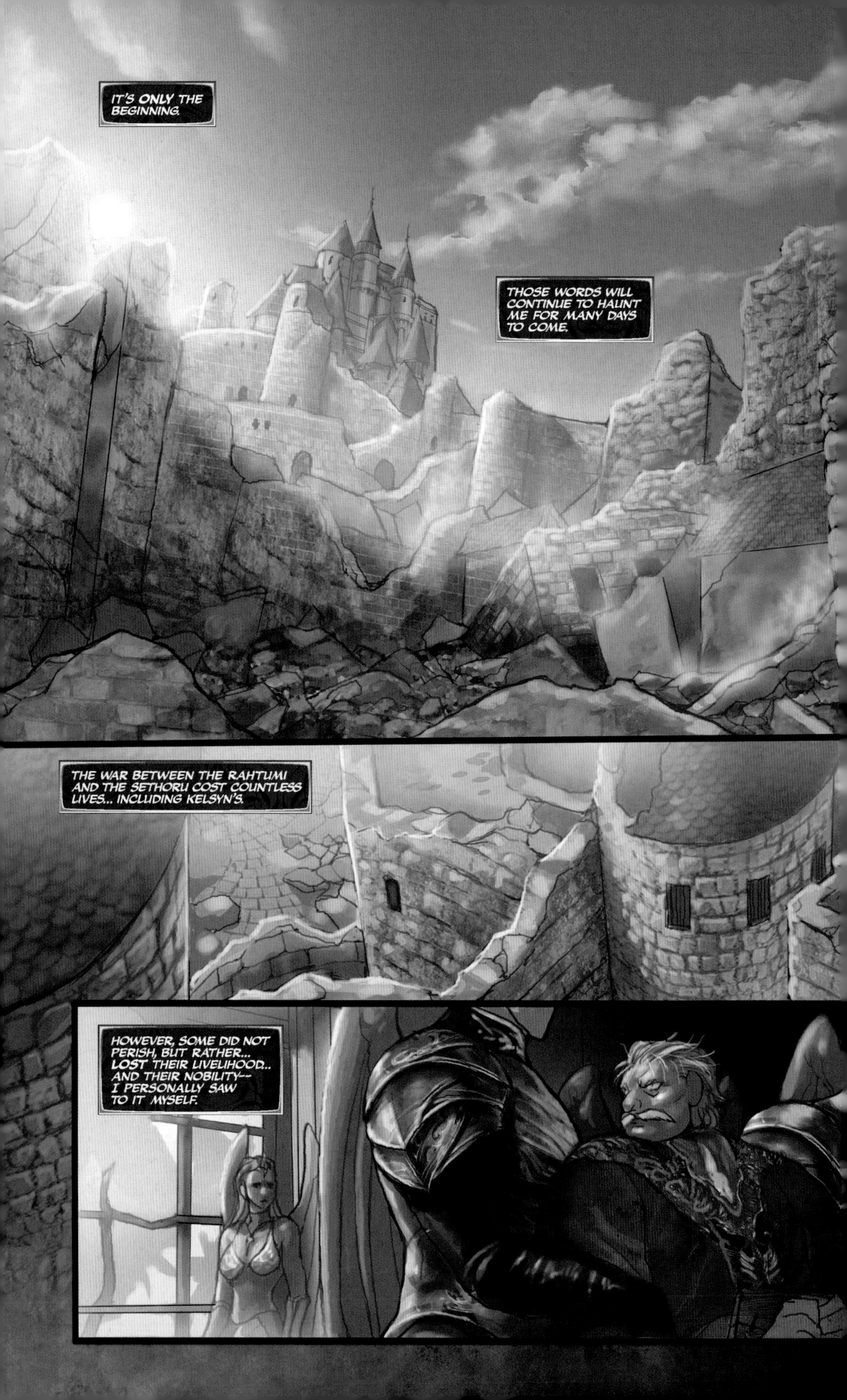
IT'S ONLY THE BEGINNING.
THOSE WORDS WILL CONTINUE TO HAUNT ME FOR MANY DAYS TO COME.
THE WAR BETWEEN THE RAHTUMI AND THE SETHORU COST COUNTLESS LIVES... INCLUDING KELSYN'S.
HOWEVER, SOME DID NOT PERISH, BUT RATHER... LOST THEIR LIVELIHOOD... AND THEIR NOBILITY-- I PERSONALLY SAW TO IT MYSELF.

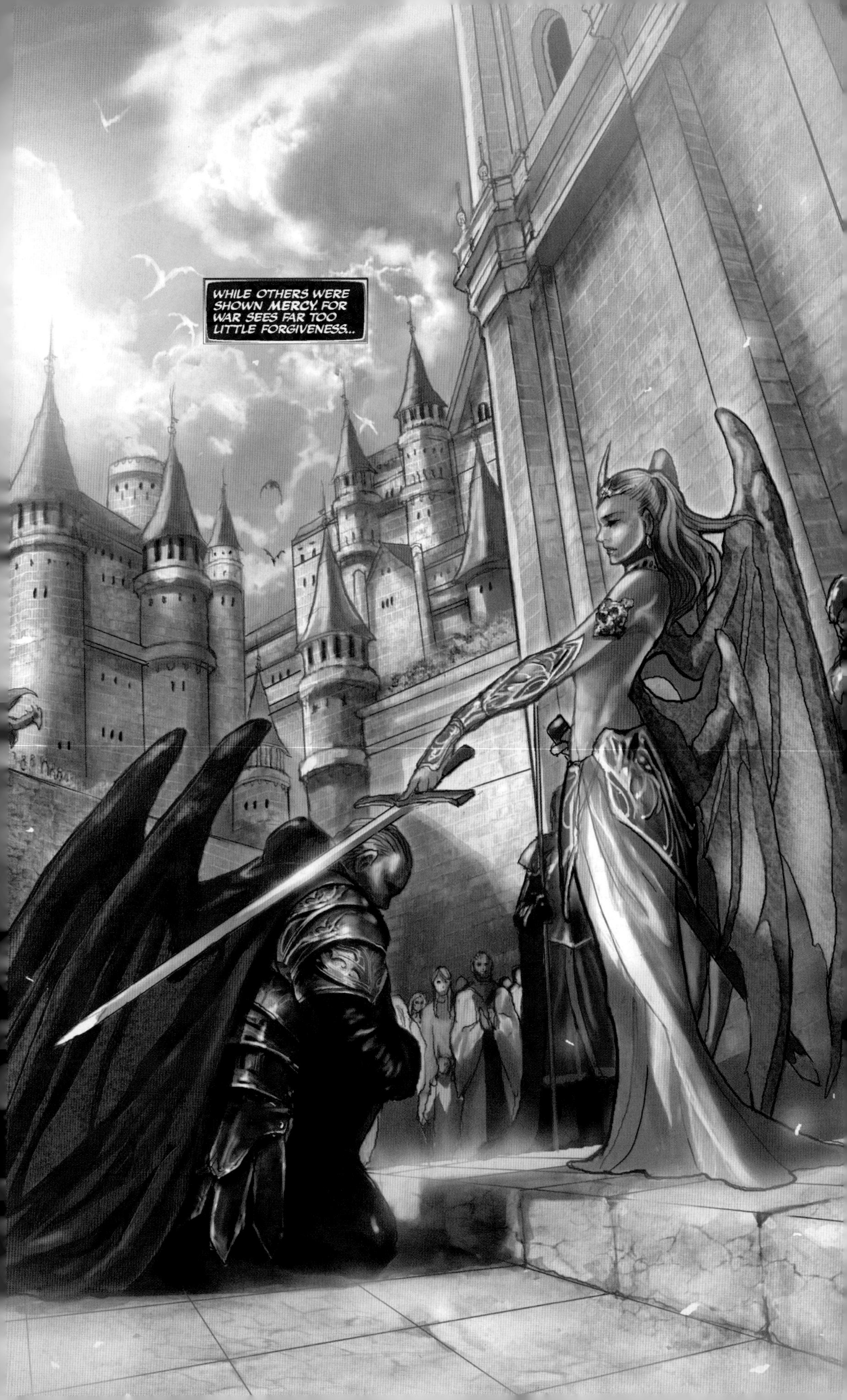
WHILE OTHERS WERE SHOWN MERCY. FOR WAR SEES FAR TOO LITTLE FORGIVENESS...

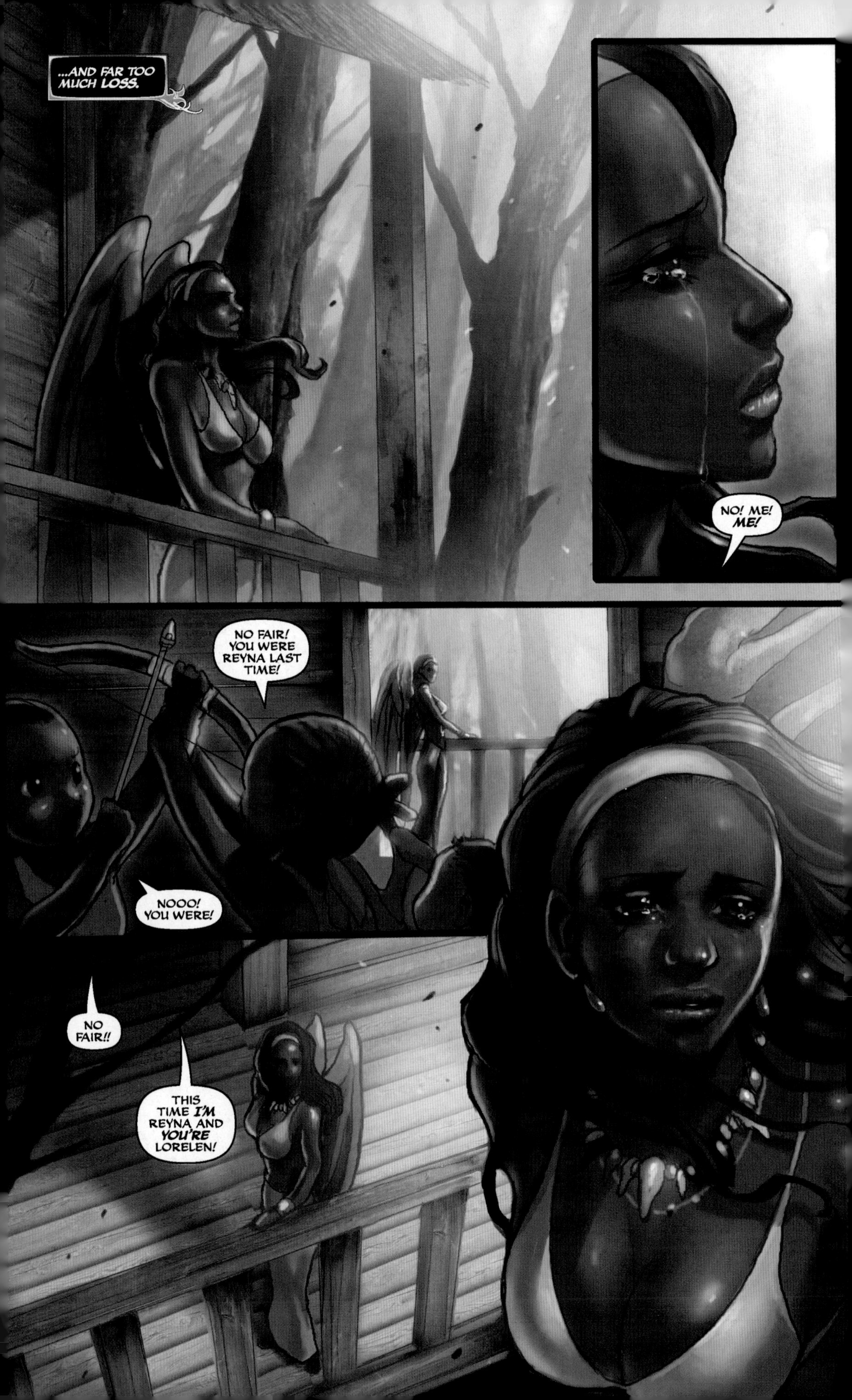
...AND FAR TOO MUCH LOSS.
NO! ME! ME!
NO FAIR! YOU WERE REYNA LAST TIME!
NOOO! YOU WERE!
NO FAIR!!
THIS TIME I'M REYNA AND YOU'RE LORELEN!

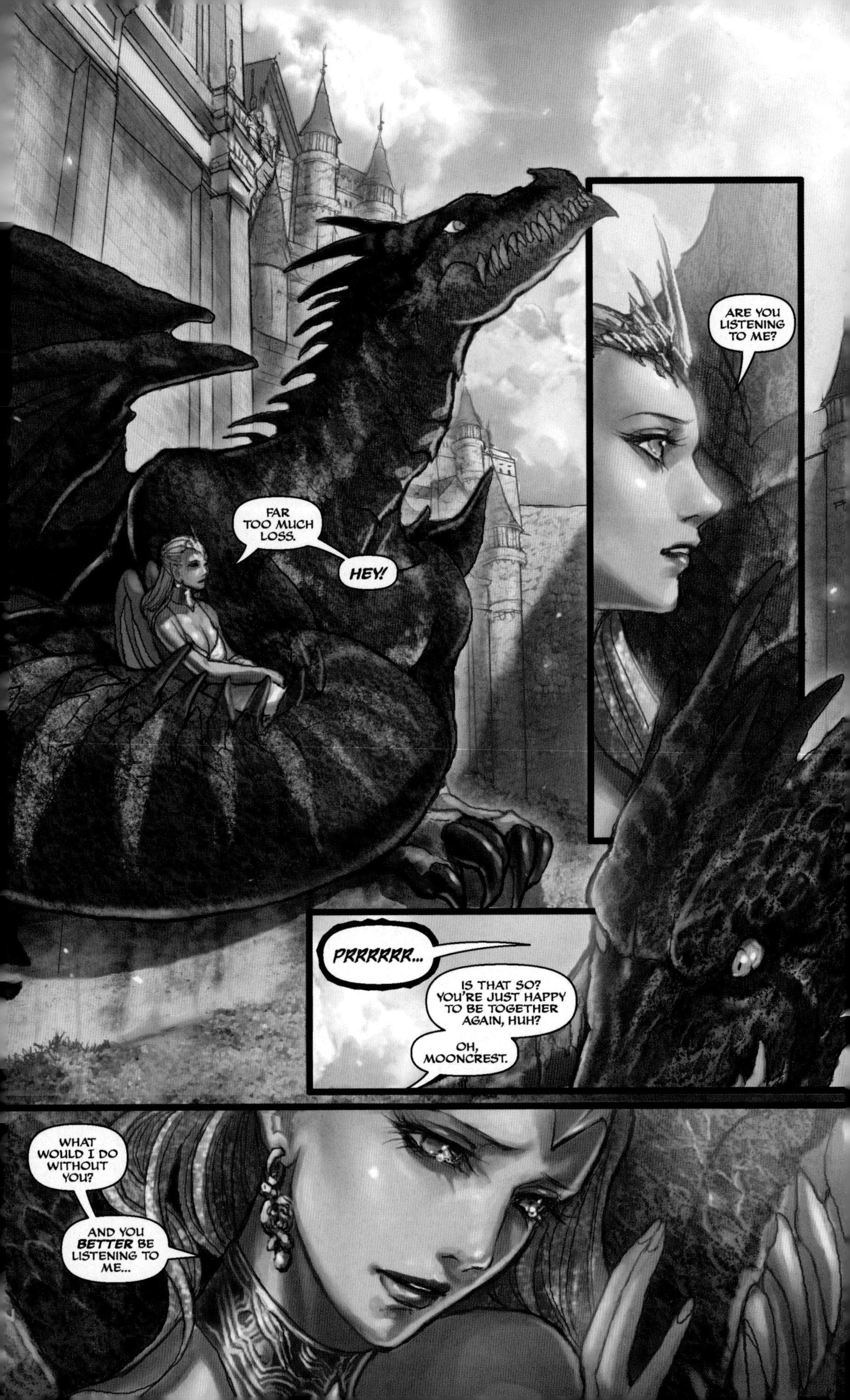
FAR TOO MUCH LOSS.
HEY!
ARE YOU LISTENING TO ME?
PRRRRRR...
IS THAT SO? YOU'RE JUST HAPPY TO BE TOGETHER AGAIN, HUH?
OH, MOONCREST.
WHAT WOULD I DO WITHOUT YOU?
AND YOU *BETTER* BE LISTENING TO ME...

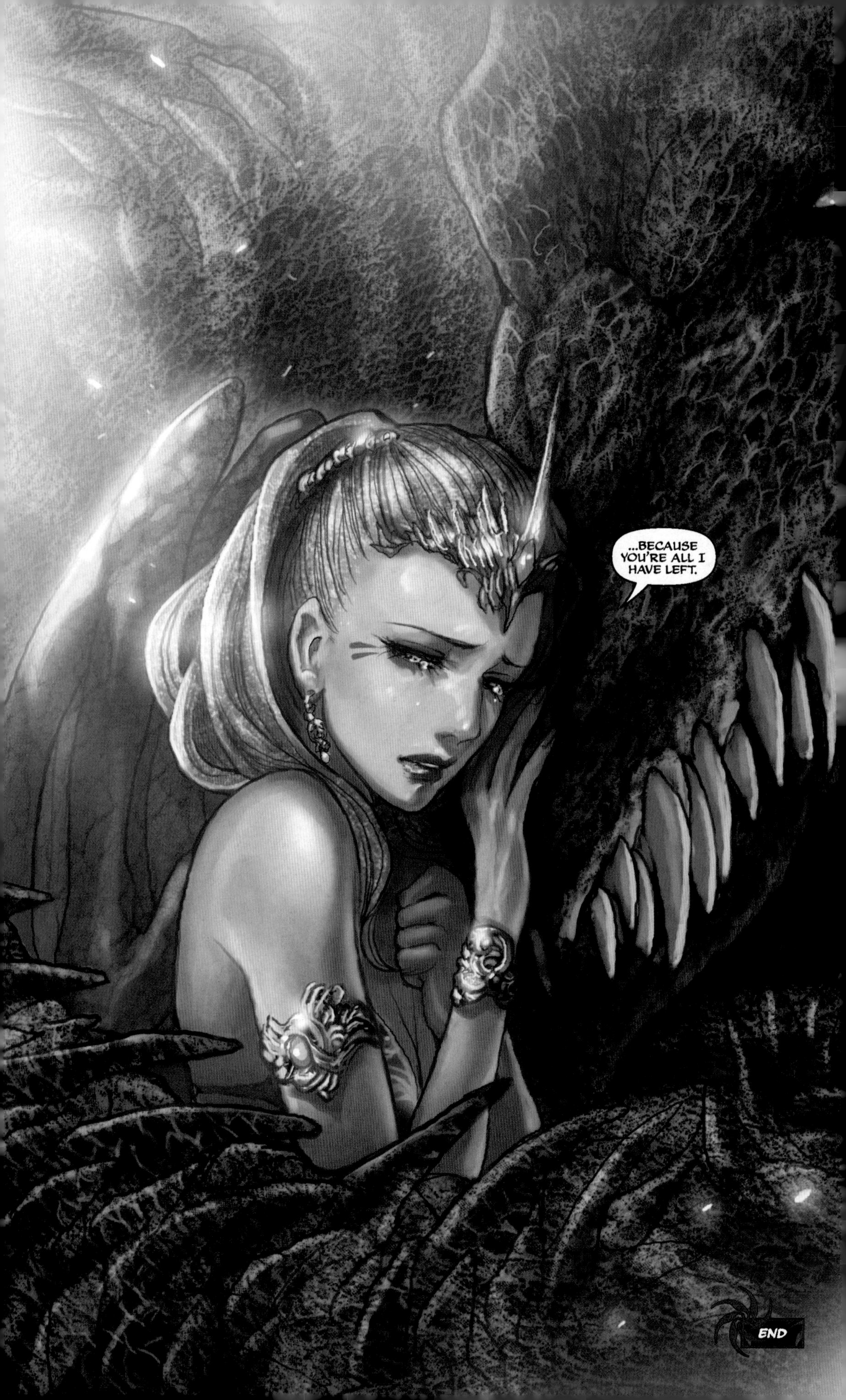
...BECAUSE YOU'RE ALL I HAVE LEFT.
END

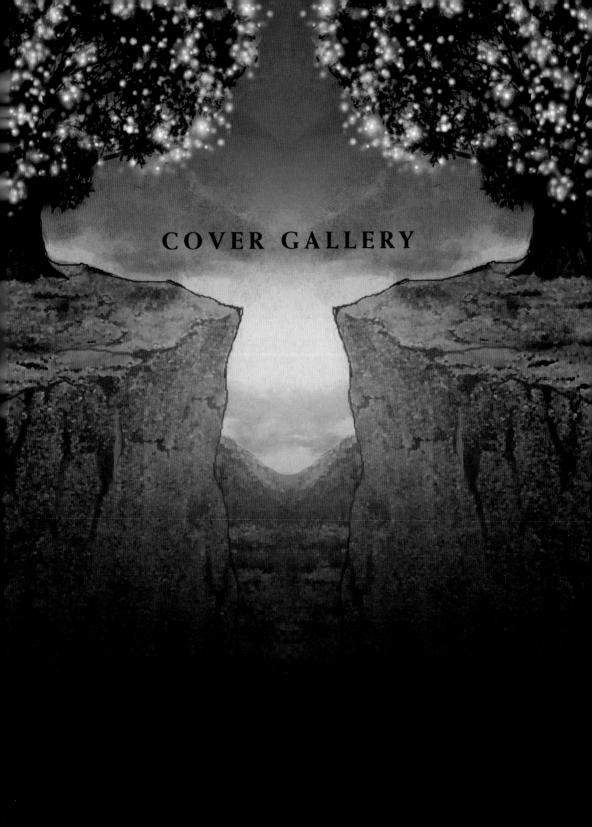

COVER GALLERY

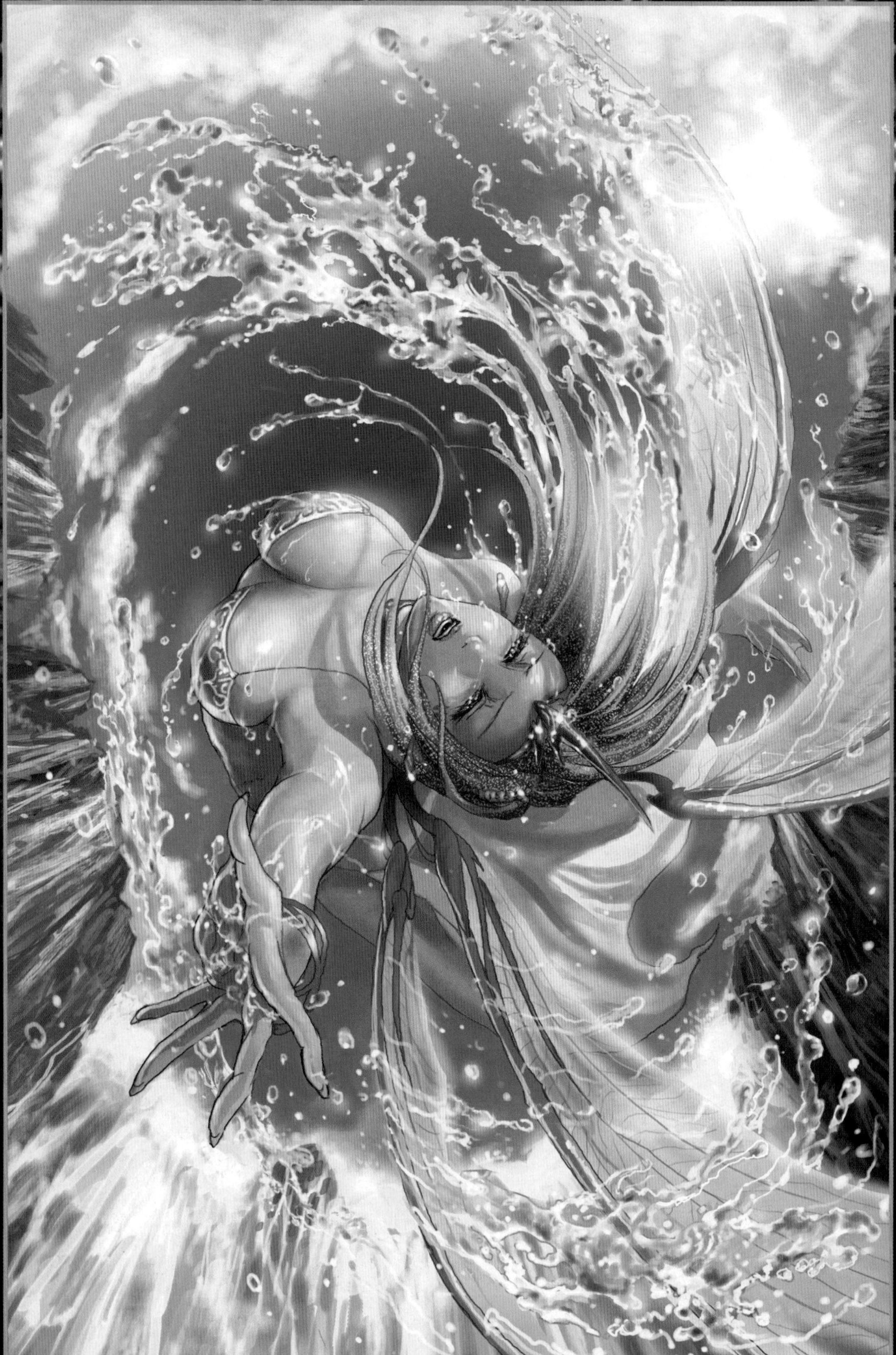

Cover A to
SOULFIRE: SHADOW MAGIC #0 by
• Sana TAKEDA •

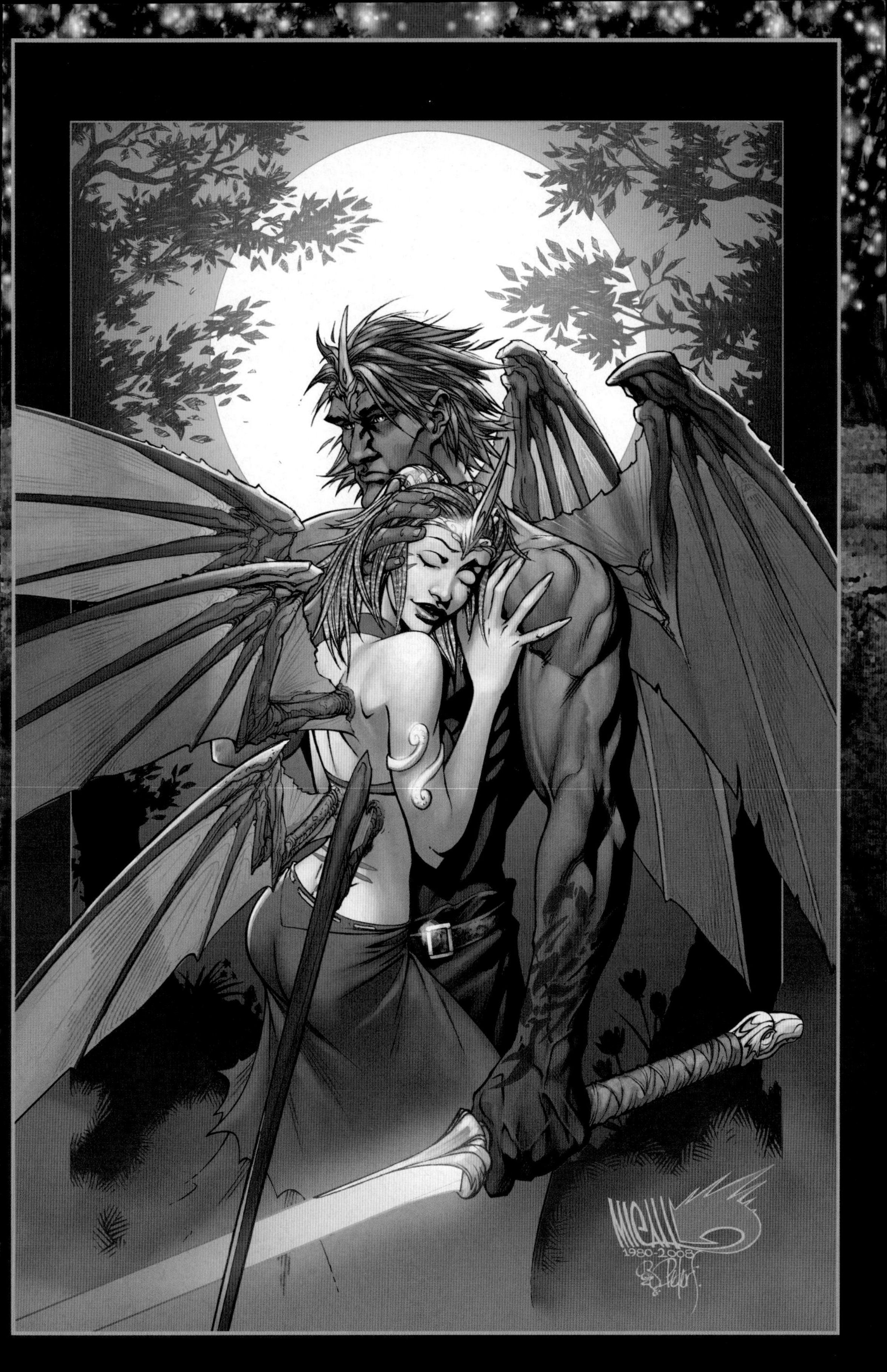
MICAH
1980-2008

Cover B to
SOULFIRÈ: SHADOW MAGIC #0 by
• Micah GUNNELL • Mark ROSLAN • Peter STEIGERWALD •

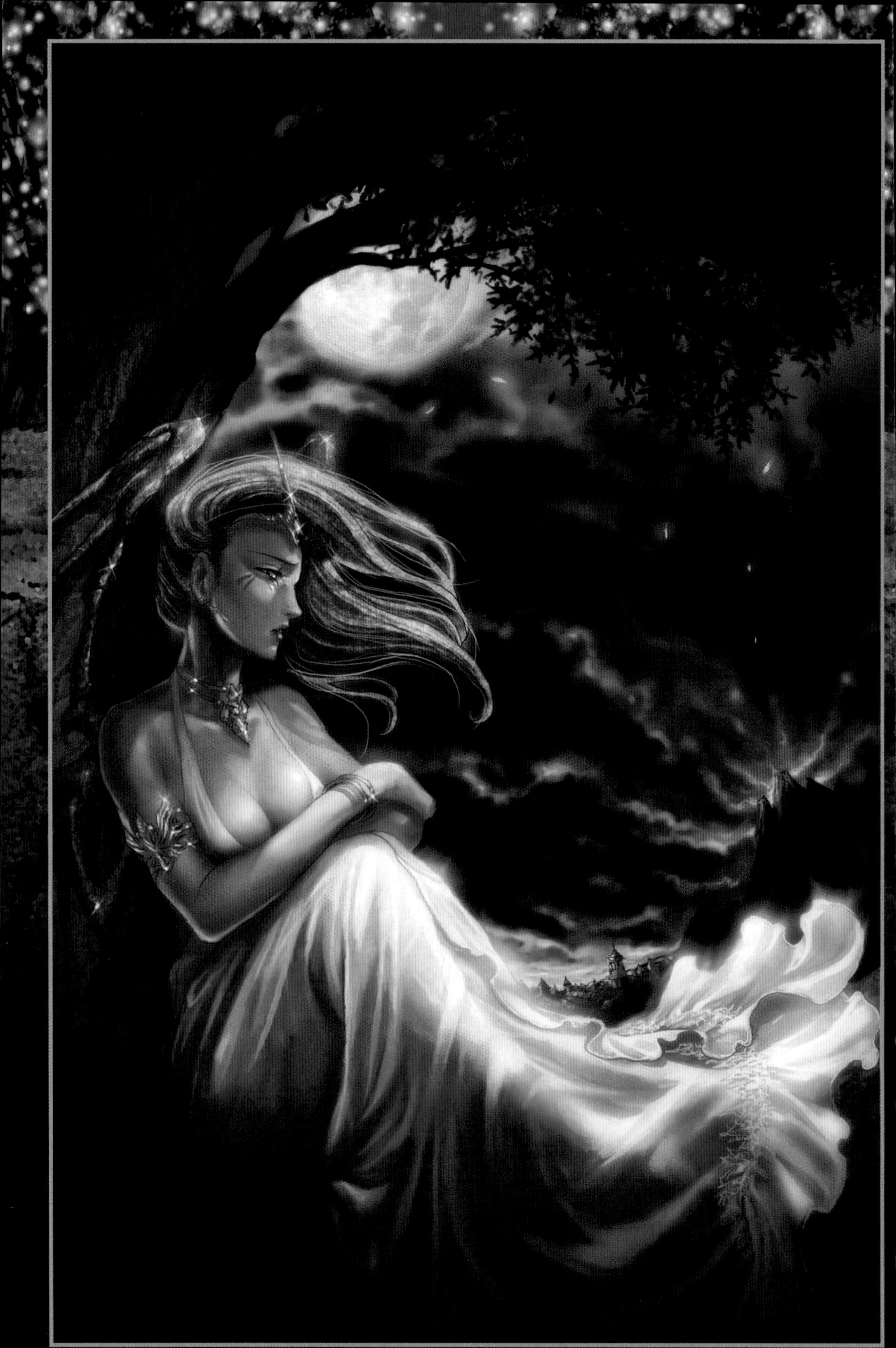

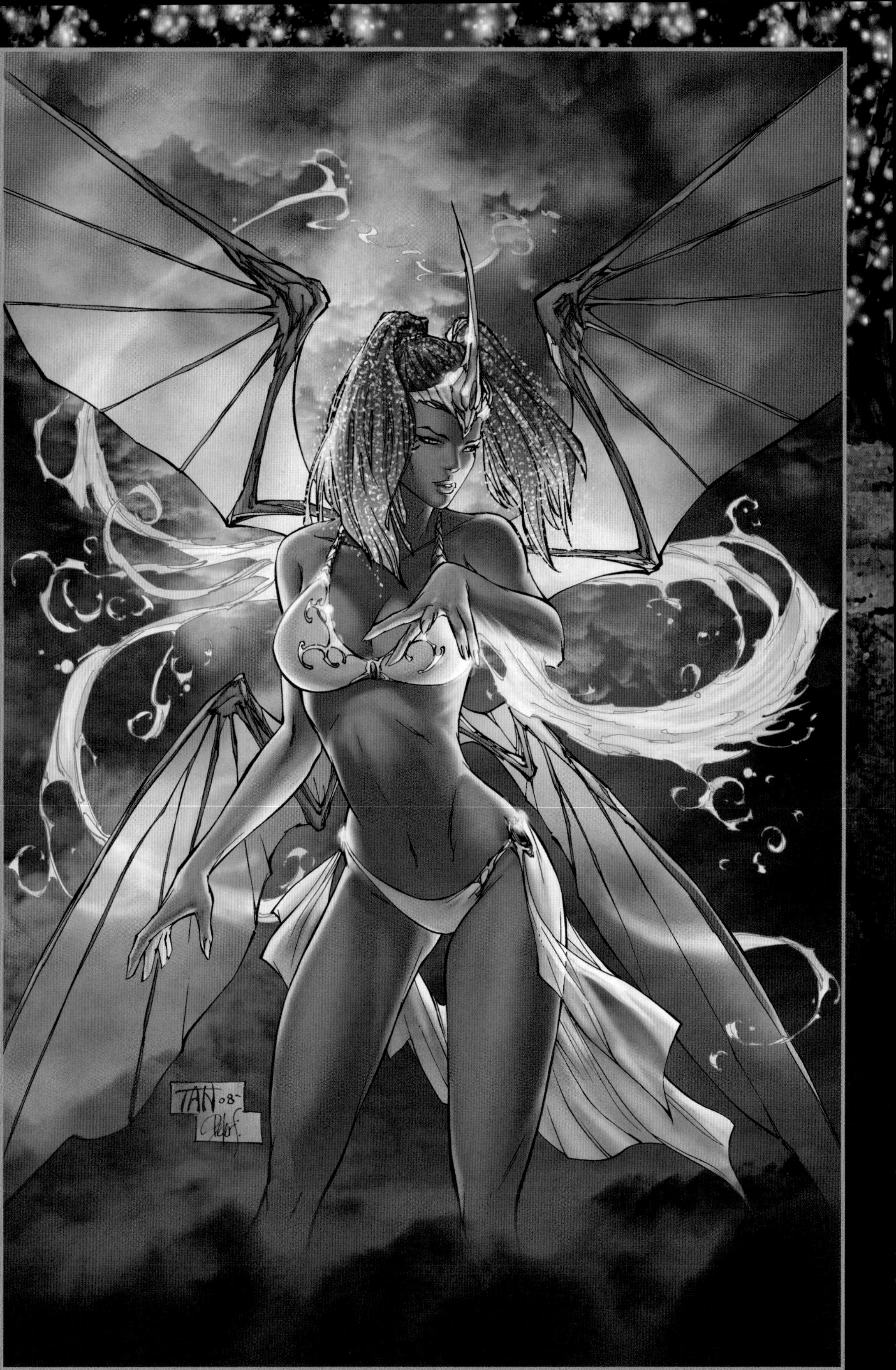
TAN 08

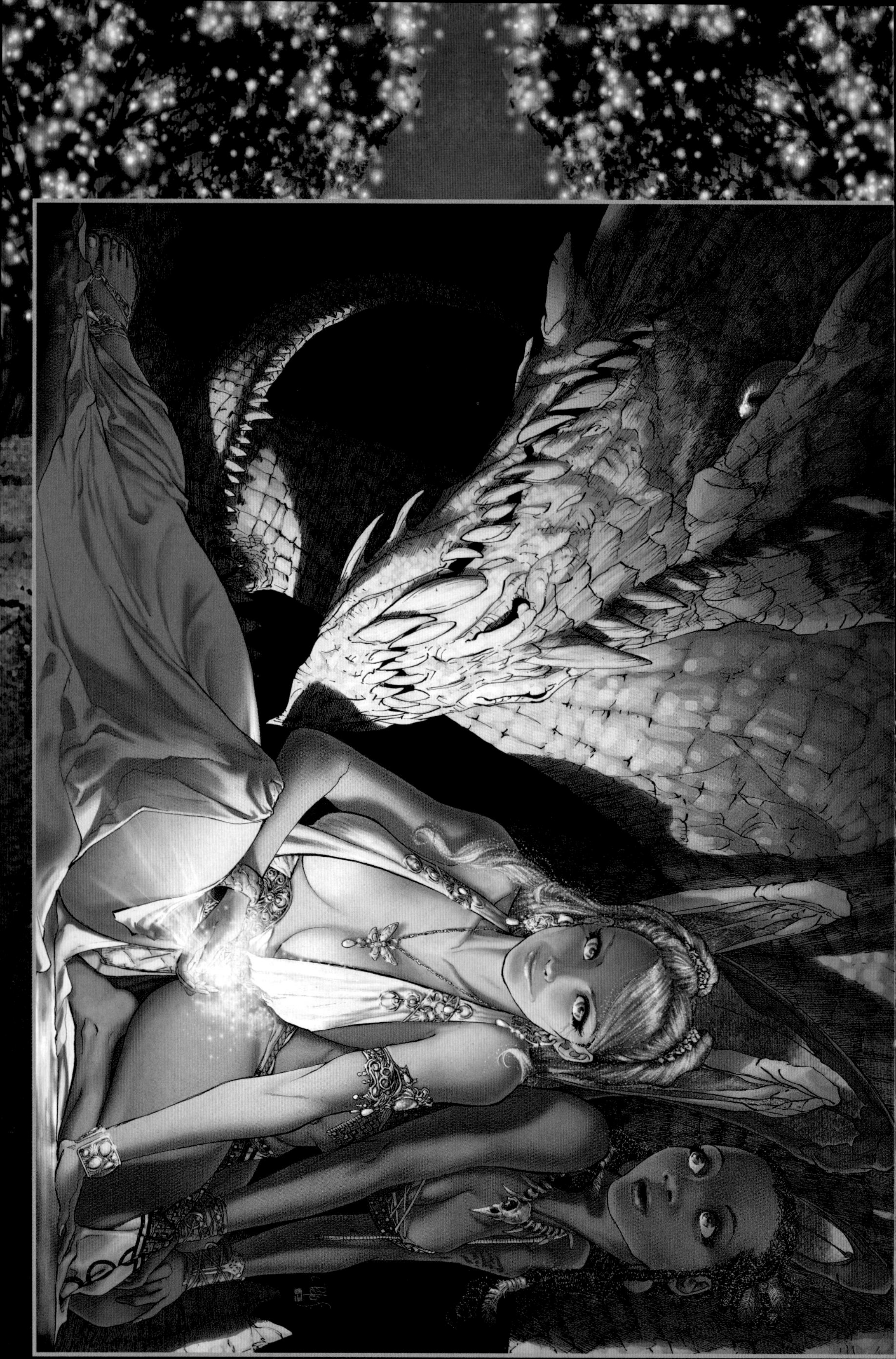

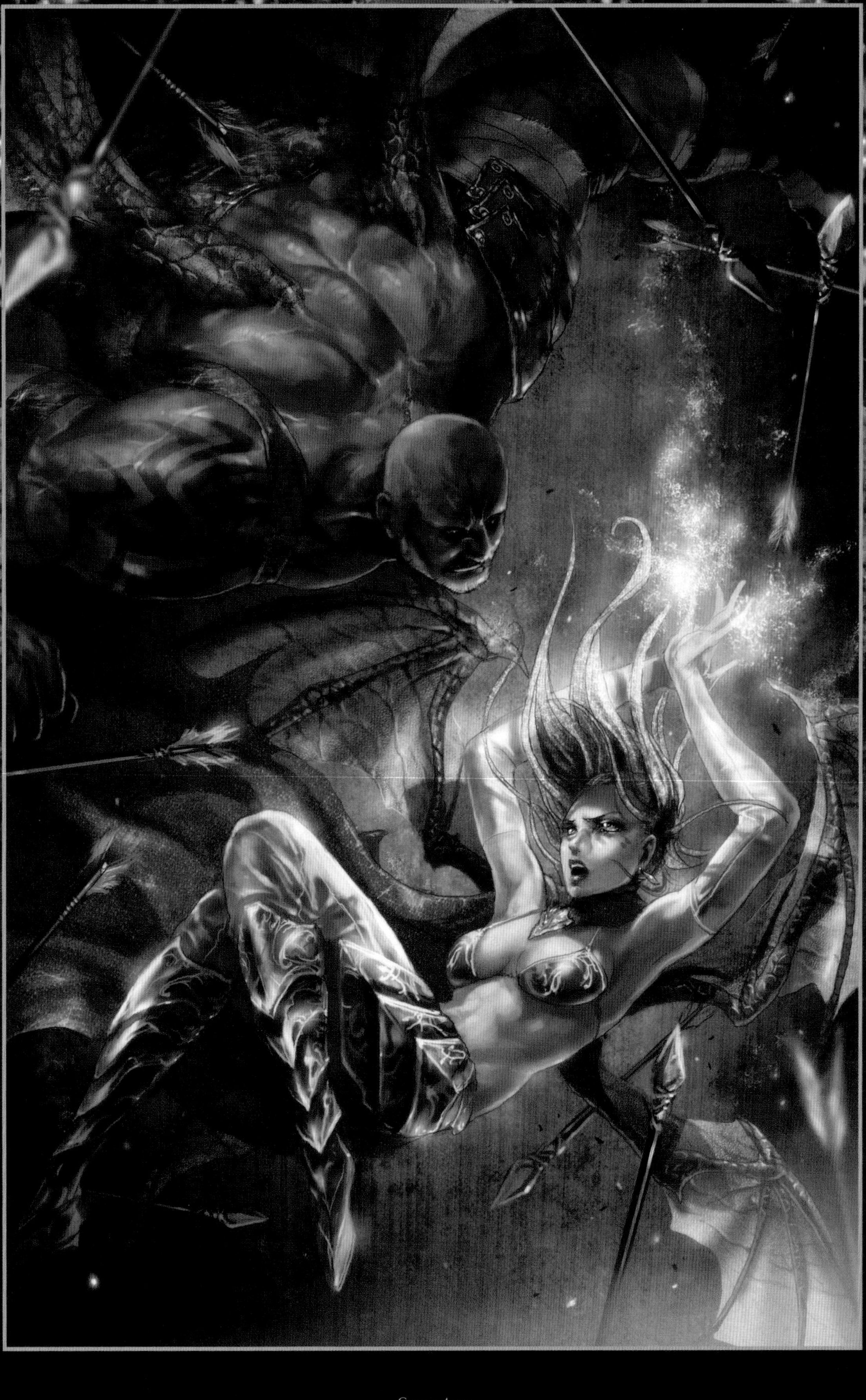

Cover A to
SOULFIRE: SHADOW MAGIC #2 by
• Sana TAKEDA •

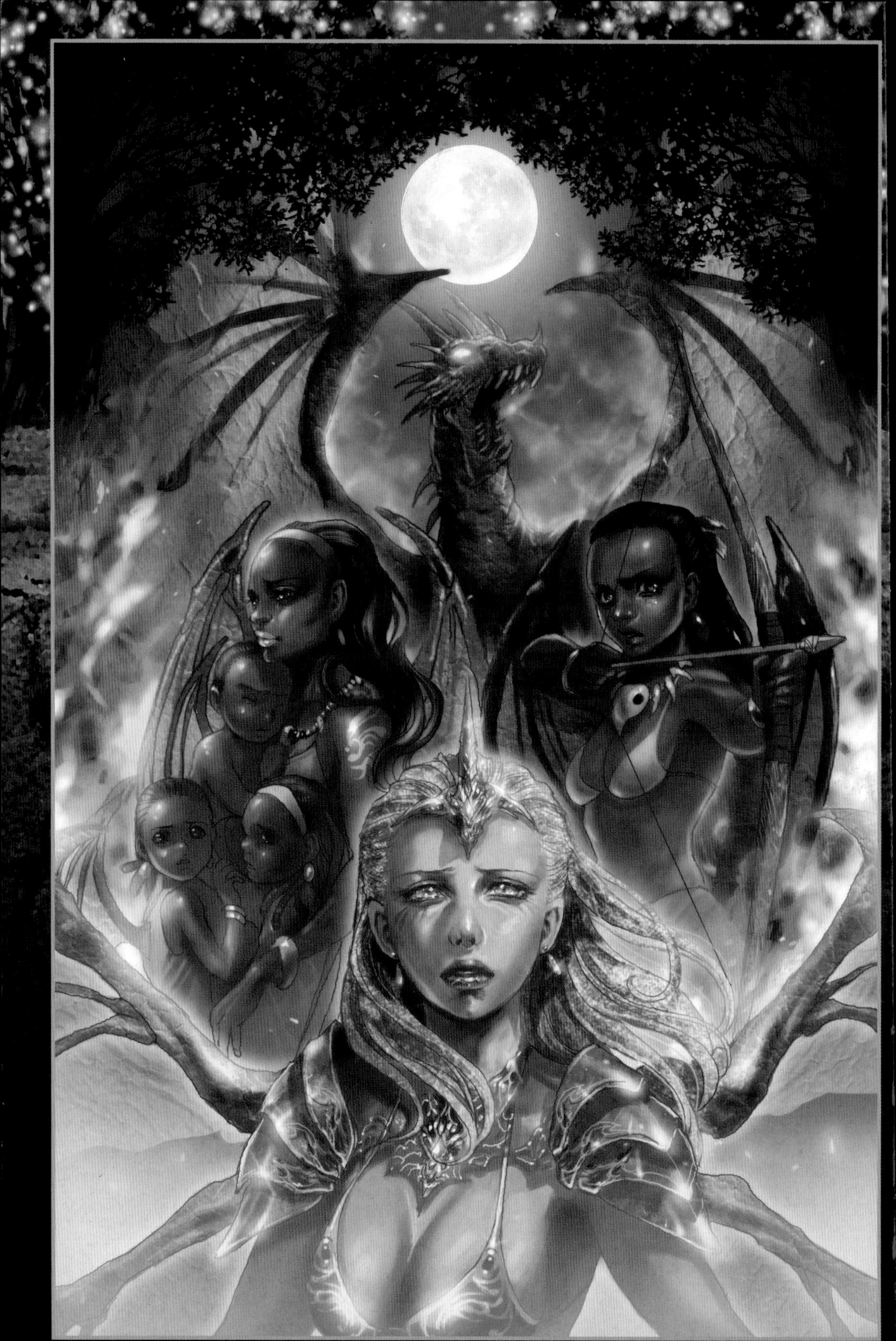

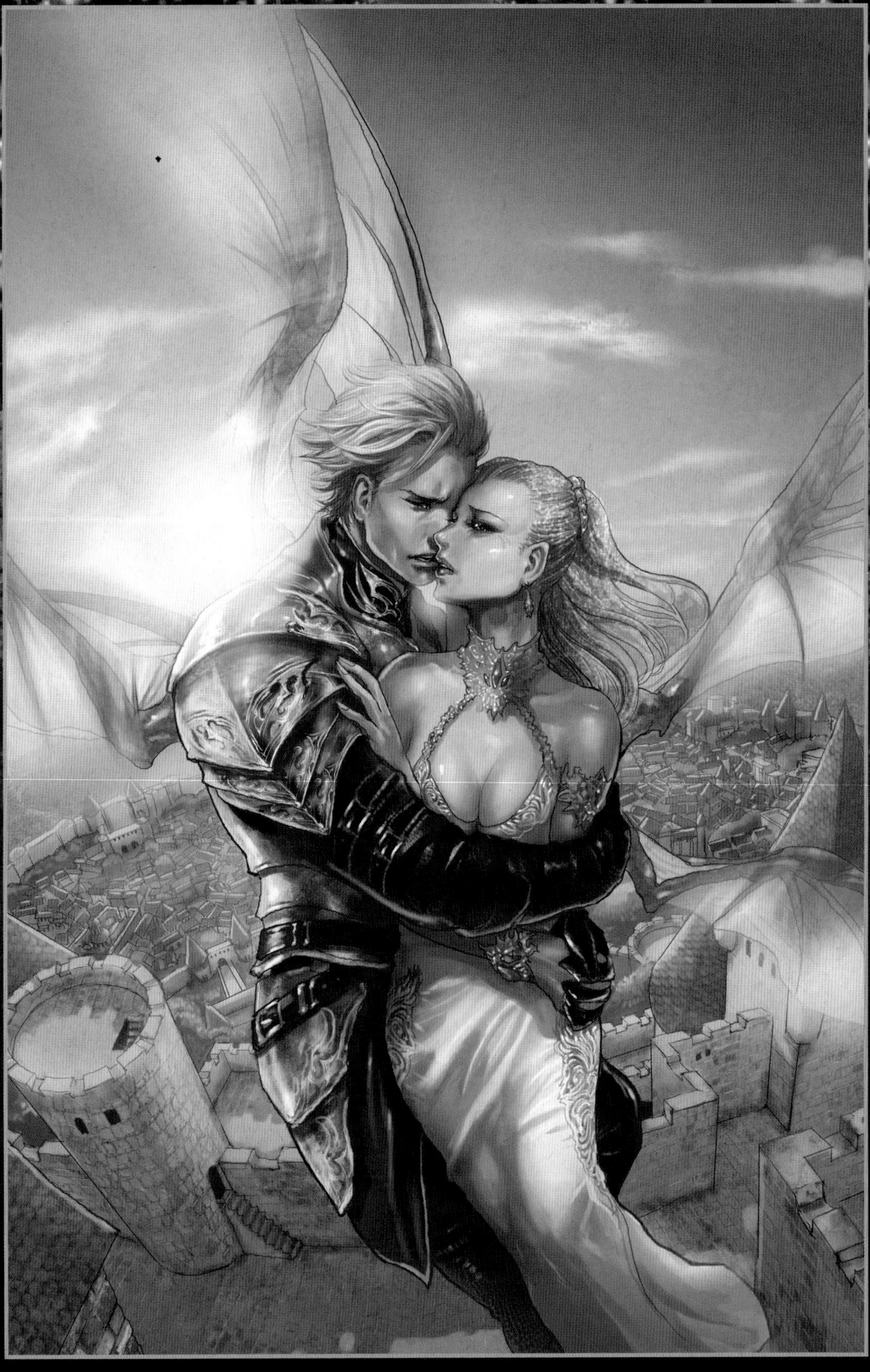

Cover A to
SOULFIRE: SHADOW MAGIC #4 by
• Sana TAKEDA •

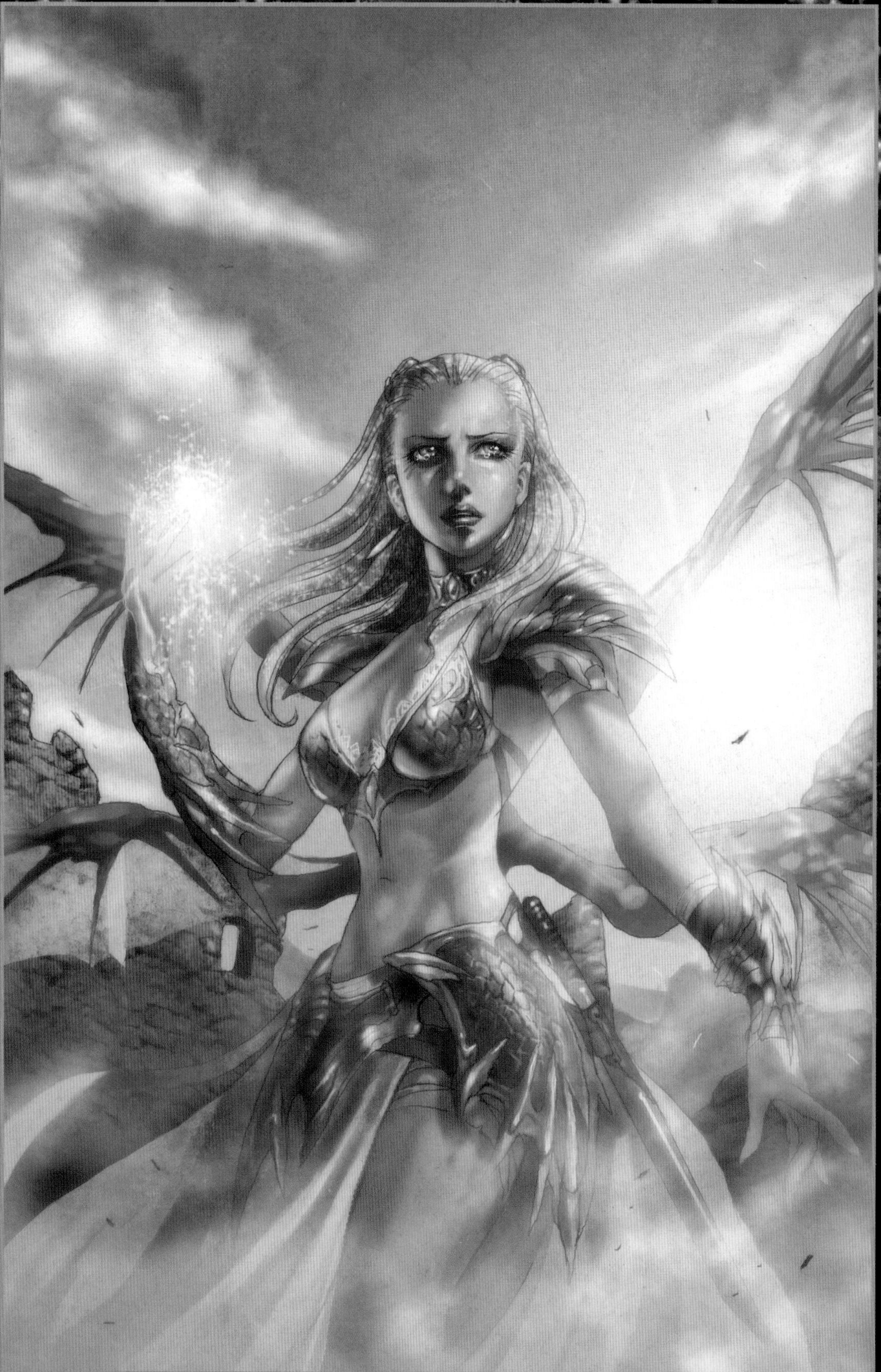

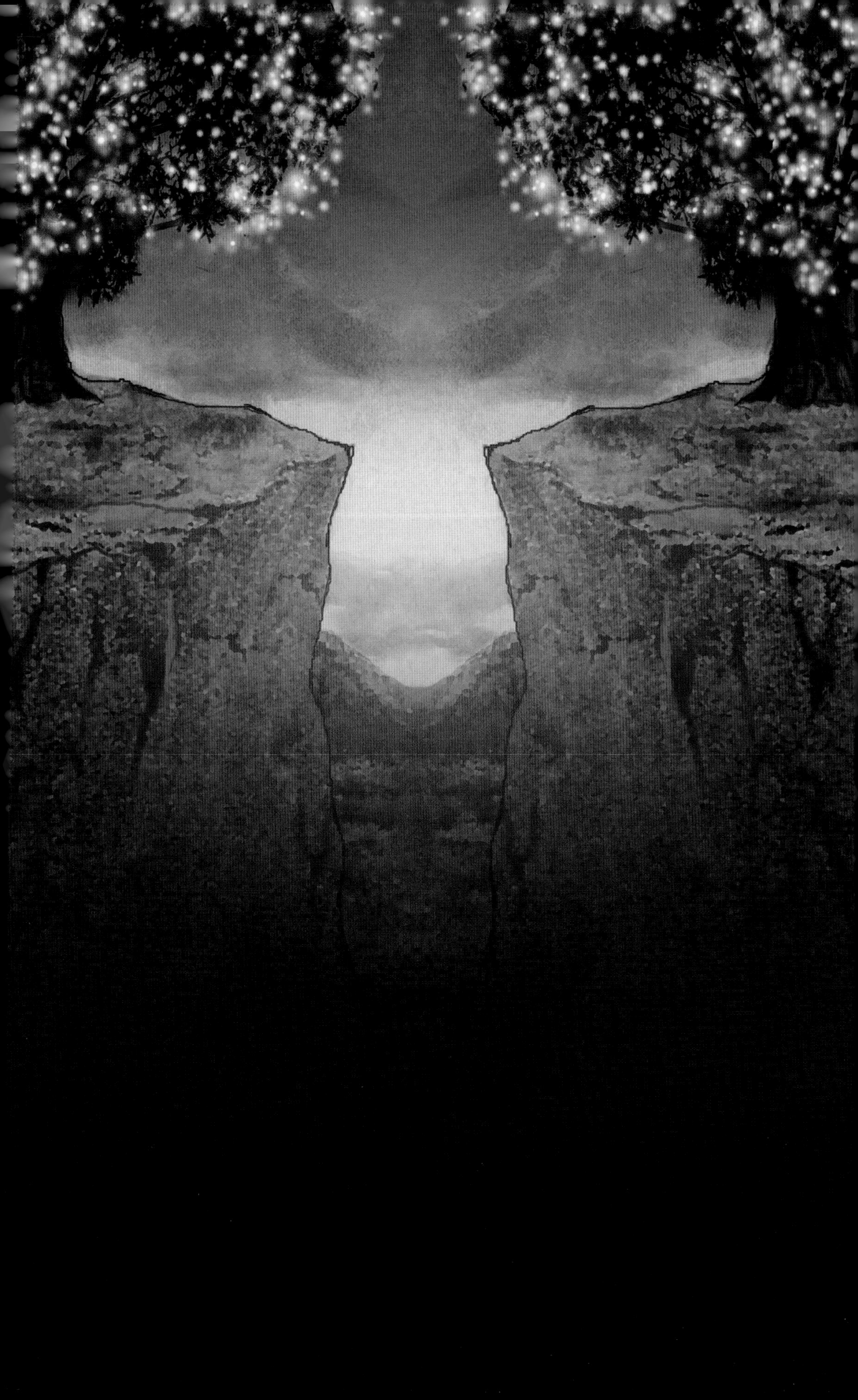

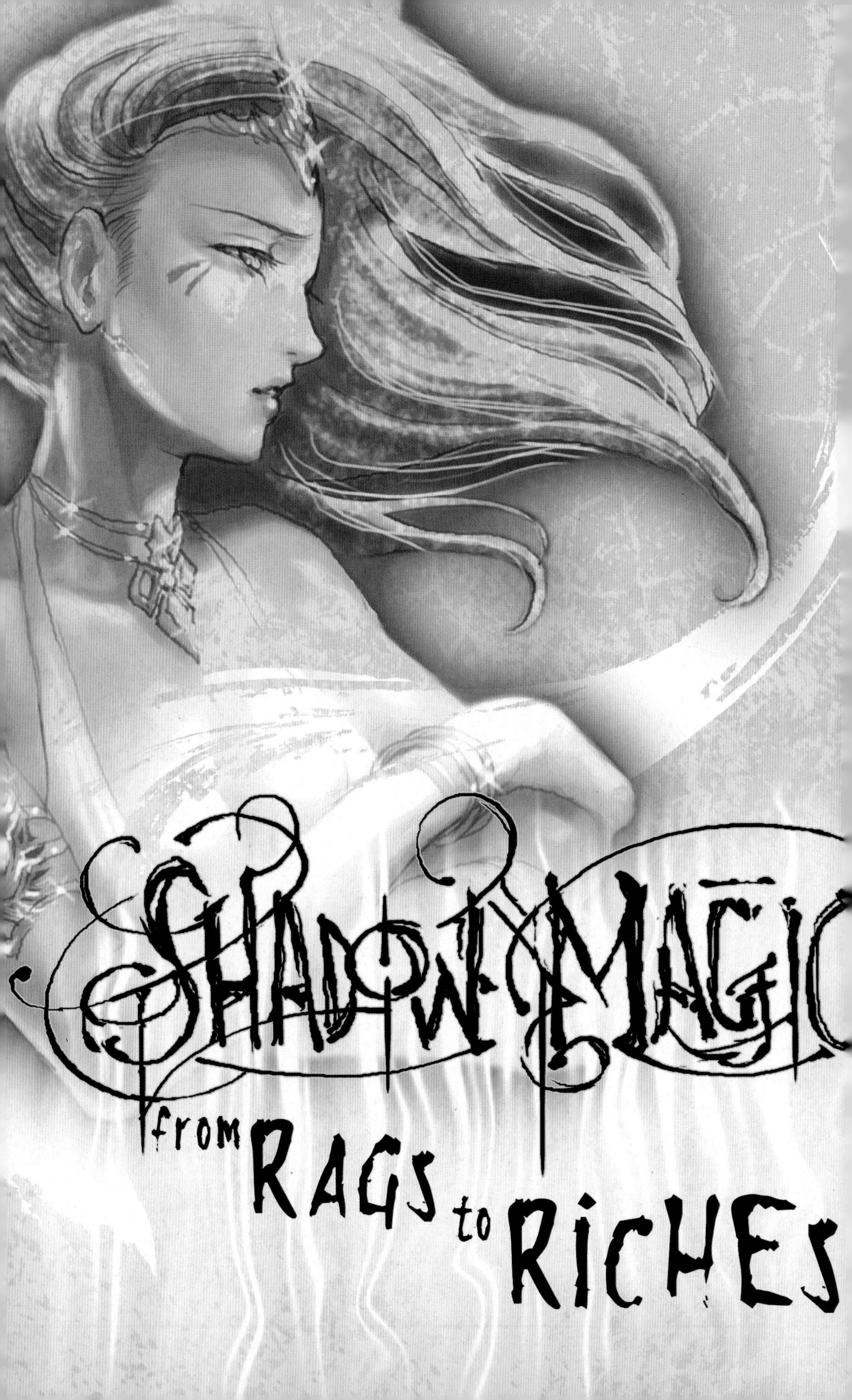
SHADOW MAGIC
from RAGS to RICHES

With the wide assortment of characters in Shadow Magic spanning across contrasting kingdoms, it was important to painstakingly develop each of their roles in the narrative. Everyone from dragon keepers to kings were given equal measures of focus during their creation, and each a visual appearance based upon their respective roots. Here's a special look at just some of the characters you'll find within the pages of **Soulfire: Shadow Magic.**

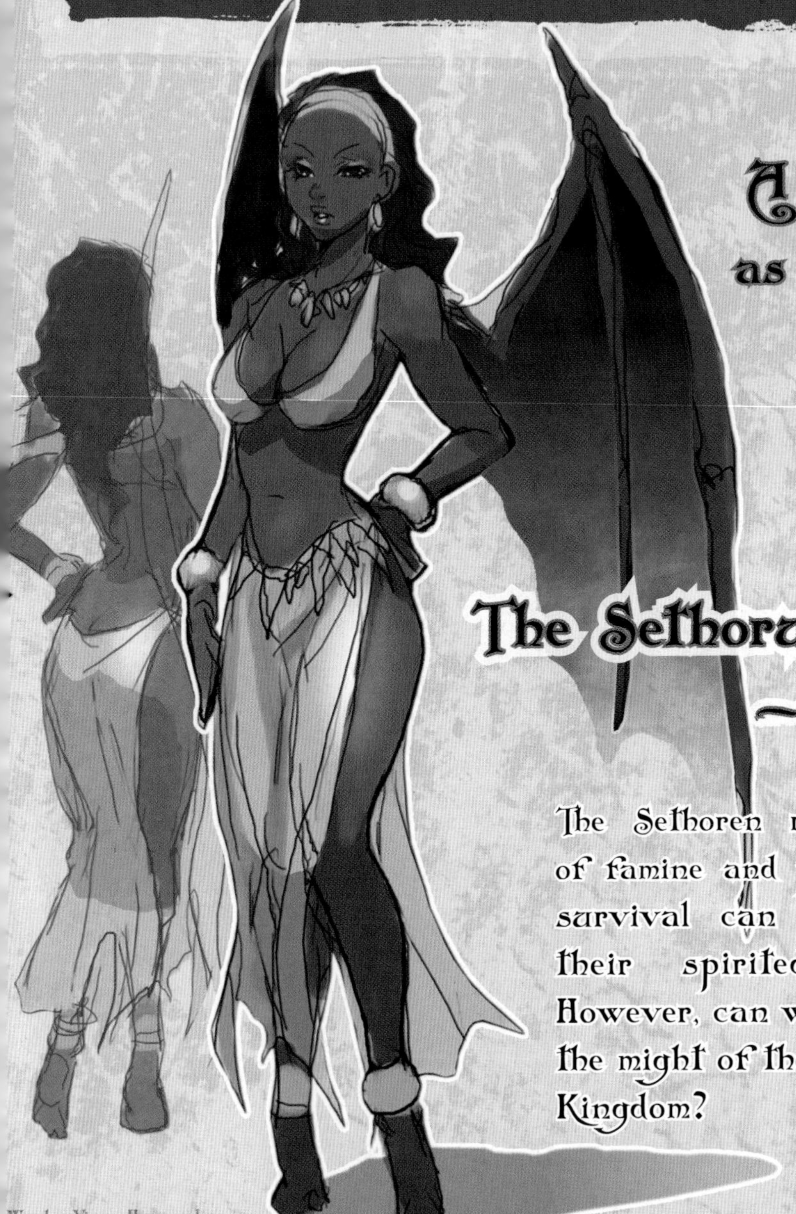

A story is only as strong as its characters...

The Sethora Villagers ~ LORELEN

The Sethoren race is the victim of famine and poverty, but their survival can be attributed to their spirited determination. However, can willpower overcome the might of the ruling Empyrean Kingdom?

Words: Vince Hernandez
Illustrations: Sana Takeda
Layout Design: Mark "Roz" Roslan

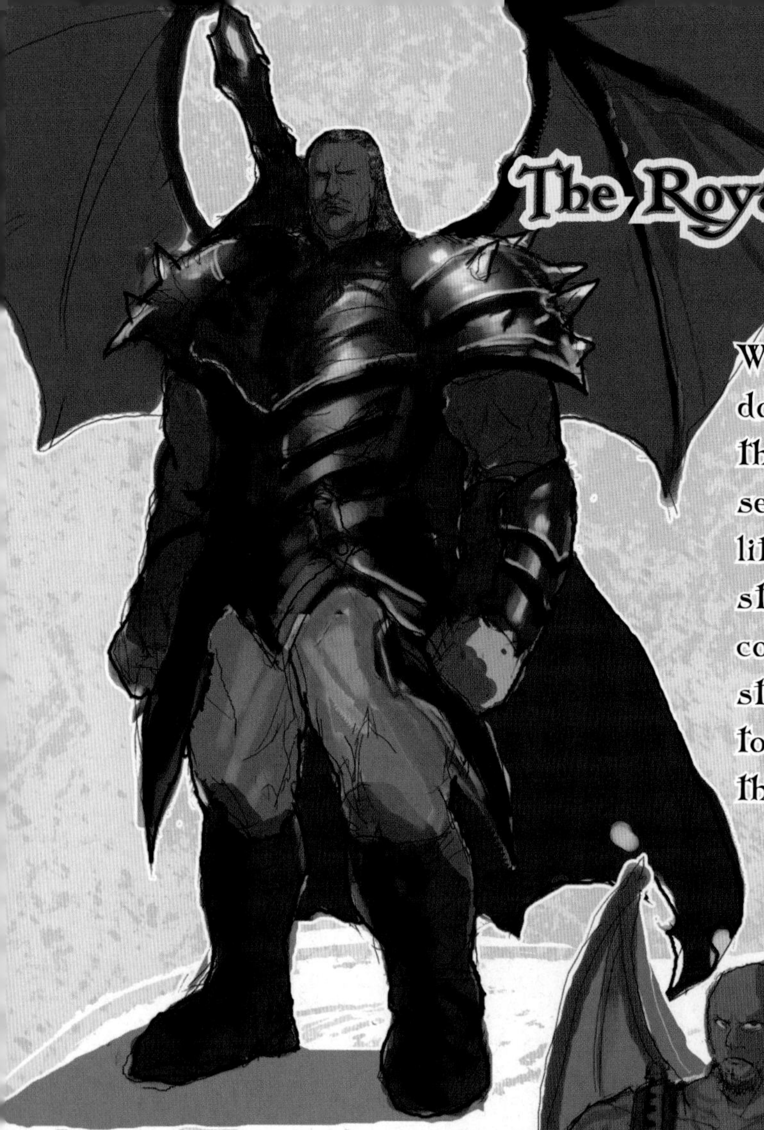

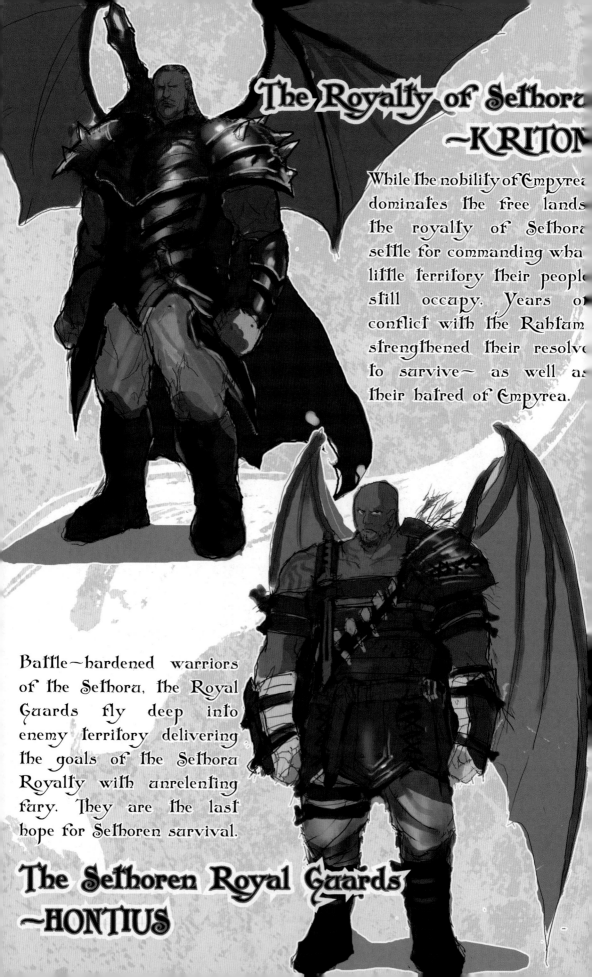

The Royalty of Sethora ~KRITON

While the nobility of Empyrea dominates the free lands the royalty of Sethora settle for commanding wha little territory their peopl still occupy. Years o conflict with the Rahtum strengthened their resolv to survive~ as well a their hatred of Empyrea.

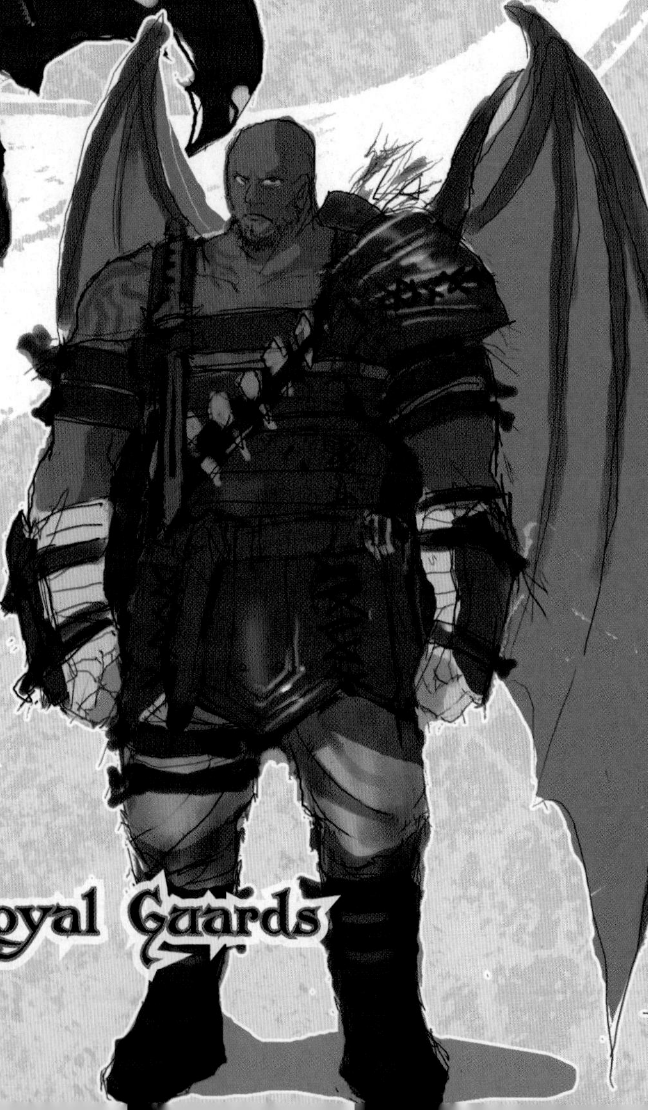

Battle~hardened warriors of the Sethora, the Royal Guards fly deep into enemy territory delivering the goals of the Sethora Royalty with unrelenting fury. They are the last hope for Sethoren survival.

The Sethoren Royal Guards ~HONTIUS

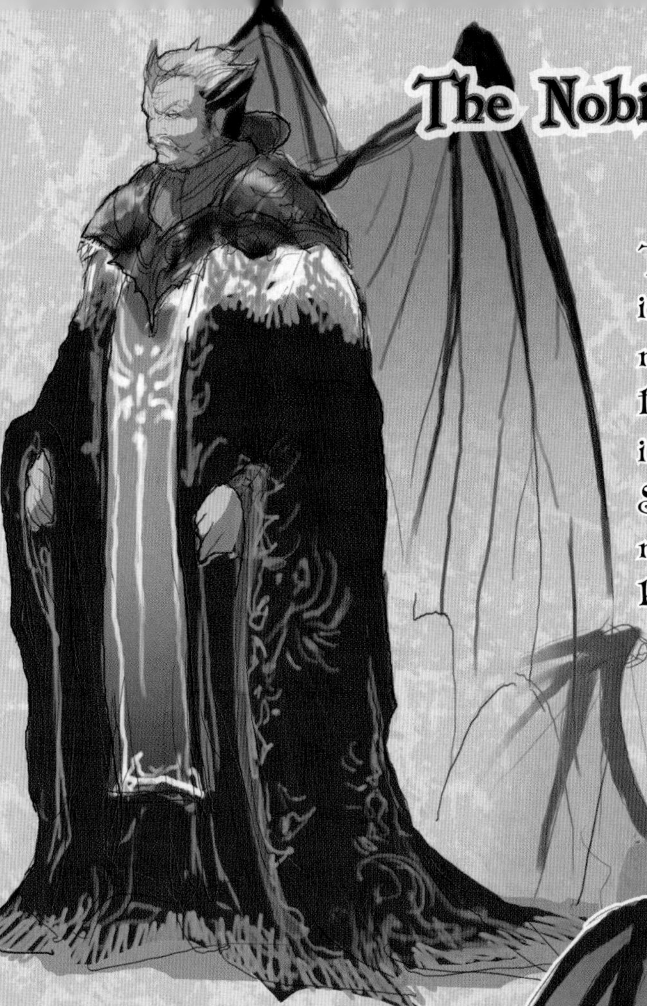

The Nobility of Empyrea ~ENDREW

The power of the land rests in the chambers of the nobility in Empyrea. When the sovereignty of their land is threatened by the race of Sethoru, the nobility will not hesitate to defend the kingdom~ and their wealth.

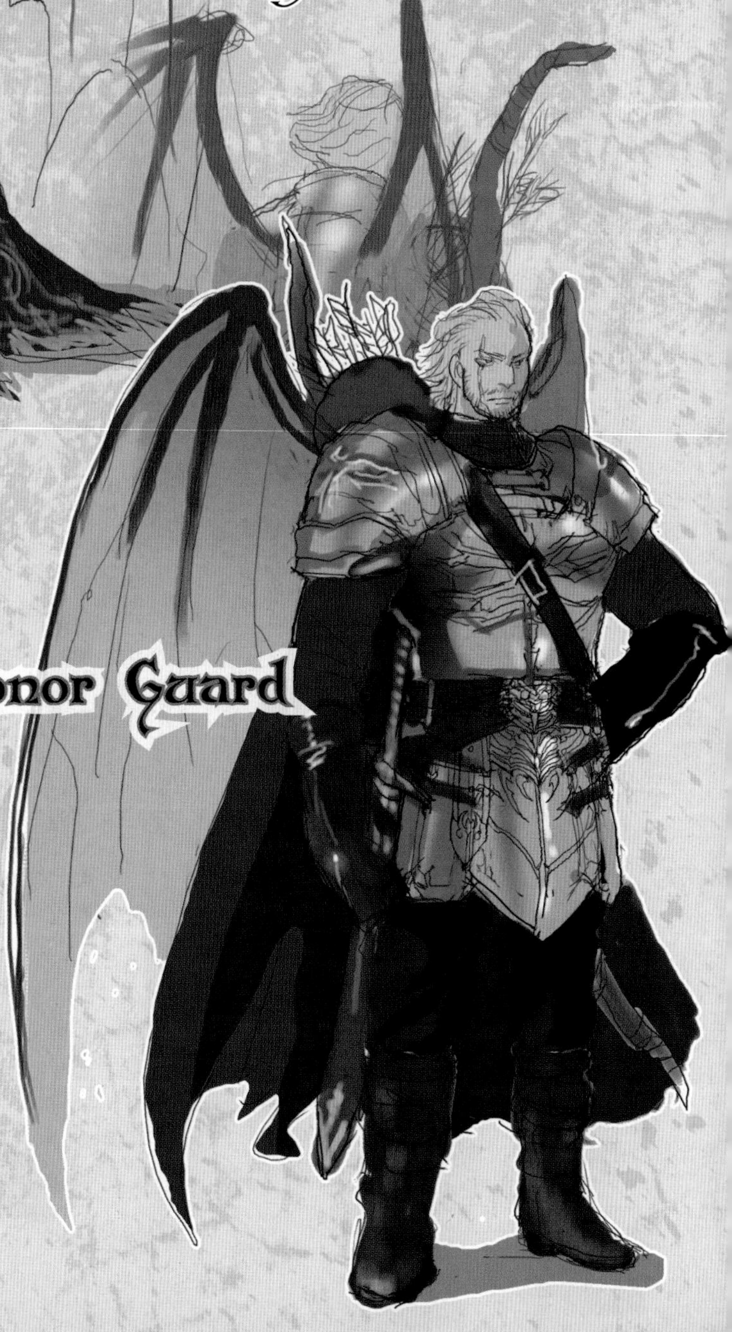

The Rahtumi Honor Guard ~TREYBOUGH

Land is nothing if not protected. The Empyrean Honor Guard reigns over the skies of Empyrea, defending the cities while also acquiring new lands for the kingdom. They are the lifeblood of the Rahtumi people.

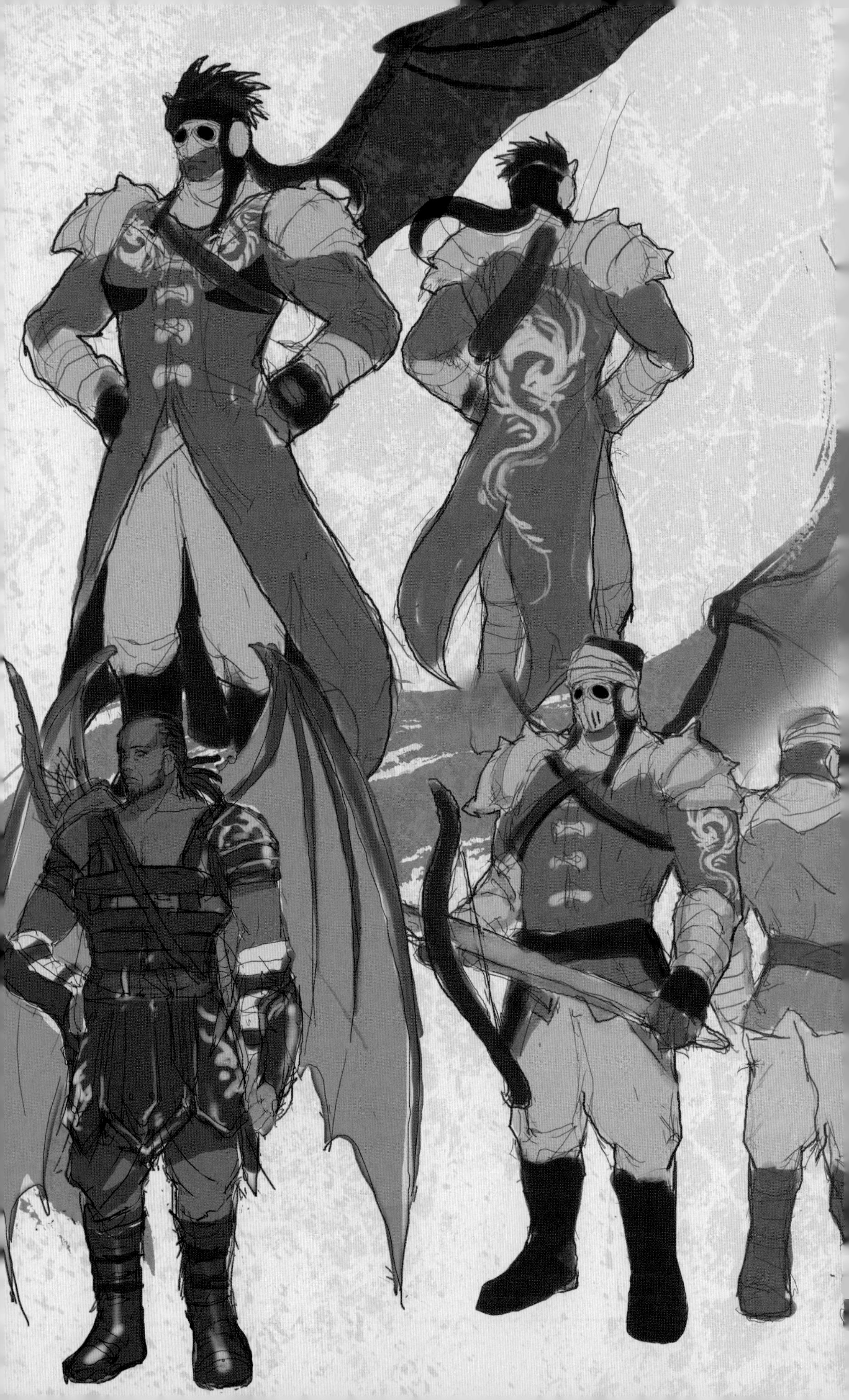

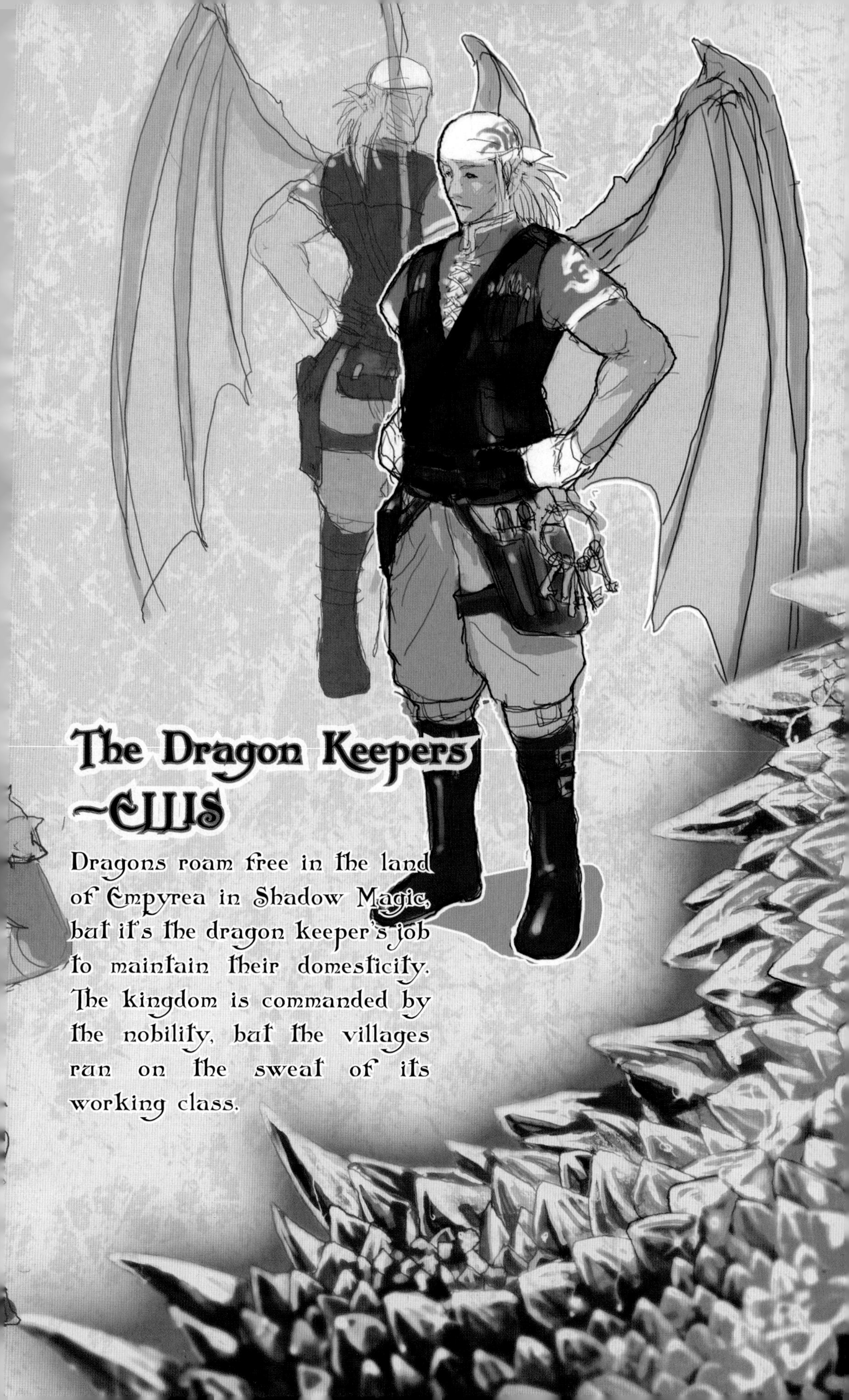

The Dragon Keepers ~ELLIS

Dragons roam free in the land of Empyrea in Shadow Magic, but it's the dragon keeper's job to maintain their domesticity. The kingdom is commanded by the nobility, but the villages run on the sweat of its working class.

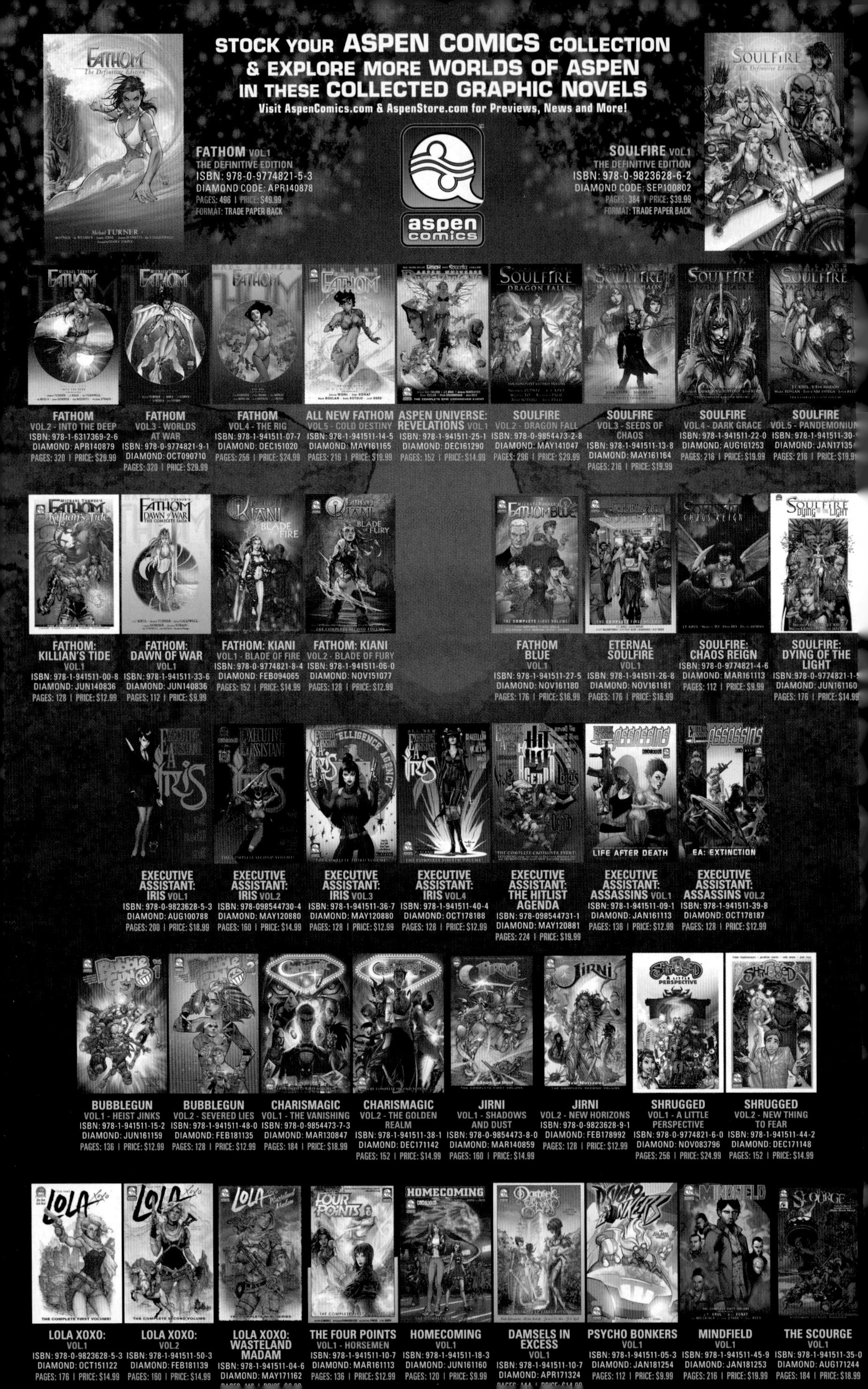

STOCK YOUR ASPEN COMICS COLLECTION
& EXPLORE MORE WORLDS OF ASPEN
IN THESE COLLECTED GRAPHIC NOVELS
Visit AspenComics.com & AspenStore.com for Previews, News and More!
FATHOM VOL.1
THE DEFINITIVE EDITION
ISBN: 978-0-9774821-5-3
DIAMOND CODE: APR140878
PAGES: 496 | PRICE: $49.99
FORMAT: TRADE PAPER BACK
aspen comics
SOULFIRE VOL.1
THE DEFINITIVE EDITION
ISBN: 978-0-9823628-6-2
DIAMOND CODE: SEP100802
PAGES: 384 | PRICE: $39.99
FORMAT: TRADE PAPER BACK
FATHOM VOL.2 - INTO THE DEEP
ISBN: 978-1-6317369-2-6
DIAMOND: APR140879
PAGES: 320 | PRICE: $29.99
FATHOM VOL.3 - WORLDS AT WAR
ISBN: 978-0-9774821-9-1
DIAMOND: OCT090710
PAGES: 320 | PRICE: $29.99
FATHOM VOL.4 - THE RIG
ISBN: 978-1-941511-07-7
DIAMOND: DEC151020
PAGES: 256 | PRICE: $24.99
ALL NEW FATHOM VOL.5 - COLD DESTINY
ISBN: 978-1-941511-14-5
DIAMOND: MAY161165
PAGES: 216 | PRICE: $19.99
ASPEN UNIVERSE: REVELATIONS VOL.1
ISBN: 978-1-941511-25-1
DIAMOND: DEC161290
PAGES: 152 | PRICE: $14.99
SOULFIRE VOL.2 - DRAGON FALL
ISBN: 978-0-9854473-2-8
DIAMOND: MAY141047
PAGES: 296 | PRICE: $29.99
SOULFIRE VOL.3 - SEEDS OF CHAOS
ISBN: 978-1-941511-13-8
DIAMOND: MAY161164
PAGES: 216 | PRICE: $19.99
SOULFIRE VOL.4 - DARK GRACE
ISBN: 978-1-941511-22-0
DIAMOND: AUG161253
PAGES: 216 | PRICE: $19.99
SOULFIRE VOL.5 - PANDEMONIUM
ISBN: 978-1-941511-30-
DIAMOND: JAN17135
PAGES: 216 | PRICE: $19.9
FATHOM: KILLIAN'S TIDE VOL.1
ISBN: 978-1-941511-00-8
DIAMOND: JUN140836
PAGES: 128 | PRICE: $12.99
FATHOM: DAWN OF WAR VOL.1
ISBN: 978-1-941511-33-6
DIAMOND: JUN140836
PAGES: 112 | PRICE: $9.99
FATHOM: KIANI VOL.1 - BLADE OF FIRE
ISBN: 978-0-9774821-8-4
DIAMOND: FEB094065
PAGES: 152 | PRICE: $14.99
FATHOM: KIANI VOL.2 - BLADE OF FURY
ISBN: 978-1-941511-06-0
DIAMOND: NOV151077
PAGES: 128 | PRICE: $12.99
FATHOM BLUE VOL.1
ISBN: 978-1-941511-27-5
DIAMOND: NOV161180
PAGES: 176 | PRICE: $16.99
ETERNAL SOULFIRE VOL.1
ISBN: 978-1-941511-26-8
DIAMOND: NOV161181
PAGES: 176 | PRICE: $16.99
SOULFIRE: CHAOS REIGN
ISBN: 978-0-9774821-4-6
DIAMOND: MAR161113
PAGES: 112 | PRICE: $9.99
SOULFIRE: DYING OF THE LIGHT
ISBN:978-0-9774821-1-
DIAMOND: JUN161160
PAGES: 176 | PRICE: $14.99
EXECUTIVE ASSISTANT: IRIS VOL.1
ISBN: 978-0-9823628-5-3
DIAMOND: AUG100788
PAGES: 200 | PRICE: $18.99
EXECUTIVE ASSISTANT: IRIS VOL.2
ISBN: 978-098544730-4
DIAMOND: MAY120880
PAGES: 160 | PRICE: $14.99
EXECUTIVE ASSISTANT: IRIS VOL.3
ISBN: 978-1-941511-36-7
DIAMOND: MAY120880
PAGES: 128 | PRICE: $12.99
EXECUTIVE ASSISTANT: IRIS VOL.4
ISBN: 978-1-941511-40-4
DIAMOND: OCT178188
PAGES: 128 | PRICE: $12.99
EXECUTIVE ASSISTANT: THE HITLIST AGENDA
ISBN: 978-098544731-1
DIAMOND: MAY120881
PAGES: 224 | PRICE: $19.99
EXECUTIVE ASSISTANT: ASSASSINS VOL.1
ISBN: 978-1-941511-09-1
DIAMOND: JAN161113
PAGES: 136 | PRICE: $12.99
EXECUTIVE ASSISTANT: ASSASSINS VOL.2
ISBN: 978-1-941511-39-8
DIAMOND: OCT178187
PAGES: 128 | PRICE: $12.99
BUBBLEGUN VOL.1 - HEIST JINKS
ISBN: 978-1-941511-15-2
DIAMOND: JUN161159
PAGES: 136 | PRICE: $12.99
BUBBLEGUN VOL.2 - SEVERED LIES
ISBN: 978-1-941511-48-0
DIAMOND: FEB181135
PAGES: 128 | PRICE: $12.99
CHARISMAGIC VOL.1 - THE VANISHING
ISBN: 978-0-9854473-7-3
DIAMOND: MAR130847
PAGES: 184 | PRICE: $18.99
CHARISMAGIC VOL.2 - THE GOLDEN REALM
ISBN: 978-1-941511-38-1
DIAMOND: DEC171142
PAGES: 152 | PRICE: $14.99
JIRNI VOL.1 - SHADOWS AND DUST
ISBN: 978-0-9854473-8-0
DIAMOND: MAR140859
PAGES: 160 | PRICE: $14.99
JIRNI VOL.2 - NEW HORIZONS
ISBN: 978-0-9823628-9-1
DIAMOND: FEB178992
PAGES: 128 | PRICE: $12.99
SHRUGGED VOL.1 - A LITTLE PERSPECTIVE
ISBN: 978-0-9774821-6-0
DIAMOND: NOV083796
PAGES: 256 | PRICE: $24.99
SHRUGGED VOL.2 - NEW THING TO FEAR
ISBN: 978-1-941511-44-2
DIAMOND: DEC171148
PAGES: 152 | PRICE: $14.99
LOLA XOXO: VOL.1
ISBN: 978-0-9823628-5-3
DIAMOND: OCT151122
PAGES: 176 | PRICE: $14.99
LOLA XOXO: VOL.2
ISBN: 978-1-941511-50-3
DIAMOND: FEB181139
PAGES: 160 | PRICE: $14.99
LOLA XOXO: WASTELAND MADAM
ISBN: 978-1-941511-04-6
DIAMOND: MAY171162
THE FOUR POINTS VOL.1 - HORSEMEN
ISBN: 978-1-941511-10-7
DIAMOND: MAR161113
PAGES: 136 | PRICE: $12.99
HOMECOMING VOL.1
ISBN: 978-1-941511-18-3
DIAMOND: JUN161160
PAGES: 120 | PRICE: $9.99
DAMSELS IN EXCESS VOL.1
ISBN: 978-1-941511-10-7
DIAMOND: APR171324
PSYCHO BONKERS VOL.1
ISBN: 978-1-941511-05-3
DIAMOND: JAN181254
PAGES: 112 | PRICE: $9.99
MINDFIELD VOL.1
ISBN: 978-1-941511-45-9
DIAMOND: JAN181253
PAGES: 216 | PRICE: $19.99
THE SCOURGE VOL.1
ISBN: 978-1-941511-35-0
DIAMOND: AUG171244
PAGES: 184 | PRICE: $18.99